MW00461348

"Detective David 'Kubu' Bengu is a wonderful creation, complex and beguiling. The exotic smells and sounds of Botswana fill the pages as well as the changes and struggles of a country brimming with modern technology yet fiercely clinging to old traditions. Compelling and deceptively written..."
    —*New York Journal of Books*

"A wonderful, original voice—McCall Smith with a dark edge and even darker underbelly."
    —Peter James #1 UK bestseller

"My favourite writing duo since Ellery Queen."
    —Ragnar Jónasson bestselling author of the *Dark Iceland* series.

"Great African crime fiction."
    —Deon Meyer author of the Benny Griessel novels

Praise for *A Deadly Covenant*, the second Kubu prequel

"As a big fan of uncovered or unsolved mysteries from the remote past, I found *A Deadly Covenant* completely intriguing and engrossing, and the Bushman scenes fascinating. Vividly painted scenery, and I can feel the oppressive heat. Talk about Sunshine Noir!"
    —Kwei Quartey, best-selling author of the Emma Djan and Darko Dawson mysteries

2023

APR

"The unmatched beauty, spirit, and mystery of Africa never fails to come to life in Michael Stanley's award-winning Botswana-based Detective David 'Kubu' Bengu series. In the newest addition to this irresistible series, *A Deadly Covenant*, societal conflicts, generational prejudices, family secrets, and political turf wars combine to obstruct a youthful Detective Kubu's investigation into old bones unearthed in a remote Botswana village and the seemingly unrelated murders that soon follow their discovery. *A Deadly Covenant* is an irresistible page-turner and a powerful contribution to the Kubu saga."

—Jeffrey Siger, international best-selling author of the Chief Inspector Andreas Kaldis series

Praise for *Facets of Death*, the first Kubu prequel

"A fabulous test of Kubu's legendary deductive talents, *Facets of Death* is easily one of the best heist novels I've read since Gerald Browne's classic *11 Harrowhouse*."

—*Bookpage* **starred** review

"The local colour is as delightful as the intriguing investigation."

—*The Times and Sunday Times Crime Club* **Pick of the Week**

"Every fan of mystery novels should be reading and enjoying this series, and not just because of the ending, which has quickly and quietly become my favorite in recent memory."

—*Bookreporter*

"The African Columbo ... a smart, satisfying complex mystery."

—*Entertainment Weekly* **A rating** review for *The Second Death of Goodluck Tinubu*

"Bringing a love of Africa similar to Alexander McCall Smith's popular *No. 1 Ladies' Detective Agency* series, the author has created an excellent new venue for those who love to read about other cultures while enjoying a good mystery. Highly recommended."

—*School Library Journal* **starred** review for *The Second Death of Goodluck Tinubu*

"*Death of the Mantis* is the best book I've read in a very long time. A fantastic read. Brilliant!"

—Louise Penny, #1 *New York Times* bestselling author

"*Death of the Mantis* is the best book yet in one of the best series going: a serious novel with a mystery at its core that takes us places we've never been, thrills and informs us, and leaves us changed by the experience. I loved this book."

—Timothy Hallinan, author of the Junior Bender series

"Impossible to put down, this immensely readable third entry ... delivers the goods. Kubu's painstaking detecting skills make him a sort of Hercule Poirot of the desert. This series can be recommended to a wide gamut of readers."

—*Library Journal* **starred** review for *Death of the Mantis*

"Kubu's third recorded case is again alive with local color and detail and, refreshingly, offers his fullest mystery plot yet."

—*Kirkus Reviews* for *Death of the Mantis*

A DEADLY COVENANT

ABOUT THE AUTHOR

Michael Stanley is the writing team of Michael Sears and Stanley Trollip. Both were born in South Africa and have worked in academia and business. Michael specialised in image processing and remote sensing and taught at the University of the Witwatersrand. Stanley was an educational psychologist, specialising in the application of computers to teaching and learning, and is a pilot.

On a flying trip to Botswana, they watched a pack of hyenas hunt, kill, and devour a wildebeest, eating both flesh and bones. That gave them the premise for their first mystery, *A Carrion Death*, which introduced Detective David 'Kubu' Bengu of the Botswana Criminal Investigation Department. It was a finalist for five awards, including the Crime Writers' Association Debut Dagger. The series has been critically acclaimed, and their third book, *Death of the Mantis*, won the Barry Award for Best Paperback Original mystery and was shortlisted for an Edgar award. *Deadly Harvest* was shortlisted for an International Thriller Writers award. *A Deadly Covenant* is the second prequel in the series.

They have also written a thriller, *Shoot the Bastards*, in which investigative journalist, Crystal Nguyen, heads to South Africa for *National Geographic* and gets caught up in the war against rhino poaching and rhino-horn smuggling.

For information about Botswana, the books, and their protagonists, please visit www.michaelstanleybooks.com. You can sign up there for an occasional newsletter. They are also active on Facebook at facebook.com/MichaelStanleyBooks, on Twitter as @detectivekubu, and on Instagram as @michaelstanleybooks.

BOOKS BY MICHAEL STANLEY

The Detective Kubu Mysteries
A Carrion Death
The Second Death of Goodluck Tinubu (A Deadly Trade - UK edition)
Death of the Mantis
Deadly Harvest
A Death in the Family
Dying to Live
Facets of Death

The Crystal Nguyen Thrillers
Shoot the Bastards (Dead of Night - UK edition)

Short story anthologies
Detective Kubu Investigates
Detective Kubu Investigates 2
African Mysteries

WHITE SUN BOOKS
61 East 11th Street, Apt 7
New York
NY 10003-4628
USA

ISBN 978-0-9979689-8-9 (paperback)
ISBN 978-0-9979689-9-6 (e-book)
ISBN 978-0-6397-0611-5 (large print)

Author website: www.michaelstanleybooks.com
Author email: michaelstanley@michaelstanleybooks.com
Publisher website: www.whitesunbooks.com
Publisher email: info@whitesunbooks.com

Cover by 100Covers

This book is dedicated to all our readers, whose enthusiasm for Detective Kubu and the cases he's had to solve has kept us writing. Thank you all.

A DEADLY COVENANT

A DETECTIVE KUBU MYSTERY

MICHAEL STANLEY

WHITE SUN BOOKS

AUTHOR'S NOTE

The peoples of Southern Africa have integrated many words of their own languages into colloquial English. For authenticity and colour, we have used these occasionally when appropriate. Most of the time, the meanings are clear from the context, but for interest, we have included a glossary at the end of the book.

A resort called Drotsky's Camp appears in this book. It is a real place overlooking the Kavango River that we visited a long time ago. However, due to COVID restrictions, we were unable to go back there while researching this book. Consequently, it should be regarded as fictitious since we made up how it looks today and how it is run.

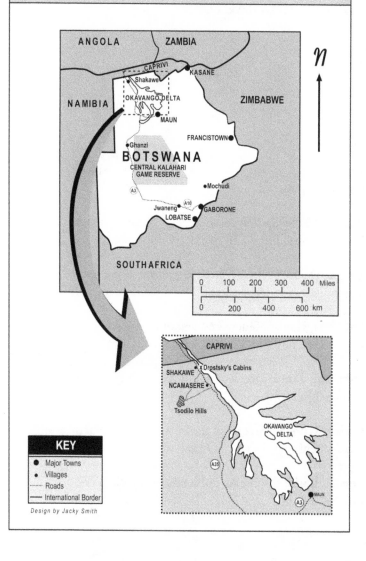

Botswana & Surrounding Countries

ANGOLA

ZAMBIA

CAPRIVI

●Shakawe ●KASANE

NAMIBIA

OKAVANGO DELTA

●MAUN

ZIMBABWE

●Ghanzi

FRANCISTOWN●

BOTSWANA

CENTRAL KALAHARI
GAME RESERVE

●Mochudi

(A3)

(A10)

Jwaneng●

GABORONE

LOBATSE

SOUTH AFRICA

| 0 | 100 | 200 | 300 | 400 | Miles |
| 0 | 200 | 400 | 600 | km |

CAPRIVI

SHAKAWE ● ×Drostsky's Cabins

NCAMASERE ●

Tsodilo Hills

OKAVANGO
DELTA

(A35)

●MAUN

(A3)

KEY

● Major Towns

● Villages

..... Roads

—— International Border

Design by Jacky Smith

CAST OF CHARACTERS

Words in square brackets are approximate phonetic pronunciations.

Balopi, Tolalo: Station commander at Shakawe police station [Taw-LAH-loh Buh-LOW-pee]

Bengu, David 'Kubu': Detective sergeant in the Botswana Criminal Investigation Department [David 'KOO-boo' BEN-goo]

Dibotelo, Kagiso: Elderly resident of Ncamasere [Kuh-HEE-sow Dib-oh-TELL-oh]

Dibotelo, Tandi: Deceased son of Kagiso Dibotelo [TUN-dee Dib-oh-TELL-oh]

Gobey, Tebogo: Director of the Botswana Criminal Investigation Department [Teh-BO-go GO-bee]

Lesaka, Endo: Counsellor at Ncamasere kgotla [EN-doe Luh-SAH-kuh]

Lesaka, Joshua: Son of Endo Lesaka [Joshua Leh-SAH-kuh]

Mabaku, Jacob: Assistant superintendent in the Botswana Criminal Investigation Department [Jacob Muh-BAH-koo]

MacGregor, Ian: Pathologist for the Botswana police

Moitsheki, Rantau: Kgosi (chief) of Ncamasere. Known as Kgosi Rantau [GGO-zee RAN-tow Moi-CHECK-ee (GG as in clearing throat; ow as in how)]

Moitsheki, Raseelo: Son of Kgosi Rantau [RUS- uh-EH-low Moi-CHECK-ee]

Mowisi, John: Local farmer [John Moh-WEE-see]

Ntemba, Abram: Detective Sergeant at Shakawe police station [Abram N-TEM-buh]

Selelo: Bushman [Seh-LEH-low]

Serome, Joy: Clerk in the Botswana Police Service Records department [Joy Sé-ROE-meh]

Tembo: Local contractor [TEM-bow]

Wata, Mami: Water spirit [MUM-ee WUH-tuh]

Zondo, Ezekiel: Deceased farmer; husband of Mma Zondo

Zondo, Jacob: Son of Ezekiel and Mma Zondo

Zondo, Mma: Mrs Zondo; wife of Ezekiel Zondo

CHAPTER 1

Amos Sebina peered through the dust at the bucket of his backhoe. He blinked and looked again. He had to be mistaken, but it did look like a skull sticking out of the sand. He turned off the engine and jumped out of the cab, shielding his eyes from the sun. He eased forward to inspect it more closely.

It was definitely a skull.

He took a step back. Was it human? Or could it be a baboon's? He didn't know the difference. He scratched his head. If it was human, why wasn't it buried in a graveyard? And if it was a baboon's, why would anyone bury it in the first place?

He retreated further. He wasn't going to touch it, because that could bring him very bad luck. He looked around for a stick but didn't see one. So he broke a branch off a bush and stripped off the leaves and twigs.

He edged closer to the bucket, reached forward and poked the skull. It didn't move.

He wanted to see more, but it would be disrespectful to stick the branch into the eye socket and try to lift it. So, he used the branch to sweep away the fine Kalahari sand. In a few minutes, most of the skull was visible, but he was none the wiser as to what sort of creature it had belonged to.

He stepped back, unsure of what to do. If he dumped the skull and continued digging, his boss would be happy, but the police wouldn't – if it was a human skull. If he stopped digging, and the skull turned out to be a baboon's, his boss would be furious and probably fire him for delaying the project.

Sebina knew that his best course of action was to tell his boss as soon as possible and let him make the decision. However, there was no way to contact him. He'd only see him at the end of the day when he came to take him back to Ncamasere, the village where he lived.

Sebina shrugged. Whatever it was had been dead for a long time. A few more hours weren't going to change anything.

He glanced at the trench that he'd been digging. He gasped and jumped backwards. Numerous bones of different shapes and sizes were protruding from the sand.

Now it was obvious that he couldn't do any more digging that day. But it was only just before noon and at least five hours before his boss arrived. More likely six. He would bake if he sat in the cab for all that time doing nothing, to say nothing of the heat he'd take from his boss.

So he decided to walk to the farmhouse down the road to see if he could find some shade. His boss had told him in no uncertain terms that the farmhouse was off limits, but to hell with that. The skull was a good-enough reason to disobey orders. He could always say he had to report what he'd found as soon as possible, and the only way to do that was to have someone at the farmhouse call the police.

Sebina picked up his lunchbox and a bottle of now-tepid water, and set off across the sand towards the road that led to the farmhouse. Maybe a car would pass, or a bakkie, that could drop him off a kilometre down the road. That would leave only a few hundred metres to his destination. However, nothing came down the road, not even a bicycle, leaving Sebina a nearly thirty-minute walk to the farm gate.

When he reached the driveway to the house, he stopped. Not only was there a high wall around the property, topped with razor wire, but his way forward was blocked by a metal swing gate with a large *DO NOT ENTER* sign, topped with more razor wire. Most frightening was the picture of two ferocious-looking black dogs, mouths open, teeth showing. With red eyes.

He looked around to see if there was an intercom he could use to alert the house. There wasn't. In a final effort, he cupped his hands around his mouth and shouted, 'Dumela! Hello!' Nobody came out of the house. He tried again with the same result.

The only response was two huge dogs racing towards the gate, barking, snarling and jumping up against the gate. Sebina backed away. He looked at the house, but no one appeared. They were either out or not interested.

'Amos Sebina,' he said out loud. 'Now don't waste your time here. The skull can wait.'

After a couple of minutes, he turned and trudged back to the backhoe. The cab would have to do until his boss arrived to take him home later that afternoon.

~

At nearly half past six, Sebina was returning to the scene once more, but this time in the back of a police Land Rover. There was still enough light, so he led Abram Nteba, the local detective, and a constable across the sand to where the backhoe stood, looking like a huge scorpion.

Sebina pointed. 'I saw the skull in the bucket first.'

The constable kept his distance while the detective edged forward.

'It's definitely a skull.'

'And there are bones in the ditch.' Sebina took a wide path around the bucket and pointed at the ground. 'See, there.'

The detective nodded. 'We'll have to call in the pathologist from Gaborone. He won't be able to do anything until the day after tomorrow even if he flies.' He turned. 'Constable, put police-scene tape around the whole area. No one is to come in. You'll stay here until morning—'

'No way. You must be mad if you think I'm going to spend the night near those things.'

'Sorry, Constable. You don't have a choice. Build a big fire. That should keep the spirits away.'

The constable backed away, fear in his eyes.

'There's a tent and sleeping bag in the back of the Land Rover. I think there's water and some cans of food too, and a little gas stove. You'll be fine. Now get moving, I want to get home, and I've still got to call the CID in Gabs.'

Fifteen minutes later the area had been cordoned off, and the constable had fetched everything he needed for the night, putting them on the ground nearly fifty metres away.

The detective laughed as he walked back to the vehicle. 'I hope the ancestors aren't angry at being disturbed.'

The constable glowered and headed off to find some wood.

'And what about me?' Sebina asked as he climbed into the Land Rover.

'I'll drop you off at your house.'

'No. What I mean is what am I going to do tomorrow and the next day. The boss will be angry and won't pay me.'

'That's too bad, but there's nothing I can do.'

CHAPTER 2

Detective Sergeant David 'Kubu' Bengu was on his hands and knees, silently cursing. The new filing cabinet that had just been delivered didn't sit squarely on the floor and rocked when he pulled out a drawer. So, he was folding pieces of paper, trying to find the exact thickness to remedy the situation. So far, he hadn't succeeded.

Just as Kubu was wondering whether he should use thicker paper, his office door swung open, barely missing him.

'Can't you knock before you come in?' he growled without looking up.

'I want to see you in my office. Now.'

By the time Kubu had scrambled to his feet, blushing, Assistant Superintendent Mabaku had disappeared. Kubu dusted his knees and headed down the corridor to his boss's office. He knocked on the door.

'Sit down.'

'I apologise for what I said, Assistant Superintendent. I thought it was Elias coming to upset my day.'

'He's very good at that. What are you working on?'

Kubu hesitated. He wasn't quite sure how to answer. If he said he was very busy, which he wasn't, Mabaku might ask him for a debriefing and find out the truth. If he said he wasn't busy,

Mabaku might shout at him for being lazy and give him a pile of uninteresting cold cases to go through.

'To be honest, sir, I'm a little bored. I've enough to keep me busy, but most of it isn't very exciting.'

'Most police work is boring, Detective Sergeant. Cases are solved by being methodical and paying attention to detail. That diamond heist I pulled you into is the exception. That type of case happens rarely. Most of your time will be spent pulling together bits and pieces, trying to create a picture that'll allow us to prosecute someone.'

'Yes, sir.' Kubu was hoping that Mabaku's question was going to lead him into an interesting case, but his hopes were soon dashed.

'I want you to go home and pack for a five-day trip to Shakawe.'

Kubu frowned. 'Shakawe? What's happened there?'

'That's the problem. We're not sure. You'll go with the pathologist. What's his name? MacGregor, I think. Ian MacGregor.'

'Has someone been murdered?'

'We don't know. A man was digging a trench for a water pipe just south of Shakawe, and unearthed a skull and some bones. The police there took some Polaroids and faxed them through. They're human all right, but that's all we know. I want you to observe what the pathologist does when he approaches a body and documents the scene. Then when he's finished, I want you to bring the bones back to Princess Marina Hospital – that's where he has his lab – and watch him do a post mortem.'

'Watch him do a post mortem?' Kubu blanched, hoping he didn't throw up when Ian cut up the bodies

'Don't worry. From what I'm told, it's only a skeleton, which means it's been dead for some time. Ten years or more, most likely.'

'When do I leave?'

'MacGregor will pick you up at ten. I'll get you rooms at the Kalahari Arms in Ghanzi for tonight. Then report to the Shakawe police station as soon as you can tomorrow.'

When Kubu returned to his office, he realised he had two problems. It was already just after nine, and there was no way he could walk back to his room, pack and return by ten. And even if he could, he'd be wet through. It was hot outside.

However, it was the second problem that he really didn't want to deal with. For the past few months, he'd become very fond of a woman from Records – a Joy Serome. In fact, 'very fond' wasn't quite accurate. He had a crush on her that made him feel like a schoolboy whenever he saw her.

He and Joy enjoyed lunch together on those Saturdays they were both free. And the next lunch was in two days, so he was going to have to postpone it.

He picked up the phone and spoke to Ian MacGregor, who promised to come a little early so he could take Kubu to his room.

That took care of the first problem.

Kubu knew he should walk over to Records and tell Joy that he couldn't make Saturday's date, but he couldn't pluck up the courage to tell her face to face. He'd mumble and bumble, and generally make a fool of himself.

He took a couple of deep breaths and dialled her number.

'Records. This is Joy.'

'Dumela, Joy. This is Kubu.'

'Oh, Kubu. How nice to hear your voice.'

Kubu wondered if she meant it.

'How are you?' she continued.

'I'm ... um ... fine. And you?'

'I'm fine too. Is something wrong? You sound a little strange.'

'Well ... um ... I'm sorry but I have to cancel lunch on Saturday. I have to go to Shakawe in an hour. I'll be away for five days.'

'No problem. I can't talk now. Call me when you get back. Have a good trip.' Kubu heard the phone being put down.

Kubu's stomach ached. Did she think he was no longer interested? Was she blowing him off? Maybe she'd found someone else. Maybe that's why she couldn't talk.

He wanted to run over to Records and give her a big hug, but knew he'd only make a fool of himself.

∼

Kubu was impressed when he saw what was on the backseat of the police Land Rover that pulled up in front of the Criminal Investigation Department at a quarter to ten. The two cooler boxes indicated that MacGregor was a man who thought ahead – something Kubu also did when it came to food.

Kubu climbed into the Land Rover and settled into his seat. 'I'm afraid I don't have any supplies.'

MacGregor shrugged. 'Not a problem, laddie. I've plenty. It's a long, hot way to Ghanzi, and we don't want to be without refreshments if we run into car trouble. You can wait for hours before anyone passes.'

Kubu nodded in appreciation, smiling at the broad Scottish burr, and proceeded to spell out directions to his room.

MacGregor glanced across. 'I think the last time I saw you was at the time of the great diamond robbery.'

Kubu nodded.

'And, if I remember correctly, you played a big part in solving the case. Not so?'

'Well, I had some lucky breaks, and I thought I saw a way to catch the brains behind the whole thing.'

'An unusual plan, I believe, which worked. From what I hear, you impressed the powers that be.'

∼

'I haven't seen much of Botswana,' Kubu said as they left Gaborone on the A10 towards Kanye. 'I grew up in Mochudi, and for the most part, all I saw was the road from there to Gabs. However, I did go on this road to Jwaneng when working on the diamond case.'

'There's not much to see except scrub and sand. And cattle, of course.'

'Tell me about Scotland and how you came to be in out-of-the-way Botswana, of all places.'

'Well, my family is from a village called Newmains, near Glasgow. There were coal mines in the area for the iron works, so some of the men in the family worked there and some in the works. My father was actually a mining engineer, so he didn't work in the mine itself. My mother was an Edinburgh lass. It took some time for her to be accepted. Glaswegians generally don't like people from Edinburgh.'

'So, why did you leave?'

'I was very lucky to win a scholarship to the medical school at Glasgow University. When I finished, I did a residency in Kenya, because I wanted to get away from the rain – it never stops in Glasgow. When I returned to Scotland, I joined a small general practice and continued studying to become a forensic pathologist. It was fascinating – we had to pass exams in toxicology, firearms and ballistics, serology, and so on. I'm sure it's very much like what you do – snooping round for clues, except most of my clues are in the human body.'

Kubu grimaced. 'But why Botswana?'

'When I left Kenya, I knew I had to get back to Africa. It had got under my skin. So I started looking around, and I saw this job advertised. I applied and was offered it. As ye ken, I've only been here four months. I love it. I dabble in watercolours, and I find the light in the desert wonderful. And the sun! There were times in Glasgow that I'd forgotten what it looked like. What about you? How did you land up at the CID?'

'My story is a bit like yours. The local priest in Mochudi persuaded Maru a Pula school in Gabs to give me a scholarship. My parents had no money, so they couldn't have afforded it. I loved the school, loved the teachers, loved learning.'

'But why a detective?'

'It's a long story, but the short story is that before I went to Maru a Pula I was at school in Mochudi. I was always being teased and bullied because I'm fat. I hated that. There was another boy there, whose name was Khumanego. He was also having a hard time because he was small and a Bushman. We became friends. Two of a kind, yet so different in looks.'

Kubu paused as he thought back to his schooldays. They seemed a long time ago now.

'Anyway, Khumanego and I would go out into the desert sometimes. He showed me that it was alive, not dead, as I'd always thought. One day he drew a circle in the sand, a few metres in diameter. He asked me what I saw. I told him I saw sand, stones and some dry grass. He was appalled at how blind I was. He taught me how to look beyond the obvious, how to explore below the surface, to notice what no one else would see. He showed me that in that small circle thrived a teeming world: ants, and plants that looked like stones – which I found out later were called lithops – and beetles and spiders.

'I particularly liked the trapdoor spider. I can remember Khumanego pointing to a crescent in the sand that I could barely see. He told me to pick up a twig and pry the trapdoor open. I was pretty nervous, but I did it. Underneath was a tunnel, the size and length of a pencil, made from grains of sand and some substance holding them together. Khumanego tapped the tube, and a small white spider scurried out and stopped on the hot sand.

'He told me how clever the spider was, living in the cool below the surface, hidden from view. Then jumping out, grabbing its prey and scuttling back into its hole. I was very impressed, but also embarrassed at how blind I was.'

'There's always a silver lining, if you're willing to look for it.'

Kubu nodded. 'My silver lining was that I vowed I'd never be blind again. Since then I've always tried to be observant and to see what others don't. To look beyond the obvious.'

They were both silent for a few minutes, each reflecting on the paths they'd taken that had brought them together in the middle of the Kalahari Desert.

'That time with Khumanego – that's when I decided I was going to be a detective.'

~

As they headed west, the terrain became more desert-like. The bushes were more stunted and further apart, not wanting to share the little water there was. Even their leaves were covered in a brown dust, and the sky had a brown haze. The only splashes of colour were the occasional road signs. Kubu wondered how people could survive in such desolation.

After a while he turned to his companion. 'What do you think happened in Shakawe, Ian? It's strange that a person is buried without any headstone or marker.'

'Not really. If you're out there alone and die, nobody may find you and bury you. And even if they do find you, they may be scared of touching a dead body or just think it's too much effort. Then, over time, the bones would get covered by the sand.'

'How long does it take for a body to decompose into just a skeleton?'

'It depends on a lot of things, such as temperature and moisture. But I'd say these bones have been in the sand at least ten years. But it could also be a hundred.'

Kubu felt a flash of disappointment. The case had become even colder than it had been before.

'How do you think he died?'

Ian shrugged. 'There's no way of knowing at this stage. That's what we have to find out.'

'What's your guess?'

Ian glared at Kubu. 'I don't guess. That only causes problems.'

Kubu retreated into silence, embarrassed by his question.

After a while, Ian continued. 'There are only two possibilities. The person either died of natural causes, such as sickness or old age, or was killed. Of course, if he was killed, it could have been accidental.'

Or on purpose, Kubu thought. He perked up again. If it was a case of murder, the perpetrator may still be alive. Suddenly the case became interesting.

CHAPTER 3

Kubu had never been on a trip that lasted nearly seven hours, but to his surprise, he enjoyed it – the wide-ranging conversation with the gentle Scot; the companionable silences; the vastness of sand and scrub. He'd expected the stunted bush to give way to red dunes as they headed deeper into the Kalahari, but although the sand started to have a pinker hue, the vegetation didn't change much.

However, some of the silences were not as benign as he would have liked. It was during those that he'd worry about Joy. He'd never felt this way about anyone else. He yearned for her, but wondered if she felt the same way. Nor did he feel confident enough to try to move the relationship forward. He was sure he'd make a fool of himself.

Certainly, she seemed eager to meet on Saturdays for lunch, and, yes, she kissed him on the cheek each time they parted. But what did that mean? Was she waiting for him to seize the initiative and kiss her? On the mouth? His heart pounded. What would that feel like?

Each time Joy intruded on his thoughts, he felt a little depressed. And each time, he took a deep breath and banished her by asking Ian a question.

The only other thing he didn't like about the journey was the surprising number of dead cows lying next to the road.

'What a waste of good meat,' Kubu said as they passed yet another carcass.

'Now there's a good idea gone wrong,' Ian responded. 'You'll notice that this road has a fence on each side. That's to keep cows and other animals off the road. But what they didn't plan on was that even the smallest amount of rain runs off the road. So, the best grass is right there, at its edge. Animals want that. Somehow the cows find a way through the fence and head for the edge of the road. Not too much of a problem during the day. But at night, it's a real hazard. They are hard to see, and often drivers aren't paying attention because it's such a boring drive.'

Kubu gazed at another carcass, legs pointed skyward. 'It certainly seems that the fence is doing a better job keeping animals near the road rather than away from it.'

≈

It was late afternoon by the time they reached Ghanzi and pulled into the Kalahari Arms hotel. Ian opened the back of the Land Rover and took out the suitcases. 'Time for a swim before dinner.'

Kubu frowned.

'What's the matter, laddie? Scared of water?'

'No. But I don't have a swimming costume.'

'How could you forget it in this heat?'

'It didn't occur to me that I could swim while on duty.'

Ian chuckled. 'Well, well. Isn't that something? A hippo who can't get in the water!'

He picked up his suitcase and headed towards the reception. 'I'll see you at the pool. You can cool off with a drink. By the way, have you ever had a steelworks?'

Kubu shook his head. 'What's that?'

'Order one. I think you'll like it. And order one for me too.'

≈

Twenty minutes later, after he'd washed his face in cold water, Kubu headed for the pool, where he found a table under a small, thatched roof. When a waiter arrived, he ordered the two steelworks.

'By the way, I've never had one. What's in it?'

'Kola tonic, lime juice, bitters and ginger beer.'

Kubu thanked the man, and when the drinks arrived, took a sip. Interesting. A little sweet, but not overly so, followed by a sharpness. That must be the ginger beer, he thought. He took a mouthful and swirled it around as he'd been told to do with wine. Different parts of his mouth reacted differently to the various tastes. Kubu liked it. And it was very refreshing.

Ian walked over, drying himself. 'Well, what do you think?'

'I like it a lot. Where does it come from?'

'I dinna ken, but it's popular in South Africa. I was given a glass when I visited Cape Town on my way here.'

'Well, please give me the recipe. It's not as good as wine, but it's a good substitute.'

'I thought you'd like it. Let's enjoy it and then go for an early dinner and bed. We have a way to drive tomorrow, and work to do when we get there.'

The next morning, Kubu and Ian had an early breakfast and were on the road again by seven-thirty. After about three hours, they started seeing signs to lodges on the Kavango river.

'I've always wanted to stay at one of those,' Ian commented. 'Good fishing, beautiful scenery to paint.'

Not long after they drove through Sepupa, Kubu pointed to a billboard next to the road.

WELCOME TO NCAMASERE
HOME OF THE KGOSI RANTAO WATER PROJECT

Across it were the words 'WATER THIEVES' sprayed in red paint.

'I wonder if that's where the skeletons were found,' Kubu mused.

Ian shrugged. 'Probably. There can't be too many water pipes being laid around here. But obviously not everyone is on board.'

As they continued through the small village of Ncamasere towards Shakawe, they speculated about the disagreement shown on the billboard. Eventually, they agreed they were wasting their breath since neither knew anything about the situation.

When they arrived at the Shakawe police station just after noon, the receptionist took them to the office of Detective Sergeant Abram Nteba, a slight man whose size was the antithesis of Kubu's. He immediately suggested that they head to Drotsky's Cabins for lunch.

'It's our favourite place – when someone else is paying. And it's also where we've made reservations for you to stay, so you can drop off your things.'

He has his priorities right, thought Kubu, even though he doesn't look as though he enjoys his food.

'Call me Abram. No formalities here. I'll go and tell the station commander we're leaving. He wants to join us. I'll tell you what I know when we get there.'

Drotsky, whoever he was, had chosen a perfect spot for a camp. The cabins were scattered under huge trees. All overlooked a large expanse of water, which Kubu learnt was the Kavango River, not far from where it spread out into a huge delta that then disappeared into the sands of the Kalahari. And the birds ... He'd never seen so many in his entire life. They were everywhere, often dozens in a tree, of every shape and size, from magnificent brown-and-black eagles with white heads to gorgeous reddish birds with blue tinges that nested in holes in the banks of the river.

As for Ian, he seemed to be in heaven, walking along the bank,

framing views with his fingers and pointing excitedly at birds that
he exclaimed he was seeing for the first time. 'Lifers' he called them.

Eventually, the station commander arrived, looking as though
he'd just changed into a new uniform, every crease in place. He
introduced himself and shook hands. 'Assistant Superintendent
Balopi. Let's eat. I've a busy afternoon.'

How does he manage to look so fresh in this heat? Kubu
wondered.

Abram ushered them all to an outdoor table, where they
placed their orders. Then he described what had happened when
the trench was being excavated.

'I've never seen anything like it. A skull grinning out of the
sand in the bucket of a backhoe, and various bones in the trench
where the hoe had just scooped up the sand. Here, let me show
you.'

He pulled some Polaroid photos out of his notebook and
handed them to Ian. 'You can keep these.'

Ian scrutinised them carefully. 'Some of these came over the fax
in Gabs, but obviously they weren't as clear as these. I'm sure the
skull is human, but that's about all I can say right now.'

He handed them to Kubu, who looked through them,
studying each carefully. Then he pointed to one. 'This is the
only one that shows how big the trench is. Not how wide or
deep, but how long. From this angle you can see that it almost
disappears into the distance.' He turned to Station Commander
Balopi. 'I know it's for water. But I don't know any of the
details.'

'Next to the river, there's plenty of water, but a few hundred
metres away it's desert. That's why they're digging the trench – to
lay a water pipe so they can farm more land. It'll help a lot of
people out here.'

Kubu mentioned the water-project sign they'd seen near
Ncamasere.

Balopi nodded. 'Yes, that's what we're talking about. The
project is the brainchild of the local kgosi, Kgosi Rantao. He's very
progressive and has a vision for the future. He realises we need to

increase food production around here, otherwise everyone will leave.'

~

After they'd finished their meal, the station commander stood up and turned to Ian. 'This shouldn't take long should it, doctor? You must have more-pressing cases in Gabs than a pile of old bones in the desert.'

'All I can promise, Assistant Superintendent, is that I will move as quickly as my investigation requires. I haven't been to the site yet, so I can't even speculate.'

Balopi nodded at Abram. 'I can't imagine it'll take more than this afternoon. I need the detective sergeant back in the office tomorrow morning.' With that, he marched off to his Land Rover.

Abram shook his head. 'He means well. It's just that he's very protective of his authority. He's a top-down man and doesn't like it when his people show initiative.' He hesitated. 'He needs a wife to soften him up a bit.'

Kubu was surprised – he thought a senior policeman would be sought after as a partner. 'Has he ever been married?'

'No. The rumour is that two dates were the most anyone lasted: the first, he was sweet, and the second, his true colours came out. As far as I know, he hasn't asked anyone out for years. And even if he wanted to...' He paused. 'I shouldn't be talking about him like that. He's a good policeman and runs a very tight operation, even if he's a bit controlling and overly exacting with paperwork and all that stuff. I even had to get his permission for us to talk to the boss of the man who found the skull. The man's pretty unhappy and angry that I won't allow them to touch the backhoe until Dr MacGregor here can take a look.'

Ian drained his coffee. 'Very well. Let's go. I've someone waiting for me.'

'My boss wants me to watch Ian deal with the body.' Kubu said. 'When he's finished, perhaps we can go and talk to the man who found the skull. And his boss.'

~

Kubu was surprised, even shocked, at the number of people pushing up against the crime-scene tape. There must have been more than twenty, including two young white men. It had always puzzled him why accidents and crime scenes were such a source of fascination.

'Where did all these people come from?' he asked Abram.

He shrugged. 'Ncamasere is a village quite near here. Probably from there.'

Ian took his briefcase from the back of the Land Rover and headed towards the backhoe. The throng of people parted to let the policemen through.

When he reached the bucket, he peered at the skull. 'It's important not to disturb anything until you're sure that you've documented it all. You can't afford to miss something or contaminate what may be useful evidence.' He turned to Abram. 'Detective Sergeant, you did exactly the right thing in securing the whole area. Well done. Don't worry about the blather you get. You've got a job to do, and that's all that counts.'

Kubu could almost see Abram swell with pride.

Ian pulled a small camera from the briefcase and took several photographs from different angles. Then he pulled out a ruler and laid it next to the skull in the bucket. 'It makes it easier for people to get a sense of the size.' He took some more photos.

Then he walked over to the end of the trench. 'And what have we here?'

Kubu looked down and saw some bones protruding from the sand and others scattered nearby. Ian took some more photographs from several angles, initially without the ruler, then with it lying on the sand next to the bones.

'I'll get the exact measurements when they're in my lab.'

Looking at the scene, Kubu felt a little despondent. He couldn't see an interesting case emerging from a collection of old bones. Nevertheless, he had to do his best, so he wandered into the crowd and started asking whether anyone had any idea of what they were looking at.

As expected, most said they'd heard a rumour of a body being found, and curiosity had led them there.

'I've never seen a body,' a young man said.

'I'm so excited,' a girl commented. 'I've never seen a real skeleton, just pictures of one.'

Ian pulled what looked like a paintbrush from his briefcase and returned to the backhoe bucket.

The crowd pushed forward, eager to see what was going to happen next. It took an angry constable to prevent them breaking through the tape. 'Get back! Get back!' he shouted. 'Or I'll arrest you.' That stemmed the tide, at least for the moment.

Ian started to carefully sweep away the sand from around the skull. Progress was so painstakingly slow that the crowd started to become restless. They wanted action, not scientific rigour.

While this was happening, Kubu continued to talk to people, with much the same results as before. No one knew anything. They were just curious.

Then the two white men approached him. They looked like young backpackers, with crumpled clothes and scraggy beards.

'Where are you from?' Kubu asked.

'We're from London on a trip through Botswana,' one responded. 'Can you tell us what's happening? My name is Fred Wray and I'm with the BBC, that's the British—'

'I know what the BBC is.' Kubu didn't believe the youngster for a minute. He looked just out of school. 'What are you? Some sort of cub reporter?'

The youngster didn't meet his eye. 'Actually, I'm just an intern there.'

'Well, I'm Detective Sergeant Bengu with the CID in Gaborone. You've seen that there's a skeleton here, and right now that's all we know.'

He turned away and was just about to go back inside the tape, when he noticed an elderly woman at the back of the crowd. She was taller than most and had her arms folded so tightly that she looked as though she was hugging herself. Kubu walked over to her.

'Dumela, mma.'

The woman glared at Kubu, then looked back at the trench. 'Dumela.'

'Mma, do you know who was buried here? Is that why you're watching?'

'I told them Mami Wata disapproved of their scheme.'

Kubu didn't respond immediately as he was trying to understand how the water spirit had anything to do with the skeleton. Eventually he continued, 'Mma, I don't understand. How is Mami Wata involved?'

'They're stealing her water, and now she reveals the past.' With that, she turned and walked away.

Kubu watched her go, then shook his head, puzzled.

As he walked back to Ian, he noticed an old man leaning on a stick, standing away from the crowd, staring intently at what Ian was doing.

Kubu joined him. 'Dumela, rra.'

The man turned his head. 'Dumela.' Then he returned to watching Ian.

'What brings you here, rra?'

The man didn't answer for a few moments. 'I hope they have found my son.' His voice was hardly more than a whisper.

'Your son? Is he missing?'

The man nodded.

Maybe there is a case after all, Kubu thought. 'When did you last see him?'

The man hesitated again. 'On the fifth of September, 1975.'

Kubu nearly choked, then filled with sadness. This man had been looking for his son for nearly twenty-five years.

'Rra, I am Detective Sergeant Bengu with the Botswana Police Force. I know it's hard for you, but please tell me what happened.'

'I've told the police many times, but they do nothing. We pay them good money, and they do nothing.'

'So, I will find a report at the Shakawe Police station?'

The man nodded.

'What is your name, rra?'

'Dibotelo'

'And the police know where you live?'

'I've lived in the same place for sixty years.'

Kubu took a deep breath. 'Rra, I promise I will see what I can find and come and tell you.'

The man shrugged.

Kubu looked to see what Ian was doing. He was in the process of lifting the skull out of the bucket. A murmur ran through the crowd.

Ian looked at it from all angles, then put it down and took more photos. Then he pulled some sheets of paper from his briefcase. From where Kubu stood, it looked as though they were filled with photographs. Ian held each sheet next to the skull, comparing what he saw.

Eventually, he put the papers back in his briefcase and turned to the crowd. He held up has hand. The crowd went silent.

'The skull is of a Bushman.'

The crowd buzzed and started dispersing. A Bushman's body wasn't of any interest.

Kubu noticed the woman who'd been talking about the water spirit. She didn't look disappointed; she looked pleased.

Then he glanced at Dibotelo. The old man was shuffling slowly away, shoulders hunched, head down.

CHAPTER 4

Kubu walked back to Ian, who was looking for something in his briefcase.

'Here they are.' Ian pulled out a marker pen and a large evidence bag. He picked up the skull, turned it upside down, and marked it with a small numeral '1', then bagged it.

He walked back to the trench. 'Now let's see what's going on here.' He jumped down and approached the bones. He pointed to one. 'That's a femur – a thigh bone.' He carefully brushed the sand away and lifted it. After examining it for a few moments, he marked it and bagged it too.

Only part of the next bone was showing, so Ian squatted down and started brushing the sand away. Suddenly he stood up. 'Sweet baby Jesus! There are more here.' He pointed to where he'd been working. 'That's another skull. This needs to be excavated by someone who knows what they're doing. Here, give me a hand.'

Kubu extended his hand and helped Ian out of the trench.

'Who will you get?' Kubu asked.

'I know someone at the university who may be able to help.'

Abram interrupted him. 'I don't understand why we can't just dig the bones out. They've been dead for a long time.'

'Detective Sergeant, we can often learn a lot from how the bones lie. They can tell us if they've been laid to rest or thrown in a grave. If they were put here at different times, we may be able to learn that too, and maybe how long between them. Answers to any of those questions could be useful.'

'When will this expert be able to get here?'

Ian frowned. 'I don't know. I have to speak to him first.'

'You mean it may be days?'

Ian nodded.

'Please, Dr MacGregor. Can we go back to the station now? You can explain the situation to the station commander. He's not going to be happy. And you can phone your expert from there.'

Ian glared at the man. 'It's not as though we'll be looking for a murderer who's just left the scene. These have been here for years.' He turned and picked up his briefcase. 'Kubu, please bring the evidence bags.' With that, he stalked back to the Land Rover.

It was only when the bags had been packed and they were on the road that Kubu could ask Ian the question that was puzzling him. 'How do you know the skull is from a Bushman? Isn't it more likely that it's a Motswana's?'

'Of course, I'm not one-hundred percent sure, but I'll give up Scotch for a month if I'm wrong.' He waved his hand at his briefcase. 'The Polaroids Abram gave me are in there. Get them out and take a look at one taken from the front.'

When Kubu had it in his hand, Ian asked him, 'What do you notice about it?'

Kubu studied it closely, but nothing seemed to be unusual. 'It looks like a skull to me. Am I missing something?'

'Look closely at the orbits – that's eye sockets, to you.'

Kubu looked carefully, but was none the wiser. 'I'm not sure what I'm meant to see.'

'There are three human groups commonly found in this area: Blacks, Whites, and Bushmen. Blacks generally have squarish orbits and Whites the shape of sunglass lenses. The ones in the skull we found are rounder, which makes me think they are from a Bushman. We'll only be able to confirm that later with the help of an anthropologist.'

Abram joined in from the back seat: 'I don't think your eyes look like sunglasses, Dr MacGregor.'

'I never said the eyes of Whites looked like sunglasses, Abram. I said the shape of the orbits were the shape of sunglasses.'

Abram shrugged. 'I thought all skulls were the same.'

'Well, they're not.'

It was late afternoon by the time the policemen arrived at the Shakawe police station. Ian immediately asked for a phone.

'Assistant Superintendent Mabaku, please.'

Ian waited to be put through. When Mabaku answered, Ian explained the situation to him.

Kubu could hear the response from where he was sitting. 'What do you mean, MacGregor? Hire an archaeologist? That's ridiculous. Go and dig up the bones. Tell me who they are, if you can, and how they died. It's simple.'

Kubu couldn't but admire Ian's patience as he explained how having an archaeologist excavate the site would have two benefits: it could help to establish the logistics of how the bodies came to be there. And secondly, it was in the overall interests of the country to document the demise of its original people.

'I don't give a damn about the demise of what you call the original people. I'm a policeman trying to solve crimes. I want to know what happened at Shakawe, and soon. The answer is no!'

Ian scowled at the handset, then returned it to its cradle with exaggerated care. 'Damned bureaucracy.'

He turned to Abram. 'Is there anywhere around here I can buy some balls of string?'

Abram pointed at the door. 'Before you do anything, Dr MacGregor, you'd better talk to the station commander.' He stood up and turned to Kubu. 'We'd better tell the contractor they won't be able to work for a while. He'll be pissed off. So will his worker, because he won't get paid if he's not working.'

Kubu frowned. He'd been close to having no money himself on so many occasions that he felt a lot of sympathy for the backhoe driver. 'If we deal with the skull in the bucket first, they can then take the hoe and continue working a little further on. Would that work, Ian?'

Ian nodded. 'I suppose so. Kubu, you go and talk to them. Explain what's going on. I've got to get organised so we can get moving first thing in the morning. Meet back here when you're finished.'

Abram looked relieved. 'Come with me, Kubu. I'll drive. But be prepared for a tirade.'

∼

On the way, Kubu asked about the strange woman at the excavation. 'There was an elderly woman watching Dr MacGregor. When I spoke to her she told me that Mami Wata was angry with what was happening because her water was being stolen. I've no idea what she was going on about.'

'Oh, that must have been Mma Zondo.' Abram tapped his head. 'She claims that she talks to Mami Wata on the bank of the river. Of course, no one else has ever seen the spirit, even though Mma Zondo swears she's real.'

'Then she said that Mami Wata was revealing the past. What does that mean?'

Abram shrugged. 'I've no idea.'

'I also spoke to an old man who was watching Ian work on the skull. He said he lost a son twenty-five years ago – just disappeared and has never been found.'

'That must have been Kagiso Dibotelo. It's very sad. He lost his wife when their son was young. He brought up the boy himself. They were very close. Then the boy disappeared. With absolutely no trace. No clues, nothing. It broke Kagiso. He's never been the same since.' He tapped his head again. 'He comes to the police station at least once a year to ask whether we've made any progress finding the body. Of course, we haven't.'

'Nobody saw the boy the day he disappeared? Nobody heard any rumours?'

'No. A total mystery. People ended up saying someone must have put a curse on him.'

'A convenient explanation.'

Abram frowned. 'You don't believe in curses?'

'Oh yes, I believe that people put curses on other people.' Kubu hesitated. 'I just don't believe they work. What works is that people believe in them. It's all in the mind. If you don't believe in them, they don't work. I learnt that on my first big case.'

Abram glanced at him, but didn't respond.

A few minutes later they pulled up at a warehouse on the outskirts of town. 'This is it,' Abram announced and climbed out of the vehicle.

∼

They found Sebina and his boss in a make-shift office at the front. The boss didn't wait for introductions. 'I'm Tembo, and I've got a contract to complete. A *government* contract with deadlines.'

The meeting had started off much as Abram had predicted.

'Now my equipment is stuck out in the desert losing money while you people dig up old skeletons. When can I get back to work, hey?' Without letting them answer he pointed at Sebina. 'Meanwhile this lazy bum sits around doing what he likes doing best. Nothing.'

Kubu jumped in. 'People have died, Rra Tembo. We're investigating a possible multiple murder. That takes priority.'

'It does, does it? I want to talk to your boss. You people get paid even if you do nothing. It doesn't work like that in the real world.'

Before Kubu could respond, Abram interjected. 'Rra Tembo,

we completely understand your situation. However, we have a simple plan so you can get back to work right away.' He paused and waited for a response.

Tembo started to say something, then just folded his arms and waited.

'The pathologist will start with the backhoe and be finished with it tomorrow morning. Then you can move it—'

'So I can resume work tomorrow?'

'As I was saying, you can move the equipment. After that you can resume work fifty metres further on and finish the small section we're working on when the investigation is over.'

'That's not convenient. The trench has to be completely straight. You can't start putting kinks in plastic pipes.'

'I'm sure the kgosi would want you to keep moving.'

Tembo took his time thinking it over. 'All right. I think we can do that. But we start first thing after lunch. One-thirty.' He glared at the detectives and pointed to the door. 'What are you waiting for? Haven't you got work to do?'

~

When Kubu and Abram returned to the police station, they found Ian with three balls of string and several bundles of stakes. There were also two constables in the room.

'The station commander had a fit when I told him what I needed to do. He clearly doesn't want people from Gabs treading on his turf.' Then he smiled. 'I told him we'd leave sooner if I had help, so he assigned these two constables to work with me.

'I've also arranged accommodation for us at Drotsky's Cabins for two more nights. At least Mabaku can pay for that. Not a thebe is coming from my budget. I can assure you of that.' He picked up his briefcase. 'We can go there now and have something to eat. We'll need to be up early, so an early night is called for.'

He turned to the two constables. 'Meet me at the excavation at seven tomorrow morning. Let's hope it's a cool day because it could be a long one.'

A while after the detectives had left and Sebina had gone home, Tembo made a phone call. He'd just been given a modified set of plans for the water reticulation system, and he was furious. He started shouting the moment the call was answered.

'What the fucking hell are you smoking? You can't ask me to do this. This isn't a storage facility, this is a full-scale dam. It's nothing like what was in the tender document. Must be ten times the size.'

'You're wrong. It's more like fifteen times. But take a look at the new location. The amount of work involved wouldn't be much more than for the original storage facility.'

'What do you know? You're an engineer suddenly?' Nevertheless, Tembo studied the plans again. 'It's in a riverbed. All the water will just leak away in the sand.'

'It has a clay base. The civil engineer says it should work.'

'But this isn't what Water Affairs approved. They'll never accept this. You'll be taking far too much water from the river.'

'That's not your problem. You've got a signed set of plans. You're just following the new instructions.'

'Forget it. It's bad enough that I'm delayed by the stupid skeletons. You'd better make that go away or I'm going to be way behind. We stick to the original plans in the tender. That's final.'

There was a long pause on the line.

'You still there?'

'I'm here, Tembo. Listen, you wanted this tender really badly. I arranged you got it. You owe me. And I'll make it worth your trouble. Estimate how much extra time you need for this. It better not be too many days. We don't want any more delays. And you don't want to be losing money.'

Tembo was about to deliver an angry reply, but then thought about the extra money. He named a figure.

There was a pause. 'That's a *lot* more than the extra cost.'

'Yes, it is,' Tembo said with satisfaction.

There was an even longer pause. 'Very well. But then you stick to the original schedule. And keep your mouth shut about this.'

'Fair enough. Have the money in my account tomorrow.' Tembo hung up. He smiled. It had been a bad day, but it had ended pretty well.

CHAPTER 5

Kubu and Ian had made a bit of a night of it, with Ian insisting Kubu join him for a single-malt whisky or two. Unsurprisingly, Kubu was a little under the weather as he and Ian drove to where the skeletons were waiting for them. He hadn't slept well, experiencing a number of bizarre dreams. However, hard as he tried, he couldn't remember them.

If this is how I'm going to feel if I drink too much, he thought, then I'm going to be very careful in future.

Ian, on the other hand, was on top of the world with seemingly no after-effects of the night before. As he drove, he was whistling melodies that Kubu had never heard before.

How does he do it? Kubu wondered.

When they arrived at the site, Abram was already there, together with the two constables, shovels at hand. Ian asked them to help him lay out a grid centred on the bones in the trench, perpendicular to and parallel to the trench, using lengths of string one metre apart. He was meticulous with the layout and keeping the string-lines parallel.

At last he was satisfied and gave a nod of approval. 'Good. Now I can record the location of any more bones we find against that grid.' He pointed to one corner. 'We'll call that row A, then B and so on. In the other direction, we'll start at 1, then 2 and so on.

We'll extend it later when the backhoe is moved.' He carefully photographed the grid from different positions.

Next, he instructed the constables to dig down to a little deeper than the deepest part of the trench, one starting at row A, going from cell A1 to A10, and the other to do row J from cell J1 to J10.

'Dig carefully, now. Don't go putting your spade through someone's head. They won't like it, and neither will I. It's soft sand, so digging should be easy. If you find nothing, move to the next cell and repeat, and so on. If you find something, let me know immediately.'

He turned and headed to the backhoe bucket to finish his work there.

Abram headed back to the police vehicle to sit out of the sun, but Kubu stayed for while, watching Ian and his team, and thinking about the situation. How should one investigate a case where the victims had died so long ago? Was it even a case for the police? Maybe there were only two Bushmen in total, who'd died from some sort of illness. Would Ian be able to identify that at an autopsy? Or perhaps there had been some sort of fight, but so long ago that no one remembered it anymore. If that was the case, there should be evidence of broken limbs or cracked skulls. Whatever the case, Mabaku would want a report laying out the evidence, the remains reburied in a more appropriate location, and a closed file.

The more interesting situation, Kubu mused, would be if there were more than two bodies, perhaps the remains of a mass murder or even of a serial killer who'd systematically buried his victims out here in the middle of nowhere.

Kubu shook his head gingerly and went to join Abram, who'd opened all the doors of the police vehicle to catch some breeze.

'How well do you know the people around here?' Kubu asked.

Abram shrugged. 'Quite well. I'm a policeman after all. Most people are poor, but a few are pretty rich. A lot have small farms near the river from here to Shakawe. The river is gold around here.

It's what we depend on. Most grow enough to live off and run a few cattle and goats, and some make a bit selling to the lodges. Tourism has also picked up, which helps, and we get a lot of fisherman coming for tiger fish. But most of that money goes to the lodge owners or tour operators. Overall, I'd say the town is making its way, better than it was ten years ago.'

Kubu thought it wasn't much different from any rural area in Botswana, except here they had water.

Abram pointed into the desert. 'Once you're away from the river, you're back in the Kalahari. Not much goes on out there. Some Bushmen come through from time to time. Also wild animals. That's about it.'

Kubu looked out over the sand and scrub, and wondered how it could ever support a community's food needs. The whole area was parched. Growing abundant crops was impossible.

He turned back to Abram. 'Tell me about this Kgosi Rantao.'

'What do you want to know? He's been chief for about ten years. He'll be around for a long time. He's only about fifty.'

'Is he popular?'

'Very much so. He's working hard to improve life for everyone in Ncamasere.'

The two men sat quietly for a few minutes, then Kubu stirred. 'I can't sit around doing nothing. Let's go back to the station, and I'll take a look at Old Man Dibotelo's son's missing-person file.'

Abram shook his head. 'You're crazy. That happened just after I was born. How long do you think they keep records around here?'

Kubu shrugged. 'I've no idea. You work here. How long do they keep records?' That stopped Abram's derision. 'Come on, I promised I'd take a look. At least it'll be better than sitting here being roasted.'

Abram was obviously reluctant to exert any energy, but Kubu eventually cajoled him into action. 'Okay, I'll take you,' Abram groaned, 'but you won't find anything that Dibotelo doesn't know already.'

Kubu told Ian he'd be back later in the afternoon, and the two detectives set off for Shakawe.

In fact, the Shakawe police station did keep its old records, unfortunately in a large storage shed at the back of the property. Not only was it scorching inside the brick structure, with a corrugated iron roof and no windows, but year after year of boxes blocked those from earlier years.

Abram groaned when he realised what had to be done. 'We may have to move a couple of hundred boxes before we find the one with Dibotelo's case.'

Kubu frowned. 'Abram, do you know how the boxes are organised? Are all the files for a year just dumped in boxes and stored, or are different sorts of cases stored separately, such as robberies, murders, missing persons, and so on?'

Abram shrugged.

Kubu was getting annoyed at how little Abram seemed to know of what happened at his own police station.

'Come on, Abram, let's pull out the closest boxes and check. Hopefully something will be written on the outside, at least.'

They were relieved when they saw that the year 1997 was scrawled on the closest boxes. It looked as though the station kept a couple of years' records in the station building itself before moving them out to the shed.

It took about five minutes for them to stack all the 1997 boxes on the ground in front of the shed. By the time they'd finished, sweat was pouring down Kubu's face, running into his eyes. His only handkerchief was sodden and barely useful to stem the flow.

He stretched his back and took a deep breath. 'Let's see if they're organised in any way.'

To his surprise and delight, each box contained several concertina folders marked on the top with their contents. At least they wouldn't have to look at every scrap of paper.

It took another few minutes to open each box and check the folder names. There was one marked Missing Persons.

'Thank God,' exclaimed Abram.

Kubu nodded. He was beginning to fade. 'Now we only have to move about twenty-five years of boxes to find the one we want,' he groaned. 'I'm going to need lots of water and food.'

Abram started walking towards the station. 'Let me talk to my boss. Maybe I can persuade him to arrange some help.'

Kubu immediately followed, looking forward to some shade and some liquid. When they reached Station Commander Balopi's office, Kubu was taken aback by how tidy it was. There were no piles of folders on the desk, no stacks of folders on the floor. The walls were bare, and there were no family photographs anywhere.

Nothing like mine, he thought. Where did he keep everything?

'Assistant Superintendent, sir.' Abram snapped to attention. 'I have a request that will help Detective Sergeant Bengu here.'

'What is it, Detective Sergeant Nteba?'

'Kubu here – that is, Detective Sergeant Bengu – wants to find the missing-person file for Kagiso Dibotelo's son.'

Balopi stared at Kubu. 'Are you completely crazy?'

'Probably, sir. But I promised Rra Dibotelo that I would look at his file and report back.'

Balopi shook his head. 'You're new on the force, aren't you?'

'Yes, sir. About four months, sir.'

'We've been telling Dibotelo for the past twenty-five years that his son's file is still open and that we are still trying to find out what happened to him.'

'But sir...'

'But you promised him you'd look into it, right?'

'Yes, sir.'

'A promise like that is made so you can get rid of him. It does not obligate you to do anything.'

There was an uncomfortable silence. 'Sir,' Kubu eventually said, 'when I make a promise, I intend to keep it.'

'For fuck's sake, Bengu, are you out of your mind?'

'Probably, sir, but I still intend to keep my promise, even if it takes me a week of moving boxes by myself to find the right file.'

'Detective Sergeant, you are not in control of how you spend your time. Did Assistant Superintendent Mabaku instruct you to look for Dibotelo's file?'

Kubu said nothing.

'Well, did he?'

'No, sir. He didn't.'

'Then why aren't you doing what he said?'

'Sir, I've watched Dr MacGregor digging for several hours. I don't believe I have anything more to learn about that.'

Balopi glared at Abram. 'And I suppose your request is that I detail some constables to help you find the right box and the right file and the right report, even though it may take moving a hundred boxes?'

'Yes, sir. That's my request. But it's more likely three hundred boxes.'

'Well, the answer is no. If you want to do it, you must do it yourselves. And be finished this afternoon. Clear?"

'But—'

'No buts. Those are my orders.'

As Kubu and Abram made their way back to the shed, Kubu looked at Abram and said quietly, 'I think I just had my second date.'

Abram laughed. 'If you stay within his limits, you'll get on fine. That's what we've all learnt to do.'

'I'm always interested in why people behave the way they do. Why they are who they are. What do you think made him like that?'

Abram shook his head. 'I don't think about things like that very much. Rumour has it that he's a chip off the old block.'

∽

In fact, it didn't take nearly as long as expected to find the file Kubu was looking for. Fortunately, behind the first three years of boxes were two aisles with boxes stacked on racks on either side. And each box was clearly marked with the date and contents. Once the recent stacks had been cleared, it was plain sailing to find the missing-persons folder from the year Dibotelo's son had disappeared.

Exhausted, Kubu took the folder inside to the conference room and settled in to find the report he needed. The first two reports were about two boys who had gone out to play and were never seen again. Initially, according to the report, the parents insisted that they'd been abducted by a tokoloshe set on them by a local witchdoctor. However, the police were of the opinion that they'd been taken by crocodiles while splashing in the shallows of the Kavango River.

The third report was the one Kubu was looking for. Dibotelo's son, Tandi, was reported missing on 7 September, 1975. He'd been last seen two days previously, heading out to check on the three cows the family owned. When he didn't return home that evening, no one was overly worried as they thought he was probably with his girlfriend. But when the girlfriend showed up the next day enquiring about his whereabouts, they realised that something was amiss. For three days, the entire community searched the area for any signs of the young man, to no avail. After a week, the police called off the search, thinking privately that he'd headed off to Gaborone for work

Underlined heavily in the report was the statement by Dibotelo that his son would never have disappeared without trace, and that on the day of his disappearance, they'd talked about lobola issues. The young man was obviously intent on marrying his girlfriend.

There were also notes in the file from the following two years about Dibotelo's visits to the police station.

Saddened, Kubu realised he had nothing to offer the father other than an assurance that the case was still active – a stretch, but credible now that he'd shaken the dust off it.

Kubu continued to page through the remaining three reports when he stopped suddenly. Did I see correctly? he wondered. He flipped back a page or two, where there was a report of an Ezekiel Zondo going missing on 23 August, 1975 – less than two weeks before Dibotelo's son. The circumstances were similar. Zondo had gone out hunting and had never returned. Kubu felt a spark of interest. Could this man be related to the woman who was raving about Mami Wata at the excavation? He'd thought she was simply curious like most of the others, but perhaps her interest was much more personal.

Kubu's heart beat faster. Could it be a coincidence? Or was there some sinister connection between the two incidents? Then reality kicked in. The police had found nothing suspicious twenty-five years ago, so why should they do so now?

∿

By the time Ian and the two constables stopped working that evening, they'd unearthed seven more skulls and many of the associated bones. A very depressed Ian reported that he was convinced they were working on a mass grave of Bushmen who'd been murdered. At least two of the deceased were children.

In addition to more artifacts, he'd also found four small chunks of metal, which he took for bullets. 'I'm nae an expert on old firearms, but there are people in Pretoria or London who'll be able to identify them. They must have been lodged in the victims' bodies at the time they were buried.'

When they returned to Drotsky's, they persuaded the receptionist to let them use the manager's office to phone Mabaku.

'I hope you're about to tell me that you've wrapped up and are heading back here.'

'Unfortunately not,' Ian replied. 'We've bad news.'

There was silence on the line.

'I've now found a total of nine skulls,' Ian continued. 'Two of them are children. The bad news is that I think they were murdered.'

'Murdered? How do you know that?'

Ian went on to explain the head injuries he'd seen.

'Could it have been a fight between two Bushmen groups?'

'Aye, it could, but I also found what I think are bullets. I dinna think Bushmen had guns when this happened.'

'Goddammit! That's all we need. You'd better continue digging to see what else you can find. Bengu can ask around to see if anyone knows anything about this.'

'How much more time do you think you'll need?' Kubu asked as they sat down for a drink. He was anxious to get back to Gaborone.

'Difficult to say. At least another day. Two if we find more bones.'

'I'll speak to Abram to see if he can point me to people who may know something.'

Ian climbed to his feet. 'Yes, we better have something to tell your boss. Well, let's go and have dinner. I've had enough for one day.'

CHAPTER 6

Kubu and Ian were about to start dinner when the lady at reception came to the table and told Ian there was a phone call for him from the Shakawe police station.

'What now?' Ian grumbled as he stood up.

When he picked up the phone, the man on duty told him that the constable guarding the excavation site had just radioed in to report that a Bushman had arrived and was refusing to leave, giving a garbled story about ancestors. Ian told the constable to relay the message that the man could stay, but not be allowed into the excavation itself. Ian and Kubu would get there as soon as possible.

It was Kubu's turn to grumble when Ian told him that dinner was being postponed. However, he was intrigued by what the man wanted and felt a buzz of curiosity as they drove to the site.

When they arrived, the sun was sinking towards the horizon in a fiery sunset – so common in the dust-filled air of the Kalahari. They found the constable sitting on a camp chair in front of a fire, sipping tea from an enamel mug, glowering at a man sitting on his haunches on the sand a short distance away. From his features, it was clear that he was a Bushman, although darker than most, probably of mixed blood. Despite the man's face, wizened from years in the desert sun, Kubu judged him to be quite young, probably around forty. He wore a crumpled jacket over a red shirt and khaki slacks. On his head he had a dirty grey hat.

The constable climbed to his feet and pointed at the man with his mug. 'I told him to sit there and not move.'

'I learnt a little of their language from my Bushman school friend,' Kubu said. 'Let me try and talk to him.'

When he reached the man, Kubu stopped and put his hand over his heart. '!Gâi//goas. Good day.' He tried to say the click sounds the way Khumanego had taught him.

The man didn't respond, but addressed Ian. '!Gâitsēs. Good day.'

Kubu tried again. '!Gâi//goas.'

'He doesn't seem to understand you.' Ian said and turned to the Bushman. 'Ian. My name is Ian. What is your name?'

The man touched himself on the chest. 'Selelo.'

'Selelo?'

The man nodded.

Ian pointed to Kubu, who was quietly embarrassed by his failure to communicate. 'Selelo, this is Kubu.'

'Kubu?' The man let out a high-pitched giggle and did a little dance with his arms mimicking a fat man. 'Kubu?' He giggled again, but then he frowned and said no more.

Ian smiled at Kubu. 'He seems to find your hippo nickname amusing.' He turned to the Bushman. 'Why are you here, Selelo?'

'When moon full, ancestors speak to me.' He looked at them with anxious eyes. 'Is it true?'

'Is what true, Selelo?'

'Ancestors happy. Tell me to come.' Then he turned away and spat into the sand. 'Ancestors sad.'

Kubu couldn't work out what the man was getting at, but didn't say anything.

Eventually, Selelo spread his arms, hands upturned, and raised them to the sky. 'Ancestors waiting.' He kept his arms raised. 'Ancestors waiting long time.'

He turned towards Kubu and lowered his arms, his face struggling to maintain composure. There was pain in his eyes. The silence stretched. When Selelo spoke again, his voice was barely audible. 'Is it true?'

This time Kubu felt compelled to say something. 'Selelo, is what true? What do you need to know?'

Selelo shook his head. 'Not Selelo. Ancestors. I am ancestors' mouth. And ears.'

Kubu didn't know what to say, so sat quietly. Ian, too, said nothing.

Suddenly, Selelo let out a wail. 'Is it true? Is it true my family found?'

He has to be referring to the skeletons, Kubu thought. 'Was your family here? Did they die here? When?'

'Many seasons.' He barely whispered. 'Too many seasons. Why I born.'

Now it was Ian's turn to try to solve the puzzle. 'Selelo, do you mean they disappeared before you were born?'

Selelo's shoulders slumped. 'Before I born. My ancestors. Ancestors of my ancestors.' Tears started to run down his face. 'Is it true?'

'Selelo, this man' – Kubu pointed at Ian – 'he found nine of your ancestors here.' He held up nine fingers. 'They were killed. Shot.' He made as though he was shooting a rifle. 'And hit.' He swung his arm as though there was a club in his hand. 'Nine killed. Maybe more. It is terrible.'

To Kubu's surprise, Selelo smiled. 'Good they found.' He pointed to the sky. 'Ancestors happy.'

He stood up. 'Stay tonight. Need to talk to ancestors so they ready.'

The constable jumped to his feet. 'No way. I'm not spending the night with him here.'

Ian waved him off. 'Selelo, what do you want to do here? The bones are no longer here. This land is being dug up. We moved your ancestors' bones somewhere safe.'

Selelo shook his head. 'No bones. Just where they die. Make sure ancestors ready to welcome.'

Kubu was uncomfortable. 'Ian, this is a police crime scene. We can't just leave him here. Mabaku will eat us alive.'

Ian took Selelo's arm and led him about a hundred metres

away. 'You can stay here, but you must promise that you won't go to the hole in the ground. If you go there, the policeman will take you away.'

Selelo looked Ian in the eye. 'I stay here.'

Ian nodded. 'We'll be back in the morning.' He started walking back to his vehicle, but the constable ran up, looking worried.

'Will I be safe with him here all night? They have very bad poisons, and maybe he's angry.'

'You'll be fine, Constable. Just leave him alone. We're heading back. We haven't had dinner.'

As soon as he was alone, Selelo started foraging for wood. He'd need a big fire if he was going to talk to the ancestors. Given the area was largely covered in scrub, it took a long time to gather what he needed. He'd hoped to find some big logs that would smoulder for hours, but was unsuccessful. When he eventually finished, there were two big piles of twigs and small branches.

Selelo took off his jacket and shirt, slipped off his grubby khaki trousers, and sat down on the sand facing the setting sun. As it dropped below the horizon, red and purple slowly spread across the dust-laden air.

When the sky turned dark and his ancestors started appearing in the sky, he closed his eyes and tried to remember his mother, but he couldn't because she had walked into the desert when he was about a year old, never to be seen again.

The family she'd left him with, his aunt and uncle, always said it was because she wanted him to have a happy life. For a long time, he'd believed the story, proud that she'd had the courage to do what she thought was right. However, as he got older, he found himself asking why leaving him was right. He wanted a real mother, not some other woman. Why couldn't she have stayed?

One day he'd summoned the courage to ask his uncle as they walked the sand to find some antelope to kill for meat. The man shook his head. 'Your mother loved you. But too much. She didn't have the courage to tell you.'

He remembered asking another time what it was his mother couldn't tell him. His uncle shook his head and said sadly, 'Her story.'

It was only at the age he was allowed to hunt by himself that he heard about the 'terrible day'. Many years earlier, his mother's family was living by The River. He'd learnt later that was the Kavango River. One day, men had come and attacked them, shooting them and hitting them with clubs. His mother's husband had thrown himself in front of her to protect her, but he had no defence against the men. As he fell, she ran into the bushes to hide, but one man had followed her, then left her for dead. It had taken his mother four days to drag herself back to the sacred Tsodilo Hills, where she lived, close to her sister. It was her sister's family that had brought him up.

Eventually, Selelo stopped reminiscing and retrieved a box of matches from his coat. He lit some small twigs, protected the flames, and set fire to one of the piles of wood. He sat down, stared into the flames, and thought about his ancestors. I look forward to meeting them, he thought. But most of all my mother.

He gazed at the stars, each an ancestor of someone. Which are mine? he wondered.

∼

A hundred metres away, the constable also had a fire, a small, practical fire to heat water and keep him company. He wasn't happy that a Bushman was so close. He'd never spoken to one, but throughout his life, all he'd heard was derogatory comments about them. 'Animals', 'filthy', 'stupid', 'will come at night and poison you'.

He looked over to where the Bushman sat. The man had built a big fire, flames and sparks shooting into the air.

The constable shook his head. How stupid, he thought. The fire will burn itself out in less than an hour, then it will be dark.

He put another log onto his fire.

～

It took nearly two hours for Selelo's fire to dwindle into a pile of glowing ashes. He stood up, pushed a few twigs into the embers, then, when they caught fire, hurried over to the second pile, setting it alight.

He stood watching it for a few minutes as the flames grew higher and hotter. It was time to tell the ancestors.

He began to sway and started singing, a song without words. Occasionally he would stamp a foot, slowly getting himself into the mood. He shuffled sideways around the fire, the whole time gazing at the flames. The ancestors were going to be happy with the news. They had missed their relatives for so many years.

Selelo upped the tempo, stamping his feet more often, sometimes slowly spinning. Always singing. He gazed up. They were watching him, bright-eyed. They were so close, he could hear them whisper. He flung his arms upward to embrace them and started to dance, slowly at first, then picking up speed. Feet stamping, body spinning.

～

The constable was nervous. He could see the Bushman moving around the fire. He could hear the man's strange singing. Nothing like the harmonies of black people, but out of tune with no melody.

He shook his head. People were right. Bushmen were very strange.

He wondered what the song was about, if it was about anything. Probably singing about the dead people the man from Gaborone had found in the trench. Was it possible they were relatives?

He looked over again. The man was moving faster, the singing becoming more frenzied.

A chill crept through the constable. Was the Bushman working himself into a frenzy to attack him?

He put another log on the fire. He wanted to see the man early if he came.

∼

Selelo danced faster and faster. Eyes closed. Spinning. Spinning. His ancestors clapped in time to the music, urging him on. Round and round he went. Round and round.

He felt himself leave his body. He was on his way. He looked down and saw himself still spinning. Upward he went, upward to meet the ancestors.

Then he was there, and he told them he'd found the missing family. Buried under the sand, not on it as they should have been. They smiled. That was what they'd been waiting so many years for. They thanked him. And reminded him of the pledge he'd made so long ago at the top of Female Hill.

He was pleased he'd been able to bring them the news they'd waited so long for. They'd been patient. Then he returned to his body.

He circled the fire one more time and gave one last shout. Raising his arms into the air, he collapsed onto the sand.

∼

The constable was becoming angry. The singing had gone on for several hours. It was annoying and disturbing. What could have been a peaceful night had become a nightmare. A frenzied Bushman close by, to all intents and purposes going mad.

He looked over at the fire a hundred metres away. How had it stayed alight so long? he wondered. It should have burnt out hours ago.

He looked at the man, spinning and singing. How did he keep going for so long?

Then he saw the Bushman throw his hands in the air and collapse on the ground.

'Thank God,' he said out loud.

About half an hour later, he glanced towards the Bushman's fire. It was still burning. He looked more closely. The Bushman hadn't moved. He was still splayed out on the ground.

'Damn!' Irritation welled up. He felt he should go and check that the man was all right. But that was the last thing he wanted to do.

Damned Bushmen.

He sat for a few minutes, hoping the Bushman would move.

He didn't.

'Damn,' he said again and stood up. He found his torch and walked into the darkness.

CHAPTER 7

A loud banging on the door roused Kubu from a deep sleep that had been punctuated by vivid dreams of his grandparents floating in the sky.

Bang, bang.

It took Kubu a few moments to realise that the noise was real and not part of his dream.

'Hold on,' he shouted. He turned on a light and went to the door. When he opened it, he saw a man wearing what looked like a bus conductor's hat and holding a knobkierie. It was the night watchman.

'Telephone call. From the police station.'

Kubu guessed that something had happened at the site, that the Bushman had probably broken his promise and gone into the excavation. He grabbed a robe from the bathroom and followed the man.

'Detective Sergeant Kubu ... I mean Bengu ... What's happened?'

'Detective Sergeant, this is Shakawe Police Station. Sorry to disturb you, but we just received a radio call from our man guarding your digging site. He thinks the Bushman is dead. He says that you ordered him to contact you if anything unusual happened.'

'Thank you, I'll get dressed and go there right away. Can you order an ambulance?'

There was a silence for a few moments. 'I don't think so, rra. The nearest ambulance is in Maun and that's at least four hours away.'

'All right, I'm on my way. I'll bring Dr MacGregor with me.'

∾

Finding the excavation site at night was more difficult than Kubu expected, but after a few wrong turns, they arrived. The constable met them and pointed to an area outside the crime-scene tapes. 'He's over there.'

'What happened?'

As they walked, following the constable's torch light, he told them that soon after dark, Selelo had built a fire. There was nothing unusual about that. But about two hours later, the constable had heard singing, if one could call it that. More like chanting. It was quite irritating. He saw Selelo dancing and spinning, sometimes faster, sometimes slower. All the time chanting, throwing his head back and pointing to the sky.

The constable had assumed that it was some strange Bushman ritual and had tried to ignore it. An hour later, Selelo was still at it, the tempo picking up, his voice becoming shrill.

'I've no idea how he could keep going for so long. And an hour after that, he was still at it, dancing and spinning and chanting. It was driving me mad. Then it suddenly stopped. When I looked over, I saw he'd collapsed on the ground. I waited for a while then went over. I tried to find a pulse, but felt nothing. That's when I radioed the station to contact you.'

Ian knelt next to the motionless Selelo. 'You did the right thing, Constable. Well done.' Ian felt for a pulse on Selelo's wrist. He shook his head. 'Nothing.' He then felt the Bushman's neck. He cocked his head as though listening. 'He's alive, but I can barely feel his pulse. Probably hyperventilated from all that dancing.'

He stood up. 'Constable, please help me get him to the Land Rover. Is there a clinic in Shakawe?'

'Yes, sir, but it'll be closed now, and I don't know where the nurse lives. I think it opens at eight.'

The two men laid Selelo on the back seat. Then Ian turned to the constable. 'Thank you. We'll take him back to Drotsky's and do the best we can.'

When they reached Drotsky's, Kubu and Ian carried Selelo to Ian's cabin, where they laid him on the couch. Ian again put his fingers on Selelo's neck.

'It's still very weak.' He turned to Kubu. 'Go and find some salt. Quickly.'

Ian grabbed some packets of sugar from the refreshment tray and emptied them into a glass of water. He dipped a washrag into the water, gently opened the Bushman's mouth, and pushed a corner of the rag into it. Then he found a blanket in a cupboard and covered the man.

A few minutes later, Kubu returned with a salt shaker. Ian unscrewed the top and added a little to the glass. He retrieved the washrag, soaked it again, and reinserted it into Selelo's mouth. Finally, he wet a hand towel and mopped Selelo's face.

'Without an IV drip, that's all I can do for now, Kubu. You may as well go and get some sleep.'

~

Kubu tossed and turned for about half an hour, but couldn't sleep. Eventually he stopped trying, dressed again, and returned to Ian's cabin.

'No real change. If anything, his pulse is a little weaker.'

'Maybe we should get an ambulance from Maun.'

Ian shook his head. 'There's not much more they can do. He's not injured, and I'm sure he hasn't had a heart attack. Just exhaustion causing very low blood pressure is what I think. If we can get some sugar and water into his stomach, that'll help.' He waved at the door. 'Go and get some sleep.'

Kubu shook his head. 'That won't happen. I'll stay and keep you company. I'll make some coffee.'

A few minutes later he handed Ian a cup. 'This would keep an elephant awake.'

Ian sipped it and grimaced. 'How much did you put in?'

'Three packets. Selelo needs you awake.'

The next hour dragged by, with both men sitting with their eyes closed, dozing, but definitely not sleeping. Occasionally, Ian would check Selelo's pulse, but there was no change.

When eventually the Bushman stirred, Ian woke at once and jumped up and checked his pulse. 'Definitely a bit stronger.'

For the first time since they'd found Selelo collapsed on the ground, Kubu felt some hope that the Bushman was going to survive.

Ian slid Selelo into a semi-sitting position and placed a pillow behind his head. He soaked the wash rag again in the sugar-and-salt solution and pushed it into his mouth. 'Hopefully some will get into his stomach and revive him.'

'Can't you just trickle some into his mouth?'

'I'm worried it would end up in his lungs. That wouldn't be good in his state.'

Over the next half hour, Selelo slowly started showing signs of recovery. His hands started to move, and his legs twitched. And eventually, he opened his eyes.

Ian removed the wash rag from Selelo's mouth. 'Can you hear me, Selelo?'

Selelo answered with a blank stare.

Ian shook him gently by the shoulder. 'Selelo, can you hear me?'

Selelo took a deep breath and closed his eyes.

'Selelo. Selelo.'

Nothing. No response.

Kubu's patience was beginning to wear thin. 'Can't you get him to drink some of your concoction?'

Ian shook his head and returned to his chair. 'He'll let us know when he's ready.'

~

By the time light started creeping through the windows, Selelo had recovered sufficiently to be able to ingest both Ian's solution and some solids. Eventually he spoke. 'They say it must stop.'

Kubu and Ian glanced at each other.

Kubu leaned forward. 'Selelo, who says what must stop?'

'Last night I spoke to ancestors. They say they happy and not happy.'

Kubu had no idea what Selelo meant.

'Who is trying to make the ancestors happy, Selelo?'

'Past must be forgotten. I must make past forgotten.'

'Do you mean that the ancestors must forget what happened to your people? The people we found?'

'Not forget. Remember. I make ancestors happy.' He paused. 'I happy for that. When young man, I promise ancestors to remember death of family. I want, but don't want to remember. I feel like bee. When it sting, it die.'

Kubu glanced at Ian, who shrugged.

'Hard for me to sting.'

With that he fell back on the pillow and closed his eyes.

Ian stepped forward and picked up Selelo's wrist. 'His pulse is strong. I think his little speech exhausted him, and he's fallen asleep. He'll be fine. I'll check him in an hour.'

'What did you make of all that?'

Ian shrugged. 'I dinna ken. I've no idea what he was talking about.'

'It sounded to me as though he was a kid when those Bushmen were killed, and he promised to always remember them. Sounds pretty normal. I'd never forget my parents if someone killed them.'

'But what was that about him being a bee?'

Kubu shook his head. 'It sounded as though he had to do something for the ancestors, but if he did it might destroy him. I wonder if that meant kill someone. In revenge.'

'He doesn't strike me as a coward, but what do I know? Maybe it was all just part of a dream he was having.' Ian yawned then stretched. 'Well, I'd better call the clinic and let them know I'll be bringing in a patient this morning.'

Kubu also yawned. 'I have this feeling there's something in all that ancestor stuff that we need to know. But what, I've no idea. I'll see you here in half an hour. I'm going to take a long, hot shower.'

When Kubu left his cabin after his shower, he saw Ian and Selelo sitting on a bench overlooking the river. He hurried up to them and sat down.

'Good morning, Selelo. How are you feeling?'

Selelo just nodded.

'How are you feeling, Selelo?' Kubu repeated.

'I go back to Tsodilo.'

Kubu frowned. 'Is that where you came from?'

Selelo nodded.

Kubu turned to Ian. 'Tsodilo is the Bushmen's most sacred site. It's a range of hills where they believe the gods placed humans on the earth.' He turned back to Selelo. 'How did you get here? That must be a two-hour drive. Do you have a car?'

'Selelo walk.'

'You walked? It must be nearly a hundred kilometres.'

'Easy walk.' He stood up. 'I go back.'

Ian took hold of his arm. 'We're taking you to the clinic. You need to rest.'

'I go back to Tsodilo.'

'Oh no, you're not. Kubu, go and order some breakfast to be brought out here, then we can leave.'

They left about half an hour later, and Kubu dropped Ian at the excavation site.

'I'm not sure whether to hope you find more bones or not, Ian. I'll drop Selelo off at the clinic then go to the station to catch up on paperwork. I'll also call Mabaku to bring him up to date.'

When they reached the clinic in Shakawe, Kubu explained the

situation to the nurse in charge and asked if they could look after Selelo. 'Dr MacGregor was worried that Selelo was going to die after his trance dance. He thinks a couple of days of rest and good nutrition should be enough for a full recovery.'

The nurse agreed, and they led Selelo to an empty ward with four beds. 'I'll try to keep the other beds from being used,' she said. 'The locals don't like Bushmen.'

Kubu turned to Selelo. 'They will look after you well here. When you're strong again, I will take you back to Tsodilo. Okay?'

Selelo didn't respond.

Kubu raised his voice a little. 'Okay?'

Selelo nodded.

'Behave yourself. I'll come and see you this afternoon.' With that, Kubu walked out and drove the short distance to the police station.

CHAPTER 8

'Have you gone out of your mind, Bengu? His ancestors are both happy and unhappy? What does that mean? And this Bushman of yours says he stings like a bee? Huh? Then MacGregor takes him to his own room in the middle of the night to look after him? All that will lead to is Drotsky's sending me a bigger bill.'

Kubu waited for Mabaku's tirade to continue.

'And where is he now? Dancing on his ancestors' grave, no doubt.'

'No, sir. Dr MacGregor suggested that he should stay at the Shakawe Clinic for a few days to recover. He was worried that the man was going to die. Those trance dances can be exhausting.'

'And how is he going to pay for the clinic? Do a dance? Sing a song?'

Kubu took a deep breath. He hadn't thought to ask the nurse about payment. 'I'm sure it's free, sir. But if it isn't, I'll pay for it myself.'

'For God's sake, Bengu. I don't know what you've been smoking up there. You were meant to watch MacGregor exhume some ancient bones, then come back to Gabs. Now we have nine or so Bushman skeletons, all apparently murdered, and a crazed Bushman who tells you stories that make no sense.'

Kubu thought it wise not to comment.

'Listen carefully, Bengu. Tell MacGregor that today is his last day digging for bones. You and the doctor drive back to Gabs tomorrow morning. Understood?'

Kubu wasn't inclined to argue. 'Yes, sir. I understand.'

There was a click as Mabaku hung up.

Kubu sat thinking about the situation. From Mabaku's perspective in Gaborone, the situation must look bizarre. A simple exhumation had turned into a mass grave, and a Bushman had appeared out of nowhere, mysteriously knowing about the skeletons, with a raft of incomprehensible stories.

Kubu could see Mabaku's point. It was a mess.

～

It took Kubu a few minutes to contact the constable at the excavation site on the radio. A few minutes more, and Kubu was talking to Ian.

'Mabaku wants us to leave for Gabs first thing in the morning. He wasn't happy with what's been happening here.'

Kubu heard Ian sigh. 'All right. We're just about finished anyway. I'll try to wrap everything up by the time you pick me up this afternoon. How's our little friend doing?'

'He's at the clinic. The nurse said they'd take care of him.'

Ian ended the conversation by suggesting that Kubu check in on Selelo a few times throughout the day.

After signing off, Kubu poured himself a cup of coffee and settled in the conference room to finish writing his notes on the various missing men. He was looking forward to being back in Gaborone, and hoped he could persuade Joy to have a drink with him after work – if she didn't have something else arranged. He felt bad for not contacting her, but he had to admit, he'd been so focussed on what was happening in Ncamasere that she'd temporarily slipped his mind. It was time to rectify the situation.

He picked up the phone and dialled the records department at CID headquarters.

'Records. This is Joy.'

Kubu's heart fluttered. 'Joy. This is Kubu. How are you?'

'Kubu. So nice to hear your voice. I've been wondering what was happening with your skeletons.'

Kubu hesitated, hoping that wasn't a mild rebuke.

'You won't believe what's happened up here. It's been crazy. There's so much to tell you.' He took a deep breath. 'I'll be back on Monday evening. Would you like to have a drink after work?'

There was no immediate response.

'Joy, are you there?'

'I'm still here. I was just thinking. I have an appointment that evening.'

Kubu's heart sank.

'But I should be able to change it.'

'That would be wonderful. I'll phone you tomorrow evening to confirm. I'd like to chat some more now, but I'm at the Shakawe police station—'

'No problem. I'm busy too. Speak to you tomorrow. Thanks for calling. Bye.'

There was a click, and the line went dead.

Kubu leant back in his chair, wondering about the call. In some ways, Joy had sounded distant. Yet she'd been willing to change something to meet him for a drink. He shook his head. It's too bad that dating isn't rational, he thought.

Kubu had almost finished his report when the constable at reception knocked on the door. 'Detective Sergeant, you need to get over to the clinic. There's a problem with your Bushman.'

'He's not my Bushman, Constable. He showed up where Dr MacGregor is working with the skeletons, then collapsed. I'm just trying to help.'

'Well, whatever. You'd better get over there. The nurse is not happy.'

Kubu picked up his papers and headed out to Ian's car. Two minutes later, he walked into the clinic, where the nurse was at the reception desk. 'He's gone. Climbed out of the window and disappeared. We've looked, but there's no sign of him.'

Kubu wasn't sure whether to feel angry with Selelo for escaping from the clinic or relieved that he was no longer his responsibility.

'You need to find him. He's very weak.'

'But if I find him and bring him back, he'll do the same thing. We can't hold him against his will.'

The nurse frowned. 'What about his family? Where does he live?'

'All he said to me this morning was that he wanted to go back to Tsodilo Hills.'

'He'll never make it. That's a hundred kilometres away.'

'Well, I'll drive around a bit and see if I can find him. That's really all I can do.' Kubu turned and headed for the door. Before he left the building, he stopped. 'Thank you, nurse, for trying to find him. Please let the police station know if he comes back.'

Half an hour later, having had no success in finding Selelo, Kubu sat in the police-station conference room and reflected on what had happened. He realised he had to accept that he'd hit a brick wall. He was sure Selelo knew more than he had told them about the dead Bushmen, but, even if he found him, he had no way of making him talk.

In addition, unless Ian could find some piece of forensic evidence that would shed more light on what had happened to the Bushmen he'd dug up, it looked as though they'd be returning to Gaborone with the skeletons, but no information about them.

That will suit Mabaku, Kubu thought. Case closed. No problems.

Kubu was despondent. He'd arrived in Shakawe not expecting anything interesting. The idea of watching Ian dig up skeletons hadn't been particularly exciting. Then Selelo had appeared, and

Kubu had become excited about what they may learn. Now Selelo had disappeared.

While Kubu was feeling sorry for himself, the station commander walked into the meeting room. As always, he was meticulously dressed.

How does he do it? Kubu wondered, thinking how crumpled his own clothes were after a day's wear.

'What's this about you helping a Bushman?'

Kubu stood up. 'Good morning, rra.'

'Reception tells me that you took a Bushman to the clinic, but he escaped. What's going on?' He pulled up a seat and made Kubu go through the whole story in detail.

When Kubu was finished, he frowned. 'I don't like things I don't know about happening in my area. These vagrants come through and steal things, a chicken or even a goat. Cause trouble. If he's gone, good riddance, but if he turns up later, keep him at the station.'

Kubu nodded and started to comment, but Balopi interrupted him.

'Assistant Superintendent Mabaku wants you back as soon as possible, so you must leave for Gabs first thing in the morning. You may as well hang around here until it's time to pick up MacGregor.' He climbed to his feet. 'We have the monthly kgotla later, so I won't see you again. Have a safe trip.'

With that, he turned and left.

CHAPTER 9

That afternoon, the residents of Ncamasere straggled towards the monthly kgotla, where they could air their grievances, raise issues and appeal to the local chief, Kgosi Rantao, for justice. Most items were dealt with right away, but some the kgosi deferred for later consideration.

At the front of a crowd nearly a hundred strong, the kgosi sat with his counsellors. They enjoyed the shade of an ancient jack-alberry tree, while the others sat on dirty plastic chairs arrayed in arcs facing the chief. Many had umbrellas, and some fanned themselves with old newspapers.

The kgosi wondered what topics would surface during the afternoon. There would be the usual complaints about stolen chickens, and neighbours encroaching over property lines. There'd be accusations of rude comments and bad behaviour, and occasionally a dispute over lobola. And he knew there were rumours circulating about the skeletons and the sudden appearance of a Bushman at the site where they'd been found. He hoped that wouldn't come up at all.

The tough issue, which would certainly be raised, was the water project. Recently, a group of residents had been complaining about the allocation of land that would be irrigated when it was completed. The kgosi felt a twinge of irritation. The project was going to be his legacy to the community – the Kgosi Rantao Irrigation Project. He'd worked hard and long to get it off the ground, and he thought it fair that those who had contributed time and money should be the primary beneficiaries. Including himself.

As the project progressed, the complaints were becoming more strident, and now the unearthing of the skeletons was causing delays and problems. He needed to ensure these were kept to a minimum. There was too much at stake.

There was already a group jostling to get to the front, arguing loudly. He could see it was going to be a long, contentious meeting, and suddenly he felt tired. Occasionally, he daydreamed about a time when he could step down and hand over to his son, then breed his cattle and enjoy his grandchildren.

However, there was an issue. Raseelo, the man sitting next to him in the seat of honour, was his first-born and in line to succeed him. The problem was that his mind seemed to race off in different directions, unable to focus and plan, unable to come to reasoned decisions, and sometimes he'd lose his temper over nothing. More concerning was his inability to understand the politics of leadership. The kgosi worried about Raseelo succeeding him. Unfortunately, his other two sons had left to work elsewhere and had no interest in returning to the town's traditional way of life.

As though reading his thoughts, Raseelo glanced at the kgosi and gave a vacant smile. Then he turned away and looked down at his hands.

All the counsellors were now present, and it was time to begin the proceedings. The kgosi stood up and banged the table with his ceremonial knobkierie. 'Dumela, borra. Dumela, bomma.'

'Dumela, kgosi,' came the reply.

The kgosi sat down and banged his knobkierie again.

'Are there any matters to be brought before the kgotla?'

He had anticipated most of the raised hands – little happened in the village that he didn't know about. He wasn't concerned about most of the issues, but he gritted his teeth when he saw one of his own counsellors, John Mowisi, raising his hand. As far as the kgosi was concerned, Mowisi was a troublemaker. The kgosi decided to leave him until the end, when people would be tiring and eager to get out of the sun. Mowisi would take it as a slight, but the kgosi didn't care.

He was just about to ask the first man to state his issue when he saw a tall woman standing at the back. He was so surprised that he looked more closely to make sure. Mma Zondo didn't usually attend the kgotla, but there she was with her hand up.

Mma Zondo was unpredictable. She was likely to ramble on about her favourite spirit, Mami Wata, now that the water project was progressing, and he was confident he could handle that. However, she made it her business to know all the dirt in the village, including some that touched him, and that was a concern. The kgosi took a deep breath. He would deal with whatever came up when it came up. There was no point in worrying ahead of time.

The kgosi had taken his time with each of the issues raised, hoping that everyone would be eager to leave by the time he dealt with the last two people who'd raised their hands. Finally he pointed at the woman at the back.

'Mma Zondo, I'm very pleased that you've chosen to be at the kgotla. We all benefit from your wisdom. You can now have your say.'

'Thank you, kgosi.' The woman had a strong voice, so no one had to strain to hear her. 'As you know, your project to steal water from the Kavango River ran into a problem this week. I've warned you before that Mami Wata is angry, and will cast spells on the people involved and cause bad things to happen in the village.'

At the mention of Mami Wata, many of the crowd rolled their eyes, not because they didn't believe in the water spirit, but because they were tired of Mma Zondo's incessant stories of her personal interactions with her. The kgosi was pleased to see some people becoming restless and preparing to leave.

'As you know, kgosi,' Mma Zondo continued, 'skeletons were found in the ditch you were digging. How strange is that? What are the chances of that happening? You could have dug the ditch anywhere else and found nothing.' Mma Zondo lifted her hands above her head. 'Do you not think it is a sign? A sign that you should abandon your madness?' She pointed at the kgosi. 'You may laugh at Mami Wata, kgosi. You may laugh at me for talking to her. But those skeletons are a warning from her. And if not from her, from your ancestors, who know all you have done.'

The crowd was no longer restless. There was some nervous whispering as people puzzled over what Mma Zondo had said. They were used to her always invoking Mami Wata, but invoking the ancestors was more serious, especially when it was obvious that she was correct about the chances of a random ditch unearthing so many skeletons.

The kgosi was also concerned. He could handle Mami Wata. But his ancestors? That may not be so easy. For a moment or two, he worried that the irrigation project was indeed at risk.

Then he pulled himself together. Of course, the project was safe. The skeletons were a short-term irritation that would disappear once the policemen from Gaborone had left. The station commander had assured him that would happen in a day or two.

The kgosi rose to his feet. 'Mma Zondo, I've told you that you are wrong. Mami Wati knows we'll not take too much of her water. You can tell her if she listens to you so well.' There were titters from some of the crowd. 'The water will be good for our village, and our ancestors want what's best for their people. As for the skeletons, the police will make their report and go home. That will be the end of it.' He paused and stared around the assembly. 'Unless people start telling them about things that do not concern them. We do not tell outsiders what happens in our village. It stays between us. Is that clear?

Mma Zondo wasn't satisfied. 'And what of the Bushman spirit who appeared from nowhere mere days after the skeletons were found? He danced and cried out to his ancestors for justice. Then he vanished!' She jerked her hands apart as though she'd discovered she'd been holding a scorpion.

The kgosi was confused by the talk of spirits and ancestors, and for a moment he was at a loss as to how to respond. The station commander came to his rescue; he was already on his feet with his hand raised.

The kgosi nodded. 'Rra Balopi. You may speak.'

Balopi turned and glared at Mma Zondo. 'The police know all about this Bushman. He's one of these vagrants who comes through occasionally and causes trouble. He collapsed from the exertion of dancing all night, was taken to the clinic and climbed out of the window to escape. Does that sound like a spirit? We'll catch him and get rid of him, and that'll be the end of it. He is nothing. I ask you not to spread stupid rumours that ignorant people may believe. It's dangerous and—'

'He is nothing?' Mma Zondo interrupted. 'He appears the moment the skeletons appear, calls on his ancestors and disappears again, but you say he is nothing? That these accusing bones rising from the earth are nothing?'

She paused, and then called out loudly to the kgosi. 'Mami Wata knows. She knows. You steal her water for your own enrichment, but she and the ancestors will not permit it!'

For a moment, the kgosi was speechless. What had gotten into the woman? Was she truly mad as some people believed? Or did she know far more than she should?

This time rescue came from the most unlikely of sources. Rra Mowisi had jumped to his feet and, without waiting to be recognised, shouted back at Mma Zondo.

'You are mad. The water project is for the good of the people. Sit down and stop talking nonsense about Bushman spirits and skeletons.' Hardly pausing to take breath he swung towards the kgosi. 'But Kgosi, I've asked many times on behalf of some of the families in the village about the allocation of the land that will be supplied with water. Many times you've told us you will let us know. But we've heard nothing. You know we think that those with the worst land now should have the highest priority, but we now hear rumours that you will allocate the land to those who already have fine land.'

There was a rumble from one section of the crowd. The kgosi

frowned. The group that had pushed to the front were Mowisi's supporters and had sat together. He would have to be careful how he responded.

In the momentary pause, Raseelo sprang to his feet and started raving at Mowisi, calling him names. After a moment, Mowisi started shouting back, and the kgosi saw the men in Mowisi's group climb to their feet. How had things gotten out of hand so quickly? He banged his knobkierie repeatedly on the table until there was silence.

'Raseelo! Shut up. Sit down.'

Raseelo lowered himself into his chair and looked down at the ground.

The kgosi turned his attention to Mowisi. 'These people who want the land. Are they willing to contribute to its development? There are many costs and much work that needs to be done. Or is all they care about getting something for nothing? What about giving also?'

Mowisi shook his head as his supporters started muttering again. 'It's being paid for by a government grant and—'

The kgosi cut in. 'We have received some money towards the development from the central government, but much of the money needed to be raised by us. You are a member of my council and have attended the meetings. You certainly know all this. Why do you waste our time?' The kgosi paused, waiting for his meaning to sink in. Mowisi was a counsellor at the chief's pleasure.

'Yes, but nevertheless—'

Again, the kgosi interrupted. 'That is enough, Rra Mowisi. It's fortunate that your father isn't here to see this day. He was a fine man who worked hard to make Ncamasere flourish in the desert. He would be deeply ashamed of you.'

Furious at how the kgosi had treated him, Mowisi sat down, but the muttering continued. Mma Zondo was still on her feet and again had her hand up, but the kgosi had had enough.

As he stood up to end the meeting, he noticed another of his counsellors with his hand up. Rra Lesaka was one of his closest boyhood friends and, as far as the kgosi was concerned, would have a place on the council as long as he wanted it. Nevertheless, he was irritated. Since his stroke a few years before, Lesaka had difficulty with speech, and he had to hold onto his son to walk. If Lesaka did speak, he was sometimes confused and rambling, telling stories that had nothing to do with the matter at hand. The kgosi hoped that this wasn't one of those times.

'Rra Lesaka,' he said, 'the day is hot, and we are all tired. Please keep what you have to say to the point.'

Lesaka struggled to his feet. 'Kgosi, my friend, this is wrong. We counsellors are here to serve the people. There are different views, but these must be put forward with careful argument and proper consideration. There must be no shouting, no calling of names. Now, I've heard Rra Mowisi ask about the land many times, and I've heard you say each time that you will let the village know what your decision is. Yet you have not done that.' He leant on the table to steady himself. 'It does not help for you to dismiss him, to brush him aside like a fly on a plate. That is not how things are done in the spirit of botho.'

There was a smattering of applause from Mowisi's supporters.

'I have supported your water project because I thought it was good for all in the village, not just for some.' He paused. 'Kgosi, you and I have been friends since we could barely walk. We've done many things together. Most we're proud of, but some we prefer to keep to ourselves. Perhaps we have to keep them to ourselves, as you have said, but now these bones rise from the ground and this Bushman ... Perhaps it is time...' He paused again, and seemed to have lost the thread of what he was saying. Eventually he concluded, 'Kgosi, you must do the right thing for all the village.'

He sat down to more applause.

The kgosi kept his thoughts to himself. 'Thank you for your wise words, my friend. I will take them into consideration.'

With that, he banged on the table with his knobkierie and declared the kgotla over.

～

Lesaka's son, Joshua, hurried to take his father's arm. He was keen to steer his father home, where he could rest and have something to eat after the tiring afternoon. But, instead of allowing himself to be led away from the kgotla, Lesaka hobbled towards the kgosi. He stood waiting until he caught the chief's attention.

'Kgosi, may I speak with you for a few moments?'

The kgosi nodded.

'In private.'

'Right now?'

'Please. Right now.'

The kgosi nodded again and led the way to a spot behind the jackalberry tree, where they found a few chairs.

Lesaka turned to his son. 'Leave us. I'll call you when I'm ready.'

Joshua began to protest, but his father waved him away. He nodded and walked several paces away. The two men lowered their voices so he couldn't hear the conversation, but their expressions and the evident tension between them was worrying. This wasn't the time for the kgosi and his father to fall out.

At last the conversation came to an end. The kgosi walked away without a word of farewell, and Joshua hurried over to his father. The old man seemed agitated, and his shake was worse than usual.

'Sit for a minute, father, and catch your breath.'

Once Lesaka was seated and appeared calmer, Joshua said that he also needed a word with the kgosi and went to look for him. He found him remonstrating with his son.

'What do you want now?' the kgosi asked sharply as Joshua approached.

'Kgosi, may I also have a few words with you? My father—'

'Not now. I have had more than enough for today.' The kgosi turned away, but after a moment changed his mind. 'You can come tonight to my house. After dinner.'

'Thank you, kgosi.'

Joshua turned away and walked back to his father. As he

helped him to his feet, he noticed that the kgosi was back in angry conversation with his son.

Joshua wondered if he'd done the right thing. Clearly tonight wasn't the best time to visit the kgosi, but now he'd have to go through with it. He'd look like a fool if he changed his mind.

CHAPTER 10

Lesaka was exhausted by the time he'd finished supper, so he went straight to bed. The kgotla had been tiring, and had been followed by the upsetting conversation with the kgosi and the annoying meeting with Mma Zondo. Before his stroke, he'd have dealt with that sort of day with no trouble, but now he was weak and had to rely on his son for many things. He resented that.

He was grateful for his son's care, but felt the boy should be making his own life, having his own family, instead of being stuck at home looking after a damaged man. The physical issues were hard enough to bear – he could walk only with difficulty, and one arm was less responsive than it had been – but worse was the impediment to his speech. His thoughts were clear, but when he phrased them and forced his mouth to form the words, they seemed to fade and the thread was lost. He knew the council no longer respected his contributions.

With some effort, he rolled over, trying to find a more comfortable position.

It's what Mma Zondo said about the ancestors that's keeping me awake, he decided. Is it their doing that I'm now in this state? Is it a punishment for what I did all those years ago?

He pushed the thought aside.

Mma Zondo had wanted him to intercede with the kgosi concerning the water project, threatening him with retribution, saying Mami Wata would reveal what had happened all those years ago. But he knew he couldn't shift the kgosi even if he wanted to. The kgosi no longer took him seriously.

He treats me like a halfwit, he thought bitterly.

He tried to clear his mind for sleep, hoping that his rest would be peaceful. Sometimes he'd wake covered in sweat and talking to the ancestors aloud. Joshua would come, but by then he'd forgotten everything.

Suddenly, he heard the creak of the front door opening. The hinges were rusty and the house was small, so he could hear everything from his room.

He was surprised by how soon Joshua was back.

Have I been lying awake brooding for that long? he wondered.

He heard the creak again as the door closed.

'Joshua!' he called out, wanting to know how the meeting with the kgosi had gone.

There was no reply.

He called out again, but again there was no response.

Then he heard his door open, and he fumbled to turn on his bedside light.

'Joshua, is that you?'

It wasn't Joshua. As the light came on, he saw a hooded man in the doorway. Before he could react, the man was on him, swinging a knobkierie at his head. He tried to jerk aside, but his body moved sluggishly and he took a glancing blow, sending searing pain through his brain. The second blow knocked him out cold. He didn't feel the knife plunging between his ribs.

When the station commander and Abram arrived at the house, Joshua Lesaka was standing at the front door. The man looked distraught. His eyes were red, and he clasped and unclasped his hands as he watched the policemen walk towards him. Without a word, he led them through the house to his father's bedroom. Then he stood aside and waited at the door.

Lesaka was sprawled across the bed. There was blood all over his face and chest, and even some on the floor. Abram gasped and took a step towards the bed.

'Be careful where you walk, Nteba!' Balopi said sharply. 'And put on your gloves.' Abram froze and started fumbling with this latex gloves.

Balopi pulled on his own and picked his way over to the bedside. He felt for a pulse, first at the wrist, then at the neck.

'I'm afraid your father's dead,' he said to Joshua. 'I'm very sorry.'

Joshua just nodded.

'Did you touch your father after you found him?'

'Yes, I thought ... perhaps...' His voice trailed off. 'Who could have done this?'

Balopi shook his head. 'We need to hear the whole story. Let's go somewhere and sit down. Do you have some water?'

Joshua didn't have much to tell them. He and his father had attended the kgotla, and his father had been tired when they returned. Then, unexpectedly, Mma Zondo had arrived to talk to him, and when she finally left, Lesaka had been upset. He'd refused to discuss it over supper, merely saying it had been a very tiring day. Then he'd gone straight to bed.

After clearing up, Joshua had headed to the kgosi's house for his meeting, returning about an hour and a half later. He hadn't immediately realised that the house had been burgled, but had felt something was wrong as soon as he'd stepped inside. He'd gone at once to his father's room to check on him, and had found him as they saw him now.

'What's missing?' Abram asked.

Joshua sighed. 'Not much. We don't have much. I think my father's wallet is gone, and we had a transistor radio. It used to be over there.' He pointed at a small table opposite, where an empty space was surrounded by framed photographs. 'Maybe a few other things. I don't know. I haven't really checked.'

'You'll need to do that,' Balopi ordered. 'We'll need a list. These things could turn up and lead us to the killer.'

Joshua nodded. 'Who would do this? My father had no strength. He couldn't do anything. The thief could have taken whatever he wanted and just left.'

'Well, the thief wouldn't have known that. Perhaps your father was asleep and woke suddenly with the man in his room. That's how these burglaries go wrong.'

Abram was looking puzzled. 'How did he get in? All your windows are burglar-proofed. Was the front door damaged?'

Joshua looked uncomfortable. 'I didn't lock it.'

'You didn't lock the front door?' Balopi shook his head. 'Do you always just leave it open?'

Joshua shook his head. 'Father wanted me to lock everything, but sometimes if I'll be away for a short while I don't bother. This is Ncamasere. You know there's never any trouble here.'

'I certainly lock my own doors. Well, let's take a look.'

They walked back to the front door and examined the path. There was no hope of finding any useful footprints – all three of them had tramped up to the door since the intruder.

Balopi looked around and then turned to Abram. 'There are at least five houses that can see the front door. Go and check if anyone saw anything suspicious. Then you can start dusting for fingerprints on the front door and in the house. I'm going to contact the pathologist. We'd better get him out here before we move the body. Just as well he's still around. And he can bring that detective of his.'

'Kubu? Why do you want him?'

'I have an idea he knows something about the perpetrator of this crime. We'll see.'

Kubu and Ian had eaten dinner early. They wanted a good night's sleep before the journey to Kang in the morning and the long drive home the day after. In any case, they were exhausted from the missed sleep of the night before.

Despite his tiredness, Kubu had a spring in his step as he

headed to his bungalow. Joy had changed her appointment, and they would meet on Monday evening. He was really looking forward to that, albeit with a twinge of nervousness.

He'd imagined that he would fall asleep at once, but the disappointment of the case disturbed him. Something awful had happened to that group of Bushmen out in the desert, and he still had no idea what. Then there was the mystery of the two men who'd disappeared at almost the same time. It seemed they would never know the answers now.

Just when he'd managed to doze off, he was woken by banging on the door. 'Oh, not again,' he muttered as he pulled on his robe. He flung open the door and glared at the night watchman. 'Yes, what is it? I was asleep.'

'I'm sorry, rra, but the doctor said I should call you. He said you must meet him at his car in five minutes.'

'What for? What time is it?'

'He didn't say, rra. It's about half past nine.'

He thanked the man and dressed quickly, grabbing his notebook on the way out. He wondered what was up, but knew Ian would only call him for something important. He just hoped that it wouldn't delay their trip home.

Balopi met them where the main road from Shakawe entered Ncamasere. He'd told Ian that he'd never find the house on his own. Once they reached it, he introduced them to Lesaka's son before taking them to the body. Ian looked at it dispassionately, starting to assess the damage, but Kubu blanched, remembering the murdered men in his first big case. This was as bad. It looked as though the man had been beaten to death in his bed.

Kubu asked what he could do to help, but Balopi told him to wait. There was silence for a couple of minutes as Ian gently handled the dead man's head.

'At least two blows. The one to the frontal lobe looks like a surface wound – lots of blood but nothing too serious. But the one to the temporal bone – that's the side of the head – it looks like it may have cracked the skull. Chances are he was unconscious when he was stabbed.'

'The blood isn't all from the head wounds?' Balopi asked.

Ian shook his head. 'He's been stabbed in the chest. At least once. Maybe that killed him. Maybe the head wound. I'll need the autopsy to decide.'

'How long ago?'

Ian glanced up. 'Give me a bit of time, will ye? I've stuff to do.'

He produced a thermometer from his bag, rolled the body onto its side, and started pulling down Lesaka's shorts.

Balopi turned away. 'Come on Bengu. I want to talk to you. We don't have to watch this.'

They left the bedroom and joined Joshua in the sitting room. He hadn't moved since they'd arrived.

'Is there somewhere I can talk to the detective sergeant?' Balopi asked.

'Here. I'll go to my bedroom.'

When he'd left, they sat down, and Balopi glared at Kubu. 'I want to know more about your Bushman.'

'Rra, he's not *my* Bushman. And I've told you the whole story.'

'You told me he said strange things.'

Kubu nodded.

'What exactly did he say?'

Kubu flipped through his notebook until he came to the notes he'd jotted down on Selelo's ravings.

'He said that they say it must stop. When we asked who said that, he started talking about the ancestors. That they were happy and unhappy. Then, that he must make the past forgotten, but that he had to remember it. However, he didn't want to remember because he felt like a bee that would die when it stings.' He looked up from his notes. 'It makes no sense.'

Balopi leant forward. 'Sting like a bee. Like sticking a knife into someone? If he's done that, he'll die all right.'

'Rra, I'm sure he didn't mean that. He didn't seem violent at all. He was confused. Or he was telling us about a dream.'

'We'll see. You don't know this area, Bengu. I do. These Bushmen are always stealing things, grabbing livestock, whatever they can lay their hands on. Your Selelo is no different. He broke in here and pinched stuff. Probably he thought the house was empty, or everyone was asleep, because all the lights were out. Then Lesaka must have heard him, and the Bushman panicked and killed him. Unless he came here to "sting like a bee" in the first place. We'll find out when we catch him.'

'Why would he want to attack Rra Lesaka? I doubt he even could. The Bushman isn't a big man.'

'Lesaka was disabled. He had a stroke a few years ago and could hardly move one side of his body. Anyone could have overpowered him, especially if he had the advantage of surprise.'

Before Kubu could respond, Ian came into the room.

'I'd say two to three hours, Station Commander. That's what the body core temperature suggests, and it's consistent with the rigor mortis. There are early signs of it starting, but it hasn't set in.'

While they were digesting that, they heard the front door open, and Abram joined them.

Balopi turned to him. 'Anyone see anything?'

Abram nodded. 'One woman saw a man walk up the street and go into the house. She thought nothing of it. It was dark, and she assumed it was Joshua.'

'Description?'

'I took it down, but it could be anyone.' He sighed. 'No one else saw anything at all. They all wanted to know what was going on, of course, so I just told them there'd been a burglary.'

'Good thinking. You may as well start on the fingerprints next.'

'Take the victim's prints now,' Ian advised. 'It'll be harder when the fingers start to swell.' Abram shrugged and headed off on this latest assignment without enthusiasm.

'Station Commander, is there an operating theatre at the clinic here?' Ian asked. 'I could probably use that facility to do the autopsy.'

Balopi shook his head. 'As far as I know, any major surgery is done in Kasane or Maun. You can check in the morning.'

'I'll do that. In the meantime, where's the morgue? I need to keep the body cool until I decide what to do.'

Balopi shook his head. 'The best I can offer is a mortuary in Shakawe, and it'll only open in the morning.'

'I don't want to embalm it, dammit! I just want to cut it open before it becomes putrid.' Ian paused. 'If we have to go to Maun, do you at least have an air-conditioned ambulance?'

Again Balopi shook his head. 'You'll have to get one up from Gabs, and it won't get here for two or three days, if you're lucky.'

Ian took a deep breath. 'Then we'll take it in the back of the Land Rover. It should be fine if we can keep it cool tonight. Our best bet is a cold room at a butchery. I assume you have one of those?'

Abram laughed from the front door, where he was dusting for prints. 'We do, but I can't wait to see the owner's face when we tell him what we want to do.'

'What about his customers?' Kubu asked, thinking of how his mother would react if she knew her sausages had been lying next to a human corpse. 'We'd better make sure no one else knows about it, or the poor butcher will go out of business.'

'We'll do the best we can.' Balopi turned to Ian. 'The butcher will be asleep at this time of night. Can we leave the body in the Land Rover until morning?'

'I'd rather not. We don't want body fluids leaking or curious insects exploring it. Please go and find the butcher now, and we'll meet him at the butchery. Abram can show us the way.'

'Nteba, go and get the body bag I told you to bring.'

Abram shrugged and walked out of the house.

Balopi stood up. 'Very well. I'll meet you there in half an hour or so.' He turned to Kubu. 'Your Bushman's got a two- or three-hour head start, Bengu. We'll never find him in the dark, so we'll have to wait until tomorrow to look for him. But don't worry, we'll catch him. Then we'll get to the bottom of all this.'

With that, he walked into the night.

After they had deposited Lesaka's body safely in the irate butcher's cooler, Ian told Kubu that they should let Mabaku know what had happened and tell him that they wouldn't be returning to Gaborone the next morning.

'You want me to do that now? It's nearly midnight. Shouldn't I wait until morning? He won't be able to do anything tonight anyway.'

'My advice, Kubu, is phone him right away. He might not like being woken up in the middle of the night, but he'll like it even less if you don't let him know straight away.'

Kubu stood quietly for a moment, thinking that if he called his boss right then, he'd be skinned alive. Eventually, he realised that Ian was probably right – that an error of commission was less likely to cause problems than an error of omission.

'Let's go back to Drotsky's,' he said eventually. 'I'll do it.'

When they reached the lodge, Kubu and Ian went to reception, hoping the phone hadn't been locked away for the night. Fortunately, it was sitting on the desk.

As he didn't have Mabaku's home number, Kubu called the CID, and it took him a few minutes to convince the constable on duty to give him the number.

Kubu took a deep breath before ringing his boss.

'Mabaku. Who's calling?'

'This is Detective Sergeant Bengu, sir, I apologise for—'

'For God's sake, Bengu, get on with it. It's the middle of the night, and I know you're not making a social call. What's going on?'

'One of the kgosi's counsellors, a Rra Lesaka, has been murdered.'

'What happened?'

'He was beaten over the head while he was asleep and then stabbed. There was blood all over the—'

'Any suspects?'

'The station commander thinks it's the Bushman I told you about.'

There was silence for a few moments. 'And what do you think?'

'I don't know, sir, but I'd be surprised.'

'And I suppose you aren't coming back to Gabs tomorrow?'

'I was going to ask you about that, sir. Doctor MacGregor has to take the body to Maun for an autopsy. That'll take all day tomorrow at the quickest.'

There was another silence. 'You stay there, Bengu, and work with the local detective, whatever his name is. I'll phone the station commander in the morning and tell him that his man is in charge, and that you're to help.'

'Yes, sir.'

'Then, when MacGregor returns from Maun, head back here as soon as you can.'

'Yes, sir.'

'Remember, Bengu, the local man is in charge. Not you.'

CHAPTER 11

First thing next morning, Ian phoned the hospital in Maun and confirmed that he could use one of their operating theatres to do the autopsy. He insisted that it had to be that day, and after some grumbling about it being Sunday, they agreed. He had a quick breakfast with Kubu, then he headed to the butcher to relieve him of Lesaka's body and to start the long trip to Maun. He was keen to do the autopsy that afternoon so he could return that evening or the next morning at the latest.

As for Kubu, he was grateful he didn't have to share the 350 kilometres to Maun and the 350 kilometres back with a corpse. Eager to get going, he phoned the police station straight after breakfast and asked to speak to Abram.

'Kubu? The station commander is busy organising the search for the Bushman. He spoke to Mabaku this morning. He put me in charge of the investigation and said you could help me while Dr MacGregor's in Maun.'

To Kubu, it sounded as though Selelo had already been found guilty. That wasn't his idea of an investigation.

'Don't you think we should question the people who spoke to Lesaka last night? Maybe they can throw some light on what happened.'

'We know what happened. The Bushman broke in to steal things, Lesaka woke up, and he had to silence him.'

'What did he use to hit him? He didn't have anything when we left him at the clinic.'

That gave Abram pause. 'He could have picked up a knobkierie after he escaped.'

'That's true, but I don't think so. Where would he get it and why would he need it? And why stab him? Ian said he was likely to be unconscious after the blows. There's more to this than a break in, Abram. It's our job to find out what.'

Abram was silent for a few moments. 'What do you want to do?'

'We should investigate as if we hadn't already decided who the culprit is. We need to find out what Mma Zondo's visit was about. It was hardly a social call after a long kgotla meeting in the afternoon. And when did Lesaka's son arrive at the kgosi and when did he leave?'

'You're not suggesting Joshua murdered his own father that way? Why on earth would he do that?'

'I'm not suggesting anything. I'm saying we should do the groundwork. We don't want some civil-rights lawyer getting the Bushman off on the grounds that we did a bad job, do we?'

This time the silence was even longer. At last Abram said, 'I guess we could go through the formalities. It beats wandering around in the desert with the constables, looking for the Bushman. All right, let's start with Mma Zondo. But it mustn't take all day. I have a lot of work. I'll pick you up in an hour.'

~

The station commander took three constables with him to the Lesaka home. They were going to search for Selelo, whom he insisted was the murderer.

'He can't have gone far even if he walked all night. Still, we need to search the whole of Ncamasere first, though I doubt he's here.' He turned to two of the constables. 'Off you go. Make sure you check every possible hiding place: sheds, chicken coops, reed growths, empty homes. Report back here when you've finished. If I'm not here, radio me for further instructions. Constable Rari and I are going to drive along the road to Tsodilo Hills to see if we can spot him.'

The two men climbed back into the Land Rover and headed south along the A35 to the turn-off. Balopi didn't think his men would find the Bushman in Ncamasere, because he was sure Selelo would have headed back to his home at Tsodilo. However, there was no harm in being thorough. He really wanted him caught. The big problem would be if Selelo reached Tsodilo Hills before they found him. There, he could easily disappear in the caves and crevasses. Then he would be almost impossible to find.

They reached the turn-off and drove slowly, carefully scanning left and right, both close by and distant. Even though the area appeared flat, it would only take a small fold in the sand to provide cover.

Balopi wondered how far along the road he should drive. He tried to calculate the furthest a man could get in the time available, but wasn't sure whether he was right. Bushmen were reputed to be able to run for hours on end.

After about fifteen minutes, he stopped and climbed onto the roof of the vehicle. He scanned the surrounding desert with his binoculars. Nothing. Constable Rari scoured the sand alongside the road for footprints, but also found nothing.

After he climbed down, Balopi carefully brushed some dust from his trousers. When he was settled once again behind the steering wheel, he called the station on the radio. 'This is Assistant Superintendent Balopi. I'm on the road to Tsodilo Hills, looking for the Bushman. Constable Rari is with me. The Bushman is dangerous, but we should be able to handle him. I'll check in every fifteen minutes. If you haven't heard from me, try contacting me. If you don't succeed, send a couple of constables after us.'

Ian could never understand why cars in Botswana either didn't have air conditioning or, if they did, it didn't work. Consequently, when he pulled up in front of the Maun Hospital, he was wet through. He felt fortunate that the road was now paved. Just a few years earlier, it would have been a gruelling six hours negotiating a dirt road littered with traps of soft sand.

Ian climbed slowly out of the van and stretched his creaking joints. He walked into the building, hoping the interior was in better repair than the outside. After a quick discussion, the receptionist took him into the small operating theatre at the back of the building that would serve as a makeshift morgue. 'We've moved an autopsy table in and covered the floor with a large tarpaulin. That should catch all the blood.'

'Thank you. Can you get someone to help me bring in the body? Then I need a quick lunch before I start. Any recommendations?'

'The Duck Inn is the most popular. It's opposite the airport. I'll get someone to help you with the body.'

The Duck Inn, once Ian eventually found it, was unlike any eatery that Ian had ever seen. To call it rustic would have been generous, but it was completely full. White men like himself, obviously professionals of some sort, sat next to young backpackers from all over the world.

Other tables were occupied by do-it-yourself travellers, probably from South Africa, who were trying to sort out their trip's expenses. Ian glanced at the table next to him. There were piles of South African rands, Zambian kwachas, Botswana pula, US dollars, euros, and various other notes that he didn't recognise. A scholarly-looking man was scribbling on a scruffy piece of paper, trying to convert all of the currencies to the same one, then calculating what each person owed or was owed. It was obviously no easy task, and the longer it took, the more beers and wine appeared, making it even more difficult.

Ian smiled. It reminded him of some of his student days and

the stupid drinking games they'd played. It was the process that was fun, and he was sure that the final accounting would be close, but no one would care.

Surprisingly, the service was quick, and he was able to head back to the clinic within an hour. Ian's only regret was that he hadn't been able to wet his whistle with an ice-cold beer.

Meanwhile Balopi was beginning to worry that they weren't going to find the Bushman. Nevertheless, he continued along the road towards Tsodilo Hills.

Suddenly, the radio burst into life. 'Station Commander. Station Commander, come in for Constable Mogwe. Over.'

Balopi picked up the handset. 'Balopi here. Go ahead, Constable. Over.'

'We have the Bushman, rra. Over.'

Balopi slapped the steering wheel. He hadn't expected that. 'Are you sure? Over.'

'He's the only Bushman we've seen, rra. Over.'

'Where are you? Over.'

'On Ditlhapi Street, not far from the kgosi's house. Over.'

'Stay there. Make sure he doesn't escape. I'll be there as soon as I can. Out.'

Back in Maun, Ian had returned to the hospital and was doing what was necessary to determine how Lesaka had died. Although the cause of death seemed pretty obvious, Ian was careful to check all the options, taking pictures as he went, and speaking into a small recorder. However, there were few surprises. The head had been hit twice with a blunt object, and there was no sign of any foreign material in the wounds. Ian decided that something like a knobkierie or a thick staff had been used. One of the blows had cracked the skull, and the victim would have lost consciousness, but Ian doubted that was the cause of death.

He started to explore the chest. By the time the autopsy was over, he'd confirmed a knife wound to the heart, probably about a fifteen-centimetre blade that had been slipped between the ribs and driven home with considerable force. It didn't feel like the work of a thief surprised in the act.

If Lesaka was unconscious, why didn't the thief just leave? Ian wondered. Unless, of course, Lesaka could identify the intruder.

Suddenly he felt very tired. He'd had very little sleep for the past two nights. He decided it would be unsafe to drive back to Shakawe and wasn't sure what he would do with the body when he got there. At least the hospital would be able to keep it cool overnight.

He took a few more pictures, closed up the body and washed thoroughly. He wasn't hungry. What he needed was a decent bed and no one disturbing him until the morning.

It took Balopi nearly twenty-five minutes to reach his constables, who were sitting under the only tree in the area. He jumped out of the Land Rover and strode up to the Bushman, who was lying on the ground with his hands handcuffed behind his back. The constables jumped to their feet.

'He's clean,' one said. 'We took a knife off him. That's all.'

He pointed at the man. 'What's your name?'

'Me, Selelo. Going to talk to ancestors.'

'Stand up. I'm arresting you for the murder of Endo Lesaka.'

'No go back. Go to Tsodilo Hills to speak to ancestors.'

'You're coming with me.'

Keeping a close eye on the Bushman, Balopi told the constable to pull the man to his feet.

The man looked harmless, but those stories of Bushman poisons frightened him. He looked around but couldn't see any other weapons. No bow and arrow. No knobkierie.

Selelo frowned. 'Selelo go home.'

Balopi pointed at the Land Rover, and the constable frog-marched Selelo to it and pushed him into the back, which was like a cage.

Balopi smiled at his constables. 'Well done, men. Let's take him to the station and get the truth out of him.'

CHAPTER 12

While Ian headed to Maun and the station commander searched for Selelo, Abram and Kubu drove to the Zondos' home. When they reached it, Kubu was surprised. He'd expected the usual bumpy dirt track to the farmhouse, perhaps with a cattle grate or a wire gate pulled closed across it. Instead, access to the property was barred by a heavy metal gate set in a two-metre wall topped with razor wire and plastered with warning signs.

Abram pulled up, and they climbed out of the vehicle. They walked up to the gate and found it secured with a heavy padlock. There was no sign of an intercom, so Abram tried rattling the gate.

Instantly, two huge dogs rushed from behind the house, barking wildly. They threw themselves against the gate with fangs bared, and Abram hastily stepped several paces back. That seemed to mollify the dogs somewhat, and the racket died down to growls. He cupped his hands around his mouth and shouted: 'Police here! Anyone at home?' That set off another round of frenzied barking.

A man appeared at the front door and yelled a command to the dogs. Both quietened immediately and sat on their haunches, but they remained focussed on the gate with their ears alert.

'What do you want?' He made no move to approach the gate or call off the dogs.

'Police,' Abram shouted back. 'We need to ask a few questions.'

Slowly, the man walked closer. As he approached the gate, he glared at Abram.

'Dumela, Abram. What's this about?' Then he pointed at Kubu. 'I saw you talking to people where the skeletons were buried. Who are you?'

'Dumela, Rra Zondo,' Abram responded. 'This is Detective Sergeant Bengu from Gaborone CID. We need to ask you a few questions.'

Zondo fumbled in his pocket for keys, sprung the padlock and pulled open the gate.

Abram held back. 'Rra Zondo, will you please shut the dogs away? I'm scared of big dogs.'

'They won't do anything as long as you're with me.' He motioned the two policemen through, then locked the gate behind them. Keeping an eye on the dogs, they followed close behind him to the rough-brick house with a corrugated iron roof.

'You have very impressive security,' Kubu commented. 'Unusual for a country farm. Do you have many problems out here?'

'Not recently.'

'In the past?'

'It can take an hour for the police to get here from town. If they come at all. We look after ourselves.'

Zondo opened the front door and led them into the house, leaving the dogs waiting on the stoep. He showed them to the living room, which had a magnificent view down to the river, marred only by a razor-wire fence that ran across the front of the property. He motioned them to sit down. 'What's this all about?'

Abram pulled out his handkerchief. 'Could we get some water, please? It's hot out in the sun.' He patted the sweat from his forehead.

Zondo grunted and fetched them each a glass of water. While Abram was gulping his, Kubu asked, 'You mentioned you saw me where the skeletons were found. How did you know there was more than one? Only one had been found when you were there.'

Zondo shrugged. 'Everyone knows everything that goes on

around here. Did you come here to ask me about old skeletons? I'm a busy man.'

Kubu decided he didn't much like Zondo's attitude. 'If you're so busy, why did you go up there on Thursday?'

Zondo took a few moments to respond. 'I needed to find out what was delaying the trenching. That's an important project. When can they start again?'

'Well, possibly nine or more of those people were murdered. We'll carry on investigating until we find out who's responsible, or we're convinced that this all happened very long ago and has nothing to do with the police.'

Abram leant forward. 'Actually, rra, we hoped we could talk to your mother.'

'What about?'

Abram started to explain, but Kubu interrupted. 'Is she here?'

Zondo frowned, then nodded and went to fetch her. He returned a few minutes later, followed by his mother.

'I know who you are,' she said to Abram. 'I remember you as a skinny boy.' She turned to Kubu. 'You talked to me the other day. Who are you?'

Abram jumped up and introduced Kubu.

She gave a curt nod. 'Jacob said you wanted to talk to me. So what's this all about?'

Abram waited until she was seated before he responded. 'Mma, I'm sorry to tell you that Rra Lesaka is no more. He passed during the night.'

She sucked in her breath. 'He died? But I saw him last night. He said he was tired but he seemed fine...' After a moment she asked, 'Another stroke?'

Kubu shook his head. 'Mma, we were called to the scene, and we're investigating what happened. When did you last see him?'

'After the kgotla, I went to his house, and we spoke for a while.'

'What was that about?'

She frowned. 'Just what business is that of yours, Detective? It was a private conversation.'

Suddenly, Abram came to life. 'We understand he was quite upset afterwards.'

Kubu glanced at him, but hid his surprise.

'Nonsense!' Mma Zondo responded. 'We chatted, and then I left. He was fine.'

'His son said he was upset.'

The detectives waited, but Mma Zondo sat them out. It was Kubu who broke the silence.

'Nevertheless, mma, we need to know what the discussion was about.'

She shrugged. 'We spoke about the water reticulation project. The kgosi wants to take water from the river and irrigate the desert. It'll do no good – the sand will swallow every drop.'

Kubu pushed some more. 'Why did you speak to Rra Lesaka about this?'

It was Jacob Zondo who answered. 'He was one of the kgosi's counsellors, and she keeps nagging about it. Everyone else wants it.'

'Even Rra Lesaka?'

'He always supported what the kgosi wants,' Mma Zondo put in. 'I was trying to get him to change his mind. Now he's dead.'

Kubu leant forward. 'You think there's a connection?'

'Of course not,' Jacob interjected. 'He was very sick. Why are you people causing trouble—'

'Of course, it's connected,' Mma Zondo interrupted. 'It has made the spirits angry and will cause much harm.'

Her son shook his head and folded his arms.

She pointed at him. 'Oh, he doesn't believe that. He believes in progress, that progress brings money. But Mami Wata has told me a different story, and there are omens.'

Kubu had heard stories of the water spirit, but regarded them as folk tales. A beautiful, but fickle, woman with a fish's tale? A mermaid? He didn't think so. But here was someone who claimed to have spoken to her. He wasn't convinced in the slightest.

'Of course I've heard about Mami Wata, mma, but I don't understand how she communicates with people.'

Mma Zondo smiled. 'I know you think it's all nonsense, Detective, but I know what I know. I sit next to the water, and she surfaces not far from the bank. Usually, we don't talk because we understand each other. When I'm worried, I sit there, and when I leave, I have the solution to my problem. She sends her advice into my head.' She tapped it. 'She doesn't need to talk.'

Kubu tried hard not to roll his eyes.

'But now she's angry. She says that stealing her water will lead to death in the village.' She turned to her son. 'Those skeletons – you think it's a coincidence that they rise out of the ground now, blocking the path of your pipeline? Is it a coincidence that Lesaka dies right after refusing to try to stop it? Of course it's not a coincidence. Bad luck will strike everyone responsible – the contractor, the kgosi, even you!'

Jacob turned to Abram. 'My mother has strong views about everything, but this has nothing to do with Rra Lesaka's death. Now, do you have any more questions or can we get back to our work? A farm doesn't run when people sit around and talk.'

Abram put down his empty glass and stood up, but Kubu wasn't going to give up so easily. 'Do you know if Rra Lesaka had any enemies?'

Jacob shook his head, and his mother agreed.

After a moment she added, 'But I think he'd just made one. Mami Wata is very angry.'

Kubu realised he was getting nowhere. He had to be missing something, and not for the first time he wished that Mabaku was with them. He would know how to extract useful information.

He changed the subject. 'We've been looking through old records. I understand a man called Zondo disappeared without trace almost twenty-five years ago. Was he a member of your family?'

Abram looked at him with surprise, and there was a moment of silence before Jacob spoke. 'You think that one of the skeletons...'

Kubu shook his head. 'The pathologist believes the skeletons all belong to Bushmen.'

'Then what has this got to do with anything?'

'Perhaps nothing. But Rra Dibotelo's son disappeared at the same time. It would be a strange coincidence, if that's what it was.'

'It was my father. I was at primary school then.'

'What happened?' Kubu asked.

It was Mma Zondo who answered. 'Ezekiel – that's my husband – he went out one day on a hunting trip, and he never came back. We searched for weeks. No trace of him was ever found.'

'Did anyone have any ideas at the time?' Kubu pressed on, half expecting her to blame Mami Wata, but Mma Zondo merely shook her head. 'Is that why you looked pleased when the pathologist announced the skeleton was of a Bushman? Pleased it wasn't your husband?'

Mma Zondo shook her head again. Then she stood up and walked over to a small side table displaying a collection of photographs. She picked up one in a silver frame. 'This is Ezekiel and me just after we were married.' Then she pointed at a second photograph, of a young version of herself holding a baby. 'And this is me and Jacob.' She glanced at her son. 'I never thought he would grow so big.'

Kubu went over and took a close look. He'd never been able to link a baby's face with its adult looks. As far as he was concerned, all babies looked much the same. Then he noticed a picture of two young men on horses. 'And who are these?'

'Ezekiel is the one on the left.' Then she pointed to a good-looking man sitting on a horse with a striking white fork marking its chest. 'He is now our kgosi. They grew up together and were close friends.'

'It must have been an amazing time to grow up around here. There must have been stories about cattle thieves and hunting expeditions into the desert.'

'There were stories. The young men were always getting into trouble in those days. Playing practical jokes on people. Getting into fights. You know, the things boys usually do.'

'Was your husband involved?'

'If he was, it was before we were married. He behaved himself after that. I made sure of it.'

'Did he know Rra Dibotelo's son?'

She shrugged. 'Ncamasere is small now; in those days it was tiny. Everyone knew everyone else.'

'Were they friends?'

'Not really.'

'And can you think of any possible connection between the disappearances?'

She glared at him. 'Detective, do you think you've discovered something new? Do you imagine no one considered that at the time? Do you think you will brilliantly solve these disappearances more than twenty years on, when the people back then could find nothing?'

Kubu flushed, realising that he had nothing new to offer. He almost apologised, but bit it back. He had a right to follow up on ideas. It was his job.

Mma Zondo looked down at her hands, and her voice dropped to little more than a whisper. 'I even asked Mami Wata. But that time there was no answer. Maybe this is something I'm not meant to know in this life.' She took a deep breath. 'There is nothing more I can tell you about Rra Lesaka,' she said in her normal tone. 'Now, is there anything else?'

Kubu realised there was one issue they hadn't explored yet. 'Mma, we're also investigating the deaths of the Bushmen. Did any of the stories you heard when you were young concern skirmishes with them?'

Kubu thought he caught a moment of surprise on her face.

'There were stories about the Bushmen and how they could live in the desert,' she said. 'In those days, people were scared of them and their poisoned arrows. Sometimes they'd try to steal our crops or animals, and the men had to chase them off. But that was all long ago.'

'We almost never see them around here nowadays,' Jacob added. 'Now, are you done?'

Abram thanked the Zondos for their time, and Jacob took them to the door.

Kubu decided that either the Zondos knew very little, or they'd successfully avoided telling him what they did know. He still had one question for the son. 'You said the trenching was important, Rra Zondo. How are you involved with this water project?'

'It's a government project. The idea is to pipe water to open up farms away from the river. One thing we have a lot of out here, Detective, is land. It's sandy, but not too bad if you work it properly. But you must have water.'

'What about boreholes? Wouldn't they be easier and cheaper?'

Jacob shook his head. 'It's not enough, and in the dry season they can dry up altogether. You must have reliable water.'

'Isn't there a danger of impacting the flow to the delta and all the wildlife there?'

'That's just nonsense,' Jacob replied angrily. 'There's plenty of water. The Namibians are planning a big pipeline to supply Windhoek. The conservationists should be fighting them instead of causing trouble for the small farmers. We'll be taking nothing in comparison to that.'

Kubu persisted. 'You *are* involved then?'

'I'm involved in this area. I want to see it flourish. I'm lucky because my land fronts onto the river, but we all need to look after each other. That's the spirit of botho.'

Abram nodded. 'Indeed. We all believe in botho.'

'Well, then you should stop interfering by digging up ancient skeletons!'

Kubu was surprised by Jacob's strong reaction, but didn't pursue it. He realised there was nothing more they would learn that day.

'Come on. I must get back to work,' Jacob said. Then he walked Kubu and Abram to the gate, past the watchful eyes of the two dogs.

CHAPTER 13

As Zondo locked the gate behind them, Kubu commented quietly, 'I don't understand the point of all the high security out here in the middle of nowhere – walls, razor wire, attack dogs and so on.'

'It's been here as long as I can remember. Perhaps Mma Zondo was worried about their safety after her husband disappeared.'

'Was there any reason for that concern?'

'Not that I know of.'

'What do you make of Mma Zondo and her water spirit?'

'She's mad. She sits on the bank of the river and talks to herself.'

Kubu digested that for a moment, then changed the subject.

'So tell me more about Zondo. Why is he so keen on the water project?'

Abram took his time replying. 'Zondo is very close to the kgosi. After his father died, they say the kgosi kept an eye on him. I guess since he and Zondo's father were such great mates, he felt some obligation to look after the boy. Now the kgosi has given him the right to more land, but much of it is far away from the river...'

'Where the pipeline is going?'

'Maybe.'

So, Kubu thought, it's not entirely botho that motivates

Zondo's support for the pipeline. But then why was Mma Zondo so against it? Did she really hear voices in her head?

Abram started the vehicle. 'What now?'

'We should visit the kgosi to check on Lesaka's story and get his take on what happened.'

'We should check with the station commander first and see what he wants us to do. Then we can go from there.'

Kubu didn't like that, but he couldn't think of any reason to object.

However, just as they reached the main road, the police radio came to life, giving them urgent instructions.

'Well,' Abram said after he'd finished the call, 'it seems we're going to the kgosi's house after all.'

Kgosi Rantao lived with his daughter and grandchildren in a large, but not ostentatious, house on the outskirts of the Ncamasere. His daughter cooked and looked after the house, and, as he liked to say, his grandchildren kept him young.

He'd barely started his lunch when he heard the sound of singing – not the joyful singing of a celebration, but angry chanting, and it was coming closer. Curious, he went out onto his stoep to see what was going on.

A group of about twenty men was approaching, clapping and stamping their feet in time to the chant. Some of them carried sticks. The kgosi was shocked to see his counsellor, Mowisi, among them, joining in the chant. He didn't like Mowisi, but never thought he was a rabble-rouser. However, maybe his put down of the man at the kgotla the day before had made him angry.

The kgosi folded his arms as he watched the crowd approach. The leader was a rhino of a man with arms as thick as some men's thighs. The kgosi knew him as a troublemaker, who wasn't averse to settling an argument with his massive fists. It was just as well it was lunchtime rather than in the evening, when he might have been drinking.

When they were close to the stoep, the leader raised his hand and shouted for them to stop. Then he turned to address the kgosi; but habit took over, and he stood tongue-tied, waiting for the kgosi to speak first, as tradition required. The kgosi let them wait for a long moment and, when he did speak, he ignored the leader and addressed Mowisi.

'Rra Mowisi, what is the meaning of this? You've raised your issues at the kgotla. We can consider them further when the council meets. Yet you bring this unruly mob to my home while I'm having my lunch.'

Mowisi protested that the men were coming anyway and that he'd only joined them to mediate. However, at that point, the leader remembered he was supposed to be in charge and interrupted.

'Kgosi,' he said in a loud voice. 'We want land. Good land with water. Yet Rra Mowisi tells us there are no promises and if we don't demand our rights now, the water will go to the people who are rich already. We want your promise that we will be given our share.'

There was a murmur of agreement from the rest of the crowd, and they pushed forward towards the house. Mowisi broke from the group and moved to the front.

'Kgosi,' he began, 'we raised the issue of the new irrigated land at the kgotla. How will it be allotted? These people feel that those with the worst land now should have the highest priority.' Again there was a rumble of approval from the crowd.

The kgosi ignored him and turned to the group. 'Borra, this is not how we work together. You have come to the kgotla. You've made your points. I'll discuss the matter with the council and tell you my decision.'

At first, there was no reaction, and the crowd fidgeted, awaiting direction. However, neither Mowisi nor the leader of the group said anything. As several of the crowd started to drift away, the kgosi glared at Mowisi and started back towards the house. That was a mistake. The leader felt insulted, and his anger rose.

'You turn and walk away from us? We respect you, kgosi, but you have no respect for us!'

There were shouts of agreement from the crowd. Several shook their sticks in the air, and one picked up one of the half-bricks marking the edge of the path.

Mowisi looked around nervously, realising that things could get badly out of hand. 'Borra!' he shouted. 'We've made our point. Our kgosi has said he'll discuss our requests.'

'He turned his back on us. He treats us like pigs.' It was the man with the brick.

There were shouts of agreement, and once more the crowd surged forward. Suddenly the brick flew through the air and smashed a window of the house. The kgosi froze, shocked. The leader turned, looking back into the crowd, and held up his powerful arms. The men came to a halt.

'Who did that?' he thundered.

No one spoke and, in the momentary silence, they heard a siren approaching. A few seconds later, a police Land Rover pulled into the driveway.

Abram climbed out of the vehicle with Kubu following. 'What's going on here? Why are you all at the kgosi's house?'

The kgosi spoke first, his voice shaking with fury. 'It's a riot! These scum broke my window. Arrest all of them right now.'

Kubu took a look around at the crowd. He and Abram certainly couldn't do that on their own. He even doubted that they could take on just the leader.

How had things got so far out of hand? he wondered.

Abram looked as unhappy as Kubu felt. 'I'll talk to the kgosi. You stay here and prevent it getting any worse.'

Leaving Kubu sweating in the sun, Abram joined the kgosi, who showed him the broken window behind substantial burglar bars. They were in conversation for some time, and several of the men lost patience and pushed forward. Kubu held up his hands and shouted for them to stop. To his relief, they did, but there were angry mutters.

At last, Abram returned with the kgosi and addressed the leader. 'Kgosi Rantao is very angry. He expects an apology from you, rra, for leading these people here and being responsible for this riot. Also, we will find out who threw the brick, and that man must arrange for the window to be fixed and pay for it.' He paused. 'However, the kgosi is wise and understands that sometimes men's tempers rule them, so he's asked me not to arrest the man now, although that's exactly what I should do.'

There was a lot of discussion in the group, and Kubu thought it could go either way. Then the leader shouted for silence. He argued for restraint, pointing out that their legitimate request had been damaged by the hooligan who'd thrown the brick.

At last, he turned to the kgosi, bowed his head, and apologised for the damage to his house, at the same time making it clear that their demands remained in full force. 'And Rra Mowisi will continue to represent us in the council.'

The kgosi clenched his jaw and said nothing, but the leader waited, and eventually the kgosi agreed.

'The man will pay for the window,' the leader said. 'I will see to it.' No one had any doubt that the man would do as instructed.

'Very well,' the kgosi said. 'By the time we meet again, I hope you have learnt some manners and can make arguments without violence. Now get off my property.'

Abram and Kubu stood between the chief and the men until they'd all dispersed, with Mowisi being one of the first to hurry off.

Kubu turned to Abram. 'We need to talk to the kgosi to confirm that Lesaka's son was here last night. Let's do it now. And we can ask him who might want to kill the old man.'

Abram shook his head. 'For God's sake, Kubu. He's in the middle of lunch. A mob has just damaged his house. You think this is a good time for an interview? We're heading back to the station.'

Without another word, he climbed into his vehicle and started the engine. Kubu had no option but to scramble into the passenger seat.

CHAPTER 14

When Kubu and Abram walked into the station in Shakawe, the receptionist greeted them with a big smile. 'We've got him. The Bushman. They found him in Ncamasere, sitting under a tree. You're to go to the station commander's office right away.'

'Guilty already,' Kubu muttered as they went to speak to the man. The door was open, so Abram knocked and walked in. 'You wanted to see us, rra?'

'I waited for you so you could be there when I interview him. Surly bastard. Doesn't say anything, except he wants to speak to his ancestors. But we'll get to the truth quickly enough. Come with me.'

The three policemen walked to an interview room where Selelo was huddled in a corner on the floor.

Balopi pointed at a chair. 'Get up and sit there.'

Selelo didn't move.

'Sit on the chair, dammit.'

Selelo gave Kubu a pleading look. Kubu could only shrug, unable to do anything even though he could see Balopi was about to lose his temper.

'If you don't sit in that chair, I'll have the detective sergeant tie you to it. Get in the chair!'

When Selelo didn't move, Kubu walked over to him and, with his back to the station commander, smiled. 'Let me help you up,

Selelo.' He leant down and gently helped Selelo to his feet and then to the chair. Selelo slumped onto the seat and looked at the floor.

Balopi sat down and turned on the recorder, giving the date and time, and the names of the four people in the room. Then he pulled a piece of paper from his pocket and addressed Selelo. 'You are not obliged to say anything unless you wish to do so, but whatever you say may be put into writing and given in evidence. Do you understand?'

There was no response from Selelo.

Kubu thought Balopi was going to hit him.

The next twenty minutes was very frustrating for everyone. Balopi was unable to extract any useful information from Selelo other than that he wanted to go to Tsodilo Hills to talk to his ancestors. Abram was frustrated because he could see that Balopi's ever-louder shouts wouldn't change the situation. Kubu was frustrated because he felt he couldn't interfere. And Selelo was frustrated because the man who was shouting at him didn't seem to understand his simple goal, namely to return home to Tsodilo Hills.

Eventually Balopi gave up in exasperation. He stood up, ended the interview, then screamed at Selelo that he was going to hang for killing Lesaka.

It didn't help that Selelo cocked his head at that moment and smiled. Abram had to hold Balopi back for fear he would assault the Bushman.

∿

A few minutes later Kubu and Abram were back in the station commander's office, wondering what he was going to do next. Eventually he addressed Abram. 'You speak to the prisoner this afternoon, Detective Sergeant. I expect you to make more progress that I did.' Abram nodded.

'Sir,' Kubu said tentatively, 'don't we have to offer him legal representation? He won't know that he can ask for it.'

'For God's sake, Bengu, this isn't Gaborone. He's our only

suspect, and no one locally would hurt Lesaka, who was revered around here. It has to be an outsider, and other than yourself and Dr MacGregor, he's the only one.'

'And what would his motive be?'

Balopi hit his desk. 'It's a robbery gone wrong. He took Lesaka's wallet. Lesaka woke up, and the Bushman had to deal with him.'

'Did he have the wallet when you found him?'

'Of course not. He would have taken the money and thrown the wallet away. I'll have some men look for it in the morning.'

Kubu decided he wouldn't ask the obvious follow-up question, but could do so anytime in the future. Instead, he changed the subject.

'Did his knobkierie have blood on it?'

Balopi glared at Kubu. 'He didn't have one – probably threw it away somewhere in the desert where we wouldn't find it.'

Kubu decided not to push too hard, but was shocked by the lack of any evidence. In fact, the case against Selelo so far had nothing to support it other than Balopi's apparent need to close it as quickly as possible.

Kubu felt despondent. He hoped that what he was witnessing wasn't widespread in the police force. He wanted justice – justice arrived at properly. He remembered what one of his lecturers had told his class: 'It's better to let a guilty person off than find an innocent person guilty.'

Kubu didn't know what to do with his doubts.

Abram's afternoon interview didn't go any better than the one in the morning. When they arrived at the interview room, Selelo was huddled even further into the corner. In front of him was food and water, obviously untouched. Kubu wondered if the Bushman was planning to starve himself to death. He'd heard how four walls were the equivalent of a death sentence to many Bushmen.

They managed to get Selelo into the chair again, but that was about all they accomplished. All Selelo would say is that he wanted to go home to speak to the ancestors.

Just as they were about to give up, Kubu asked Selelo what he'd done after he climbed out of the clinic window. That brought a smile to Selelo's face.

'Easy out. Walk straight home.'

'Why did you go to Ncamasere on the way?' Kubu asked gently.

Selelo frowned. 'Easier to walk on road. Desert hard.'

'Are you sure.'

Selelo shook his head. 'Not stupid. Know how to get home.'

And that was all they could get out of him.

～

The station commander was angry they hadn't made any progress. 'Well, it doesn't really matter. I'll file charges of robbery and murder—'

'But we don't have any evidence,' Kubu spluttered.

'We'll have enough and...' Balopi paused '...we'll have a signed confession. I'm drawing one up now. I'll explain it to him tomorrow, and he'll sign it. He'll see it's in his best interests.'

Once again, Kubu decided to keep quiet. He needed to think the situation through carefully, because this was not how he thought justice should be served.

'Abram,' he said, 'please could you drop me at Drotsky's. It's been a long day, and I have to bring my notes up to date.'

'With a beer in hand, I suppose.'

Kubu shook his head. 'A glass of wine.'

～

By the time they arrived at the guest house, Kubu had decided that he couldn't let his concerns go unaddressed. So he immediately went to reception and asked once again to use the manager's phone. He hoped Mabaku would listen to what he had to say.

'Mabaku.'

'It's Detective Sergeant Bengu, rra. I'm very sorry to disturb you again.'

'What's happened now?' Kubu could imagine Mabaku rolling his eyes.

'Well, rra, they found the Bushman, Selelo, in Ncamasere, not too far from the deceased Lesaka's house.'

'And?'

'Rra, I feel very uncomfortable saying this, but I don't think that Selelo is being treated properly.' He paused, but Mabaku said nothing. Kubu took a deep breath. 'Rra, the station commander didn't offer Selelo the chance to have a lawyer present when he was questioning him, and he's found no hard evidence – no stolen wallet, no murder weapon, nothing. Now he says that he's preparing a confession for Selelo to sign tomorrow. Selelo won't have a clue what it's all about. I doubt he can read and write. I know I'm new on the job, sir, but this doesn't feel right.'

There was silence on the line.

Eventually Kubu said 'Rra?'

'Give me a minute to think about this, Bengu.'

A short while later, he spoke. 'You were right to contact me, Bengu, but I have to warn you that what you've done will not go down well if it gets out. Telling tales about superiors is a quick way to find yourself ostracised by your colleagues and at the bottom of the promotion list, no matter how good you are. Have you told anyone that you were going to speak to me?'

'No, rra.'

'Well, make sure you keep it that way. I'll take it from here, and I'll keep your name out of it.'

'Yes, rra. Thank you, rra.'

After he hung up, Kubu sighed with relief. He was very lucky to have Mabaku as his boss.

CHAPTER 15

Mabaku started Monday morning by worrying about what Kubu had told him the previous evening. What had started as a single skeleton accidentally unearthed in the desert had escalated first to a whole graveyard of Bushman skeletons, and now to murder. Even worse, a probably innocent man was being railroaded for it.

His phone rang, and he recognised the voice of the director's secretary, Miriam.

'Assistant Superintendent Mabaku? The director wants to see you.'

Mabaku grabbed his notebook and hurried to Director Gobey's office, where Miriam waved him in.

The director looked harassed as he waved Mabaku to a chair. 'I've just come from a meeting with the commissioner. This Bushman thing is a mess, Jacob.' He frowned. 'Have you heard of a group called Bushman Survival?'

Mabaku shook his head.

'It's an organisation pushing to save Bushman culture and lobbying for Bushman land rights. It's based in London, and they picked up on the Bushman skeleton story from some radio report there. Heaven knows how that came about. Now they're claiming we're ignoring the Shakawe Massacre, as they call it.'

'That's complete nonsense.'

'I know that. But there's more. They're saying that the Bushmen were killed for their land.'

'What for? There's plenty of empty desert up there. And Bushmen don't own land anyway. Their land is wherever they happen to be at any point in time.'

'Somehow they've linked it with the Ncamasere water project. So now they claim the water project is being used to irrigate the stolen land and reap fat profits for the local kgosi and his cronies.'

'That's ridiculous. The attack on the Bushmen took place ages before anyone even thought about a water project.'

'Of course, but they sent a long fax to the president demanding an internationally supervised investigation. It's outrageous.'

'I completely agree, rra.' Mabaku wondered if this meeting was merely about Gobey letting off steam. 'We should just ignore these people. Let them stir up trouble in their own countries instead of spreading lies about us.'

Gobey nodded. After a moment he asked, 'Did you forbid the pathologist up there from getting in an expert to study the site with the skeletons?'

Mabaku's head jerked up. 'Who told you that?' He would hang MacGregor out in the sun for biltong if the man had gone behind his back to the director.

'It was part of the complaint from Bushman Survival. They said the police blocked it. Is it true?'

'Yes. The man wanted an archaeologist to come up and spend days at the site. At that point, MacGregor had found just two human skeletons, and we didn't even know it was the result of violence. It could have been a fatal disease – anthrax for instance. It would have wasted time and cost a fortune. You would have been furious if I'd approved it.'

'You could have asked me.'

'You would have thrown me out of your office.'

Gobey glared at him for a moment, and then gave a half-smile. 'I probably would have, at that.' He sighed. 'This whole business is heading for an international PR disaster. Some newspapers are picking it up now too.'

Mabaku decided he'd better add Kubu's news to the mix. 'I'm afraid there's more bad news, Director. Dr MacGregor and Detective Sergeant Bengu took care of a Bushman who had collapsed at the skeleton site. The next morning, they took him to a clinic in Shakawe, but he disappeared from there, and an old man in Ncamasere was killed that night, apparently a robbery gone wrong. The local police think the Bushman was responsible, and they've arrested him, although there's really no evidence it was him. I'm afraid they mean to get a confession out of him one way or another.'

'That will just make it all worse. You know that human-rights group, Ditshwanelo, has persuaded the High Court to investigate the trial and sentences of those two Bushmen, Maauwe and Motswetla. They were tried for murder with inadequate legal representation, found guilty and sentenced to death, although they had no real understanding of what was going on. Ditshwanelo is sure to pick up on this case as well, and then Bushman Survival will be all over it too.'

Gobey stood up and walked to the window as if to find inspiration. After a moment, he came to a decision.

'It sounds as though the locals are more interested in closing the case than finding out what actually happened. You need to get up there as soon as possible. Take over. Get this sorted out. If this Bushman is guilty, make sure you get the evidence to back up any charge. If not, catch the guilty party and put this all to bed. And come up with some feasible explanation about the so-called Bushman massacre.'

'Yes, Director. I won't let you down.' Mabaku rose to his feet, anything but delighted by the prospect of spending weeks at the other end of the country trying to unscramble this tangle. He hated anything that smacked of politics.

Gobey returned to his seat. 'Sit down, Jacob. I'm not finished.'

Mabaku was sure that he didn't want to hear more, but he had no option. He lowered himself back into the chair.

Gobey opened a file and handed a document to Mabaku. He glanced at it and saw that it was a photocopy of a letter addressed to the office of the minister of water affairs. Judging by the definition of the letters, it'd been typed rather than printed. It was unsigned.

'Go ahead. Read it.'

Mabaku did so. It was a series of complaints about the Kgosi Rantao Water Project, making various insinuations of corruption and malpractice. It was the sort of letter the police received from time to time when someone with a grievance wanted to create trouble. Nine times out of a ten, they were filed and no further action was taken.

Mabaku reread the letter, then glanced up at the director. 'You're taking this seriously?'

'Normally, it wouldn't get a second look. But now the newspapers are picking up Bushman Survival's drivel, so the letter writer might see another way of getting publicity. The problem is that there's European Union aid money involved here. It's not a lot, but Botswana has a first-rate reputation for squashing any hint of corruption. Maybe this letter is the rubbish it seems to be, but we can't take any chances. Find out who wrote it and whether they actually know something. If it's some crackpot, put the fear of God into them. Then we can keep out of it. We don't want to stir things up unless we have facts to back us up.'

'Do we have any clues? Fingerprints? Postmark?'

'It was mailed in Shakawe five days ago. That's consistent with the date on the letter. That's all. No prints. But you should be able to match that typewriter – if you find it.' He paused. 'Keep this to yourself, Jacob. Don't talk to the local police about it. Who knows who is involved? And that detective of yours is too young and inexperienced. He might let something slip.'

'What about MacGregor?'

'Absolutely not. He's from Scotland. We don't know where his loyalties lie. Maybe he was behind the leak of the whole Bushman story.'

Mabaku snorted. 'So I must solve a murder case, perhaps from scratch, find out the facts behind a hundred-year old massacre and investigate possible corruption at a civil-engineering project without any help. A couple of days should be enough for that. Anything else?'

Gobey didn't smile. 'How do you know the massacre took place that long ago? Can the pathologist tell?'

Mabaku shook his head. 'He says he can't tell how old the skeletons are. They'd need at least ten years in the desert sand to get to this state, but after that...'

Gobey nodded. 'So we could be talking about a mass murder by some person or persons still alive. Maybe it's about time you took it more seriously, Assistant Superintendent. The commissioner is most unhappy with the whole situation.'

'Yes, rra.' Mabaku hesitated. 'While I'm away, please could you have one of the detectives look into the water project, its permissions and its financing. We may as well check all the paperwork here in Gabs.'

Gobey made a note on a pad lying on his desk. 'All right, then. On your way out, see Miriam about getting you onto tomorrow morning's flight to Maun.'

∼

Kubu started Monday morning out of sorts, worrying about what he'd told Mabaku the previous evening. He'd expressed his opinion about how a case was being handled, criticising a superior. He hadn't realised what a chance he was taking. Apparently, had it been anyone other than Mabaku, he could have been pushed to the bottom of the ladder, possibly forever. He was slowly learning that there was more to policing than examining evidence and solving cases. Logic wasn't the only thing that played a role.

As he ate his breakfast, overlooking the Kavango river, he wondered what he should do next. Ian was probably on his way back from Maun – that would take him at least half the day. Abram was likely at the station, maybe even interrogating Selelo once again. Kubu couldn't imagine he was going to learn anything new. Or perhaps Abram was with the station commander, coercing Selelo to sign a document he almost certainly didn't understand.

Kubu wondered what promises were being made in return for a signature or, more likely, a thumbprint – promises that may not be kept when the confession was obtained. He shook his head. The whole situation was similar to the dreadful case of Maauwe and Motswetla that he'd read about in the newspapers. Was Selelo going to be the next Bushman found guilty for who he was rather than for what he'd done?

Kubu was gazing unfocussed into the distance when a waiter told him that there was a phone call for him at reception.

'Detective Sergeant Bengu,' he said, a little breathless from the quick walk.

'It's Assistant Superintendent Mabaku. I've decided to come to Shakawe myself to see what the hell is going on. I'll be at the Shakawe police station about three tomorrow afternoon. Make sure you're there.'

'Yes, rra. What about Dr MacGregor?'

'He should be there also. What are you doing today?'

Kubu hesitated. 'Actually, I'm not sure, rra. I don't have transport, and I'm quite a way from town.'

'I want you to start digging around to find out who is against the water project. Then go and talk to them to find out why. Understood?'

'I'll do my best, rra.'

'You'd better. And don't tell anyone that we've spoken or that I'm coming up to Shakawe. Little surprises often work wonders.'

'Yes, rra. Goodbye, rra.'

The only people Kubu had been in contact with who were opposed to the water project were Mma Zondo and the man at the protest outside the kgosi's house, Rra Mowisi. Even then, Mowisi wasn't really against the project, but rather disagreed with how the soon-to-be-irrigated land was to be distributed.

Kubu had already spoken to Mma Zondo and knew her position with respect to the water project. So he needed to find out where Rra Mowisi worked and, once he'd done that, figure out how to get there.

When Kubu phoned reception at the Shakawe police station, he was told exactly where to find Mowisi – at a smallholding just west of the A35, just north of Ncamasere. 'You can't miss him. There'll be an old Toyota bakkie parked off the road. I think it was white once.'

Things continued to go well for Kubu because when he asked the manager of Drotsky's whether she could drop him off just north of Ncamasere, the woman took the easy path and handed him some keys. 'It's the Land Cruiser out back with Drotsky's painted on the sides. Bring it back in one piece. Please.'

Kubu had never driven such a magnificent vehicle and suffered a few brief pangs of envy of people who could afford such luxury. 'May as well enjoy it while I can,' he thought. 'It may be the only time I get to drive one.'

Kubu found Mowisi easily enough and invited him to sit in the air-conditioned cab. Mowisi accepted and climbed in, grateful to be out of the heat.

'What's this all about? I did nothing at the protest. You saw that. You were there.'

'This isn't to do with the protest, rra – not directly, anyway. What I'm interested in is why some people are totally against the water project, and why some, like you, think ordinary people won't get any of the new, irrigated land.'

'Not many are against the project. Mma Zondo, of course, and a few others who don't think we should siphon off water from the river. Of course, they're not farmers, and none of them do anything about it except gossip in the bar occasionally.'

'Do you know who they are?'

'By sight, but not by name. I can get their names if you want.'

Kubu asked Mowisi to leave the names with the constable at reception at the Shakawe police station. Then he asked about Mowisi's personal position.

'As I've said before, I'm in favour of the project because it will help our community.'

'But?'

'But it's corrupt.' He hesitated for a moment. 'Please don't tell anyone that I said that.'

Kubu nodded. 'Please go on.'

'As much as the kgosi tells us it's for the good of the community, it will only benefit him and a few of his friends. They'll get the best of the new farms. People like me, who work hard for the community, probably won't get anything.'

Kubu thought back to some of his training on interviewing skills. He wanted to draw Mowisi out.

'So how does that make you feel, rra?'

Mowisi looked out of the window at his land. 'I'm very angry. It's not fair. The kgosi is the kgosi of everyone in Ncamasere, not just his friends.' He opened the window and pointed out. 'Just look at it. It's nearly desert. Sometimes nothing grows at all, but those with water...'

He remained looking out for a few moments then brought his arm back in and raised the window. As he opened the door, he turned to Kubu. 'Rra, one day there will be enough people against the way the kgosi is handling the project to force him out of office. Believe me.'

Kubu then drove to the police station, where he hoped Abram could give him some other names to talk to. However, he was told Abram was with the station commander interviewing the Bushman again.

Beating him up, most likely, Kubu thought.

He poured himself a cup of coffee and sat down in an empty conference room to bring his notes up to date. He leant back and took a sip, thinking that if Lesaka hadn't been murdered, he and Ian would be nearly home.

He took another sip, then nearly spat it out as it hit him. He had a date with Joy that evening, and she had rearranged her schedule just for him. And he'd forgotten to phone her the previous night.

He felt as though he had an ostrich egg in his stomach. He gasped for breath. He'd blown it. She'd never speak to him again.

He tried to calm himself by breathing deeply. Then, when he felt a bit more composed, he closed the door and picked up the phone.

CHAPTER 16

When Abram eventually opened the conference-room door and sat down opposite Kubu, neither said a word. Kubu was roiling inside after his conversation with Joy, and Abram had just left the interrogation room, where his boss had extracted a confession from Selelo. Neither liked how their respective afternoons had gone.

Eventually Abram spoke. 'Coffee?'

Kubu shook his head. 'Tea, please. With milk and two sugars.'

Abram stood up and left the room, returning a few minutes later with two cups.

'Any biscuits?' Kubu asked hopefully.

'No.'

They sipped their drinks in silence until Kubu spoke up. 'Abram, who is really against the water project around here?'

Abram looked puzzled, not expecting the question. 'Mma Zondo, of course. She's the most vocal. The men at the protest at the kgosi's house aren't really against it. They just want to benefit.' He took a sip of his coffee. 'I can't think of anyone else. Why do you want to know?'

Kubu shrugged. 'We seem to have reached a dead end with Lesaka's murder—'

'But we have a confession.'

Kubu looked at Abram. 'You were there. Will it hold up in court?'

Abram didn't answer.

Kubu took another sip of his tea. 'Is someone putting pressure on the station commander to close the case?'

Abram shrugged.

'Abram, all I'm doing is looking at other possibilities. Maybe someone who's against the water project thinks that murdering Lesaka will put pressure on the kgosi. It's a long shot, but who knows?'

'Well, if you want to waste your time, go ahead.'

'Talking of the protest at the kgosi's, I spoke to Mowisi this morning. I didn't learn very much, but he made a comment that caught my attention.'

'What did he say?'

'He said he thought the kgosi would be thrown out if he continued favouring his friends.'

Abram shook his head. 'I'm surprised he said that. The kgosi's popular, and I've heard no rumours of anything like that.'

'Why would Mowisi say it then? He can't do anything to get rid of the kgosi, can he?'

'No. The kgosi isn't elected; he's the chief. But he does need the support of the people.'

Kubu mulled this over for a few moments, then changed the subject. 'Who do you think vandalised the water-project sign on the road near Sepupa? That's quite far from town.'

'We think it was some youngsters who camped here over Easter. We picked them up and the station commander tore strips off them. They didn't admit it, but they won't try a stunt like that again.' He paused. 'Surely you can't think that's connected to Lesaka's murder.'

Kubu had to admit to himself that he wasn't making much progress with Mabaku's order. Other than Mma Zondo, nobody seemed opposed to the water project, and if anyone would know, it would be Abram. And there was something else that didn't make sense: the station commander's insistence that Selelo had committed murder.

'I think whoever killed Lesaka intended to do so,' Kubu said. 'But for what conceivable reason? The station commander says he had no enemies. So why was he murdered? The only thing I can think of is his support of the water project.'

'But how would killing him have any impact? It's not that there's going to be a vote or anything.'

Kubu stood up and paced up and down. 'I know it makes no sense. I'm just looking for an angle that does.'

After a while, he sat down. 'Maybe I've got it all wrong. Maybe it has nothing to do with the water project. What else was Lesaka involved in?'

'Nothing. Nothing at all. He hardly did anything after his stroke.'

There was another silence. Eventually Kubu stood up. 'I wonder when Ian will get here. I want to go back to Drotsky's. Meanwhile, I'm going for a walk. See if I can shake some sense into my head.'

With that he left the room and walked out of the station into the Kalahari heat.

~

What started out as a walk to think about what Kubu regarded as a stalled investigation, soon turned into a walk of self-doubt.

When he'd spoken to Joy, apologising profusely for his over-sight in not calling the previous evening, and even more profusely for upsetting her previous arrangement, he felt she'd been abrupt, even dismissive. How that had hurt.

'No problem,' she'd said. 'I'm sure he's still free.'

That left Kubu desperately searching for something to say. Eventually he stammered that he'd call when he returned.

'Okay,' she'd said. 'Bye.' And she'd hung up.

As he replayed the call in his head, all the pain and disappointment returned. This time he was sure he'd really blown it.

He stopped in the middle of a small field and breathed deeply.

He wanted to cry – he wanted to phone her again and beg a second chance. But he knew she would think him a sissy if he did that.

What was he to do?

At that moment, he heard someone shouting from the edge of the field. 'Kubu. Kubu, come and help me.'

Kubu looked round and saw Ian leaning out of his Land Rover, waving him to come over. Kubu didn't want company; he wanted to be left alone to wallow in his misery.

'Kubu, come on. Lesaka's going to walk out of here soon.'

Kubu walked over and climbed into the car.

Ian looked at him. 'What on earth were you doing standing in the hot sun? That's not like you. You normally home in on any air conditioning.'

'Just thinking. We have problems with the investigation.' As Ian drove to the undertaker, Kubu explained that Selelo had confessed.

'Confessed, my foot. How badly beaten up was he?'

Kubu said that he hadn't seen the Bushman since the previous day. Apparently the station commander and Abram had got him to sign. Then he took a deep breath. 'I want to tell you something, but you have to promise not to tell anyone. You can't even mention that I told you something in confidence.'

Ian looked at him quizzically. Then nodded.

Kubu then related how he'd spoken to Mabaku about his concerns regarding how the Lesaka investigation was being handled. And now Mabaku had decided to come to Kasane.

'He'll be here tomorrow afternoon. He wants us to be at the station when he arrives. And we're to tell no one that he's coming. I suppose he wants to surprise the station commander.'

'I hope this means he's taking the Bushman massacre seriously as well.'

A few minutes later they arrived at the undertaker's premises. Ian explained that Lesaka's body was evidence in a murder investigation and should be kept in a manner that would allow further inspection.

'For how long, rra?' The undertaker was clearly worried that he could end up being a long-term storage facility. 'Who is going to pay?'

'I'll let you know when I know. Probably tomorrow or the day after.'

The undertaker reluctantly took custody of the body, wheeling it to the back of the building on a stretcher.

'I need a beer,' Ian exclaimed. 'Let's head back. I'm hot, and I'm parched. Is that okay with you?'

'Definitely,' Kubu replied. 'The quicker, the better.'

Kubu led the way back to Drotsky's in the Land Cruiser. When they arrived, he decided to talk to the manager while Ian showered and changed. Places like Drotsky's, with a bar and restaurant, were often good for gossip. So he walked over to the main lodge.

'You want to know about the water project?' the manager asked after Kubu explained the situation.

Kubu nodded.

'I'm not sure I can add anything to what you probably know. Kgosi Rantao wants to have a legacy and decided irrigating part of the desert near here would be a good one. It would expand the farming area, which would be a good thing for the community.'

She paused.

'What do you think of it?'

'Opening up extra farm land would be very good, and I don't think it would affect us here one way or the other. The water is to be taken from the river quite a long way away.'

'Do you know of anyone who doesn't want it?'

'Well,' she said, 'I'm sure you know about Mma Zondo and Mami Wata.'

'I do.'

'But other than that, I'm not sure.' She shrugged. 'We've had a few guests who seemed to think it was a bad idea.'

'In what way?'

'Well, for example, there was a small group of environmentalists just last week – at least that's what they called themselves. They were worried that allowing one project like that would encourage every community along the river to do the same. Then it was possible that the delta would be affected.'

'Were they part of an organisation?'

The manager shook her head. 'I don't think so. Just a group of like-minded friends enjoying our wonderful area.'

'Did they talk about Kgosi Rantao or any of the other locals involved in the project?'

She shook her head. 'Why are you interested in this?'

Kubu explained that he'd been told of a few small issues in the community, and since he had a little free time, he was sniffing around. He then thought for a few moments, wondering what else he could ask. When he couldn't think of anything, he stood up. 'Thank you so much, mma. If you hear anything at all, please let me know.'

Just as he was turning to leave, she spoke. 'There was one thing that was unusual, just a few days ago. Two young men rented a campsite. They were telling people at the bar that they were BBC reporters. And one of them actually used my office to call London. He reversed charges so he didn't have to pay, but he was on the phone for nearly fifteen minutes. Must have cost a fortune.'

'What did he talk about?'

'Well, I wasn't in the room, but the line must have been bad, so he was almost shouting. Everyone could hear him. He was telling whoever he was talking to that the water project was violating Bushman burial grounds, and that the Botswana government was turning a blind eye.'

'He was at the site when Dr MacGregor identified the first skull as being a Bushman.'

'Well, that's not all. The next day, someone called to speak to him, but he wasn't around. They left a London number and asked him to call back. I passed on the message that evening, and he spoke for another quarter of an hour or so. Unfortunately, I didn't hear anything that time, because I was at dinner.'

Kubu thanked the manager, asking her to get him the two men's details: names, addresses and so on. Then he found a table overlooking the river. As he waited for Ian, he pulled out his notebook and jotted down what he'd learnt. It wasn't much. Mabaku was going to be disappointed.

CHAPTER 17

Mabaku was hot and irritable by the time he arrived at the Shakawe police station. The CID in Maun had lent him an old vehicle with no air conditioning for the four-hour drive to Shakawe. He was lucky to get even that. They were short of vehicles and had parted with one grudgingly, insisting it be back by the end of the week.

'I'm Assistant Superintendent Mabaku of the CID,' he told the constable at reception. 'I want to see the station commander at once.'

His tone must have convinced the man, because he merely nodded and headed off without a word. He returned with the station commander, whose face showed that this was a surprise – and not a welcome one. Nevertheless, he stuck out his hand.

'Assistant Superintendent Mabaku? I'm Assistant Superintendent Balopi. We didn't know you were coming up here.'

Mabaku shook the offered hand. 'Didn't Gaborone inform you? Let's go to your office. But I'd like a glass of cold water first. It was a long, hot trip from Maun.'

Mabaku downed the first glass and took a second with him to the station commander's office.

'Your people are around here somewhere,' Balopi told him. 'The pathologist is writing up his report on the autopsy. No surprises there. The poor man was bludgeoned in his bed and then stabbed through the heart. I don't know what Bengu's doing. Now, what's this all about?'

'Various things, but let's start with the murder. You have a suspect?'

Balopi smiled. 'Oh, much better than that. I hope you didn't come all the way up here for that. We have the culprit in custody, and he's given a full confession.'

'Indeed.' Mabaku wasn't impressed. 'I'd like to see the confession.'

'Very well.' Balopi retrieved a file from his desk and extracted a single printed sheet. Mabaku read it carefully.

The Bushman, who was identified only as Selelo, admitted to breaking into a house. He said he was looking for food and money. However, as he was searching the home he disturbed a sleeping man, who woke up and started yelling, so he hit him with his knobkierie and then stabbed him. He stole the man's wallet from the table next to his bed and escaped, scared that someone might have heard the commotion. On the way out, he grabbed a portable radio. Once out of the house, he panicked and dumped the radio in some bushes. Later, he buried the knife, wallet, and knobkierie in the sand near the road, but wasn't sure where. At the bottom of the page there was a smudged thumbprint.

Mabaku laid the confession on the desk. 'And you have physical evidence to support this? Or witnesses?'

Balopi nodded, looking smug. 'A neighbour saw the man enter the house at the time that corresponds to the pathologist's estimate of the time of death. She didn't see him clearly, but it could easily be this Bushman. He isn't as small as they sometimes are. And we found the radio in some bushes nearby, just as he said.'

'Fingerprints?'

Balopi hesitated. 'We took prints from all over the house. And the portable radio. We'll need to send them to Maun for analysis. But it hardly seems necessary.'

Mabaku could hardly believe his ears. 'Hardly necessary? Station commander, this is murder we're talking about. Your evidence is a witness who saw a man, who might or might not be this man, enter the house. That's hardly surprising. Someone killed Lesaka. Then you found a radio discarded in some bushes. Quite likely any thief would discard it since the robbery had gone so badly wrong. Without fingerprints, you have nothing.'

'I have the confession.'

'Oh, yes, so you do. I want to interview the suspect myself, Assistant Superintendent, and I want Detective Sergeant Bengu and Dr MacGregor with me.'

Balopi stood up. 'Are you suggesting I haven't done my job properly? We've solved this case, and it took us two days. And with no help from you clever people in Gaborone.'

Mabaku also rose to his feet and leaned towards him. 'Rra, in the first place, this is not your job. This is a CID job. In the second place, yes, I'm not satisfied with the investigation so far. This confession will never stand up in court. You may be a bit out of the way here, but surely you've heard about the case before the High Court right now of the two Bushman who signed a confession they didn't understand? With that, and the mass grave of Bushmen up the road here, we need to be especially careful instead of extremely casual. Now, get this man to an interview room. I want to talk to him.'

Balopi looked as though he would explode. 'I insist on being with you. And also *my* detective, Detective Sergeant Nteba, who actually knows about this case.'

'All detectives are part of the CID, no matter where they are based,' Mabaku reminded him. 'But I have no objection if the two of you want to join us. But you must let me ask the questions. It's my job, not yours.'

Balopi muttered something and stalked out of the room, shouting for the duty officer.

Mabaku realised he'd made an enemy, but he didn't care. It appeared the situation was even worse than Kubu had described it.

∼

Mabaku found Ian and Kubu waiting outside the office. From the looks on their faces, they'd heard at least part of the exchange.

Ian smiled. 'This is a surprise, Assistant Superintendent. Welcome to Shakawe. Glad you're here. It's a real dog's dinner, this business.'

'The director wants it sorted out, so I want to see this Selelo now. We can discuss it all later.'

When they'd all crowded into the interview room, Mabaku took the seat at the table and the others sat behind him. Once again, Selelo cowered on the floor in the corner. He had an angry cut on his lip and a bruise on his forehead. Eventually, he allowed Kubu to coax him into the chair. He stared down at the table, unwilling to meet Mabaku's gaze.

Once Mabaku had switched on the recorder and introduced the interview, he turned to the Bushman. 'Now, Selelo, I want to know if you killed that man in the house in Ncamasere. You must tell me the truth. You won't be hurt, whatever you say.'

At first Selelo said nothing. Then he muttered, 'No kill man. Going home to speak to ancestors.' Suddenly he lifted his head and met Mabaku's eyes. 'Why kill? I not know this man. Bushmen not kill.'

'You were stealing. You broke into his house.'

'Where house? Here? I go home.'

'In Ncamasere. You were there.'

Selelo shook his head. 'Go home. Tsodilo. Only stop in Ncamasere to rest. Tired after ancestor dance. Men find me there.'

Balopi jumped in. 'Ncamasere's not on the way to Tsodilo from Shakawe.'

'Road longer, Road easier than desert. Quicker.

'You took a radio?'

'Radio? What for radio?'

Balopi broke in again. 'You threw it in the bushes, didn't you? You admitted it yesterday. Stop lying!'

Mabaku turned and glared at the station commander. 'I'll ask the questions. Do you have the confession?'

Balopi shoved it at him.

'Selelo, did you put your thumb on this paper?'

Selelo hesitated. 'Man make me.' He rubbed his right wrist.

'Do you know what's written here?'

Selelo shook his head.

'Can you read it?'

Again Selelo shook his head.

Mabaku raised his voice. 'Selelo, you must tell me the truth now. Did you break into the man's house to steal?'

Selelo shrank back, shaking his head quickly from side to side. 'Selelo not steal. Selelo not kill.'

'What did you do with your knobkierie?'

'Not here. Tsodilo.'

'And the knife?'

'Men took.'

Mabaku turned to the others. 'He had a knife when you arrested him?'

After a moment, Abram said, 'He did, but it didn't look—'

'He admitted what he did with the knife,' Balopi interrupted. 'He buried it.'

Ian spoke for the first time. 'I'd like to see the knife he had with him.'

Abram nodded and left to fetch it.

Mabaku turned back to Selelo. 'You had another knife. Did you bury it?'

'Other knife? One knife. No bury. Men take.'

Mabaku felt Selelo was genuinely confused by the question. He turned to a different issue.

'What cut your lip?'

'The man.' Selelo glanced at Balopi.

'He fell off the chair. You can see he doesn't know how to sit properly.'

Mabaku kept his eyes on Selelo. 'Is that true? Did you fall off the chair?'

Selelo said nothing.

'I asked you if you fell off the chair.'

Again there was no response.

The tense moment was interrupted by Abram returning with Selelo's knife, sealed in a plastic evidence bag. He gave it to Ian, and the pathologist immediately shook his head. 'The blade isn't long enough. He couldn't have used this.'

'Well, he must have had another knife,' Abram responded, and Balopi nodded.

Mabaku had had enough. 'All right, Selelo. I'll talk to you again later.' He stood up. 'Let's go. I'd like to discuss this in your office, Assistant Superintendent.'

~

The previous meeting in the station commander's office had been tense. This one was all out war. The two men stood and shouted at each other.

'You beat that man into signing that confession!'

'Nonsense. With you being so soft, he saw an opportunity to wriggle out of it. You people in the capital don't know what it's like out here.'

'It doesn't matter what it's like. It's a question of whether he's guilty or not.'

'We deal with these people all the time. They're not like the Bushmen of the past, who lived off the land and kept to themselves. The modern ones want alcohol and live by thieving. He's one of those. And he murdered my friend in cold blood.'

Mabaku lowered his voice. 'Lesaka was your friend?'

'One of my close friends. A harmless man, who was helpless because of his stroke. The bash on his head might have killed him, but that bastard had to stick a knife into him to finish him off. He has a bruise or two? So what? *He's* alive. For the moment.'

'You can't be on the case. You're not impartial.'

'You're damn right I'm not impartial. He's scum. Lesaka was a good man, who worked hard for the community his whole life. And was rewarded with a knife in his chest by a petty thief. And you worry because the Bushman has a couple of bruises?'

The whole thing is a mess, Mabaku thought. The man wants

revenge for the death of his friend, and he's lashed out at the first possible suspect.

Balopi collapsed into his seat and waved Mabaku to do the same.

'Look, Assistant Superintendent, I'm a hundred percent sure we have our man. If you insist, we'll send the fingerprints to Maun. More time wasted.'

Mabaku nodded. 'We'll collect everything you have and get it to Maun tomorrow morning. Bengu or Nteba can do that. While we wait for the results, we can search for the knife, the wallet and the knobkierie.'

Balopi shook his head. 'Mabaku, you have no idea, do you? There's sand everywhere. We'll never find them. He's lying that he doesn't know the location, but you won't make him talk, will you? Just asking him nicely is your style.'

Mabaku took a deep breath. He was tired, and this was getting them nowhere. He stood up. 'Station commander, we'll check the fingerprints. That Bushman wouldn't be wearing gloves; he's not a professional thief. If he broke into Lesaka's home, he'll have left prints all over the place. As well as on the radio. If there's a match, we have him. If we don't find any, it's not him. And then our job is to catch the real culprit.'

~

Kubu had arranged a room for Mabaku at Drotsky's, and as soon as the assistant superintendent had checked in, he announced he was going to take a shower. Ian suggested meeting for drinks over-looking the river in half an hour, and Mabaku gave a curt nod.

'I must say you two have done yourselves proud here. I hope I'm not expected to pay for all this from my budget.'

He headed off without waiting for a response. Ian, whose idea was exactly that Mabaku would pay for Drotsky's, decided this wasn't the moment to bring that up.

Half an hour later, showered and changed, Mabaku was in a much better mood. He ordered a cold beer – emphasising the cold to the waiter – and relaxed in a chair overlooking the water. A small herd of lechwe was drinking not far away and, as usual, spectacular birds were active in the trees and at the water's edge.

'It is beautiful and peaceful here,' Mabaku commented. 'Pity humans come and mess it up with murders and irrigation projects.' He sighed. 'Dr MacGregor, did anything new come out of the autopsy?'

Ian described what he'd discovered, but concluded that his original assessment was correct. Lesaka had been knocked unconscious by a blow from a blunt instrument like a knobkierie and was subsequently stabbed through the heart.

'Could the Bushman have done that?'

Ian hesitated. 'On the basis of the autopsy? Certainly. I'm sure he can handle a knobkierie and knows how to use a hunting knife. But the knife they found on him isn't the right sort of weapon at all.'

'He might have had another knife, I suppose,' Kubu put in. 'But where would he get a knobkierie? He didn't have one when I took him to the clinic. Why would he even want one? He was going home.'

'Well, that's his story,' Mabaku pointed out. 'Doctor, could he have used some other sort of weapon? A brick or something he found in the house?'

Ian thought about that for a moment, and then cupped his hands and put them together. 'The blow was from something roughly this size and shape. I suppose a smooth rock could have done it, but I found no traces of stone or sand on the scalp. And then I'd be more doubtful if the Bushman would have the strength. He's wiry, but the second blow cracked the skull. Without any leverage that would take a great deal of force.' He paused. 'I can't think what he might have used from the house. And if he did grab something, he would have discarded it there. Why take it with him?' Ian shook his head. 'It doesna make sense to me.' He took a long draw of his beer.

'Bengu, what do you think?'

By this time, Kubu knew his boss pretty well. He wasn't asking for an opinion, he wanted an assessment based on observations, facts and deductions. He tried to arrange his thoughts.

'Well, I don't believe the story about him breaking into the house to steal. Lesaka's house isn't even close to the main road. If he walked to Ncamasere from Shakawe, there were plenty of nearer houses he could have burgled if he was hungry or wanted money. Then there's the mystery of where he got the knobkierie or whatever it was. And would he really just bury the evidence next to the road in the middle of the town where he might be seen? It doesn't make sense.' He paused for a moment. 'And why take a radio on the way *out* and then immediately throw it away?'

'To put us off the trail?'

Kubu thought about that while he finished his beer. 'There are some puzzling aspects. Why did he go to Ncamasere in the first place? He's a Bushman. They can find their way through the desert without roads or maps. He said the road is easier, but I'm told it's a lot longer that way. If he deliberately went to Ncamasere to kill Lesaka – maybe something to do with the 'stinging like a bee' story I told you about – then the story makes some sort of sense. But one thing doesn't fit at all. If he murdered Lesaka, he could disappear into the desert and probably never be found. Instead, he hung around in the town, and made no attempt to get away when the police came.'

'What about the confession?'

'Rra, you know what I think about that.'

Mabaku nodded and seemed satisfied. After a few moments, he added, 'Let's have another beer. I'm still parched.'

Once they'd ordered, he asked Ian what he'd discovered about the skeletons, and Ian brought him up to date.

'No idea who could have caused the deaths or how long ago they took place?'

Ian shook his head. 'I can't even say for sure that they all died at the same time. If we'd had an expert investigate, it might have been different.'

Mabaku frowned and leant forward. 'Did you tell anyone else about that mad idea of yours?'

Ian bristled. 'It wasna mad. But, no, I did not. Why do you ask?'

'Because some overseas Bushman-rights group knows about it and is claiming we're ignoring what they call a massacre.'

Ian looked shocked. 'That's impossible.'

'You think they made it up?'

'I only raised it with you.'

Mabaku stared at him without replying.

'Detective Sergeant Nteba and I were there as well,' Kubu put in tentatively. 'We were in a vacant office, so no one else could have overheard what Ian said.'

'I presume *you* didn't repeat what you heard to anyone?'

'No, rra. Of course not.'

'Well, then it's Nteba who can't keep his mouth shut. What sort of policeman is he? I'll teach him a thing or two about police procedure when I see him.' Mabaku banged his empty glass down on the table and looked around. 'Where's that damn beer?'

Fortunately the waiter was just arriving with the new round. Mabaku finished half of his beer, then turned to Kubu. 'You found no one who remembers anything about Bushmen deaths in this area?'

'No, rra.'

'What about the kgosi? They tend to know about everything that's happened in their areas in the past.'

Kubu admitted that he hadn't spoken to the kgosi as yet.

Mabaku grunted. 'First thing tomorrow we're going to do that. We'll ask him about Lesaka's background too. If Selelo wasn't the culprit, then it was someone from around here. In that case, we need to find the motive, and that will link with something in Lesaka's past.' He drained the rest of his beer. 'I'm famished. Lunch was a stale sandwich. Let's get something to eat.'

CHAPTER 18

Once they'd finished their steaks, Kubu decided to ask Mabaku about the puzzling task he'd given him the previous day. 'Assistant Superintendent, do you think someone who's against the water project is somehow linked to Lesaka's death?' He frowned. 'Or to the Bushman massacre?'

'Who said they're linked to either? Maybe nothing is related. The discovery of the skeletons was just chance, and Lesaka was in favour of the project anyway. On the other hand, maybe he did know something about the deaths of the Bushmen. Or maybe he knew something about the way the water project was being managed that someone didn't want him to divulge. Or maybe it's all related.' Mabaku managed to cut a few last scraps off his T-bone and polished them off. 'What did you find out?'

Kubu related what he'd learnt and then shrugged. 'What it comes down to is that the only person really opposed to the water project is Mma Zondo. The others just want it modified in their own favour.'

'Could this Zondo woman have been involved in Lesaka's death? You said she visited him the day of the murder, and he was upset afterwards.'

Kubu thought about the way Mma Zondo had reacted to the news. It seemed unlikely. However, she was clearly unbalanced. There were stories of people committing violent acts because they claimed invisible voices told them to do so. Most Batswana attributed that to witchcraft, but the scientific opinion was mental disease.

'Well?'

'No, rra, I don't think so.'

'And defacing that sign on the way up here?'

Kubu shook his head. 'Abram says it was a group of students who visited over Easter. Just a prank.'

'Well, we need to interview Mma Zondo again. We'll go tomorrow after we see the kgosi.'

Kubu still couldn't see the connection between Lesaka's death and the water project. After a moment, he said tentatively, 'The problem is that although Lesaka was supporting the project, his death doesn't affect it at all.'

'Maybe it was meant as a warning to the kgosi. Do you have any better ideas?'

Kubu admitted that he did not.

After breakfast the next morning, Kubu set up an appointment with the kgosi at his home, and Mabaku arranged with the station commander for Abram to take the fingerprint file and radio to Maun. The station commander offered to join them at their meetings in Abram's stead, which surprised Mabaku, but he politely declined. 'That won't be necessary, thank you, rra. Bengu knows his way around here by now.'

In fact, Kubu was quite worried that he'd get lost, but the receptionist gave him careful instructions and they found the house quite easily. Kubu recognised it at once, having been there with Abram at the demonstration. He noticed that the broken window had been fixed, and the brick had been replaced along the walk to the house.

Kubu rang the doorbell, and after a few moments, the kgosi's daughter first unlocked the front door, then the security door, then invited them in. She took them into the lounge, where the kgosi was sitting on a couch next to a younger man. They rose when Mabaku and Kubu entered.

The detectives greeted the kgosi with the respectful handshake, touching their right arms with their left hands, and waited until he was seated again before they joined him.

'Kgosi,' Mabaku began, 'we're very grateful for your time this morning. As you know, we're investigating the death of Rra Lesaka, and we'd appreciate your help with—'

'But you've arrested that Bushman,' the young man interrupted. 'We know what happened.'

Mabaku frowned and glanced at the kgosi, but he seemed impervious to the rudeness.

'The Bushman is a suspect, and we're questioning him. However, I doubt he's the murderer.'

'But, we were told—'

This time the kgosi interrupted. 'Raseelo, we're wasting time. Perhaps you should give me a few minutes with these detectives alone. We will call you if we need you.'

Raseelo glowered and seemed about to object, but rose and left the room without another word.

The kgosi turned back to the detectives. 'I apologise for my son. He sometimes forgets his manners. Anyway, I will help in any way I can.'

Mabaku thanked him and asked how well he knew Lesaka. He was surprised when the kgosi chuckled. 'Forgive me, Detective. You see Endo – Rra Lesaka – was one of my oldest, closest friends. We grew up together, went to school together, we did everything together. When I became kgosi, I knew I could always rely on him, not only to support me and cover my back, but also to tell me when I was wrong. He did so the day he died. That sort of friend is worth his weight in gold.'

'I'm sorry for your loss, kgosi, but then we've come to the right person.' Mabaku paused. 'When a man is murdered, there can be many motives. But the answer is always to be found in their past – things they've done or threatened to do or omitted to do. Can you give us some insight into Lesaka's background?'

The kgosi took his time describing Lesaka's life. They were distant cousins, nearly the same age, and so met when they were young. 'We were rowdy youths, I'm afraid. We played pranks, went hunting with our friends, kissed girls, behaved badly.' He smiled. 'I hope none of that led to his death, because then I'm also in danger.'

Mabaku didn't smile, and the kgosi continued. 'Endo fell in love with a girl called Refilwe, and she liked him too. After that he never looked at another woman. Her family demanded a big lobola, but he found the money. I lent him some myself. Soon he had a son and then a daughter, but Refilwe died with the third child.' He became pensive. 'My wife also died in childbirth. Neither of us married again.' The story went on for a while until it reached a day a few years past when Lesaka had collapsed at dinner and was subsequently diagnosed with a major stroke. 'It took a year before he could walk again. Joshua, his son, was wonderful. He devoted his life to his father and never allowed him to become despondent. He's devastated by the death.'

There was silence for several moments before Mabaku said, 'Kgosi, forgive me, but the picture you paint is of a saint, not a man. There must have been things he did that he was ashamed of, perhaps a love affair, money he owed, fights he had. No one is perfect. I'm asking for insight, not a eulogy.'

The kgosi frowned. 'Detective, I am kgosi here, and I've been kgosi for ten years. I know everything that goes on here, and many problems are brought to me at the kgotla or in private. Yes, Endo was not a saint, and had problems and quarrels as we all do. None of them could have led to murder.'

'He had no enemies?'

'He wasn't always popular with some of the other councillors. Rra Mowisi, for example, disagreed with him often.'

'What about?'

'Mowisi always suspects someone is trying to take advantage of him. He's a troublemaker. Endo would support me – because I was right. So Mowisi would attack him at the council. I suppose you could call him an enemy. But that doesn't make him a murderer.'

Mabaku was disappointed. He'd hoped that the kgosi would be more forthcoming. If he was right about Selelo's innocence, there had to be someone who had more against Lesaka than a simple disagreement at a council meeting.

Kubu said he had a question, and Mabaku nodded for him to go head. 'Kgosi, did you see Lesaka's son, Joshua, the night Lesaka was killed?'

'Yes. He asked to see me after the kgotla, but I was tired so I told him to come to my house after dinner.'

'What time was he here?'

'I'm not too sure. He came around eight and stayed about half an hour perhaps.'

Kubu noted the answers, satisfied that they agreed with what Joshua had told him. Mabaku looked at him expectantly and waited a moment, but when Kubu didn't continue he turned back to the kgosi.

'Why did he come and see you, kgosi?' Mabaku asked.

'It was a private matter. Nothing to do with any of this.'

'Kgosi, it's for me to decide if it's relevant. What did you talk about?'

The kgosi didn't look pleased, but his reply was casual enough. 'His father had criticised me at the kgotla. I was tired and a bit upset by it, so I was short with him. Joshua was worried we'd fallen out and wanted to smooth things over. I told him I probably deserved the rebuke, and there was nothing to worry about.'

'Did anyone else know about the meeting?'

'Anyone else?' The kgosi frowned. 'Well, we arranged it right after the kgotla. A few people were milling around talking, but I don't think they would have overheard. I can't recall who was there right then. I told my daughter to expect him, of course. And I don't know if Joshua told anyone else. You will have to ask him.'

After a moment, Mabaku changed the subject and asked about the water project. The kgosi's face lit up, and he leant towards them.

'It will change everything. The land will become fertile, people will want to stay here, not go in search of a better life elsewhere. Shakawe is already becoming a tourist and cultural centre for this part of the Okavango, and we will become the agricultural centre.' He paused. 'People say it can't be done. That the land is too sandy, too poor, but people are very lazy. They say something can't be done because they don't want to do the work to make it happen. Look at the Israelis. They too are faced with arid, sandy conditions. So they worked out what to do and then they just did it. We can be the same. We just need the water. That's what this project is about.'

'And who manages the project?'

'A civil-engineering company appointed by the council.'

'But who controls the project from the council's side? Checks that the work is being done properly and so on.'

'An outside consultant oversees it from time to time. He comes from Maun.'

'And the finances?'

'I do that myself. We have various sources of money, and the accounts are reported to all of them, and, of course, there's an external auditor. Why are you asking about this?'

'Kgosi, I'm trying to understand the background here. Was Lesaka involved in the financial aspects?'

The kgosi shook his head. 'After his stroke, I didn't want to bother him with things like that.'

'So you do it all yourself? It's a lot of work.'

'Yes, it is. That's what I said. You have to do a lot of work to make something big and worthwhile happen.'

'But some people are against it. Your Rra Mowisi, for example.'

The kgosi shook his head dismissively. 'No, he's not against it. He just wants to do nothing and then benefit unfairly. That is his nature. But he supports the project.' He shrugged. 'Some of the older people worry about tradition, but, again, that's really just another name for laziness.'

Kubu realised that the kgosi's statement was similar to what Mowisi had told him the afternoon before, although the motives ascribed were quite different. He glanced at Mabaku for permission, then asked, 'What about the sign that was defaced on the road south of here?'

'It was some stupid kids showing off. I must have it cleaned up. Thank you for the reminder.'

'And what about Mma Zondo and the water spirit?'

The kgosi chuckled. 'Mma Zondo has a fixation about Mami Wata. She believes the water spirit will be offended, and some of the fishermen share her beliefs. But the water we take won't affect the river. I'm confident Mami Wata will forgive us.' He smiled again.

'But what if Mma Zondo is so fixated that she's willing to do anything. Even kill.'

This time, the kgosi hesitated before replying. 'I think she's harmless, but I suppose it's possible I'm wrong. But, anyway, why kill Endo?'

Mabaku chipped in. 'Perhaps as a warning. To you.'

The kgosi shook his head. 'I doubt that. Her warnings come verbally and at great length.'

'Kgosi,' Mabaku said, 'if we are right and the Bushman is not the culprit, then someone in this area wanted Lesaka dead. There were no other outsiders here, apart from Detective Sergeant Bengu, our pathologist, and a few tourists passing through. You say Lesaka always supported you. You also say he had no enemies of his own, so maybe your enemies became his enemies. Maybe this was intended as a warning to you. I think it would be wise to give that thought.'

The kgosi was unperturbed. 'I will do so. Is there anything else?'

'There is one other matter. I'm sure you know much about what went on here in the past. Our original interest here was the discovery of the skeleton at what has turned out to be a mass grave of Bushmen. Can you help us with any background for that?'

The kgosi hesitated. 'Bushmen have been around this area since long before we came. There's plenty of land here, and we never had any issues with them. Do you know how old these skeletons are?'

'We haven't dated them accurately yet, but around fifty years.'

Kubu was impressed that Mabaku could say this so glibly, when in reality they had no idea.

'I was three years old then, Assistant Superintendent.'

'It appears at least nine men, women and children died violently. Surely people would have talked about it for years.'

'I never heard anything. Perhaps it was a battle between different Bushman groups. Fifty years ago, this was wild country. There were still lions around here in those days. Perhaps the skeletons are even older than you think and date back even to before Ncamasere was founded.' The kgosi looked at his watch. 'Now, is there anything else?'

With the meeting clearly over, Mabaku thanked him for his time, and the detectives took their leave.

～

As they walked to the vehicle, Mabaku asked Kubu what he'd made of the interview.

Kubu thought for a few seconds. 'Everything is too perfect. Lesaka had no enemies. Everyone supports the water project except Mma Zondo, and she's mad. There have never been any issues with Bushmen. I think the kgosi was holding back.'

'I think so too.' After a moment he added, 'It was good work pushing him on Mma Zondo and asking him about Lesaka's son's visit.'

'Thank you, rra,' Kubu responded, feeling proud.

'But you should have followed up. You left it to me to ask what they talked about, and who knew about the meeting. If someone knew about that meeting, they knew that Lesaka would be alone for a while that night. That's important information.'

Kubu said nothing. He'd been pleased that he'd checked on Joshua's story but now was ashamed that he'd missed the implications.

Mabaku unlocked the car. 'You said the kgosi was popular, but the house is well protected. Security doors, bars on the windows. It seems excessive for a house out here, even if the kgosi does live in it.'

'I noticed that too. It's certainly not usual in Ncamasere. However, Lesaka's house had burglar bars.'

'Drotsky's seems pretty relaxed. But I suppose no one throws bricks at their windows. Well, let's go and talk to the mad woman with the water spirit.'

CHAPTER 19

M abaku took a step back as two ferocious dogs threw themselves at the gate in front of him. 'What the hell's happening in this part of the country? Every house is like a fortress.'

Kubu was also keeping his distance. 'They say they need to protect themselves because it takes the police so long to get here if they're called.'

Mabaku scowled. He didn't like anyone criticising the police. However, Kubu knew Mabaku liked even less the idea that the police were not doing their job. He was sure that the subject would surface sometime in the near future.

Kubu cupped his hands around his mouth and shouted. 'Police. Anyone there?'

Almost immediately, he saw Jacob Zondo walk out of the house and whistle for the dogs. They quietened immediately and sat near the gate, still focussed on the visitors.

Jacob walked up to the gate. 'What do you want now?'

'Rra Zondo, this is my boss, Assistant Superintendent Mabaku. Rra, this is Jacob Zondo, Mma Zondo's son.'

Mabaku acknowledged the man with a nod. 'We'd like to speak to your mother.'

'She already told the police all she knew about Rra Lesaka.'

'Please open the gate and take us to her,' Mabaku said quietly.

Kubu knew when Mabaku's voice went quiet, it was often the precursor to all hell breaking loose. Mabaku didn't like people making assumptions about him or obstructing what he wanted to do.

Jacob must have sensed the menace and opened the gate. 'Don't worry about the dogs. They're well behaved if I want them to be.'

～

A few minutes later they were seated inside, waiting for Mma Zondo. Kubu could see Mabaku taking everything in.

I'd love to know what's going on inside his head, thought Kubu. I have so much to learn.

A few minutes later, after introductions had been made, Mabaku told Jacob they wanted to speak to his mother in private.

'That's not necessary,' he replied. 'My mother and I have no secrets.'

However, Mabaku insisted and Jacob stalked out of the room.

For about fifteen minutes, Mabaku probed why Mma Zondo was so opposed to the water project. Kubu thought her answers were consistent with what he and Abram had learnt on the previous visit. Basically, she claimed it was Mami Wata who was against it, not her.

Kubu could see that Mabaku wasn't happy with her answers. His voice was getting a little louder.

'And where do *you* stand regarding the project, mma? You, personally?'

Mma Zondo didn't flinch. Nor did she answer.

He's going to lose it soon, Kubu thought. And he was right.

Mabaku jumped to his feet and glared at the woman. 'How convenient it is that you don't have to take responsibility for what you say or do.' He took a step towards her. 'Maybe Mami Wata, or whatever you call her, told you to kill Rra Lesaka because he supported the project.'

She stood up too, holding her ground.

He took another step forward. 'Bengu here tells me that you visited Rra Lesaka just before he was murdered.'

Mma Zondo nodded.

'Did Mami Wata tell you to murder Lesaka?'

Mma Zondo didn't respond.

Mabaku raised his voice. 'Well, did she?'

'No, she did not. And I didn't kill him. I'd never do that.' She took a deep breath. 'And what right have you to come into my home and accuse me of murder? Please leave. Now.'

Kubu wasn't sure what to expect next. For several long seconds, Mabaku and Mma Zondo glared at each other.

She's tough, Kubu thought. Not many people stand up to Mabaku.

Eventually, Mabaku stepped back and sat down. 'Had you known him for a long time?' He asked in a normal voice.

She also sat down. 'Oh yes. My husband, Ezekiel, and Lesaka were close friends before Ezekiel died. They grew up together.'

'And your husband just disappeared?'

'Yes. He rode out one day to hunt and never came back. After a while, we assumed he was dead – because he would never have abandoned us. It was a difficult time. However, I was consoled by Mami Wata.'

Mabaku stood up and Kubu braced for another outburst. However, he walked over to the small table with photographs. He picked up the one of two young men on horses. 'One of these is your husband?' he asked.

'The one on the left.'

'And is that Lesaka on the right?'

'Oh no. That boy is now the kgosi – another of Ezekiel's boyhood friends.'

'Are you still friendly with the kgosi?'

Mma Zondo shook her head. 'No. The only time we meet is at the kgotla, and then we usually disagree.'

'About what?'

'Everything. The fact that there even is a water project, and also the way it's being run.'

Mabaku returned the photograph to the table and sat back down. 'What's wrong with how it's being run?'

'Well, it seems that the kgosi's friends are all going to get the best land. That's not how it should be.'

'Anything else?'

Kubu was puzzled. His boss seemed to be trying to sniff something out.

Mma Zondo hesitated, then asked, 'Isn't that enough?'

Mabaku took his time to answer. 'Mma Zondo, a few days ago, the office of the minister of water affairs received an anonymous letter posted in Shakawe.'

Kubu sat up. This was something new. He glanced at Mma Zondo, but her expression hadn't changed.

'The letter alleges that the project is being run badly and, worse still, that it's rife with corruption.' He paused. 'Do you know anything about such a letter?'

It was a few moments before she replied. 'No, Assistant Superintendent, I do not.'

'Have you heard any rumours about corruption, about money being siphoned off?'

She shook her head.

Mabaku stood up yet again and walked to a window overlooking the river.

Eventually, he swung round. 'Has Mami Wata mentioned any corruption?'

Kubu was taken aback. It must have been very difficult for Mabaku to ask that question, given how much he'd disparaged the water spirit and Mma Zondo's relationship with her.

Mma Zondo didn't answer.

'Well, did she?' Kubu could see that Mabaku was struggling to keep his temper under control.

'No, she did not.'

Mabaku gazed at the woman for a few moments, then turned to Kubu. 'Please find her son and bring him here.'

Mma Zondo stood up at the same time as Kubu. 'He doesn't know anything.'

'About what?' Mabaku snapped.

'I assume you want to ask him about the letter.'

A smile flitted across Mabaku's face. 'If you don't know anything about the letter, why would you have ever discussed it? I think you're lying, Mma Zondo. About what, I'm not sure yet, but I promise I will find out. I always find out.'

Kubu opened the door to go and search for Jacob, but instead found him standing there, apparently listening.

'What do you want? I've work to do.'

Mabaku asked him if he knew anything about a letter that had been sent to the minister of water affairs.

Jacob frowned and shook his head. 'No, I don't.'

'Has your mother ever mentioned it to you?'

'No.'

Mabaku glared at Mma Zondo, then turned back to Jacob.

'This letter was posted in Shakawe and alleges that there is corruption in the water project. Do you know anything about that?'

'No, I don't. I haven't even heard any rumours about such things.'

'Are you sure?'

'Of course I'm sure.'

Kubu wondered where this was going.

After a few moments, Mabaku indicated that it was time to leave. 'Thank you, mma. Thank you, rra. We'll be talking again soon.'

Kubu immediately thought about what was waiting outside. 'What about the dogs?'

Mma Zondo said she'd escort them to the gate. She opened the front door, and, sure enough, the dogs were outside, but they remained seated until Mma Zondo snapped her fingers. Then they ran to the gate and back, then milled around.

Mma Zondo unlocked the gate, and the two detectives walked out. Just as the big padlock snapped shut, Mabaku turned.

'Thank you for your time, Mma Zondo. I apologise for the intrusion.'

She nodded.

'I do have one final question. Do you have a typewriter?'

Kubu wasn't sure what the look was that passed across her face. Confusion? Surprise? Puzzlement?

Eventually she answered. 'What a strange question, Assistant Superintendent. But, no, I don't have one.'

As they walked back to the car, Mabaku asked Kubu if he'd been keeping notes of the meeting.

'No, rra. I didn't know you wanted me to, rra.' Kubu was embarrassed to admit it.

'Did you see me taking notes, Detective Sergeant?'

'No, rra.' Kubu decided he would only make things worse if he continued.

'If I dropped dead right now, you'd have no record of the conversation. Right?'

'Yes, rra. I mean, no, rra. I would have nothing. I apologise, rra. It won't happen again.'

They climbed into the car and headed for the police station.

When he'd recovered his composure, Kubu had to satisfy his curiosity. 'Rra, you asked me to find out about people who were against the water project. Was that because of the letter you mentioned?'

'Yes. What did you think of that woman's response?'

'I'm not sure I would trust anything she said.'

Mabaku glanced across at Kubu. 'Why's that?'

'Well, rra, I think she's a little mad, what with her Mami Wata. I think you were right when you said she wouldn't take responsibility for anything. If she didn't want to answer something directly, she could say it came from her spirit.'

'So you think she knows about the letter?'

'I just don't know, rra. And the same with the corruption.' Kubu paused. 'What do you think, rra?'

'I have to admit I'm also not sure, but my gut tells me that she knows more than she's telling. But how to get her to tell us? I don't know at the moment.'

It took another ten minutes or so to reach the Shakawe police station. As they were getting out of the car, Mabaku told Kubu not to mention the letter nor the suggestion of corruption.

'Always keep something back, Bengu. Never show your whole hand.'

Not for the first time Kubu felt how fortunate he was to have Mabaku as a boss. Every time he was with him, he learnt something new.

As they walked into the station, the receptionist told them to go to the station commander's office right away. Kubu could see Mabaku stiffen. He didn't like being told what to do, particularly by a station commander in an out-of-the-way village.

As soon as they walked in the door, Balopi went straight for Mabaku. 'I hear you've been bullying Mma Zondo, Assistant Superintendent.'

Mabaku didn't respond.

'What right have you to come to my jurisdiction and try to get people to tell lies about the kgosi?'

'I haven't talked to anyone about the kgosi.'

Kubu noticed that this was Mabaku's quiet voice – his dangerous voice.

'Jacob Zondo just phoned and said you were putting pressure on him and his mother to admit they were working with the kgosi in some corrupt scheme.'

Kubu wanted to jump in and say his boss had done nothing of the sort. However, he held his tongue.

Mabaku answered even more quietly. 'The Department of Water Affairs recently received a letter suggesting there was corruption in the water project. I was merely asking if they knew anything about it. They said they didn't. The only time the kgosi came up was when I looked at a photograph. I thought it may have been of Mma Zondo's husband and Rra Lesaka. It wasn't. It was of Mma Zondo's husband and the kgosi – when they were very young.'

Kubu thought the station commander wanted to continue his attack on Mabaku, but was at a loss for something more to say.

'I thought you were here for the Lesaka case,' he eventually spluttered.

'I am,' Mabaku replied. 'But there are other things the director wants me to look into. When appropriate, I'll tell you about them.'

The station commander jumped to his feet. 'You'll tell me now,' he shouted. 'This is my police station. I'm in charge of this area.'

Mabaku pointed at the man. 'I'll remember you shouted at me, station commander. Come, Bengu, we've things to do.'

～

Mabaku marched straight to the reception desk and asked whether the conference room was available for an hour or so. When he was told it was, he walked down the passage, beckoning Kubu to follow.

Once seated, Mabaku pulled out his notebook and found what he wanted. Then he picked up the phone and dialled. It was obviously picked up right away, because Mabaku immediately asked if Abram Nteba had arrived from Shakawe.

He's checking on the fingerprints, Kubu thought.

A few moments later, Mabaku asked Abram whether the fingerprints had been processed yet.

'In an hour?' Mabaku asked. 'Can't they do them any quicker?'

Mabaku listened to the answer. 'All right, I'm at the station in Shakawe. When you have the results, call reception here and ask to be put through to me directly. I'm in the conference room. I'll wait for your call.'

After hanging up, he turned to Kubu. 'This place is worse than all the stories you hear about small towns. Mma Zondo's husband was a close friend of the kgosi, who was a close friend of Lesaka, who was a close friend of the station commander, who should have recused himself from the investigation.'

He stood up. 'Where do I find the coffee?'

Kubu directed him to the urn, and Mabaku returned a few

minutes later with two cups of black coffee, a third cup with some milk and a few sachets of sugar. 'Help yourself.'

Once he'd added milk and sugar to his coffee, Kubu told Mabaku that he hadn't understood what the station commander had reported about their visit to the Zondos. 'We didn't do any of the things he said we did.'

'Detective Sergeant, the station commander was behaving like many animals: trying to define and defend his territory. He regards us as intruders, and he's right, of course. However, if he were competent, he'd work with us rather than feel threatened. Collaboration is always more effective in police work.'

'Do you think he'll change his mind?'

Mabaku shrugged. 'Probably not. By shouting at me, he's shown his ego is too involved. He'll find it very difficult to back down.'

Kubu pondered Mabaku's words for a while, then decided that being a detective was much more complicated than he'd realised. He'd thought it was going to be like solving a big jigsaw puzzle, slowly putting pieces together until you saw the whole picture. Now he was finding out that he also had to learn about all sorts of interpersonal dynamics and then navigate through them. As an only child, he hadn't had much practice at that.

When the phone eventually rang, Mabaku picked it up and identified himself. Then he listened, jotting down notes as he did. After a while he asked one question. 'Are you sure, Detective Sergeant?'

When he heard the answer, he put down the phone. 'The only fingerprints they found at Lesaka's home were Lesaka's and his son's. There were no fingerprints on the radio. It'd been wiped clean. So, there's no evidence at all that the Bushman was involved.'

'What are you going to do now, rra?'

Mabaku motioned towards the door. 'Go for a walk, Detective

Sergeant. I have a phone call to make. Come back in twenty minutes.'

~

It was closer to thirty minutes later when Kubu knocked on the conference-room door.

'Come in.' Then, as Kubu walked in, Mabaku stood up. 'I said twenty minutes, not thirty.'

'I didn't want to interrupt—'

'If I was going to talk for more than twenty minutes, I'd have asked you to come back in twenty-five. Come on, let's go and have a friendly chat with the station commander.'

They walked to the other side of the building and, since the door was open, Mabaku knocked and walked in.

'What do you want?'

'You must release the Bushman, station commander. Forensics in Maun found none of his fingerprints anywhere, not in the house nor on the radio. The confession you beat out of him won't stand up in court. In fact, no prosecutor would ever let it get to court. It's worthless.'

'I refuse to let him go. This is my station, and I'm in charge here. You don't know what you're doing. He's guilty, I tell you. I know the likes of him.'

Mabaku pulled a piece of paper out of his pocket and dropped it on the station commander's desk. 'The number at the top is Director Gobey's number. If you have any questions about the forensics I've just told you about, he says he'll be happy to explain them to you. The number below it is the assistant commissioner's. If you decide not to release the Bushman, you have to confirm that with him first.'

With that he turned and walked out.

Kubu hurried after him, marvelling at how his boss had made it impossible for the station commander to do anything other than release Selelo.

'Rra, shouldn't we wait for Selelo and give him a lift back to Tsodilo? It's a long way.'

Mabaku opened the door of his car. 'No, Detective Sergeant, we shouldn't. We are detectives, not social workers. He made it to Shakawe, and he'll make it back.'

CHAPTER 20

'Where are we going?' Kubu asked as they drove away from the police station.

'To talk to Joshua Lesaka. He's at home at the moment. I checked when you were out walking. I want you to conduct the interview.'

Kubu knew Mabaku was putting him on the spot for not being thorough at the kgosi's, but was determined not to give him another chance to criticise.

'Yes, rra. Please let me know if I miss anything.'

~

They walked up the short path to the front door, and Mabaku banged on it with his fist. A few seconds later it opened, and Joshua invited them in. Kubu was amazed at the transformation. When he was last in the house, it was neat and tidy. Now, there were pots and pans everywhere, and paper packets, and flowers.

'Excuse the mess,' Joshua said. 'I'm trying to get ready for the funeral on Saturday, and the whole of Ncamasere will be there. So four of us will be doing the cooking at different homes. It's very complicated.'

He waved them to the seats around the table and moved what was on it to one end.

'Have you found who killed my father?' he asked as soon as they'd sat down.

'Unfortunately not, rra,' Kubu replied. 'We're trying to narrow the field of suspects, so we've a few questions for you, if you don't mind.'

'I don't think I can help you. I told you everything I know.'

Kubu pulled out his notebook. 'One thing we're trying to understand is whether the person who killed your father knew that you were going to be at the kgosi's. The kgosi didn't tell anyone about your upcoming visit, so we need to know whether you did.'

'No. I only told father at supper that I was going. And he went straight to bed, so it couldn't have been him.'

Kubu noted that down. 'Could someone have overheard you and the kgosi when you made the arrangement?'

Joshua shook his head and said it was unlikely, since most of the people at the kgotla had left already.

Kubu was thinking about what else to ask when Joshua exclaimed, 'Maybe there was someone.' He paused. 'Yes, someone could have overheard – the kgosi's son, Raseelo. When I walked up to the kgosi, I thought they were having an argument. And Raseelo stayed there while the kgosi told me to come and see him after supper. He would have overheard us.'

'Did Raseelo know your father? Had they spent any time together before that?'

Joshua shrugged. 'My father and the kgosi were close friends. They visited each other's homes. My father would have met Raseelo there. And at the kgotlas, of course.'

'Did your father ever mention him to you?'

'Not that I can remember. Perhaps a comment about his bad behaviour. But that's all.'

'Nothing to indicate hostility?'

'No, nothing like that.'

Kubu couldn't think of anything else to ask, and Mabaku didn't step in, to Kubu's surprise. So, the two policemen chatted to Joshua for a few minutes, mainly about the arrangements for the funeral, which was going to start on Friday night. The actual burial was scheduled for three on Saturday afternoon. Joshua hoped that they would be able to join in some of the celebrations of his father's rich life.

'We'll be there,' Mabaku said. 'Probably only at the burial though. To pay our respects.'

As they walked to the car, Mabaku didn't say anything about Kubu's performance. Kubu hoped that lack of criticism was approval.

'Rra, I'm surprised you said we would go to the burial. I didn't think you knew him, and I certainly didn't.'

'Murderers sometimes attend their victims' funerals.' With that he climbed into the car and motioned to Kubu to do the same.

A couple of blocks away, Mabaku pulled to the side of the road and asked Kubu what they should do next. Kubu had been wondering exactly the same thing and was hoping that Mabaku would make the decision. However, it seemed that his boss had dropped it straight into his lap.

'I know what I'd like to do,' Kubu said, 'but I'm not sure that it's the right thing.' He glanced at Mabaku, hoping for a response. None came.

'I would like to speak to the kgosi's son, but that would mean getting the kgosi's permission. I don't think he'd be pleased if we told him we wanted to speak to his son in connection with Lesaka's murder. Actually, I think he'd throw us out on our ear.'

'Detective Sergeant...'

Kubu stiffened, prepared for a reprimand.

'Detective Sergeant, the police's need for information supersedes everything. You have to ignore any feelings you may have for the person you want to question. If you think we should speak to the kgosi's son, let's do it now.'

Kubu began to feel a pain in his stomach. He was sure that

Mabaku was going to leave it all up to him. For a moment he felt as out of control as he did when thinking about asking Joy out.

'And you want me to ask the kgosi? And question his son?'

Mabaku smiled. 'Of course.'

Kubu and Mabaku walked onto the veranda of the kgosi's house, and Kubu knocked on the door. A few moments later, the door was opened by a surprised-looking kgosi.

'What do you want now?' he asked Mabaku.

'Kgosi, rra,' Kubu stammered, 'when we spoke to you earlier, you said you didn't think anyone had overheard you making the arrangement to meet with Rra Lesaka's son.'

The kgosi nodded.

'We've just spoken to Joshua Lesaka, and he thinks it's possible that your son may have overheard.'

The kgosi bristled visibly. 'Are you suggesting my son was involved in Endo's murder?'

'No, rra. Not at all, rra. But if he did hear the arrangement, we need to speak to him to check his whereabouts while you were talking to Joshua that evening.'

'You don't need to talk to him. I can vouch for him. He was here in the house all evening.' He looked at the two detectives as though daring them to continue.

Kubu felt flustered and wasn't sure what to do. Fortunately, Mabaku came to his rescue. 'Thank you, kgosi. That's all we need to know. Good afternoon.'

He turned and walked off the veranda, with Kubu gratefully following.

When they were both in the car, Mabaku spoke. 'Sometimes, a tactical retreat is called for. Pushing any more right now would have been counter-productive. But that box hasn't been ticked yet. We only have the kgosi's word that his son wasn't involved. And he is what you may call biased.'

~

Selelo had come to the conclusion that he wouldn't be able to fulfill the ancestors' wishes. He would be dead before he could do anything.

As he lay on the floor of his cell, he could feel the walls slowly edging towards him, squeezing the air out of his body. He had no strength to push them back. He was sure that the food pushed through the door was poisoned to save the angry policeman from killing him himself. All he'd put in his mouth over the past few days was a little water.

He didn't understand what had changed. When he did the trance dance where his ancestors had been found in the sand, the ancestors in the sky had been happy. They'd welcomed the news and told him that the circle was nearly closed – that he could join them when he closed the circle. He was happy to be part of the circle of life.

Why had the ancestors abandoned him? he wondered.

And why was the policeman so angry with him, shouting at him and hitting him when he said he wanted to go back to Tsodilo? And putting black paint on his thumb and pushing it onto the white sheet?

Selelo didn't understand.

And then there was the hippopotamus, who tried to help. Even in his depressed state, the thought made Selelo giggle. Hippopotamus? What a name.

The hippopotamus was kind, and he could tell that he didn't like the man who hit him.

But the hippopotamus had left, and the man who hit him kept hitting him.

Selelo closed his eyes and tried to will his spirit out of his body. He didn't want to live if his world was going to be four walls that kept creeping closer. He needed air and sand and sky to live.

Suddenly, there was a noise at the door, and it was flung open. Selelo barely opened an eye as he lay curled up on the floor. He closed it immediately when he saw who it was and prepared for pain.

He felt the man grab his arm and drag him along the floor, out of the room. He was determined not to show the pain, not to give any satisfaction. He was sure this was the end.

Suddenly, he was in sunshine. The man kicked him down the stairs at the front of the building and shouted at him.

'You're free now, Bushman. But you'll be back in that cell as soon as they leave for Gaborone. You'd better start running now.'

Selelo didn't understand what the man was saying, but the message was clear. The man was angry. More than angry.

He staggered to his feet, barely able to stand. He held onto a small tree for a few moments as he tried to understand what was happening.

It seemed that he was free once again. Perhaps he shouldn't have been angry at the ancestors. Perhaps they wanted him to have the experience so he could be better prepared.

He took some deep breaths and walked slowly away, praying to the ancestors to support him. He needed to find food if he was to fulfil his destiny. Food and sleep.

CHAPTER 21

Selelo found water quite easily – at Shakawe's one and only garage. He'd nearly had his fill drinking from the tap next to the petrol pumps, before the attendant shooed him away. However, he hadn't been able to find food and was scared to ask the people he saw in case they called the police. So he sat down at the back of a building and waited for the ancestors to appear.

Dusk came and went, and night fell. Slowly the ancestors appeared in the sky. Selelo had faith they would help him find the energy he needed to complete the task they'd set for him. Then the moon rose, and he took it as a good omen that it had restored itself after being nibbled night after night by the sun.

He was close to sleep when a door opened a few paces from him, and a woman walked out carrying a large black bag with both hands. Selelo cowered against the wall. The woman put down the bag and lifted the top of a big box that stood nearby. She held the top open with one hand and tried to pick up the bag with the other, but struggled to lift it. Meanwhile the smell of food wafted from the door. It was torture. Selelo wondered if he had the energy to dash in and take some, then disappear into the night.

As he thought about it, the woman gave up and allowed the box to close with a bang. She dropped the bag and returned to the house, closing the door. Selelo was too late.

As he lay there, ruing his weakness, it occurred to him that there may be food in the bag. He'd seen that before. From his time at Tsodilo, he'd noticed that both Blacks and Whites wasted so much food – something no Bushman would ever do. He'd seen them throw away enough food from one meal to feed a family for days. Maybe...

He pulled himself to his feet and staggered over to the bag. He grabbed it and pulled. It was heavy, but he was able to drag it along the ground. As quickly as he could, he moved behind the box. He could only hope the woman didn't return.

A few moments later, he heard a man's voice, then footsteps. They stopped, then moved to one side. Selelo thought the man was trying to find the bag. Shortly after, the footsteps moved to the other side of the box. Then silence. Selelo closed his eyes. The man would look at the back of the box next.

~

Selelo was embarrassed by how much he'd eaten. The bag was full of good food, some of which he'd never seen. Bits of cooked meat – that he recognised. The stiff porridge he knew, but wasn't sure about the reddish sauce that covered it. And those big green leaves, whatever they were, tasted good but didn't fill him. Once he started, he couldn't stop until he had a pain in his stomach.

I've eaten like a lion, he thought, which doesn't know when the next meal will be.

After the man had left, Selelo had pulled the bag behind some bushes a couple of hundred metres away. He'd torn the bag open and feasted. Then he'd fallen asleep until the rising sun woke him. He was still tired, but the thought of his quest filled him with energy. He'd need it. It was a long walk to Ncamasere.

~

It took most of the day to reach the tree where the police had found him. He'd walked parallel to the road, but not on it. He felt safer that way. When he reached the tree, he rested in preparation for that night's dance.

He looked around, wondering whether he was too close to the houses. If they heard him, they would certainly call the police. He couldn't risk that. He decided that once he had regained his strength, he'd walk into the desert until he was sure he would be alone. Then he would dance, inviting his ancestors to witness the closing of the circle, the fulfilment of his destiny.

He closed his eyes and slept. And as he slept, memories filled his head – memories of walking to Shakawe from Tsodilo Hills all those years ago. In search of a horse with a white stripe that forked on its chest. He had looked everywhere, but hadn't found it. He remembered the disappointment – remembered wondering whether the horse was even real, or just part of a dream.

Then he remembered doing the same thing again a few years later – this time to Ncamasere. Again, he'd searched and was about to give up when he'd seen it. It was in a large enclosure with other horses.

He'd waited for several days before a man took the horse and put a saddle on its back. Then he rode it round and round, talking to it, stroking its neck.

In the dream, the man grew bigger and more ugly, then switched to someone who looked like a warrior – strong and determined. Was he the man he sought? He had no way to be certain.

Selelo woke with a start. He'd had that dream so many times, and it was always the same, ending with uncertainty. He wished it were otherwise.

∾

The sun was setting when Selelo walked away from the village into the desert. When he was far enough away not to be disturbed, he started moving slowly in a circle, whispering a song. He began to move quicker, and as he did, the song became louder. It was a prayer to the ancestors, asking for their blessing and support as he tried to close the circle.

Suddenly he stopped as he felt a pain in his heart. He was filled with uncertainty. He'd been so sure he could do what he was called to do, but now he felt like running away. He gazed up at the ancestors, asking for guidance.

He knew none would come. It was up to him.

He took a deep breath and started dancing again, gradually speeding up until he was spinning so fast he left his body. He rushed to ask the ancestors for advice. Was he capable of doing what they wanted? Were they sure he should do it?

Being with them filled him with courage, and he was pleased.

He returned to his body and collapsed on the ground exhausted, knowing he'd be ready when he awoke.

CHAPTER 22

On Thursday evening, when she felt it was time, Mma Zondo put on her coat, collected a torch and headed for the front door. On her way, she walked past her son, who was in the lounge watching television.

'Are you going out?' he asked.

'I'm going to the river.'

'To talk to your water spirit, I suppose.'

'She's not my water spirit, Jacob. But, yes, it's full moon, so she'll be there. Everyone knows I talk to her at full moon, except you apparently.' She paused. 'I'll tell her that I've stopped the plan to take her water. Something awful would have happened if I hadn't.'

Jacob jumped out of his chair and walked up to her. 'What do you mean you've stopped it? You wrote that letter the detective asked about, didn't you?'

She glared at him. 'What if I did?'

Jacob shook his head in frustration. 'Mother, you have to stop interfering. This new policeman, Mabaku, he's not like the other two. He won't be put off. He'll find out what you've done.'

'If they look for corruption, they will find it. I don't trust the kgosi.'

'The kgosi is a powerful man. You're meddling in things you don't understand.'

She glared at him. 'While you know everything, I suppose.'

'I know what's important for this family and the farm.'

'Nonsense. We have plenty of water.'

'We could irrigate much more land, but we have to support the kgosi if we want him to support us. This farm could be—'

'This is *my* farm, Jacob. Just remember that. Your father left it to me. One day, it will be yours, then you can make the decisions, but for now you have to do what I say. And so does the kgosi.'

Jacob looked at her with disbelief. 'The kgosi won't listen to you, Mother, he—'

'I spoke to him today. Now he will listen.'

'Mother—'

'Don't wait up for me. Mami Wata will come when she's ready and not before. I'll sit and meditate in the meantime.'

'Meditate?' he sneered. 'Like the time you fell asleep, and I had to shake you awake in the morning?'

She shoved past him to the door. 'I was *not* asleep.' She let herself out and banged the door behind her. The dogs started barking, but soon quietened when they realised who it was.

She was furious as she walked towards the river. The night her son had referred to was the time that Mami Wata had shown herself clearly. Mma Zondo felt a chill at the memory. She'd actually seen Mami Wata just that once, and that was more than enough.

Usually, she'd sit at her favourite spot on the river bank and let her mind wander, trying to keep it as empty as she could. Then, when Mami Wata arrived, the spirit would speak to her by putting thoughts directly into her mind. Although she couldn't see her, by the sudden ripples Mma Zondo could tell exactly where she was beneath the murky surface of the water.

However, that night had been different. The news of the water project was out, and Mma Zondo had been very worried. She hadn't known how Mami Wata would react. She'd intended to ask the spirit about it and wait for an answer, but it didn't work out that way. She shuddered as she relived the memory.

She'd waited a long time and started to believe that the water spirit wouldn't come. Then suddenly she'd been there – not in her mind as usual, but right in front of her, rising from the river. She was a powerfully built woman with heavy breasts, and her hair was in strings that seemed to move on their own, like weed in the water, or even snakes. Her black eyes were deadly, and Mma Zondo had known that a look could kill her. She has come for me, she'd thought, terrified. Now she will take me under the water, and no one will see me ever again.

That had been her last thought before she'd fainted.

When she'd regained consciousness, someone was shaking her and calling her name.

'No, no, it will not happen, I promise,' she'd cried out, but when she'd opened her eyes, she'd seen her son, his face creased with worry.

'You fell asleep, Mother. You've been here all night. You're lucky a crocodile didn't find you.'

'No! It was Mami Wata. She was here, as close as you are. She was terrible.' She'd shuddered uncontrollably.

'You had a nightmare. And now you're chilled. You'll probably catch a fever.' He'd reached down to help her up, but she'd pushed him away and struggled to her feet.

'It was no dream. I know what dreams are. This happened. It's the water project. She's very angry. It must stop at once.'

Her son hadn't listened to her, and the kgosi hadn't listened to her, and even Lesaka hadn't listened to her. And now the Bushman skeletons blocked the pipeline and Lesaka was dead. Each was a clear warning and a threat. How could they not see it?

'I *will* stop it,' she said aloud as she headed towards the river.

As if they'd heard her up at the house, the dogs started barking. She shook her head in disgust. The stupid dogs would bark at their own shadows.

Although the moon lit the path, she shone her torch from side to side as she walked, trying to spot any hulking shapes in the surrounding bush. Hippos came out of the water at night. She was also alert for unusual night sounds, but all she could hear was the continual buzzing of cicadas and a variety of chirps from the frogs that seemed to be all around her.

She continued on the path and soon came to a section heading down to the river, water glinting in the moonlight. From there she picked her way along the river's edge, scanning with the torch to make sure no crocodiles were waiting for her in the shallows.

Eventually, she came to the large jackalberry tree where she always waited. A section of the trunk had split off long ago and lay conveniently positioned for someone to sit. It was a little raised from the riverbank so there was a good view, and the moon was high on the other side of the river, lighting the water with a silver sheen.

She settled herself comfortably on the log and tried to relax, but she was upset by the argument with Jacob. Ezekiel had been a strong man, who'd listen to his ancestors for guidance, but Jacob was weak, easily led, expecting to have things given to him rather than going out to get them. Perhaps, if his father had lived, her son might have been different.

She put the thought aside and tried to clear her mind to commune with Mami Wata. She was confident the water spirit would approve of her threatening the kgosi, but still she was nervous.

Suddenly she heard a sound behind her. She swung round, grabbing for her torch, but in her haste, she fumbled, and it rolled away.

A man walked out of the bush.

She was surprised when she recognised him. 'Oh, what on earth are you doing here?'

He smiled and muttered something as he walked closer.

～

Despite his exhaustion from the previous night's trance dance, Selelo was up before his ancestors disappeared. As someone skilled at creeping close to skittish animals to shoot a poisoned arrow into them, Selelo had no difficulty in moving into the outskirts of Ncamasere undetected. There he found some small bushes, where he hid. Scant as the cover was, he knew that as long as he didn't move, it was highly unlikely that anyone would notice him. Movement was always the giveaway.

The most difficult part of his vigil was keeping awake. Had there been a steady flow of people, he would have kept alert, but since people walked past only every now and again, he was forced to make up stories or quietly sing songs to ensure he didn't miss anyone.

At six that morning, the fisherman launched his boat and headed downstream. The other fishermen talked jealously about how he usually caught more fish, how lucky he was. Sometimes there were even mutterings about witch doctors, but that was nonsense. The truth was that he knew his business and that he came out very early – as soon as it was light – while the others were still too afraid of the hippos and the crocodiles. He took his chances, and he did well.

He knew just the right spot for bream in this part of the river and, when he reached it, he cut the motor and let the boat drift. His landmark was the remains of a huge wild fig that had been uprooted by a flood long ago. The solid trunk, bleached stumps of branches and a tangle of broken roots, were all that remained.

As he approached, he saw splashing in the water near the tree. He cursed. A crocodile must have caught a bushbuck, careless about its choice of drinking spot. He didn't care about the buck, but the disturbance would scare off the fish. He'd have to move further downstream. He started the motor again and, curious about the crocodile's catch, moved closer, careful to avoid submerged branches.

He spotted the crocodile – a large one – tugging to free a carcass that had become wedged in the roots. As he approached, the thrashing increased, and after a particularly powerful tug, the body jerked forward and the head flew up. The fisherman gave a horrified yell as he realised it was human.

He revved the motor, moving the boat in towards the tree trunk. The crocodile swung round to face the threat, then disappeared below the water where he knew it would wait not far from its meal.

He tied the boat to the stump of a branch, climbed onto the trunk, and moved to the body. To his horror, he saw that it was a woman, and then he recognized Mma Zondo. He stepped back, wondering what to do. He doubted that he'd be able to move the body without getting into the water, and he certainly wasn't going to take on the crocodile.

There was also Mami Wata to consider. Many people laughed at Mma Zondo for her beliefs, but he didn't. As a fisherman, his relationship with the river spirit was respectful, so he couldn't imagine that she would want a believer fed to the crocodiles.

He crossed himself and asked Mami Wata for her help. Then he leant down, grabbed Mma Zondo below the arms, and tried to drag her out of the tree roots, pulling her against the current. He gave a huge heave, and the body moved towards him, then came loose so suddenly that he almost lost his balance. When he saw what the crocodile had done to her, he nearly let go and threw up. Biting his mouth closed, he yanked the body, centimetres at a time, onto the tree trunk. It was exhausting work, but he managed it. Finally, he rolled her into the boat.

He rinsed his mouth with handfuls of water, started the motor, and headed back to the beach where the fishermen kept their boats. All he wanted was to get rid of the body and clean himself and his boat.

Today no one would be jealous of his catch.

CHAPTER 23

Ian's job in Shakawe was done, and he was about to head back to Gaborone. He sat looking out at the river while he waited for the others to join him for breakfast. Kubu, never late for a meal, was first to arrive.

'I've got used to having breakfast with all this,' Ian said by way of greeting. 'It's really very special here. But I'll be glad to get home. And the bodies are piling up for me in Gaborone.'

Mabaku turned up a few minutes later and suggested they eat at once. 'You'll be keen to get moving, Dr MacGregor. See what you can do in Gaborone. Talk to that expert of yours and have the bullets you found looked at by forensics. We haven't heard the last from Bushman Survival, so we'd better have all our ducks in a row.'

Ian nodded, and they settled down to eat.

After a while, Mabaku said, 'Bengu, you and I need to get to work. I can't see anyone but Mma Zondo sending the corruption letter. I think we need to work on her some more and find out if she really knows anything, or if she's just stirring up trouble.'

He was working on his second cup of coffee and a slice of toast with marmalade, when the manager hurried over.

'Assistant Superintendent, there's an urgent call for you.'

'What is it?'

'It's the police station commander. He said that I must get you right away.'

Mabaku went with her to reception and picked up the phone. 'Assistant Superintendent Mabaku.'

'Mabaku, it's Balopi. There's been another death.'

∼

'Accident, be damned!' Mabaku said as they set off in the Land Rover. 'Mma Zondo suddenly gets killed by a crocodile after years going down to the river? I don't believe it. She's right at the centre of this whole mess.'

Ian concentrated on driving. 'Let's wait till we take a look at the body. She's not young, and walking along an African river at night isn't a very smart thing to do. Even if it is full moon.'

When they reached the road where the station commander was waiting, they followed him along a labyrinth of dirt tracks until they reached the Kavango. A silt beach gave easy access to the river, and a couple of boats had been pulled up some distance from the water. Next to them, Abram was guarding something covered by a blanket.

Ian grabbed his forensic bag, walked to the blanket and gently pulled it back. Kubu flinched. The crocodile's attack had left the legs in shreds, and a bite had been taken out of her left side. Her face was bloated.

Ian took a deep breath. 'Sweet baby Jesus. Quite a send-off for me. Well, let's take a look.'

Kubu felt the contents of his stomach lurching. He swallowed hard.

∼

Ian took his time, and Kubu managed to keep his breakfast down. Mabaku watched carefully, while Abram and the station commander stood well back.

At last, Ian turned to the detectives. 'I saw the results of a crocodile attack once before, and this is pretty consistent with that.

Multiple lacerations, puncture marks from the teeth. Pieces of flesh ripped off. Very unpleasant.'

Abram pointed out a man sitting on the side of a boat. 'That's the fisherman who found her. She was lodged against a sunken tree, and a crocodile was tearing at her flesh.'

'There is one odd thing though.' Ian turned her head to show them Mma Zondo's face. 'There's this heavy bruise on her forehead. That's pre-mortem. Before death.'

Balopi shook his head. 'A crocodile moves like lightning and could have grabbed her by a leg and yanked her into the water. She probably hit her head on a stump on the way down.'

Abram shuddered. 'It's awful to think that she was alive as it dragged her into the river...'

Mabaku was unconvinced. 'She would have screamed her head off. Someone would have heard her.'

'It's quite far to the house from the river,' Balopi said. 'The poor woman.'

'Did you see any other bruises?' Kubu asked.

'No obvious ones.' Ian stood up and looked down at the body without speaking.

'Can you determine the cause of death, Doctor?' Mabaku prompted.

Ian hesitated. 'The other crocodile victim I examined had drowned. Apparently, that's generally how crocs kill their prey, but there didn't seem to be much water in her lungs when I compressed her chest.'

'What does that mean?'

'Well, it's hard to say. Maybe just that she was face down in the boat.' He paused. 'There's often frothing around the mouth directly after a drowning, but after all this time...'

'So you think she did drown then?' Balopi asked.

Ian didn't reply.

'Will you be able to find out definitely at an autopsy?' Mabaku asked.

'It depends. Generally, asphyxiation is pretty hard to prove, but I could exclude other things.'

Balopi shook his head. 'Come on, it's straightforward. The fisherman saw the croc, for God's sake. We don't need an autopsy to tell us the obvious.'

'An autopsy is definitely necessary,' Mabaku said firmly. 'Seems you're going back to Maun, Doctor.'

Ian sighed, wondering if he was ever going to return to Gaborone. He turned to the station commander. 'Did you bring a body bag?'

'Yes, it's in the vehicle.'

'Well, help me get her into my vehicle, and then I'll be off.' He turned to Mabaku. 'Assistant Superintendent, can you contact the hospital and tell them I'm on my way? It'll save time when I get there. And you better tell Drotsky's I'll be back tomorrow.'

Balopi frowned. 'It's your time you're wasting.'

Mabaku ignored him. 'Time of death?'

Ian shrugged. 'It's hard to say for sure, but assuming she was in the river all the time, it would have been last night before midnight.'

'Does her son know?' Kubu asked.

'I'm on my way there now,' Balopi responded.

'We'll all go,' Mabaku said. 'I want to see where it happened and then talk to him.'

'What for?' Balopi asked.

'If you're right about her head hitting something, there should be evidence of that. Maybe she slipped. Or maybe there was a struggle.'

For once, the gate to the farmhouse was open. The dogs were shut away somewhere, but they still barked their heads off as the policemen walked to the front door. Jacob was talking to a group of men, but he immediately came to meet them.

As he looked at the faces of the four policemen his expression became apprehensive. 'Have you found her?'

Balopi replied. 'I'm afraid we have, rra. I'm so sorry to tell you that she has passed on. It was a crocodile.'

'Oh, no. Are you sure? Are you sure it's her?'

'I've seen her myself. We just came from there. A fisherman found her body this morning.'

Jacob seemed to struggle for composure for a few moments, and then cleared his throat. 'I can't believe it. Every time she went, I told her how dangerous it was, but she always ignored me. She said Mami Wata would look after her...' He paused. 'I must go to her.'

'They're still sorting things out at the moment,' Balopi said. 'Maybe later on, in Shakawe.' After a moment he added, 'Rra, I want to tell you how deeply sorry I am about your mother.'

'Thank you. I need to let my wife know – she's with the boys at her sister's in Gaborone. They go to school there.'

Mabaku changed the subject. 'May we ask you a few questions just to fix the timing and so on? Then we'd like to take a look at the area along the river.'

Jacob nodded and led them into the house.

'Rra,' Mabaku began, 'when was the last time you saw your mother?'

'It must have been a bit after nine last night. That's when she usually goes down there. I was watching something on TV that starts at nine.'

'When did you realise she was missing?'

'Only this morning. Sometimes she stays there quite late. Once she even fell asleep down there. Maybe that happened again, and a croc found her... It's so awful to think about.'

'And then you went looking for her?'

'Yes. She has a favourite spot, so I walked there and looked around. I found her torch, but there was no other sign of her. That's when I really became concerned, so I got the farm workers to help, and we searched along the river and everywhere we could think she might have gone. Then I phoned the police station.'

Kubu was jotting everything down in his notebook. He'd learnt his lesson.

'Could you ask someone to show us the way to the river?' Mabaku asked.

'I'll take you there myself.'

Jacob led them to a gate in the security fence to the side of the house. He fished a set of keys from his pocket and opened the heavy padlock. From there he followed a path that led down to the river, then along the bank. When he reached the jackalberry, he pointed out the log where his mother liked to sit. 'She was definitely here last night. That's where I found her torch this morning, lying in the mud over there.' He pointed to the mud bank running down to the water.

'There's no sign of crocodile tracks,' Kubu commented.

Abram wandered a bit downstream, and then called out, 'Take a look over here.'

They all hurried over to join him, and he pointed out crocodile tracks in the mud, coming out of the river and returning.

'It's a big one,' he informed them. 'Look how wide apart its footprints are.'

Balopi nodded. 'He was probably the culprit.'

Jacob hesitated, then said, 'But it's not dragging anything. There are no slip marks. It looks like it came to sun itself on that mud bank yesterday.'

While the others argued about the spoor, Kubu and Mabaku walked back to the log.

'Suppose Mma Zondo wasn't grabbed by a croc, but attacked by a person,' Kubu said. He paused as he visualised her sitting on her log, staring out at the river.

'She would have seen anyone approaching her,' Mabaku pointed out.

'Maybe he came up from behind, and she turned just as he was going to strike her. Or maybe she knew him and let him get close.'

'That's possible.'

Kubu searched around the log, and found a few strands of dry grass with brown spots that might be dried blood. He pointed them out to Mabaku.

'Probably mud, but it's worth checking. Did you bring an evidence bag?'

Kubu was pleased he'd thought to shove a couple into his pocket before they left. He nipped off the grass stems and bagged them.

The others joined them, still discussing the crocodile tracks, and Kubu showed them what he'd found.

'Could be anything,' the station commander said.

'Bengu and I will go upstream for a bit and you two go downstream. See if you can spot anything. Rra Zondo, please wait here.'

'I'd rather come with you.'

'We won't be long. We'll meet back here in at most fifteen minutes.'

After a few minutes, Kubu and Mabaku came to a point where the bank fell off steeply into the water. Mabaku stopped and peered over, careful not to approach too close to the crumbling edge. 'It would be easy to throw a body in here.'

Kubu was examining the ground between the path and the river edge. 'It's scuffed here. Plants have been pulled up.'

'Maybe a bush pig rooting around.' However, Mabaku came over and looked more closely. 'Or maybe not.' He pointed. 'Here are some more pieces of grass for you to bag.'

Kubu broke off several stems that had brown stains on them, and sealed them in his second bag.

They went a little further, but discovered nothing more of interest. When they returned, they found Jacob sitting on the log, staring out at the river. Balopi and Abram joined them a few minutes later, but had nothing to report.

'I need to get back to the station,' Balopi said, and turned to head back.

Mabaku ignored him and addressed Zondo. 'Is there any way to get down here other than from the farmhouse?'

Jacob nodded. 'There's another path. You get to it through a gate in the fence around the farm. It's not locked because the workers use it. It joins the path we came down about a hundred metres back.' He paused. 'Or, of course, you could come by boat.'

Shortly after that, they walked back, taking the alternative path, which brought them to a gate in the perimeter fence not far from the house. The gate was unlocked, but when they opened it, the rusty hinges creaked, setting off a frenzy of barking.

'Did the dogs bark last night after your mother came down here?'

'As a matter of fact they did. It's unusual. They usually settle at night because there's no one around. It was a short time after my mother left the house, I think.'

'But you didn't hear anything else during the night – like shouts or screaming?'

He shook his head. 'Nothing. I would have investigated if I had.'

As they left, Balopi shook Jacob's hand. 'Rra, once more, I'm sorry for your loss. We'll let you know when you can come to collect the body.'

～

On his way to Shakawe, Abram dropped Kubu and Mabaku at Drotsky's. After they'd told reception that Ian would be staying a few more nights and had phoned the hospital in Maun, Mabaku said he'd like another cup of coffee. He selected a table on the veranda and signalled the waiter over. They ordered, then he said to Kubu, 'Someone could have come along that side path and attacked her.'

Kubu nodded. 'And set off the dogs.'

'The question is why.'

'Maybe she did write that letter. And maybe she really did know something about corruption.'

'But then why didn't she tell us when she had the chance?'

Kubu had no answer for that. 'You said yourself that she was at the centre of everything. It can't be a coincidence. Lesaka was murdered a week ago. And nine Bushman skeletons...' He trailed off. That was the whole point about coincidences. They happened.

'Maybe it was opportunistic.'

Kubu waited for him to go on, but Mabaku didn't continue.

'Opportunistic?' Kubu prompted.

'Yes. Someone saw a chance to commit a murder for their own reasons and have it blamed on all these other issues even though there's no connection.' He paused to sip his coffee. 'I wonder what her son gains from her death, for example. We need to look into that.'

'Her *son*?' Kubu was shocked.

'Murders are often committed by a family member. And he had opportunity. He knew she was at the river. All it needed was a bash on the head to knock her out and then drag her to where he could throw her into the water.'

Kubu was revolted at the idea a son could do that to his mother. 'But what if she survived? It's an awful risk.'

'Wait for Dr MacGregor's autopsy report. Whoever murdered her would have made very sure that she didn't live to bear witness.'

Mabaku finished his coffee and stood up. 'Come on.'

Kubu hastily drank the rest of his. 'Where are we going, rra?'

'Back to the kgosi. I'd like to see how he reacts to this news.'

CHAPTER 24

Once again, Mabaku and Kubu met the kgosi and his son in his lounge, but this time the kgosi looked depressed, and the energy he'd displayed at their last meeting was missing. He waved them to the seats opposite without any greeting.

'You've come about Mma Zondo, I suppose.'

'You've heard then,' Mabaku responded.

The kgosi nodded. 'It's terrible. I'm very shocked. First Endo and now her. These are people I grew up with.' He hesitated. 'She put her trust in Mami Wata. She forgot that spirits don't always repay favours.'

'You think Mami Wata was involved?' Kubu interjected.

'No. I think she was not involved. That's the point.'

'Then who was involved?' Mabaku asked, but the kgosi just looked at him.

'For God's sake, man, it was a crocodile!' Raseelo burst out. 'This isn't Gaborone. People here die of thirst in the desert, and drown in the river, and get taken by crocodiles. Now you're cutting her up like a side of beef instead of giving her to her son to mourn and bury with proper respect.'

The kgosi frowned, but didn't rebuke him.

How did he know that? Kubu wondered. It had to be Abram or the station commander who told him.

As if reading his thought, Mabaku asked Raseelo, 'Who told you all this?'

Before he could reply, the kgosi spoke. 'Detective Nteba phoned us. Is it true that you insisted on an autopsy?'

Mabaku leant back in the chair and folded his arms. 'Yes, it's true. This was an unnatural death, and it's our business to investigate it, especially coming so close to the murder of someone else in a small community.' He paused. 'Did she have enemies?'

The kgosi shook his head. 'She made a lot of noise, but she wasn't a threat to anyone.'

'And would anyone benefit from her death?'

'I don't think she had a lot of money. The farm will go to Jacob now, of course.'

'He doesn't own the farm?'

'He was a young child when his father died. Mma Zondo inherited the farm.'

'That's unusual. Land normally goes to a male heir.'

'It's what Ezekiel wanted, so my father arranged it so Jacob would inherit it from her. But Jacob runs it anyway these days, so it makes no difference.' He sighed. 'Frankly, Detective, I think Raseelo's right. The obvious explanation is the true one. It's dangerous to wander along the edge of the river at night. Even during the day, we've had people attacked by crocodiles.'

Mabaku took his time before his next question, and Kubu could see he was irritated, probably both by Raseelo's rudeness and the kgosi's dismissive attitude.

'Kgosi, do you really believe this is all coincidence? First the discovery of the skeletons, then the murder of Lesaka, rumours of corrupt practices with the water project, and now Mma Zondo's death?'

Raseelo jumped to his feet. 'What rumours? How dare you. My father is in charge of the water project. He's kgosi here. You should leave. Now!'

'I asked your father what *he* thought.'

Kubu could tell that Mabaku's temper was close to flashpoint.

'Raseelo,' the kgosi said heavily, 'these men are doing what they see as their job. Please sit down.'

Reluctantly, his son resumed his seat.

'I asked you a question, kgosi.'

The kgosi stared at Mabaku for what seemed a long time. At last he said, 'I told you I manage the finances of the water project. Everything's in order. I'll give you the auditor's details, and I'll thank you not to spread any slanderous rumours.' He paused. 'As for the rest, yes, I think it is coincidence, unfortunate but coincidence.'

'And I think you're lying to us.'

Raseelo jumped up again, his fists clenched at his sides. 'Get out! Before I throw you out.'

Mabaku didn't move. 'Where were you last night, Raseelo?'

The sudden change of tack seemed to throw the man. 'Me? I was here with my father.'

'And where were you the night that Lesaka was murdered?'

'Also here with my father.'

'I've already told you that,' the kgosi snapped.

Mabaku ignored him. 'Even when your father was talking to Lesaka's son?'

'No, of course not. But I was with my sister in the kitchen. You can ask her if you don't believe me.'

Mabaku rose to his feet. 'We certainly will.' He turned to the kgosi. 'We may have more questions later, kgosi, once we have the results of the autopsy.'

The kgosi glared at him, but said nothing.

When they were back in his Land Rover, Mabaku asked, 'Well, Bengu, we've made two enemies here now. What with the station commander, we won't win any popularity contests in Ncamasere.' It was clear from his tone that he wasn't going to lose sleep over it. 'What did you make of the two of them?'

Kubu thought for several seconds. They hadn't learnt much except about Raseelo's alibis and that Jacob Zondo didn't own the farm. He tried to assess the kgosi and his son based on their reactions.

'Well?'

'There was the issue of Jacob Zondo inheriting the farm. From the times we interviewed Mma Zondo, I'd guess he'll be pleased to have full control himself.'

'I thought you didn't believe a son could murder his mother.'

'I still don't. But if it is murder, we have to consider the possibility.'

Mabaku nodded. 'This is where good old-fashioned leg work comes in. If Jacob Zondo has something to hide, talking to enough people and looking at enough documents will expose it.' He paused. 'What about the kgosi and his son?'

'I think you're right. They're hiding something.' He paused. 'I don't think the kgosi was involved in the murder. He seemed too shocked. As for his son, he's capable of anything. I don't think he's all there. I thought he was going to physically throw us out.'

Mabaku smiled. 'Luckily for him, he didn't try.'

True to his word, Mabaku set out to gather any information relevant to Mma Zondo, particularly anything that might connect her to Lesaka. They began at the police station. The station commander was busy, but Abram was available and happy to share the local gossip he'd picked up over the years. He shared Kubu's distaste for the idea that Jacob may have been involved in the death of his mother, but admitted that they'd had a heated disagreement about the water project at a kgotla a few months earlier. Also, it was common knowledge that Jacob fretted about the ownership of the farm. After a few beers, he would complain about the things he'd like to do to modernise and expand, and how his mother refused to agree although she had little real interest in the operation.

Mabaku commented that it added up to friction, but hardly a motive for murder.

As for the community's feelings about Mma Zondo, Abram said she was not disliked. Some of the older people even respected her relationship with Mami Wata, and several of the fishermen would ask her advice if the water became unusually low or the fishing was bad.

Finally, Mabaku asked if Abram had informed the kgosi of Mma Zondo's death. Abram confirmed that he had. She was a senior member of the community, and the kgosi would be expected to express his condolences to Jacob in person as soon as he knew.

'And you told him that we'd sent the body for an autopsy?'

Abram nodded. 'He wanted to know about the funeral, so I had to explain that there would be some delay.'

After lunch, Kubu suggested they talk to Mowisi, but they learnt nothing new. Mowisi expressed formal regret about Mma Zondo's death, but was dismissive. Nothing significant would change, he felt, and he knew of no link between her and Lesaka. Nevertheless, he suggested they go to Lesaka's funeral the next day. After the burial, when the sorghum beer was flowing freely, people sometimes said more than they would have on other occasions.

After that, Kubu and Mabaku returned to Drotsky's to be in good time for the call from Ian.

'We need to make some progress, Bengu,' Mabaku told Kubu as they sipped coffee at a table overlooking the river. 'I need to let the director know what's happening after I hear from MacGregor. This is all costing a fortune, and the only thing we really have to show for it so far is saving Selelo's skin.'

Kubu shared his boss's frustration. 'Rra, I feel there's something going on in the background here. In Mochudi, where I grew up, my parents were always talking about family feuds and bitter enemies. Here, everyone tries to seem very open and forthcoming, but it's all too smooth. No serious disagreements – except for who gets the new, irrigated land – no serious enemies, no cliques. If this were Mochudi, we'd have more to look into than we could handle!'

Mabaku laughed, but then became serious again. 'I feel it too. Lesaka's life was perfect. Mma Zondo was a pillar of the community – except for her fixation with the water spirit, and there's even some sympathy for that. No one knows anything about the Bushman skeletons, even though the event could have happened while some of the people here were children. Normally, places like this keep war stories alive for generations.'

Just then Mabaku was summoned to the phone.

'This may be it, Bengu. Either the start of a new twist in these cases, or we may be packing up and heading home.'

As Kubu waited for Mabaku to return, he hoped that Mma Zondo had indeed been taken by a crocodile. He'd like to head back to Gaborone and leave the Lesaka case to Abram.

He'd been missing Joy and, despite his uncertainty about her feelings for him, wanted desperately to see her again. He'd thought about her a lot and was trying to see the relationship rationally.

When he was feeling self-confident, he convinced himself that he needed to be more direct with her. Is this going somewhere? he'd ask. That would force the issue. If she liked him, wonderful. If she didn't, he'd be sad and move on.

Then doubt would creep in. Move on to what? He didn't know any other women. And no one else had ever made him feel the way he did now.

His brain told him to treat her like anyone else, but his heart laughed. It knew who was in charge.

Kubu's stomach started to ache.

At last Mabaku returned. Kubu tried to see from his face whether the news was good or bad, but no one was any good at reading the assistant superintendent's face. Kubu wasn't sure what he'd regard as good news anyway. He was keen to get home to see Joy and his parents again, but the whole trip would then feel like a waste of time and effort.

'It was murder all right,' Mabaku told him as he sat down. 'No doubt about it, MacGregor says. There was a lot of technical stuff – you know what he's like – but the bottom line is that a knife wound killed her. Upwards from below the ribs into the heart.'

'A stab wound to the heart again...'

'Yes. MacGregor believes it's the same weapon. Of course he didn't put it that way, but that's what it comes down to. Knife, similar length, similar width.'

'He's certain it couldn't be a puncture wound from one of the croc's teeth?'

'Absolutely. I asked him that, and he said he was a hundred-percent sure. Not like him at all.'

Kubu felt his excitement build.

'After that, I phoned the director and told him, and he's given us the green light to stay another week. He even asked if we needed more support, but I told him we had it covered, so that better be true. I also phoned the station commander and let him know. He sounded very surprised and unhappy, and started carrying on about that Bushman again. He'll be safely back in Tsodilo by now, I hope. I said we'd be at the station tomorrow morning for a meeting, but I didn't tell him what we're going to do next.'

'And what's that?' Kubu asked, hoping that whatever it was would be in the morning or at least after dinner.

'We're going to see Zondo. We can ask some more questions, and then go through his mother's possessions and papers and so on.'

'Don't we need a warrant for that?'

'Only if he refuses to allow us to do it. That would be interesting. Come on, let's go.'

By the time Kubu was on his feet, Mabaku was already striding towards the vehicle.

CHAPTER 25

When Mabaku and Kubu arrived at the Zondo farm, they found a number of cars parked outside, and once more, the gate to the house was open.

'They seem to have become lax about their security,' Kubu noted.

'Well, many people will be coming over to condole with Zondo. It's probably easier this way.'

Someone they didn't recognise met them at the door and went to fetch Jacob. When he arrived, he looked surprised and not particularly pleased to see them. Nevertheless, he invited them in, adding, 'There are quite few people here right now.'

'Thank you, rra, we won't intrude,' Mabaku responded. 'We'd just like to talk to you for a few minutes privately.'

'Very well. We can go to my room.'

The house was busy with people setting out sandwiches and talking quietly.

Jacob took them through to a bedroom. He sat on the bed and offered the two chairs in the room to the detectives.

Mabaku cleared his throat. 'Rra Zondo, we have some distressing news. It was bad enough this morning when we believed your mother had been taken by a crocodile, but now we know that she was actually murdered.'

The surprise and shock on Jacob's face immediately convinced Kubu that he'd had nothing to do with his mother's death.

'That's impossible. Why do you think that?'

'Our pathologist was with us, investigating the Bushman skeletons. Your mother's death was unnatural, and coming so soon after Lesaka's murder, we asked him to perform an autopsy. He did so today. There's no doubt about it.'

'But who would want to kill her? Why?'

'We were hoping you'd have some suggestions on that.'

Jacob shook his head. 'Why are you so sure it's murder?'

'The injuries that killed her couldn't have been inflicted by a crocodile. Anyway, the bites were post mortem.'

Jacob shook his head again.

Mabaku moved on. 'Your mother was doing her best to stop the water project, something almost everyone around here wanted. That would have made her very unpopular with some people.'

Jacob brushed that aside. 'No one took her seriously. She made a nuisance of herself, but there was nothing she could do to stop it.' But then he hesitated, and for a moment seemed about to say something more.

Mabaku picked it up at once. 'Are you absolutely sure about that?'

Again, Jacob hesitated. 'Well, what she said when she left here last night was that she'd tell Mami Wata that she'd stopped the water project. Not that she was trying to stop it, but that she had. I remembered the letter you mentioned and accused her of writing it. We had a bit of an argument, but she didn't deny it.'

'So perhaps she'd found out about some kind of corruption and was blackmailing someone?'

'But it doesn't make sense. The kgosi manages the funding himself, and she had nothing to do with the project, so how could she have discovered anything?'

'Do you have anything to do with the project?'

'No.'

'Rra, please think about this very carefully and let us know if you remember anything at all that might help. Will you do that?'

'Of course.'

'Have you cleared your mother's room as yet?'

'No, I'll have it done before her body returns the afternoon before the funeral for her last night in this house. When do you think that could be?'

'We'll let you know as soon as we can. We'd like to look at your mother's room and go through her papers, and so on.'

'What, now?'

'If you don't mind. Time is always very important in a murder case. We'll keep to her room so we won't disturb your guests.'

Joshua looked unhappy, but he shrugged. 'Very well. I'll show you where it is.'

The room was much bigger than Jacob's and clearly the master bedroom of the house. It was obvious from the décor that Mma Zondo had turned it into a woman's room: there were no traces of her late husband. Everything was neat and tidy, and the bed was carefully made. A worn bible lay on a bedside pedestal. On one side of the room was a double, built-in cupboard, and on the other was a writing table with two small drawers, a chair, and several family photographs, similar to the ones they'd seen in the lounge.

Kubu went to the cupboards and opened them. One contained a variety of women's clothing, dresses hanging up, and underwear and blouses neatly folded on shelves. The other had a variety of items on its shelves, with the hanging space stacked with boxes, the highest ones threatening to collapse when the cupboard door was opened. One thing caught Kubu's attention immediately. He called his boss over.

'A typewriter,' Mabaku said with satisfaction. 'Get it onto the table.' He produced the copy of the corruption letter from his pocket and a blank sheet of paper, which he quickly rolled into the machine. 'I thought we'd find the typewriter here.'

Next, he typed the first paragraph of the letter, and compared the result with his photocopy. 'Definitely the same. Look at that break in the "e" there, for example.' He pulled the sheet out of typewriter. 'Well, we seem to have solved one of the mysteries. Now all we need to do is find out who killed her.'

He went back to searching the writing table, and Kubu started dredging the boxes.

It was about an hour later when they decided that there was nothing more to be found. In particular, nothing pointed to any evidence of corruption in the water project. All they had to show for their search was the typewriter and a wad of bank statements that Mabaku wanted to go through later on.

'Bring the typewriter, and we'll take our leave of Zondo.'

Kubu hesitated. 'Won't people gossip if they see us carrying out a typewriter and private documents? It could be embarrassing for Zondo.'

Mabaku gave a sardonic smile. 'No one is doing any gossiping so far. Maybe this will set them off. Come on.'

By the time the ancestors appeared once more in the sky, Selelo hadn't seen him – the man on the horse. In fact, not a single person attracted his attention. They were all too young or too old.

As he moved back into the desert, Selelo was disappointed, but he told himself that it was like hunting. Rarely did an eland or kudu present itself when a Bushman was hungry. Sometimes he was starving before an animal appeared. His current quest may end up being no different.

CHAPTER 26

Selelo pushed aside the reeds that covered him where he lay in the small depression he'd made in the sand. The sun wasn't up yet, and he wanted to be back in the village before people were about. This time he'd have to find a place to hide closer to the centre, where he hoped there would be more people.

As he walked, he wondered what he could use as a weapon. The police hadn't given him back his knife, and his bow and arrows and spear were at Tsodilo Hills. If he found the man he was looking for, he could go back and get them, if he had the strength. Otherwise, he could try to steal a knife. And if he couldn't do that, it wouldn't be the first time he'd killed using a rock.

He approached the first houses cautiously. He knew he could hide from anyone who saw him – the people around here seemed to be blind. But the dogs – he couldn't hide from them, and he'd no way to silence them.

He made his way between the houses, keeping as far away as possible from those he thought might have dogs. For the most part he stuck to the edges of roads so he didn't have to climb many fences. He was a few hundred metres from the general area where he wanted to hide for the day when a dog ran up to a fence near him and yapped.

'Shhhhh,' he whispered.

However, this made the dog bark even louder. Selelo backed

away and lay down in a shallow ditch running alongside the road. The dog continued to bark.

He heard a loud whistle and a command. The dog kept barking. Another whistle, followed by an angry shout.

Selelo prayed to his ancestors that the man wouldn't bother to find out what was bothering the dog.

Another loud shout. The dog stopped barking. Then Selelo heard a yelp. Then silence.

～

Kubu and Mabaku returned to the Zondo farm in the morning and spent several hours trying to find footprints, any trace of the missing murder weapon, or any further indications of what had taken place. They asked Jacob more questions, but learnt nothing else. Mma Zondo had gone to the river just after 9.00 pm, and shortly after that, the dogs had barked. Jacob had discovered that she was missing around six the next morning. He'd recalled nothing that might point to the killer.

They did discover that a vehicle had pulled off the road near the farm. Unfortunately, the ground was quite firm, and the tread marks were not very clear. They looked like the heavy off-road tyres everyone used in the area. Nevertheless, they took several photographs, hoping it might lead somewhere. Other than that, they returned empty-handed.

～

It was much easier for Selelo to keep awake that day because there were more people walking along the road. From his hiding spot, he inspected every man who walked by, but even though there were many, not one resembled the one he was after. Selelo started to wonder whether he was still alive. People died all the time, he thought. It was quite possible that he was too late.

After a while, Selelo realised that everyone was walking in the same direction, from his right to his left. That didn't make sense.

Suddenly the number of people dropped until there was no one to see.

The only thing that made sense was that they were all going to a meeting of some kind. Perhaps his man was there.

He moved slowly in the direction everyone had headed, keeping an eye open for more dogs. Fortunately he saw none. Then, in the distance, he saw a crowd of people outside a big house with a tower. He didn't think they could all fit into it.

As he came closer, he realised that he would never be able to get close. It was safer to hide where he was and wait for people to walk by. He wouldn't be able to see everyone, but at least some would walk past. Maybe he'd get lucky.

As he waited patiently, some of the people carried a box out of the house and put it in the back of a car. Then everyone started walking down the road away from him, and Selelo decided that the Mantis was playing tricks on him that day. And as one couldn't fight the Mantis, he decided to head back to the desert.

As he retraced his steps, Selelo realised he would have to find food once again. He had noticed that several houses had boxes outside like the one he'd found on the night he'd been released from jail. Only these boxes were much smaller. He'd be able to open them.

As he reached the edge of town, he saw a house with one of the boxes. There was no fence, so he took a chance there was no dog. He scavenged through the box and found more than he could possibly eat at one time. So, he saved some for the following day and walked back to his bed in the sand.

Kubu and Mabaku met up with Ian at Drotsky's around lunchtime. He'd driven back from Maun and delivered the body to the undertaker in Shakawe. He decided to work on his report while the others attended Lesaka's funeral in the afternoon.

The funeral was long and tiresome. It seemed that everyone in the village was there, and all the older men wanted to make long speeches extoling Lesaka's virtues and praising his achievements. Eventually, when the grave was finally filled in and the wailing had ceased, everyone adjourned to Lesaka's house for refreshments. There, Kubu and Mabaku had a chance to circulate, meet Lesaka's daughter, ask a few questions and generally keep their ears open.

At one point, Mowisi came over to them. 'I see you took my advice, Detectives. I hope you discover something more than just what a wonderful man, father, friend and workmate Lesaka was.'

'You were very generous with praise yourself,' Mabaku commented.

'Well, it's expected.'

'We asked you before if you knew anything about a connection between Mma Zondo and Lesaka. We now know that she'd written a letter claiming that there was corruption in the management of the water project. Did you know that?'

'No, I didn't. I disagree with the kgosi on many matters, but I strongly doubt that it's true. I think she was just trying to stir up trouble to delay the project.'

'You've heard that she's dead?'

'Yes. Awful to be taken by a crocodile.'

'The crocodile came later. She was murdered. We believe by the same person who killed Lesaka.'

Mowisi looked shaken by that news and for once seemed at a loss for words.

'Perhaps you'd like to think about that, Rra Mowisi. Let us know if you think of anything that might connect the two deaths. And be careful.'

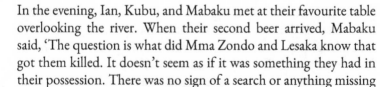

In the evening, Ian, Kubu, and Mabaku met at their favourite table overlooking the river. When their second beer arrived, Mabaku said, 'The question is what did Mma Zondo and Lesaka know that got them killed. It doesn't seem as if it was something they had in their possession. There was no sign of a search or anything missing in Lesaka's case, other than his wallet, and that was almost certainly misdirection. So it must have been something they knew.'

'The corruption?' Kubu suggested.

'It could be. If Lesaka was half the man they described today, he would have exposed it. As for Mma Zondo, if she had information, she would have used it for blackmail to stop the water project. Judging by those bank statements, she wasn't short of money.'

'Makes sense,' Ian put in. 'And explains the common murder weapon.'

Kubu had been following a different line of thought.

'Rra, remember you suggested that maybe *everything* was related? Suppose that's right. The murders, the corruption in the water project, the Bushman massacre, the earlier disappearances – even Selelo.'

'Selelo?' Ian exclaimed. 'He's harmless. You can't think he really was the murderer.'

'No, although he did turn up as soon as the skeletons were discovered. I was thinking more about the heavy security some people have – Lesaka, the Zondos and the kgosi. I wonder if Dibotelo and the station commander have it too. The younger members of those families don't seem to care about it that much. Joshua Lesaka left the door unlocked for his father's murderer, and Jacob Zondo doesn't bother with the security gate anymore. Perhaps it was the older members of the families who feared attack.'

'Attack by whom?' Mabaku asked, looking puzzled.

'I don't know. But two people were attacked even before the skeletons were found – Ezekiel Zondo and Dibotelo's son. Admittedly many years ago – but perhaps that's when the security was installed.'

Mabaku was looking at Kubu in an odd way, and Kubu was afraid he thought his ideas very stupid. However, when Mabaku spoke, he sounded impressed. 'So you think they installed the security in case of retaliation for the massacre. And maybe it was the men who carried out the attack on the Bushman group all those years ago. But what about the corruption?'

'I don't know. Maybe it doesn't even exist. If Mma Zondo knew about the massacre – perhaps her husband admitted to her that he'd been involved – then she had a way of blackmailing the kgosi and Lesaka.'

'But why now? Why not when the water project was just being talked about?'

'Because the blackmail was useless without the skeletons.'

Mabaku drained his beer. 'It's all speculation, Kubu. But there could just be something in it. At least we have a new way of looking at all this now.' He put down his glass and rose to his feet. 'Let's eat.'

As Kubu headed after his boss, he felt a warm glow. Maybe he was right and maybe he wasn't, but for the first time he'd spotted a possible explanation before his boss. And for the first time, Mabaku had treated him as a colleague rather than a trainee. He'd called him Kubu.

～

Ian had no difficulty persuading Mabaku and Kubu to join him in an after-dinner drink. 'This is my treat,' he said. 'It's time you learnt something about uisage beatha – the water of life.'

'I've been drinking whisky for years,' Mabaku said. 'I know what it's all about.'

'Aye, you may. But we call it Scotch if it's made in Scotland. Otherwise you may get something from Ireland or, even worse, America.' He gave a histrionic shudder. 'I would bet, though, that you drink a blend, right?'

Mabaku nodded.

'Have you ever sipped a fine single malt?'

'I don't remember. If it's expensive, probably not.'

'Well, Kubu and I had a few when we arrived. So, he's a little ahead of you. However, he's never had an Islay single malt. Islay is an island off the west coast and produces Scotch with a strong peaty taste. You'll love it or hate it.'

At that moment, a waiter put a glass in front of each man.

'Did you have what I asked for?' Ian asked.

The man nodded.

'Excellent.' He picked up his glass and held it in front of his nose. 'Breathe in deeply.'

Mabaku frowned as he did so. 'Strange smell.'

'Now take a sip and swirl it around your mouth – thus.' Ian sipped the golden liquid and looked as though we was chewing it.

Mabaku and Kubu followed suit.

Mabaku immediately spluttered. 'It's like jet fuel.'

Ian turned to Kubu. 'I don't think the Assistant Superintendent likes it. What do you think?'

Kubu nodded. 'I see what you mean about peaty. It's very strong.'

'Take another sip. Let it linger in your mouth.'

Mabaku grimaced. 'That explains why the Scots are so dour. You couldn't be happy drinking that stuff.'

Ian was about to reply when the waiter returned. 'Phone call for Assistant Superintendent Mabaku.'

Mabaku stood up. 'Who's been murdered now?'

∽

When he reached the manager's office, he picked up the phone. 'Mabaku.'

For the next few minutes he listened without saying anything. Eventually he asked, 'Tomorrow?'

He listened to the answer.

'How many?'

Again he listened.

'Does the station commander know?'

Mabaku listened to the answer with a frown. 'Yes, rra, I will. I'll phone you tomorrow evening. Earlier, if need be. Thank you, rra.'

∽

Mabaku sat down at the table, where Ian and Kubu looked at him enquiringly. He picked up the unfinished glass of single malt and downed it.

'I think we need another round, Dr MacGregor.'

Ian waved the waiter over and ordered three more single malts. 'Laphroaigs, of course, please.' He turned to Mabaku. 'It isn't really another murder, is it?'

Mabaku shook his head. 'Almost as bad. There's going to be a protest at the site where you excavated the Bushman skeletons. Some people will be there to honour those who were murdered and others to protest that the Bushmen's final resting place is in the process of being dug up for a water pipe.'

He wiped his brow. 'And others will be here to protest against the water project for potentially harming the whole Okavango Delta.' He paused. 'The director says to expect between twenty and thirty people camping out for a week. Including the media.'

CHAPTER 27

As Selelo walked into Ncamasere on the third day, he gazed at his ancestors as they faded slowly into the lightening sky. If he didn't find who he was looking for, he decided, he'd return to Tsodilo Hills and retrieve his hunting gear. Then he'd return to Ncamasere to resume his search.

As he threaded his way between the houses, he decided to return to the big house with the tower. People seemed to gather there. When it came into sight, he found a spot much closer than the previous day from which he could look at the passing foot traffic. The front door of the house was open, and Selelo was tempted to sneak inside to see if he could find food. He decided not to when he saw a man walk up to the door and disappear inside.

As the sun rose, more people walked through the door, mainly women. However, there were some men, and it was those he was particularly interested in. He scrutinised each closely, trying to match their faces with what he remembered about the man on the horse. It was frustrating because he wasn't sure of his memory.

Then three people walked towards the building. Ha! He was sure that was the face – the one on the right. And the shape of the body was the same. It had to be the man. He didn't recognise the others. The three walked into the building, and a few minutes later, the door closed and soon he heard singing. Selelo thought it sounded as though everyone was falling asleep. Nothing like when he sang to his ancestors, telling them his stories with excitement.

When he could see no one on the road, he crept to one of the windows and peeped in. There were a lot of people, and he couldn't see the man. He went to another window with the same result. He wondered whether the man had left from another door.

After what seemed a long time, the singing stopped and the door opened. People walked out and stood at the side of the building talking to each other. Selelo was now too far away to see people's faces clearly, but after a while he saw the man, who talked to a group of people for a while, then walked away. Following him was difficult, but that didn't worry Selelo – he'd had plenty of tracking practice over the years.

The man walked down one road, then turned onto another. Selelo scuttled ahead to some bushes where he could hide and look at the man as he walked close by.

At last, the man was only a few metres away. Selelo's shoulders slumped, and he groaned silently. It wasn't the man he'd seen earlier – they were only dressed the same way. The man he wanted had to be back at the big house.

The station commander was not in a good mood as he looked at the gaggle of tents that surrounded the area where the Bushman skeletons had been found. The demonstration had sprung up over night, and tents meant they were planning to stay for a while.

Off to one side of the tents, close to the trench where the bones had been found, was a small group of about fifteen untidy kids holding posters:

Kalahari genocide!
Save the Bushmen!
Save the Delta!
Stop stealing water!
Get rid of the police!

The last poster did not improve Balopi's mood. He was proud

of the work his station did. However, he would enjoy dragging some of the protestors into an interrogation room and showing them a thing or two.

Separate from the main group, a man and a woman were playing a board game under a canopy in front of their tent. They jumped up when they saw him arrive and picked up cameras. That's the reporters, he thought. Ready to complain about police brutality.

He turned to two constables standing nearby. 'Keep an eye on this scum. If they put a foot wrong, arrest them.'

'Yes, rra,' they answered in unison.

'I'll be back in an hour or two. I have to go into town and find the Bushman who killed Rra Lesaka and maybe Mma Zondo.'

As soon as it was safe, Selelo made his way back, only to find most of the people had left. And the man he was looking for wasn't there anymore. It had to be the Mantis again – playing tricks as usual. Leading him on, only to make fun of him at the end.

As he stayed hidden, wondering what to do next, he heard footsteps coming down the road behind him. Two people. He glanced back, making sure to move his head slowly. He gasped. It was the policeman who had beaten him and one of his men.

Selelo closed his eyes and tried to shrink inside himself, to make himself invisible.

The footsteps came closer. Then one changed direction, moving behind him. The other continued towards him. Then they stopped. Someone grabbed his arm and dragged him to his feet.

Selelo opened his eyes and looked into the eyes of the station commander, who said with a smile, 'I told you we'd catch you again. People around here don't like Bushmen. When they see one, they let me know. This time you won't get away. The men from Gabs won't even know we found you.' He nodded at his companion. 'Constable, handcuff him and take him to my house. There's a shed in the garden. Lock him in there.' He put his hand in his pocket to retrieve the key.

Selelo saw his chance and dropped to the ground, causing the constable to lose his grip. Then Selelo jumped up, pushed the man into the bushes and scampered away. Balopi roared for Selelo to stop, and both policemen started to chase the diminutive Bushman.

Selelo knew that he couldn't run faster than the men chasing him, but could certainly outlast them. So he began a game of attrition. He would run ten metres or so and change direction, always trying to have obstacles in the way of the pursuers. Then he'd change direction again. And again. He would pull things in the way of his pursuers and sometimes throw something at them – a plant, a ball, even some clothes hanging on a line.

One time, he ran around the corner of a house and picked up a rake propped up against the wall. As the constable ran around the corner, Selelo swung the rake at the man's legs. The constable fell to the ground, yelling in pain. Selelo ran across the street and looked back. He'd begun to distance himself from the policemen. The man who'd hurt him was helping the other man to his feet.

Selelo ran behind a house, then, keeping it between himself and the policemen, ran away until he reached another house. He hid behind it, then crawled along a ditch next to a road. Soon, he was confident that the men were no longer on his trail.

I have to be more careful, he thought. If they catch me, they'll kill me.

As he lay there, he decided he'd better stay one more day before going home to Tsodilo Hills. He needed to find the man on the horse first. Then he could plan in good time.

If Balopi was in a bad mood when he surveyed the tents earlier in the day, he was fit to be tied when he returned after Selelo escaped. He stormed over to one of the protestors. 'I can't stop you standing here, but tomorrow you will let the contractors continue with their work. If you interfere with them, I'll arrest you on the spot.'

The man – more like a boy – smiled at him, but said nothing.

'And you will keep the area clean. No litter, no shit, no trouble.'

As he said that, a young woman walked over and slipped a necklace of dried seed pods over his head. She kissed him on the cheek and said, 'Ke a go rata. I love you.'

Balopi pushed her away.

'Kagiso,' she shouted. 'Peace.'

The rest of the group raised their hands and shouted back, 'Kagiso.'

Balopi spun away and stalked back to his car. He was furious. He knew how to deal with tough men, but felt he'd been outsmarted by the protestors. He ripped the necklace from his neck and flung it onto the ground. Now he hoped they'd give him reason to arrest them.

'City boys and girls!' He'd show them.

CHAPTER 28

The civil engineer had chosen the site of the reservoir for the Kgosi Rantao Irrigation Scheme carefully. It was a depression carved by an ancient river, now long dry, that had deposited a clayish silt in that section of its bed. In the Kalahari, water soaks away quickly through the sand, but there the water table was close to the surface, and the clay would make a good base.

The bulldozer driver's job was to push the sand that had filled the depression over the eons into a dam wall at the deeper end. On Monday morning, he'd reached the stage where he'd moved all the sand and now needed to lift it to construct the wall.

Before he continued, he took a look around to see what would be his best strategy, and that's when he saw the boot. An old boot, dried out and eaten by sand. It was odd to find a discarded boot in the middle of nowhere, but what struck him as even stranger was that it was sticking out of the sand at a funny angle, with the sole upward. He bent down and tried to lift it out of the ground.

It didn't budge. When he pulled harder, it moved a little, and he could see it was attached to something. He pulled harder still, and the boot broke loose with a scatter of small bones. He gave a horrified yell.

The company owner, Tembo, came running up. 'Hey! What the fuck's the matter with you?' He saw the shock on the driver's face, then his eyes followed the man's to the dehydrated boot and skeletal leg reaching out from the sand. His heart sank.

'What the fuck!'

The driver took a few steps back and crossed himself. 'This project's cursed, boss. Dead people everywhere we go. I'm not working here. Forget it. Call a witch doctor to sort it out.'

Tembo frowned. More delays, more costs, he thought. The project had become a nightmare. He'd been stupid to agree to a deal involving money passed under the counter and with no way to exit, but now he had to make the best of it somehow.

'Listen, man, we've had enough. Another round of those fucking Gabs cops, and this project is down the drain. And your job with it. You understand?'

The driver looked at him blankly.

'This wall needs to be a lot higher. Know what I mean? Pile it up here another several metres. That should do fine.'

The man shook his head, not sure he understood. 'You want me to bury the body? Hide it?'

'It's just a Bushman like all the others. The police have plenty of them; they don't need another one, for God's sake.' Tembo glared at him. 'This is just between you and me, understand? You'd better not let me down on this. You hear me?'

Again the driver shook his head. 'No way, boss. Call the police right now, or I will. I'm not touching that thing.

Tembo looked as though he would explode. 'This fucking project! It's going to cost me everything! I'll call the fucking police, but you can pack up your stuff. I'm not paying you another thebe!'

When the report came in to the Shakawe police station, Mabaku was waiting for Director Gobey to phone him. There'd been trouble at the sympathy protest in Gaborone the day before, and Gobey wanted a confidential report on the situation at Ncamasere. Kubu was following up with the bank on the Zondo finances, and

Ian was double-checking his inventory of the Bushman skeleton bones.

Abram brought them the news.

'They've found another skeleton at the dam construction site. It's about a kilometre away from where they found the others. A bulldozer uncovered it.'

Ian let out a muffled curse, but there was no response from the detectives for a few moments. Then Mabaku said, 'It must have been a bigger battle than we thought.' He sighed. 'Detective Sergeant, please take the pathologist to the site. You'd better take Bengu along as well. I'm waiting to speak to the director. I'll catch up later.'

Ian was already on his feet. 'My equipment's in my vehicle. Kubu, you come with me, and we'll follow Abram.'

Tembo and the bulldozer driver met them at the site and led the way. As they climbed up the earthworks of the dam wall, it was obvious to Ian that the skeleton had been shifted during the construction. It must have been lifted with the sand and pushed by the bulldozer into its current position. He could forget about any useful information from its location.

Once they came to the skeleton, his thoughts were confirmed by a bone sticking out of the ground and a boot and foot bones scattered around it. He stared at it, puzzled. The boot looked wrong – there'd been nothing similar at the other site. He was intrigued.

'I doubt this is a Bushman. Look at that boot – it's worn and bleached, but good quality. Maybe this is one of the attackers; maybe he was fatally injured in the fight and buried here by his colleagues. Perhaps this could give us some answers.'

Tembo shrugged. 'All I want is to get it out of here. I don't care who it is. I have to get this project moving again, and no one's willing to work while it's here.' He glared at the bulldozer operator.

Abram looked puzzled. 'You don't think it's another Bushman?'

'Well, it's too early to say for sure.' Ian turned to the driver. 'Is this how it was when you found it?'

The man explained about trying to move the boot, and Ian shook his head. 'A pity you interfered with it, but it's clearly been shifted by the earthworks anyway. Let's see what we've got.' He started digging carefully around the protruding bone.

It was painstaking work because the skeleton was in multiple pieces. Ian progressed methodically, first tracing the leg bone back to the pelvis, then coming across parts of the backbone and the ribs. The breakthrough was when he felt something round and smooth, and soon he lifted out the skull. He used a brush to clean it off, and a soft cloth to remove the remaining sand. After he'd studied it for a few minutes, he gave a low whistle.

'Laddies, take a look at what we have here.'

Kubu and Abram had been digging up the stony sand close by, but had found nothing. They gratefully abandoned their shovels and crowded closer to see what the pathologist had discovered.

Ian held up the skull. 'It's nae a Bushman. Look at the eye orbits – it's a Motswana. I'm not surprised after that boot, and I suspected the leg bones were too long for a Bushman anyway. But here's the really interesting part.' He held the skull at a different angle so that they could see the teeth. 'That's a filling. And here's a crown. A crown with a gold cap. This is likely to be one of your missing locals, Kubu.'

Kubu was drenched with sweat and looked decidedly wilted, but Ian could see his interest kindle immediately. Suddenly the game had changed.

'What happened to him?' Abram asked. 'Was he hit from the front with something?' There was substantial hole in the forehead.

'I don't think so. Look here.' Ian turned the skull around so they could see the back, where there was a smaller hole with a web of cracks around it. 'He was shot from behind. That's the entry wound. The front hole is larger. That's common.' He peered at the hole. 'I think there's bevelling there. Again that's common for the entry wound. We'll be able to check in the lab.'

'Can you tell what sort of bullet it was?' Kubu asked. 'Could it be the same as the bullets you found at the other skeletons?'

'Hard to say. I'd guess this would be a rifle from the damage.' He stood up and looked around at the pile of sand making up the dam wall. 'We'll never find the bullet now.'

'So maybe he was picked off from a distance, and then buried here,' Kubu suggested.

'It's possible, but there's a lot of speculation in that. Abram, would you hang on here and cordon off the area with crime-scene tape. Kubu and I will take what we've got so far to Assistant Superintendent Mabaku. Then I'll be back here with a couple of constables to relieve you.'

Tembo was furious. 'So how long is this going to take? Another day wasted? Two? You have the bones. What else do you want to do here?'

'It's not all the bones. There must be more. And there may be clothing and artefacts with the body.'

'How long? Another day?'

'As long as it takes.'

Tempo took a deep breath. 'Well, I guess we can finish that missing section of pipe in the meantime.'

Abram recalled the protest under way and looked miserable. 'Rra, that may not be such a good idea...'

Mabaku was busy on his call when they returned to the police station, so Kubu reviewed the files of the two men who'd gone missing in 1975, while Ian rounded up help to exhume the rest of the skeleton.

Both files contained descriptions of the clothes the men had been wearing but, other than the boot, they hadn't found any remnants so far. To Kubu's disappointment, neither description included footwear, nor was there any reference to dental records. Mma Zondo's husband had a scar down the side of his neck from an altercation with a warthog he'd been hunting, while Dibotelo's son had a scar on his right arm. There was nothing in either file about old injuries, like broken limbs, that might be identifiable from a skeleton. At the time the reports were filed, the police had clearly expected that the men would be found reasonably soon.

When Mabaku finished his call, Ian filled him in.

'You're quite sure it's a Motswana?' Mabaku asked.

Ian hesitated. 'With that gold crown? There's no way it would be a Bushman.'

Mabaku picked up the skull carefully, but Ian wasn't pleased. 'Be gentle with that, rra. It'll be brittle after all this time and easy to break, especially near the bullet hole.'

The assistant superintendent gingerly replaced the skull on the table. 'We need to know who this was.'

Kubu reported on what he'd found in the files for Ekeziel Zondo and Tandi Dibotelo.

Mabaku looked harassed. 'Yesterday night you asked who'd been murdered, Dr MacGregor. Well, someone has. It seems we now have to find out who. My bet would be on Zondo. He might have had the money for that sort of dental work.'

Kubu nodded. 'Rra, you may be right, but can we go to Dibotelo first? I'd like to see what his house looks like in terms of security.' The real reason, he admitted to himself, was that it would be wonderful to put an end to Dibotelo's long search for his son.

'Very well. It's on the way, I suppose. Take some Polaroid pictures of the boot and the skull, and let's go. You can lead the interview. Start by asking him about the Bushmen.'

'The Bushmen?'

'Try out your idea on him. If he lost an adult son twenty-five years ago, he's been around a while. If he knows anything about the massacre, then he must have thought about the possibility of a revenge attack, especially so soon after Zondo's disappearance.'

Kubu realised he should have had that idea himself. As he took the pictures, he thought about how he'd handle the interview. It didn't take long for him to decide there was only one way to obtain information from Dibotelo – by linking it to his son.

CHAPTER 29

I n Ncamasere they were directed to Dibotelo's house on the outskirts of the town. They found him in a small vegetable garden surrounded by a rusty barbed-wire fence to keep out the voracious goats that ran free in the streets. He was using a hoe to clear out weeds. They saw immediately that the house had no burglar bars.

He accepted their greetings and then took them inside. 'The weeds grow even though the vegetables shrivel. We need more water, but it all goes down the river to please the tourists. No one thinks about the people here.'

'The kgosi is trying to get more water here,' Kubu ventured.

Dibotelo frowned at him. 'And who will that benefit? Not people like me.'

He took them to a small living room and offered them glasses of cold water. While he was fetching it, Kubu studied the room – tidy and clean, with every item carefully positioned. At one side of the room was a two-person dining table where several black-and-white photographs were carefully displayed. One was a picture of a much younger Dibotelo with an attractive young women holding the hand of a smiling boy. There were others of the same boy at various ages, and a few of older people. There were none showing the kgosi or Lesaka.

When Dibotelo returned, Kubu asked him, 'Rra, we've been

thinking about your son's disappearance. We need to consider every possibility. I'm sure you know that he disappeared shortly after Ezekiel Zondo did. Did you consider the possibility that the two events might be related?'

After a few moments, Dibotelo cleared his throat. 'Why would they be related? Ezekiel Zondo wasn't my friend.'

'But you must have wondered. What do you think happened to Zondo?'

'I'd guess he fell off his horse, wandered away and got lost in the desert.'

'Did you join the search?'

He shook his head.

Kubu was intrigued. It didn't sound as though Dibotelo cared much about the Zondo incident.

'Rra, when I met you, you were at the site where the Bushman skeletons were found. In the end we found nine. All had been shot or battered to death. Some were children. We now think that happened fifty years ago, or even more recently. You've been here for that long. You must've heard something about it.'

'Why do you ask me this?'

'Because we think it could be connected with your son's death.'

Dibotelo straightened up at the last words. 'You know that Tandi is dead?'

'After he's been missing for twenty-five years we must assume that. Now, what do you know about the massacre of those Bushmen?'

Dibotelo hesitated. 'I know nothing.'

'But you heard something.'

There was a long pause.

'Rra,' Mabaku said. 'If we are to solve the mystery of your son's disappearance, you have to help us.'

The silence continued. Kubu was about to say something, but a slight shake of Mabaku's head told him to wait.

At last Dibotelo said quietly, 'There were rumours that four men had fought with a group of Bushman and many had been killed. It happened many years ago.'

'Who were these men?'

'I don't know.' Then he quickly added, 'Not from around here.'

'And what was the fight about?'

'Maybe over a girl.'

Kubu found that hard to believe. At least nine people dead over a fight for a woman?

'Who told you this rumour?' Mabaku interjected.

'I don't remember. It was very long ago. At least ten years before Tandi disappeared, so you see it can't be connected.'

They tried several more questions, but either Dibotelo had told them all he knew, or he'd decided not to tell them anything further. Eventually, Kubu changed tack.

'Rra, there has been a new development.'

Dibotelo leant forward, suddenly tense. 'You've found him?'

Kubu hesitated, scared to raise the man's hopes. 'A skeleton has been found. Not where I met you, but where the water will be stored for the project. About a kilometre away. The pathologist, Dr MacGregor, believes that it's from a Motswana man.'

'God be praised. You've found him. Thank you. Thank you. It's been a long wait, but now Tandi can finally be laid to rest. When can I fetch his bones for the funeral?'

Kubu was stunned by his reaction, but Mabaku stepped in. 'Rra, we don't know who these bones belong to. We need to ask you several questions. Then, when the case is settled, we can give you the remains, if indeed it is your son.'

'It's him,' Dibotelo said without any trace of doubt. 'Long ago, when I'd lost all hope of seeing him alive, I consulted a witch doctor – a very powerful and respected man, not from around here, but from Maun. He said that Tandi was gone, that the desert held him and would not give him back.' He hesitated for a second, then asked, 'Where did you find him?'

'The people building the dam found him,' Kubu said. 'Rra,

what we need is for you to tell us some things about your son on the day he vanished. Do you remember what he was wearing?'

'Of course. But I told the police all that. He was looking for some cattle. He had on a khaki shirt and shorts. And closed shoes. The puff adders were bad that year. Otherwise Tandi often had bare feet.'

'Could you describe the shoes?'

Dibotelo seemed at a loss. 'I'm not sure. I remember they were shoes because of the snakes.'

Kubu passed across one of the Polaroid pictures. 'Could this be one of the shoes?'

'This is a boot, not a shoe.' He studied the picture again and then looked from the one detective to the other. 'But maybe. It was a long time ago.'

'Rra, did Tandi have any injuries? Maybe a broken limb as a child. How were his teeth?' Kubu held his breath.

'He sprained an ankle once, and he broke one of his forearm bones as a child. But it healed. All children do these things. He was perfect. Till the desert took him.'

'His teeth?' Kubu repeated.

'There was nothing wrong with his teeth! I took him to the clinic. He had a few fillings, like all people.'

'Was one of those fillings made of gold?'

'Are you mad? Where would I find that sort of money?' His voice was shaking. 'Why do you keep asking me these questions?'

Mabaku answered. 'Rra, I'm sorry but this skeleton is not your son. It was wearing boots. And has a gold crown on one tooth. I'm so sorry to disappoint you.'

Dibotelo looked frantically at Kubu. 'Of course, it's him! This tooth is a mistake, just because it's with the bones doesn't mean—'

'It's still in his mouth, rra.'

'I want to see him. Then I will know.'

'Maybe later. The pathologist is still doing his work.'

The detectives rose to go, and Dibotelo saw them out, still asking to see his son. But when they firmly took their leave, he appeared defeated. 'Why did you come? Why did you raise all this again? Ask me all these questions about Bushmen? Made me hope...' He started to sob and turned away.

'Rra, I'm so sorry,' Kubu said, but the man was already walking back to his house.

Kubu truly was sorry. He realised he'd made a stupid mistake. As Mabaku had said, the gold pointed to the better-off Zondos, not to the lonely man with his small house and garden. He'd wanted to be helpful, to be the one to help Dibotelo reach closure. But it'd been thoughtless and hurtful.

Mabaku gave him a quizzical look, seeming to know how he felt. 'That was useful. For the first time we have someone who doesn't just shrug off the Bushmen as something that happened a hundred years ago that nobody knows about. He was quite cagey. I think he knew more, but didn't want to say.'

Kubu nodded. He'd come to the same conclusion, but it didn't make him feel any better.

'I think we'll pay a visit to the kgosi next.'

'Not to Jacob Zondo?'

Mabaku shook his head. 'He has enough on his plate at the moment. The kgosi will know if his good friend had a gold crown. And once again I'd like to see how he reacts to the news.'

CHAPTER 30

Although he'd meant to spend the full day searching for the man, at midday Selelo decided to move on. He'd seen the policemen again, and they were obviously looking for him. A lot of people were about in the town, and he was afraid someone might spot him. He decided to try his luck somewhere else, but he was no longer hopeful.

As he crept away, he felt dejected. He'd failed to close the circle. He realised he had no plan, nothing to do but hide and find food and water. He'd become the hunted instead of the hunter.

It was time to go home, get strong, fetch his weapons and wait until the ancestors led him back. When they were ready, they'd lead him to the man. Until then he was just drifting like tumbleweed in the wind.

He heard a noisy vehicle approaching from behind him and ducked behind some low shrubs. He crouched and froze, expecting that the driver would pass and move on. But shortly before it reached his hiding place, the vehicle groaned to a halt. After a moment, its engine started to whine like a swarm of angry bees. Then it stopped. Then the angry bees again. Then it stopped again. Then a third time.

A man got out, walked to the front of the vehicle and opened it, allowing him to peer inside at the engine. Selelo was very nervous after what had happened the day before and wondered whether he should move further away. However, his momentary hesitation cost him his chance because another vehicle was approaching.

It pulled over on the verge, and two men climbed out. They walked over to the broken-down vehicle and started talking to the driver. After a short time one of them took the driver's seat and the angry bees started again, even more persistently this time. Suddenly, the vehicle roared to life, coughing and spluttering with dark smoke coming from the back.

Selelo had recognised the men at once. The fat man was the hippopotamus. The hippopotamus had been kind to him. The other man had spoken to him harshly, but hadn't hit him. He wondered what they were doing and was afraid they were also searching for him. He prayed they wouldn't scan the area. Even a black man would spot him behind these two lonely shrubs.

Selelo remained motionless and, to his relief, the first vehicle soon drove off, followed shortly after by the two policemen. Selelo thanked the ancestors for keeping him hidden.

He felt an urge to follow the policemen, almost like impala that followed lions, knowing they were safe as long as they kept the predators in sight. The men had taken a turn a bit further down the road, and without a conscious decision, he found himself following them.

∼

Shortly after they'd turned off the main road, Mabaku and Kubu pulled up at the kgosi's house. In response to their knocking, Raseelo opened the door, and when he saw them, shouted at them to leave the property at once.

Mabaku was unusually tactful. 'Rra, we've important news for the kgosi. He'll want to hear this immediately.' He made it quite clear that they wouldn't leave until they had what they'd come for.

Raseelo said nothing, but after a few moments, turned and led them through the house to the kitchen. He pointed at the chairs around the kitchen table. 'You can wait here. The kgosi is with some people.'

'I don't think you heard me properly,' Mabaku said quietly. 'This is urgent. We need to speak to him immediately.'

Raseelo clenched his fists at his sides, but managed to control himself. 'Wait here.'

After a few minutes, the kgosi joined them. He was frowning and didn't offer a greeting. 'What's so urgent that it interrupts my council meeting?'

'Kgosi, another skeleton has been uncovered by the contractor. It isn't another Bushman. It's a Motswana.'

The kgosi looked shocked and after a few moments took a seat at the table. 'Who is it?'

'We think you can help us with that.'

Kubu produced the Polaroids of the boot and the skull, and passed them to the kgosi. He studied them only for a few moments. 'It's Ezekiel. Ezekiel Zondo. Another of my oldest friends. What's going on?' He seemed to shrink, slumping in the chair. 'It's almost as if Mma Zondo was right after all. The living dying, and the bones of the dead rising...'

'You're sure about it being Zondo?'

He nodded. 'The gold tooth. He went all the way to Gaborone for it. He was very proud of it and was the only man in this area who had one. He said gold brought luck and kept the tokoloshes away. But it didn't work for him, did it? How did he die?'

'He was shot in the back of the head, probably with a rifle.'

By the time Selelo reached the turnoff, there was no sign of the policemen. They've gone on, he thought. I won't find them now. Nevertheless, he continued along the road, promising himself that after this he'd rest until the night and then head for the desert.

That's when he spotted their vehicle parked in the driveway leading up to a big house. Intrigued, he crept closer, checked that the vehicle was empty, and then found a place where he could hide and wait. He was good at waiting.

~

'Kgosi, we'll inform Jacob Zondo about this shortly. But first could you tell us about Ezekiel's disappearance? We've read the police reports taken at the time, but he was your friend. Perhaps you know something more?'

'What does it matter now?'

'The case is still open. It was a missing-persons case. Now it's a murder case.'

'Very well. He set out for a day of hunting—'

'Alone?'

The kgosi nodded. 'Later in the afternoon, his horse returned without him. His wife told the farm workers to look for him and sent someone to fetch me. I gathered a few other men, and we tried to follow the horse's trail but lost it as it was getting dark. The next morning we tried again with a Bushman tracker. He had no difficulty following where the horse had gone. At a certain point another horse had joined his, and they'd proceeded together for some way. We thought he might have met up with someone he knew, but no one ever came forward. Then the second horse went a different way, and Ezekiel rode on alone.'

'How did you know which horse to follow?' Kubu asked.

'The tracker knew. Eventually, we came to one of those calcrete ridges, and even the Bushman battled to find the tracks there. He did pick them up again a couple of hundred metres further on, but he said the horse didn't have a man on its back anymore. We thought it must have thrown Ezekiel, although he was an excellent rider. The bush was quite thick around there, and we spent the rest of the day searching the area, but there was no trace of him. We tried again the next day with as many people as we could find to help. Nothing.'

'Did the police investigate the scene?'

'Balopi was with us. He made notes, and he and another

policeman came back for several days and searched for any traces of what had happened.'

'What did *you* think had happened to him?'

'The only thing I could think of was that he'd been thrown by his horse, hit his head on the calcrete and wandered out into the desert. Maybe a lion took him. There were still a few around in those days.'

'Without leaving any tracks?'

'Sometimes you can miss them. The tracker thought he saw a few boot prints on the calcrete, but then lost them. After a few days the wind hides everything.' He hesitated. 'Mma Zondo claimed it was Bushmen. She heard that from a witch doctor she'd consulted about her husband's disappearance.' He stopped and seemed to be deciding whether to say anything more. Mabaku waited patiently, and after a short while the kgosi continued.

'When Zondo and Dibotelo first disappeared, none of us thought of Bushmen. We'd heard stories, rumours about an attack many years ago. But Mma Zondo said it was the Bushmen seeking revenge. That we were the targets.'

'Why should they attack you? Were you involved in some way?'

'Of course not! But apparently the witch doctor said that these Bushmen hold all black people living here responsible.' He frowned, and his voice rose. 'This Bushman the station commander arrested, and you released, could be one of them. Balopi says you're protecting him, and now Endo and Mma Zondo are dead!'

Mabaku was surprised by the emotion in the kgosi's voice. The calmness that had characterised their previous conversations was gone. The man sounded scared. It was hard to believe that the diminutive Bushman who'd cowered in the corner of the interview room could frighten anyone.

'Kgosi, there's no evidence whatsoever that that Bushman is involved in anything. We found none of his fingerprints anywhere in Lesaka's house or on the radio he supposedly stole. He's threatened no one.'

'He said he would sting like a bee. That's a threat. He needs to be questioned about this, at least. Why is he hanging around here if he isn't up to something?'

'Actually, he's gone back to Tsodilo.'

'Not at all. He was spotted in town yesterday. You don't want to see what's under your nose.'

This was news to Mabaku, unwelcome news. The kgosi seemed better informed about the Bushman than the police, but then again people talked to him. He wondered if Balopi knew that Selelo was hanging around his home town while he was monitoring a demonstration down the road. One thing was clear: Selelo was after something. He wouldn't mind another interview with the man, but he didn't see much hope of that at the moment.

'Was it after her husband's disappearance that Mma Zondo put in the security at her house?' he asked.

The kgosi nodded.

'In case Bushmen attacked her?'

'Their farm was really isolated in those days. She was a widow with a young boy.'

'What about yourself and Lesaka?' Kubu asked. 'Your houses are in town. Did you also get security then?'

'It was about then.'

'So who were the people who followed Mma Zondo's lead on the security?' Mabaku asked.

'How should I know? I did. I didn't believe in her witch doctor, but something was going on. Why not be safe? Endo also did, but in the end it didn't help because his son was lax about it. Others did too, I suppose. Most people shrugged it off or couldn't afford it anyway.'

'Kgosi, I've heard a rumour that four men attacked a group of Bushmen near here and killed many of them. And that it happened relatively recently – less than fifty years ago.'

'Who told you that?'

'It doesn't matter. Have you heard rumours like that?'

'No, I haven't. That probably also came from Mma Zondo's witch doctor. I'm sure I'd have heard about it if something like that happened here in my lifetime.' He frowned. 'All this is irrelevant. What are you going to do about this Bushman?'

Mabaku promised to look into the matter, but then returned the interview to the murder of Ezekiel Zondo.

'If Zondo was shot somewhere in the area where the tracks were lost, how far is that from where the new dam is being built?'

'It's not that far. Probably a kilometre. A Bushman, or whoever it was, must have shot Ezekiel and then carried his body on horseback.'

'But no one found any tracks?'

'We didn't look there, and people travelled a lot on horses in those days. There would have been tracks all over.'

It seemed strange to Kubu that no one at the time had considered the possibility of an attack by someone from Ncamasere. 'Did he have any enemies?'

'People who didn't like him? Yes. People who'd want to kill him? I can't think of any.'

Kubu digested that, then asked, 'What about Tandi Dibotelo? He disappeared soon after.'

'His case seemed to be quite different. He went out one evening and disappeared. At the time I thought he'd left to make his fortune in the big city. And to avoid marrying his girlfriend. She was already pregnant, and this was his way out. Now I'm not so sure.'

'His father seemed very close to him. Would he really disappear without telling him?'

'No one can predict what young people will do.'

'Rra, we'll need to talk to the tracker who searched for Zondo with you,' Mabaku said. 'Do you know where we can find him?'

'He left long ago. He was old then. I'm sure he's dead by now.'

Mabaku asked a few more questions, but learnt nothing more. Eventually, he thanked the kgosi for his time and apologised for interrupting his meeting.

The kgosi shrugged. 'I left Raseelo to handle it. He should learn. Come, I'll see you out.'

When the door of the house opened, Selelo crouched lower and froze as he would if he were hunting. If he didn't move, he was sure they wouldn't see him. The hippopotamus and the other man from the police came out first, and then a third man followed and spoke a few words to them before turning back into the house. The detectives walked to their vehicle and drove away.

Long after they'd gone, Selelo still hadn't moved. The man who'd come out of the door was the man he'd come to find. There was no doubt about it. He'd seen him as clearly as the day he was on the horse.

The ancestors had led him right to the man's house as soon as he'd put himself in their hands. And he'd learnt something else too. The policemen were working for the man and would try to protect him. Selelo didn't care. Now he knew where the man lived, he could take his time, make his plans. He was confident that with the ancestors' help he would succeed.

CHAPTER 31

When Selelo recovered from the surprise of seeing the man he was searching for, he decided to tell the ancestors his good news. He would go to the place where his ancestors had been found in the sand, dance for them, then return to Tsodilo Hills the following day.

Now he knew where the man lived, he could take his time, build up his strength and return to Ncamasere to close the circle when he felt ready.

After ensuring that the coast was clear, he worked his way to the edge of the village, then headed for the excavation, which was a short way away. He was several hundred metres from it when he saw a group of people. He wondered if they'd found more bones. That would be good and bad – good for pleasing the ancestors, bad for the fact that more of his people had died.

Again he tried to blend into the background, to become invisible to eyes that didn't know how to look. He took his time moving closer, and when he was about twenty metres away, he settled behind a small bush. He looked at the people. They were all young, and he didn't recognise anyone. He checked again and was certain that the angry policeman wasn't there.

Selelo was puzzled because many of the young men and women carried big pieces of paper on a stick. There was writing on them, but since he couldn't read, he didn't know what they said.

Every few minutes, one of the women started to sing, and the others joined in. What were they doing there? he wondered. Were they happy that his ancestors had been found, or were they angry that the bones had been taken from the sand, or was it something else altogether?

He also noticed that there were two policemen not far away, sitting on the sand under a tree. They were obviously watching what the young people were doing. And to one side, there were some big cars like the ones that came to Tsodilo Hills with people from over the seas.

As he sat there, he wondered what to do. He wanted to go to the hole in the ground, pray for those who'd died there, then go into the desert to dance. However, he was sure that if he did that, the policemen would come and drag him back to the room that kept getting smaller. He would die if that happened again.

He decided to wait and watch.

⁓

As the sun became low, Selelo watched one of the men walk over to a car and open the door on the side. A big black dog jumped out and started running around, jumping up on some of the people. Selelo shrank into the ground, keeping his eye on the dog. It was obvious that the dog was young, because it ran up and down, round and round. Sometimes it just spun. Selelo smiled. A beautiful animal.

One of the men picked up a stick and threw it. The dog bounded after it and soon returned, stick in mouth, tail wagging. The man threw it again. This time it landed a few metres from Selelo. He held his breath. The dog dashed over and just as it was about to pick up the stick, it noticed him. It moved towards him cautiously, tail wagging gently. Selelo hissed at it, but it didn't go away. It wasn't fooled by the snake sound.

'Bosigo! Come here.' One of the men tried to summon the dog, but it edged closer to Selelo.

'Bosigo, what have you got?'

The dog put its nose on Selelo's shoulder. He didn't know what to do. So he did nothing, hoping the dog would remember the stick and continue the game. Now the dog was nudging him, hoping for affection.

'Bosigo.' The voice was closer now. Selelo heard a whistle, but the dog was determined to make friends.

Then the man was next to him, and Bosigo was pulled abruptly away.

'My God. Are you all right?' Selelo could sense the man looking at him. He looked up.

'Come over here,' the man shouted to the others.

Selelo could hear people approaching, and soon he was at the centre of a circle. Everyone was staring. He slowly stood up, hoping to see a way to escape. He was worried they'd call the policemen.

He put his hand on his chest. 'Me, Selelo. Go to Tsodilo Hills.'

The man with the dog put his hand over his heart and smiled. 'My name is Baruti. I am your friend,' he said in English. Then he switched to Setswana. 'Ke tsala.' He pointed at the others. 'Ditsala.'

Selelo relaxed a bit. It seemed that the people crowding around him were friendly, and they hadn't called out to the policemen. Had they done that, he would have disappeared into the desert.

He looked at the faces peering at him and wondered if they'd ever talked to a Bushman before. Most Batswana he'd encountered hadn't.

He put his hand on his chest again. 'Me, Selelo. Go to Tsodilo Hills.'

The man called Baruti answered. 'You can't go to Tsodilo Hills tonight. It's too far. I can take you there tomorrow.'

Selelo said nothing as he thought about how this affected his plan. Perhaps the ancestors had put these people here to help him. Perhaps he could steal a knife when everyone was asleep, then go into the desert to dance. That way, he wouldn't have to go to Tsodilo to get his bow and arrows, and his spear. And he would be ready to close the circle when the sun climbed into the sky.

'Stay with us tonight. We have plenty of food, and I'll take you to Tsodilo Hills tomorrow morning.'

Selelo smiled. 'Selelo hungry.'

~

One of the policemen lifted a carton of Shake Shake beer to his mouth. He knew he wasn't allowed to drink alcohol while on duty, but he felt he and his colleague deserved a beer, given their assignment of the past couple of days. As he wiped his mouth with his arm, he glanced over at the protestors, who'd gone back to their circle of tents. They had a big fire burning and were obviously preparing their dinner.

Then he looked again. The light was fading, but one of the figures standing next to the fire looked like a Bushman – he was much shorter than the others and dressed differently.

'Look. Look over there.' He pointed at the protestors. 'What do you see?'

The other policeman stared into the gloom. 'Aii, it looks like a Bushman. We'd better check. The station commander is looking for one.'

The two started to walk towards the protestors.

Selelo was the first to notice them. If they saw him, they would arrest him and take him back to the rooms where they'd beaten him. He needed to distract them.

He grabbed the arm of the man with the dog and pointed at the oncoming men. 'Police come to take Selelo. Want to kill Selelo.'

'Police coming,' Baruti shouted. 'They're after Selelo.' The protestors moved forward and created a wall, and the two reporters grabbed their cameras and moved where they had a good view of any confrontation.

'We need to speak to the Bushman,' one policeman told the group.

'There's no Bushman here,' Baruti answered.

'We saw him. Please move aside. We just want to talk to him.'

'He told us the police wanted to kill him,' one of the protestors shouted.

Baruti glared at him. 'You can't come any closer. This is our camp. Go back to yours.'

The policemen took a step forward. The protestors linked arms.

'You'll have to arrest us first!' one shouted.

'Murderers!' another screamed.

~

Selelo couldn't see the policemen anymore. They were hidden behind the people who'd found him.

They won't let me stay here, he thought. They'll call the policeman who beat me.

He decided he needed to change his plans again.

He walked over to a table that had been set up in the sand. A woman had been cutting some meat for the meal. Although he was hungry, it wasn't the meat that attracted him. It was the knife. He picked it up, glanced at the protestors who were confronting the policemen, and slipped away into the gloom.

~

The one constable took hold of the other's arm. 'Let's get out of here. We can't do anything. We'll radio the station commander to deal with the problem.'

The protestors waited until the constables had returned to their camp site before they turned back to theirs.

'Where's Selelo?' Baruti asked.

'He's probably hiding from the cops,' another replied.

'Selelo. Selelo!' Baruti shouted. 'They've gone. You can come back now.'

The protestors spread out to look for him. 'It's safe. Come back,' they shouted.

After a while, they returned to their fire.

'He's gone,' Baruti said. 'They scared him off.'

'I don't blame him,' another commented. 'It's terrible how they are treated.'

Half an hour later, a police Land Rover pulled up next to the excavation site. The two constables walked over to brief the station commander. After a short conversation, the three headed to the protestors' camp.

'Where's the Bushman,' Balopi demanded.

The protestors surrounded the policemen, and the reporters once more positioned themselves for a good view.

'I want to search the camp.'

'There's no Bushman here.'

'Move aside. We're going to search your tents.'

'Can I see your search warrant?'

'Get out of the way or I'll arrest you.'

'Go ahead.'

Balopi tried to push his way through the protestors, but they linked arms again.

'This is a peaceful protest. If you touch us, we'll sue for assault.'

'Rra,' one of the constables said, 'shouldn't we call for back-up?'

'Let me through,' Balopi shouted. 'The Bushman is wanted for murder. I'll arrest you for obstructing justice.'

'Arrest us. Arrest us,' the protestors started to chant.

Balopi had had enough. The Bushman had made a fool of him, and the protesters had made a fool of him. Now he was going to do his job. He whispered instructions to the constables.

Deciding Baruti was the leader, he moved towards him as if he were going to talk, but as soon as the constables joined him, he punched him hard in the stomach. At the same time, one of the constables barged the woman holding Baruti's hand. The cameras went into action.

Baruti doubled over and the woman staggered, but they

managed to keep holding hands. Then the other constable joined in and shoved Baruti so hard he lost his balance and fell.

The next moment Bosigo was on the constable, growling and biting his leg.

Balopi pulled out his handgun and shouted, 'Call it off or I'll shoot it!'

Baruti managed to get the dog under control, while the constable nursed his bleeding leg. One of the girls tried to help him, but he brushed her aside.

Balopi and the other constable broke through the cordon and headed for the tents. A few protesters ran after them and tried to stop them, but they were roughly shoved aside. Soon the policemen were checking the tents and peering into the vehicles, but they found nothing.

Balopi wasn't surprised, and he knew they'd never find the Bushman in the surrounding scrub. However, he'd shown who was in charge. He hoped the reporters had good pictures of the dog attacking his constable.

He told the man who'd been bitten to come with him and the other constable to return to his camp and keep watch. Then he turned to Baruti.

'I need to take this man for medical attention now, but I intend to charge you with obstructing the police in the performance of their duty and assaulting a police officer. That carries a long jail sentence. If you have any sense, you won't be here when I come back for you.'

As he headed to his vehicle with the constable limping after him, the protesters started their chant:

'Bye-bye. Bye-bye.'

Balopi smiled. He'd shown them who was boss.

CHAPTER 32

As Selelo crept away from the protestors and policemen, he felt better about what was ahead of him. Now he had a knife, there was no need to make the long trip to Tsodilo Hills to fetch his bow and arrows and spear. The knife was a good weapon and very sharp.

Just as important, he wouldn't have days of travel to wonder whether he'd understood the ancestors properly. He had no doubt that they wanted him to complete the circle, but to do so, he would have to kill a man and so kill himself too. The longer he waited, the greater the doubt that would fill his head.

It wasn't difficult for him to find the spot where he'd spent the previous nights. It was now familiar to him, the depression in the sand where he slept, the bushes that hid him from intruders, the sounds of the night, and, of course, the array of ancestors keeping watch over him.

I'll give them a dance they'll be proud of, he thought. A dance of death.

~

The sun's first rays woke Selelo the next morning. He was exhausted. It had taken a long time – much longer than usual – of dancing and spinning and singing for him to leave his body so he could talk to the ancestors. When he returned to his body, he knew they were waiting for him to close the circle, waiting to be proud of him.

He was ready to do it. He knew he had the energy, and now he had the will. It was time.

~

The morning did not start well for the station commander. The assistant commissioner phoned him, and he was furious.

'Balopi, I told you to leave the protestors alone unless they started interfering with people or damaging property. But, no, you start beating them. It's all over the radio news this morning. The papers will pick it up later and make a big deal about police brutality. This is exactly what they wanted. No one was taking any notice of the protestors until now.' He paused. 'Tell me there were no photographers there.'

Balopi squirmed. 'I think there were a couple, rra; but, rra, we were the ones being attacked. They set their dog on us – a huge, vicious animal. My constable needed stitches afterwards.'

The assistant commissioner calmed down. 'Oh. That's different. And this happened before the punch-up?'

Balopi took a deep breath. 'Um, well, at about the same time. You see, rra, they were sheltering a suspect in the murders. That Bushman.'

There was silence for a few moments. Then the assistant commissioner exploded. 'The Bushman? The one you falsely arrested before? That will be all over the papers too. Do you have the slightest evidence to link him to the murders?'

'Well, rra, who else—'

'You don't, do you? Nothing at all? For God's sake, Balopi, have you gone mad?'

There was a lot more before the call ended. By then the assistant commissioner had made three things absolutely clear: the station commander was not to go near the protesters, he was to leave the Bushman strictly alone unless he had strong, concrete evidence against him, and his job was on the line.

As he put down the phone, Balopi was fuming. What right had the man to talk to him like that after his thirty years of service? It was all the fault of that interfering head-office detective. If Mabaku hadn't stuck his nose in, all would have been well. He hammered his fist on his desk in impotent fury.

Selelo was becoming anxious. He'd lain hidden outside the man's house for several hours now, but the man hadn't appeared. It was frustrating. He prayed that the man hadn't left, hadn't gone away. That would be a typical Mantis trick. He steeled himself to ward off the temptations of doubt. He would wait as long as he had to.

Another hour passed, then a woman came to the house and banged on the door. When it opened, she went inside. Selelo couldn't see who had opened it. However, he now knew someone was inside. Who could it be other than the man?

It was not long before the door opened again, and the woman walked out. With the man! The two walked towards the road, talking. Selelo thanked the ancestors for providing the opportunity, then crept closer, every nerve on alert. He would take the man down when the woman left.

Selelo moved slowly towards the house. He was now only a short distance away. If he had his bow, the man would be close enough.

Eventually the woman left, and the man watched her walk down the road.

It was time.

Selelo ran forward, knife pointed.

The man saw him, shouted, stepped back, tripped and fell. Selelo jumped on him, knife to his throat.

'You kill my people. I kill you.' He pushed the knife a little harder.

The kgosi was desperate. 'No! You're wrong. I never killed anyone.'

Selelo pushed some more. A trickle of blood dropped to the ground. 'Say you kill my people.'

'I didn't. Someone else. I'll tell you who.'

'Not good you kill my people. More bad you do to my mother.' Another push. More blood.

'Please don't kill me. I'll tell you what happened.'

Tears welled up in Selelo's eyes. 'Hard to kill you.' For a moment his resolve weakened. Then returned. 'Must kill you. What you do to my mother.'

'I did nothing. You have the wrong man.'

'Right man. See you on horse. Mother say white chest.'

'I don't know what you're talking about.'

Tears started to flow from Selelo's eyes. 'Kill you now.'

'Help!' The kgosi started to struggle, but stopped as the knife dug deeper. 'Don't kill me. Please. I didn't do anything.'

'Terrible what you do to my mother.' Selelo let out a cry of anguish. 'Make you my father. You my father! My father. Because what you do to my mother.' He pushed a bit harder. 'She hate herself because what you do. Walk into desert to join ancestors. What you do kill her.' He took a deep breath. 'You die now, then I die.'

A shot rang out, and Selelo collapsed on the kgosi, blood dripping from his shoulder.

Raseelo ran from the house, rifle at the ready. 'Father, are you all right?'

The kgosi pushed Selelo off and remained lying on the ground, sobbing with relief. He nodded.

Raseelo walked over to Selelo, who was groaning in pain, and kicked him in the head. He raised the rifle and aimed it at the Bushman's head. 'Now you die.'

'No, Raseelo. Don't shoot him.' The cry came from the kgosi's daughter, now running towards them. 'Don't be a fool, Raseelo.'

Raseelo hesitated. Then a shout came from the neighbour's garden. 'What's going on? Kgosi, are you all right?'

The kgosi climbed slowly to his feet, gingerly fingering his throat, where blood still oozed from the broken skin. 'I'm fine, thanks to the Almighty.' He pointed at the man on the ground who was writhing in pain. 'He tried to kill me. Thank God Raseelo shot him before he cut my throat.'

Raseelo kicked Selelo again in the head. 'Bastard. I'll show you.' He kicked Selelo again.

'Stop it, Raseelo. Now!'

'But—'

'Stop now!'

Raseelo shrugged and gave Selelo another mighty kick before turning away.

The kgosi walked over to Raseelo. 'Give me the rifle.'

Reluctantly, Raseelo handed it over.

'You saved my life, Raseelo. Thank you. Thank you.' The kgosi put his hand round his son's shoulders. 'Go and get some rope so I can tie him up.'

∾

After they'd trussed him, the neighbour tried to stop the bleeding from Selelo's shoulder.

'I don't think it's too bad,' he said to the kgosi. 'It's not bleeding too badly.'

The kgosi turned to his son. 'Raseelo, call the station commander in Shakawe and tell him what happened. Tell him we'll go to the station after we've dropped the Bushman at the clinic. He should have a constable there to guard him. I'll be back in a few minutes. I must put something on the cuts on my throat.'

Raseelo nodded and gave Selelo one more kick before walking away.

∾

'Rra, I have good news,' Raseelo said when he was put through to the station commander. 'We've caught the Bushman. He tried to kill my father, but I shot him before he could.'

'I hope he's dead.'

'He isn't. I had to aim high so I didn't hit my father. I hit him in the shoulder. My father says that we're taking him to the clinic in Shakawe and will come to you afterwards. He suggests you should have someone guarding the Bushman at the clinic.'

'Is the kgosi okay?'

'Yes. He has some cuts because the Bushman was going to slit his throat, but I got him before he did.'

'Did anyone else witness what happened?'

'My sister did, and the neighbour.'

'Please tell them to come to the station as soon as possible. I'll need a statement from both of them.'

'I will, rra. We'll be there in half an hour.'

Kubu, Mabaku, Ian and Abram were in the police-station meeting room reviewing what they'd discovered about the various cases, when the station commander walked in. They could see at once that he was pleased about something.

'Well,' he announced, 'I was right all along. You have a lot to answer for, Mabaku. One death and another only prevented by quick action by a civilian. Your career in the CID is over. I can't pretend I'll lose any sleep over that.'

Mabaku swung round to face him. 'What on earth are you talking about Assistant Superintendent?' It was his quiet voice, the dangerous one.

'A few minutes ago I had a call from the kgosi's son. Your Bushman attacked the kgosi with a knife. He was raving about the kgosi killing people. Obviously the little shit is a psycho. Fortunately the kgosi's son managed to shoot him before he had a chance to cut the kgosi's throat.'

'Is the kgosi all right?' Kubu asked.

'He's been cut up a bit. We'll see when he gets here.'

'How does he know it's Selelo?'

'How many Bushmen have you seen around here, Detective Sergeant?'

'Is he dead?'

The station commander shook his head. 'I hope he does die and saves us the trouble of an execution. They're taking him to the clinic, then they'll come in to give statements.'

'So it was Selelo all along...' Abram said.

'Of course it was. If I hadn't been overruled, he'd be rotting in a cell here, and Mma Zondo would still be communing with Mami Wata.' He glared at Mabaku and waited, but no one responded. 'Right. I'll call you when they arrive. I'm sure you'll want to sit in on the interview, Assistant Superintendent.'

After he'd left, there was silence. Then Ian said, 'I wonder where he got the knife. I hope they bring it in with them. That could connect him to the other murders.'

Mabaku shook his head. 'It doesn't add up. How did he enter Lesaka's house, wander around, pick up the radio and leave no fingerprints? He can hardly speak Setswana. How would he know about fingerprints?'

After a moment, Abram responded. 'The fact that he doesn't speak Setswana doesn't mean he's stupid. We know nothing about him. He just appeared from nowhere.' He paused, then added, 'Maybe it is a vendetta, as the kgosi suggested, and finding the skeletons set it off again.'

'He didn't shoot Zondo twenty-five years ago. He's not old enough.'

Abram shrugged. 'Maybe the vendetta runs across generations.'

Kubu said nothing. He had no idea what was going on, but he was still sure Selelo hadn't murdered Mma Zondo and Lesaka.

CHAPTER 33

When the kgosi and his son arrived at the police station, the station commander brought them to the meeting room. Clearly, he wanted all of them to appreciate his triumph.

Kubu was surprised by how the kgosi had changed in the week since they'd first met. The previously confident man now looked old and tired.

'What's he doing here?' Raseelo demanded, pointing at Mabaku.

'He's the senior detective investigating the murder cases,' Balopi replied.

'Well, he did a lousy job. By the grace of God my father survived. No thanks to him. He—'

The kgosi frowned. 'All right, let's get on with it.'

Balopi nodded. 'Of course. Please tell us exactly what happened, kgosi.'

'I showed out a visitor, and as I was returning to the house, the Bushman pounced, held a knife to my throat, spouting all sorts of nonsense, saying he was going to kill me.'

'What exactly did he say?' Mabaku asked.

'That I'd killed his people. That now I must die. Even that I was his father!'

'His father?' Balopi asked. 'He said you were his father?'

'Yes, when he had the knife to my throat.'

'How could you be his father?'

'He was raving. He said I'd attacked his mother. It was all nonsense.'

Kubu thought the accusation about killing Selelo's people was more significant. 'Why would he think you'd killed Bushmen?'

The kgosi frowned. 'I just told you. He was raving. He's mad.'

'Why didn't he kill you at once?' Mabaku asked.

'He wanted me to admit to everything, but I refused. Then when he dug the knife into my throat, I shouted for help. Raseelo heard me and had the presence of mind to bring a rifle. He shot him just as he was about to kill me.'

Raseelo confirmed that he'd heard his father shouting. He'd grabbed the gun and rushed out to find the kgosi on the ground with the Bushman on top of him, holding a knife to his throat. He'd shot the man in the shoulder. 'I wish I'd killed him. I wanted to. They wouldn't let me finish him off.'

The detectives asked about the details, and it was clear that the kgosi and his son were telling the truth. When the interview was over, Abram wrote down a statement from each of them.

'I'll have the statements typed up and bring them over for you to sign this evening,' Balopi said. He turned to Mabaku. 'I'll be charging the Bushman with attempted murder. Do you have any comment about that, Assistant Superintendent?'

Mabaku shook his head.

Raseelo snorted. 'I should think not. We'll be lodging a complaint about you with the commissioner of police, Mabaku.'

'Did you bring the knife?' Ian asked. 'I need to see it. There are still the two murders to resolve.'

Balopi nodded. 'I have it.' He asked Abram to fetch it from his office, then added, 'It's obvious the Bushman is the culprit. But you Gaborone experts wouldn't spot a murderer if you tripped over him, would you?'

Turning to the kgosi, he said, 'I'll take you to your car. I can't tell you how sorry I am about this whole business. It should never have happened.'

~

Abram returned with the knife sealed in a clear-plastic evidence bag. Ian examined it carefully, then made some measurements. He looked sombre when he'd finished.

'Of course, I can't say this was the knife used to kill the others, but it's pretty much the right length and width. That'll be human blood on it, but it'll be from the kgosi. Forensics should run their tests and check DNA, but it's a long shot that they'll be able to match anything to Lesaka or Mma Zondo.'

While they were digesting that, he stood up. 'I'm going to see the Bushman. I want to be sure he's getting proper medical attention.'

'And we need to be sure it actually is Selelo,' Kubu said.

Mabaku nodded. 'I want to hear his side of the story, but that will have to wait. I need to talk to the director right away. He should hear about this from me, not Balopi. The two of you go.'

~

This time the station commander enjoyed his call with the assistant commissioner.

'There's no doubt about it? There were witnesses?' his boss asked when Balopi had finished his story.

'The kgosi's son and daughter were there, and a neighbour shortly afterwards. It's a miracle the kgosi wasn't killed like the others.'

'You have the knife?'

'Yes, and the pathologist is pretty sure it's the one used in the other murders. We'll send it off for detailed forensics.'

'So we were right about that Bushman all along.'

Balopi smiled. 'Yes, rra, *we* were right.'

'I'm surprised that the CID's best man had the wool pulled over his eyes so easily, but then nothing is as good as the man on the ground who knows his stuff. I'll report to the commissioner right away. Good work, Assistant Superintendent.'

Balopi was still smiling when the call ended. It was amazing how quickly his fortunes had turned around. It couldn't have worked out better if he'd set it up himself. He could almost feel sorry for Mabaku. But he didn't. Not in the slightest.

∼

When Ian and Kubu reached the clinic, they found the Bushman with his left arm handcuffed to the bed and his right bandaged and in a sling. There were bruises on his face, and a plaster covered part of his forehead. An armed constable was on guard outside the door. There was no doubt that it was Selelo.

The doctor was checking him when they walked in. 'You can't come in here. This man's seriously injured.'

When Ian identified himself, the doctor relented and was willing to discuss his patient. After they'd talked through the situation for a while, Ian summarised the medical jargon for Kubu.

'He was shot in the right shoulder – pretty much as the kgosi's son described. He was lucky; the bullet went straight through without doing too much damage along the way. The scapula is shattered, and the movement of his shoulder may be permanently affected. He's also been beaten up. The kgosi didn't mention that. His son's doing, I'd guess. He's sedated, and he'll be in quite a lot of pain once the drugs wear off. I'm going to hang on here for a while until he wakes up.'

Kubu said he would stay as well.

∼

Selelo had been feigning unconsciousness in the hope the policemen would leave. The pain had dulled, and he felt as he did when he danced, detached as though he was watching himself from outside his body.

He'd discovered that his wrist was encased in a metal ring that was fixed to the bed he was lying on. The ring was tight, and he realised he'd never get his hand out through it. He was fixed to the earth, but surely, he thought desperately, it only holds my body, not my spirit. Surely I can still join the ancestors.

That thought brought sorrow. He had failed. He should have killed the man at once. Then the other man would have killed him, and by now he'd be with the ancestors. He'd needed to be sure, to hear the man admit that he was his father and that he'd attacked his mother and killed his ancestors, but he shouldn't have delayed. He should have trusted – believed – that the ancestors had guided him to the right man.

So he had failed. He would join the ancestors because the policeman would certainly kill him now, but would they accept him?

He groaned.

Kubu leant over the bed. 'Selelo? Selelo? Are you awake? Are you in pain?'

Selelo opened his eyes and saw that it was the hippopotamus. He always seemed to turn up when something was needed. Was he also somehow a tool of the ancestors?

'Water. Thirsty. Water.'

Kubu filled a glass and helped Selelo drink.

'Tired.'

'You can sleep.'

Selelo shook his head weakly. 'Tired of here. Want be there. With them.'

'With who?'

'Ancestors. Be with ancestors. Not here.' He rattled the handcuffs. The room was much bigger than his cell had been, but he knew that soon it would start to shrink.

'I'm sorry, Selelo. You're in very bad trouble. Why did you attack that man?'

'Man bad. Father. Kill ancestors. Attack mother.'

'He killed your father?'

Selelo shook his head. 'Man is father. Selelo father.' He shook his head again. 'Tired.' He closed his eyes.

∽

As Selelo drifted between waking and sleeping, the story his uncle had told him years before returned to him.

After he was born, his mother left him with his aunt and uncle, who always said it was because she wanted him to have a happy life. But why?

'Her story,' he said aloud. 'Mother story.'

It was only at the time he was allowed to hunt by himself that he heard the true story about the killings and the rape of his mother. How the men had thought she was dead and how she'd dragged herself away. She'd managed to reach another group of Bushmen some distance away and warned them. They helped her reach her sister, who lived at the sacred Tsodilo Hills. It was her family that had brought him up.

'Four men. Horses. Guns. Kill.'

He was shocked when he heard the story, scared that he wasn't even a proper Bushman, but his uncle had assured him that he was. The ancestors would accept him if he danced for them. So he did. And after that he knew there was a task for him, and if he succeeded, everything would be all right.

Some time later, he asked his uncle if his mother had identified the man who raped her. At first his uncle refused to discuss it, but at last he showed him a pencil sketch of a horse. The horse's chest was shaded in, except for a bold white stripe that forked at the neck. 'The man who had this horse,' his uncle told him.

'Horse. White mark on chest. Like two rivers meet.'

And later still the ancestors had told him he must kill this man, then he could join them. So he'd searched for the horse and found it, then searched for the man and found him. And it was that man he had to kill.

'Man with horse attack mother. Must kill. Ancestors tell me.'

∼

The story came out in a mixture of Setswana and Selelo's own language, with Kubu sometimes gently prompting him to repeat what he'd said. Slowly, Kubu pieced it all together.

When Selelo had finished his story, his breathing became heavy and regular. Kubu realised that now the Bushman could sleep.

CHAPTER 34

When Ian and Kubu returned to the police station, Mabaku was in a foul mood. Obviously, the call with the director had gone badly. Kubu thought that he'd cheer him up by telling him what he'd learnt from Selelo.

'Rra, I had a long conversation with Selelo between the times he was falling asleep. He told me that he wanted to kill the kgosi. He said it was because he—'

'You did what?' Mabaku exploded. 'He's been arrested for attempted murder, and you're discussing the case with him. He has the right to a lawyer. Did you offer him one?'

'No, rra. I didn't think—'

'Obviously. Did you even caution him?'

Kubu admitted that he had not. 'But, rra, I didn't question him. He was just talking. He was half asleep from the drugs. It wasn't an interview at all.'

'And you just sat there without encouraging him, without asking him to clarify something he'd said? Not a chance you sat there with your big mouth shut.'

'I'm sorry, rra. It won't happen again.'

'Well, it can't be used in evidence, and it may cause problems later on, especially if he's charged with the murders. Was anyone else there?'

'Only Ian. He was worried about him.'

Mabaku mulled over what had happened and eventually decided that what was done was done. 'Well? What did he say?'

Kubu explained the story of the massacre, and the rape by the man on the horse with the strange white marking.

'Rra, it was the kgosi. He said the mark was Y-shaped "like two rivers joining". When we interviewed Mma Zondo, she showed us a photograph of her husband and the kgosi on horses as young men. I was struck by the odd forking white mark on the kgosi's horse's chest.'

'There are probably many horses like that. And even if it is the kgosi's, what does that prove? The Bushman wasn't even there. This was his mother's story.'

Kubu thought about that. 'That's true. But now we have a line to consider, don't we? If the kgosi was involved in the massacre...'

Mabaku nodded. 'But we'll have to find another reason for looking into that. The director would fire me if I used your information and it got out.

'We'll have to start with a proper interview of the Bushman tomorrow morning, and he'll need to have a lawyer there representing him. Get on to Abram and see if he can arrange to get someone appointed. We must move this forward quickly now.'

Selelo looked around the hospital room at all the people gathered there. He was pleased to see the hippopotamus. He usually helped. There was also the other man who'd asked cross questions before, but hadn't hit him. He'd said his name was Mabaku.

And there was the angry man who beat him. He was also there.

Then there was the man who called himself Lawyer, a strange name. Selelo didn't understand why he was there. He'd said that Selelo didn't need to answer questions if he didn't want to. But why wouldn't he? He'd tell the truth. If he didn't answer the questions, then the angry man would certainly beat him again.

Mabaku pressed something on a black box next to his bed. Then he made a speech, and asked him if he understood. He said he did even though he didn't, because he was afraid of the angry man. He just wanted it all to be over as soon as possible.

Then Mabaku asked what had happened the day before, and he told the story of what he'd done. Next, Mabaku asked why he'd attacked the kgosi, and he explained that the kgosi and three others had killed many of his people. Then the kgosi had attacked his mother. The kgosi was his father.

Selelo looked at the men around his bed. He could tell that they didn't believe him. That didn't matter. It was true.

'What a load of bullshit.' Balopi took a step forward, and Mabaku put his arm out to stop him. 'How can you let him say such nonsense? Look at him. Does he look like a Motswana?'

'How do you know the kgosi is your father?'

Selelo shook his head. He'd already told the hippopotamus what had happened. 'Uncle tell me.'

Mabaku asked him several more questions that didn't make sense. He couldn't understand why they continued, because he'd told them the truth. They should believe him.

Eventually Mabaku took a deep breath. 'Where did you get the knife, Selelo? Did you bring it from Tsodilo?'

'Knife from people. People where the ancestors died.'

Eventually, they understood that he'd stolen it. He didn't like to steal things, but he had to have it. He tried to explain that too. They didn't care about that, but they seemed to be very interested in where he got the knife. It seemed a small matter to him.

Then they asked if he'd killed two other people. He knew nothing about them. He said so, but they asked him over and over again. Eventually the man who called himself Lawyer started talking a lot, and soon after that, they all left. Selelo knew they would come back.

He closed his eyes – he was very tired. He thought about his ancestors and wondered when he could join them. He hoped it would be soon. The walls were starting to close in around him again.

≈

'I've never heard such nonsense,' Balopi said as they sat down around the meeting-room table. 'You can't believe a word he says.'

'Let's look at this step by step,' Mabaku said. 'Do we all agree that Selelo attempted to murder the kgosi?'

'Of course he did.' Balopi was struggling to keep his temper under control.

'What about Lesaka?' Mabaku continued.

'You're wasting our time, Mabaku. Who else could have done it?'

'For one minute, station commander, let's pretend we're in court. Please lay out your evidence. "Who else could have done it?" is unlikely to persuade anyone. Let's start with motive. What was his?'

'It's obvious. He thought Lesaka was one of the men who killed some Bushmen.'

'Evidence, Balopi, please. That's not evidence. In fact, he denies knowing Lesaka.'

'Well, of course he does.'

'What is your evidence that he had a motive to murder Lesaka? Or Mma Zondo, for that matter? Selelo said it was four men, not three men and a woman, who attacked the Bushmen.'

'He just wanted revenge on any Motswana he could find. He wasn't there. He wasn't even born.'

'Okay, assuming he wanted revenge, what evidence do we have that he was at Lesaka's? None, as far as I know. And even if he was there, what evidence do we have that he killed Lesaka? None, as far as I know.'

'The knife, dammit. It's the same knife. He buried it in the desert after killing Lesaka. Now he's used it again.'

'And how do we know that?'

'Your pathologist said so.'

Kubu couldn't take it any more. 'No he didn't. He didn't say that it was the actual knife used on Lesaka and Zondo. He said the blade *could have* inflicted the wounds on the other two. As could any knife with a similar blade.'

The tone of the meeting didn't improve. Balopi insisted that they had enough evidence to convict Selelo for two murders and an attempted murder. The Gaborone detectives insisted that they only had enough evidence for the attempted murder.

Eventually Mabaku held up his hand to stop the bickering. 'There is something we can do now,' he said. 'We can go and tell the kgosi what the Bushman said, and see if he can shed some light on the Bushman massacre. I know we've asked him before, but another round of questions won't harm anyone.'

∽

Mabaku, Kubu, Balopi and Abram piled into a police Land Rover and drove to the kgosi's house in Ncamasere. He was startled when he opened the door to Mabaku's knocking.

'What's this about?'

'We interviewed the Bushman who attacked you this morning,' Mabaku said. 'We'd like to ask a few follow-up questions, if you have a few minutes.'

The kgosi nodded and invited them to his lounge. 'Please sit down, I'll have my daughter make some tea.'

He returned a few moments later and sat down. 'So what do you want to know?'

'The Bushman insists that you were one of the men who killed a group of Bushmen many years ago – perhaps those that we dug up recently.'

'Dammit, Assistant Superintendent. Why do you believe him over me?'

'I didn't say we believed what he said. We're just following up on what he said – to see if it's true or not.'

The kgosi shook his head. 'I can assure you that I did no such thing. Why would I?'

'He has a second accusation: he says you raped his mother, and that you are his father.'

The kgosi jumped to his feet. 'That's ridiculous. If I wasn't there, wherever "there" is, how could I have done anything to his mother?' He turned to the station commander. 'How can you let the Bushman tell such a pack of lies? Lock him up and throw away the key.'

'That's what I want to do, but these ... these detectives from the big city believe everything he says.'

Kubu wondered how his boss was going to react. However, Mabaku said nothing.

'I tell you what, Assistant Superintendent,' the kgosi continued, 'I'll take one of those tests to check if I'm his father. You can arrange that, can't you?'

'For God's sake, kgosi, there's no need to do that,' the station commander said. 'We all believe you.'

'You don't understand, Balopi. It's the only way to get these lies off my back. If rumours start floating around that I did such a terrible thing, my reputation would be ruined. The water project would be in jeopardy.' He turned to Mabaku. 'You'll arrange that, won't you? Maybe with your pathologist?'

CHAPTER 35

O n the way back to the police station, Mabaku sat in the front with Balopi. Not a word was said between them, but Kubu and Abram could sense the tension. Kubu rolled his eyes, and Abram managed a tentative smile.

When they arrived, Balopi stalked off to his office and slammed the door. Abram, embarrassed by the ill-feeling between the two assistant superintendents, said he had work to do. Kubu and Mabaku headed for the conference room, where they found Ian waiting for them. On the table was a large evidence bag containing what was clearly a badly damaged human skull.

'They found bits of another skeleton while you were busy with the kgosi,' he told them. 'I went out with a constable to take a look. It was near where we found Ezekiel Zondo's remains. We've taped off the area, and the constable is digging around, looking for the rest.' He gave a wry smile. 'The contractor is beside himself. His whole team has walked off the job. They won't work at the dam site, and they won't touch the area where the Bushman skeletons were found. I'm afraid the kgosi's project is going to be delayed for quite some time.'

'Is it a Motswana?' Kubu asked.

Ian nodded. 'It is. The skeleton was badly damaged in the excavation, most of it is broken up, but luckily the skull survived in reasonable shape.'

'It must be Tandi Dibotelo,' Kubu said. 'Unless it's a child?'

'No, it's an adult.'

'Can you take a guess at the cause of death?' Mabaku asked.

Ian frowned. 'I don't make guesses. Look at this.' He held up the skull so that they could see the jagged hole in the forehead. 'He's been shot. Given the state of the skeleton, I was initially concerned that the damage to the skull might be post mortem, but on careful examination I can tell that's not the case. Look here.' He showed them how the forehead bone had warped inward at the top of the cavity. 'It was flexible when the damage occurred. After all these years, it would have just shattered had it been hit by the bulldozer. This was caused by a bullet.' He turned the skull around so that they could see the back. 'And there's the exit damage.'

'A rifle, same as Zondo?'

'Could be. Or a handgun at close range. But I'm certain he was shot.'

Kubu looked pensive. 'And at the same location as Zondo, who disappeared a few weeks earlier. If it is Dibotelo, there must be a connection between the two.'

Mabaku nodded. 'Of course, we don't know that they were murdered there. The killer could have brought the bodies there to bury them.'

Kubu turned to Mabaku. 'Rra, you said we needed another way to implicate the kgosi because I'd questioned Selelo inappropriately. This seems to be the kgosi's words against the Bushman's. But what if we tell Dibotelo that we've found a skeleton of a man who'd been murdered and that it could be his son, maybe he'll open up about what he heard concerning the massacre.'

Mabaku thought for a few moments. 'Let's go and ask him. Thanks, Ian. You better report all this to the station commander. Then please see what else you can discover from the skeleton. Also, if you have time, please check with the clinic whether they can do blood typing.'

Ian looked puzzled. 'Blood typing? You mean finding out if someone has A, B, or O blood type?'

Mabaku nodded. 'The kgosi denies he's Selelo's father and is willing to have his blood tested. I'm sure you can persuade Selelo to give some blood too.'

'But—'

'Tell me later when we link up at Drotsky's.'

On the way out, Mabaku signed out the knife in its evidence bag. Kubu guessed they would also be paying a visit to the protesters.

As they headed to Mabaku's vehicle, he felt his excitement building. The case was finally starting to fall into place.

~

Once again, they found Dibotelo dealing with his vegetable garden.

'This was your idea, Kubu,' Mabaku pointed out. 'Let's see what you can make of it.'

Kubu nodded. This was his chance to redeem himself for the mistake he'd made by talking to Selelo. He called out to Dibotelo, and the man walked over.

'You again. What do you want now?' It wasn't a promising start.

'Dumela, rra,' Kubu responded, 'can we talk inside?'

Without a word, Dibotelo turned and led them into the house.

'Rra,' Kubu began once they were settled, 'we have more news.'

Dibotelo's body tensed.

'We've found another Motswana skeleton. It's badly damaged, but we believe it may be your son.'

For a few moments, Dibotelo said nothing. Then, in a choked voice, he asked, 'Damaged? How?'

'The bones were discovered at the dam site where Ezekial Zondo's remains were found, but the earth-moving machines had broken the skeleton. However, our pathologist recovered the skull. It's damaged in a different way. I'm very sorry to tell you that the man was shot, probably murdered.'

'It is Tandi? You're sure?'

Kubu shook his head. 'We've no way to be sure at the moment. They're still collecting bones. But no other adult Batswana are missing in the area, so it seems likely that it's him.'

'Murdered.' Dibotelo's body shook with supressed sobs.

Imagining how his own father would feel if he was told of his son's death, Kubu said, 'Rra, we're very sorry for your loss.'

It took a while for Dibotelo to pull himself together. He shook his head. '*My* loss was a long time ago, detective. I'm weeping for *his* loss, for the life he had stolen from him.'

Despite his sympathy for the man, Kubu realised Dibotelo had given him an opening for his questions. 'Rra, we now think that the murders may all be connected, starting with the massacre of the Bushmen. We have to catch this murderer so the victims receive justice – including your son – but also to stop him from killing again. We need your help. You told us you'd heard rumours. We need to know who told you those rumours and just what was said. If we can trace the killers of the Bushmen, we believe we'll find the murderer of your son.'

Kubu held his breath, but he needn't have worried. Dibotelo responded at once.

'Last time, I told you that the men came from outside this area. That wasn't true. What I heard was that it was four local men.' He paused. 'And that one of them was the son of the kgosi at that time. The man who is our present kgosi.'

'And the others?' Mabaku asked.

He shook his head. 'I don't know. But they would have been his friends.'

Kubu took up the questioning again. 'So, who were his friends?'

Dibotelo shrugged. 'He was the kgosi's son. All the young men wanted to be his friends.'

'Lesaka, Zondo?'

He nodded. 'They were his best friends.'

'And who else?'

'I don't remember. It was so long ago. I recall he was always with Zondo and Lesaka in those days. Later...' He shrugged.

'They fell out later?' Mabaku wanted to know.

'They were not as close once he became kgosi. Zondo liked to drink with his friends, and I think he talked too much for the kgosi's liking. Even at the last kgotla, the kgosi warned us not to talk to outsiders, although Lesaka said maybe it was time to speak of these things. The kgosi was clearly upset by that.'

'And who told you about the kgosi and the other three attacking the Bushmen?'

'It was a man who was also a friend of the kgosi then. He said he heard it from one of the attackers. But he hadn't been with them himself, when they attacked the Bushmen.'

'What's his name? Where can we find him?'

'I can tell you his name, but he left here many years ago. He said he'd never come back, that he'd change his name. I think he was scared. I never saw him again after that.'

Kubu wrote down the details, but wasn't optimistic they'd find the man. He imagined that thirty years earlier it would have been easy to switch names if you wanted to disappear.

'Why did he tell you about all this?' Mabaku asked.

'We were drinking friends. Now, I never drink. It only leads to trouble.'

Kubu tore a sheet from his notebook and passed it to Dibotelo. 'Rra, Lesaka and Mma Zondo were both murdered. The kgosi has an alibi for the murders. So we need to know who the fourth attacker was. He must have been one of the kgosi's friends. Please make a list of all the men from around this area who are about the same age as the kgosi. And the addresses if you have them.'

Dibotelo nodded. He wrote for several minutes, stopping to think from time to time, then asked for another sheet of paper, then wrote again. Finally, he handed over the pages. Kubu sighed. There were more than twenty names. 'Did all these men know him?' he asked.

Dibotelo nodded. 'He was the kgosi's son.'

Mabaku rose to his feet, and Kubu realised that they'd learnt all they were going to. He thanked Dibotelo for his time and was about to turn away when Dibotelo grabbed his shoulder. 'I know why you came here today.'

Kubu looked at him without speaking.

'You wanted to know about the four men.'

After a moment Kubu nodded. 'But it is true, what we've told you about Tandi.'

'I believe you,' Dibotelo responded. 'And it's all right now. I will have his bones, and I can honour him and bury him. Then I can rest.'

'We will find the man who killed him.'

Dibotelo shook his head. 'I can rest,' he repeated.

'What do you think?' Kubu asked tentatively when they left. He hoped Mabaku didn't have a problem with anything he'd done.

'I think he's telling the truth. And I think Selelo is telling the truth. That makes the kgosi a murderer and a rapist, and quite likely corrupt as well, but we don't have a shred of evidence against him. Selelo heard a story from his uncle, who supposedly heard it from Selelo's mother. Dibotelo heard a rumour from a man who's probably impossible to find, and anyway wasn't present at the event. It's all hearsay.'

Kubu realised he was right. They may have their suspicions, but they had nothing the people of Ncamasere would believe, let alone a court. 'What Lesaka said at the kgotla could be a motive for his murder. Maybe it wasn't the first time he'd suggested coming clean.'

'That's true, but the kgosi didn't murder Lesaka or Mma Zondo.'

'What about Raseelo? He seems to be violent enough.'

Mabaku nodded. 'But he also has alibis, although they rely on his family. And what would be his motive? Murdering two people to cover up for his father?'

'If the kgosi is disgraced, he may be denied succession.'

Mabaku thought for a moment. 'I suppose it's possible, but he wasn't involved in Zondo's death twenty-five years ago.' He shook his head. 'I think it was the fourth man. And his name is probably on Dibotelo's list.'

As they climbed into the Land Rover, Mabaku said they were going to stop at the excavation to ask about the knife. 'The protesters will still be there. I doubt they'll have left because of the station commander. He'll never charge them – they'll laugh in his face. And I'm sure he doesn't like that.'

When they arrived, the protestors immediately formed a group, linking arms. The two reporters grabbed their cameras and readied themselves for more action. Mabaku told Kubu to wait, then walked towards them. He stopped about ten paces away. 'Good afternoon. I am Assistant Superintendent Mabaku from Gaborone. I'm not here to cause any problems, but to ask some questions. Is there someone who can act as spokesman?'

'Go away! Go away!' The group broke into a chant. 'Go away!'

Kubu waited for his boss to explode. However, Mabaku just stood in front of the group. After a while, he shouted, 'I have news of Selelo, the Bushman. He asked me to come and talk to you.'

Kubu wondered whether it was legal to tell a lie.

The group continued singing, but a man in the centre leant over and spoke to the woman next to him. That must be the leader, Kubu thought.

Eventually, the man raised his hands and told the rest to stop.

'You said you had questions. Then you said you had news. Which is it?'

'Both,' Mabaku replied. 'First the news. Selelo has been arrested for attempted murder—'

'Bullshit!'

'Bushmen don't kill!'

'Go away!' The chant broke out again.

To Kubu's surprise, Mabaku just stood patiently.

'Let me finish before you make up your minds.'

The chanting continued for a few minutes, then petered out.

'Selelo tried to kill the local kgosi – and there are several witnesses. There is no doubt.'

Members of the group muttered to each other.

'Why should we believe you?' It was the man in the middle talking.

'It's your choice to believe or not to believe. All I can do is give you the facts. And the fact is that Selelo tried to murder the kgosi.'

'That's not true,' the woman retorted. 'He said he wanted to go to Tsodilo Hills.'

'Did he say why he came here instead of going to Tsodilo Hills?'

'He was hungry.' It was the man who answered. 'He wasn't strong enough to walk there.'

'When did he leave?'

'When the policemen came to kill him,' one of the other protestors shouted.

Mabaku shook his head. 'I don't understand. Which policemen?'

Several of the protestors pointed at the constables, who were sitting in front of their tents.

'Did the constables tell you they were going to kill Selelo?'

'Selelo said they were going to,' one replied.

'What happened then?'

'We stopped them.'

'And what did Selelo do?'

It was the leader who replied. 'He must have been scared, because he disappeared. We never saw him again.'

Mabaku thought for a few moments. 'I appreciate your answering those questions. I just have one more.' He hesitated. 'After Selelo had left, did you notice anything missing?'

A woman with a gaudy apron responded. 'What sort of thing?'

'Anything. Food, clothing.'

Kubu noticed how defiant the woman looked.

The woman shook her head. 'Nobody's mentioned anything.'

Mabaku looked around at the group. 'Anybody notice something missing?'

There was no response.

'You are probably wondering why I've asked you that question,' Mabaku said quietly. 'You may not know that two people in the area have been murdered recently. Both stabbed to death. When we arrested Selelo after he attacked the kgosi, he had a knife that could have caused the wounds that killed those two.' He paused, then continued. 'If Selelo has had that knife all the time, he'll be charged with two counts of murder and one of attempted murder. The sentence for the two murders would likely be hanging.'

Several of the protesters looked shocked.

'On the other hand,' Mabaku continued, 'if Selelo acquired the knife recently, there would be no evidence that he committed the murders, and he'd only be charged with attempted murder, for which there'd only be a prison sentence.'

There was a buzz of conversation among the protestors, and Kubu saw the leader and the woman next to him in animated conversation. Eventually the man held up his hand. 'We don't believe you. We think you're trying to trap Selelo for something he hasn't done.'

Mabaku looked around at the men and women in front of him. 'Thank you for your time. If you are concealing information, which I think you are, please come to the trial and watch your friend sentenced to death. I'm sure you won't enjoy living the rest of your life knowing you could have prevented such a fate. That will give me some satisfaction.'

With that, Mabaku turned and walked back to the Land Rover.

Just as he started the engine, the woman with the apron ran over and banged on the window. She was crying.

Mabaku wound the window down, but said nothing.

'He took a knife,' she sobbed. 'My kitchen knife.'

Kubu expected Mabaku to explode, but he didn't. 'Please describe the knife,' he said.

'It's a carving knife about twenty centimetres long with a black plastic handle.'

'Does it have any marks on it that you'd recognise?'

The woman nodded. 'I dropped it into a campfire last year. The handle was damaged.'

Mabaku picked up the evidence bag next to him. 'Is this it? Please don't take it out of the bag.'

The woman grabbed the bag and inspected it closely, holding the plastic close to the handle. She nodded. 'That's mine. He must have taken it when the other policeman was beating up Baruti.'

Mabaku nodded. 'Thank you, mma. Will you make a statement to that effect?'

The woman said she would, and the detectives left feeling satisfied with the afternoon's work.

≈

As soon as they returned to Drotsky's Cabins, Mabaku and Kubu joined Ian for a cold beer. He was seated at their favourite table overlooking the Kavango river, making pencil sketches of the vista.

'I didn't know you were so good,' Kubu said as he looked over Ian's shoulder.

Ian nodded his thanks and continued shading the steep sides of the river.

'What did you find out about the blood testing?' Mabaku obviously hadn't started unwinding.

Ian looked peeved as he closed his sketchbook. 'Do you want a lecture on ABO blood typing or just the bottom line?'

'Just tell me what you know.'

'It's clear that you don't fully understand how blood types are passed from one generation to another. Because, if you did, you would know that learning anything useful was highly unlikely.'

Mabaku frowned, but didn't say anything.

Ian drained his beer and signalled the waiter for another. 'After I found that the clinic could do the blood typing, I explained to Selelo what I wanted to do and asked his permission to take blood. He was only too pleased to let me. I left the sample at the clinic and drove to the kgosi's house. He, too, was keen to let me take a few millilitres of his blood. I returned to the clinic, and they typed his blood also.'

Ian took the new beer from the waiter, poured a glass, and took a large mouthful. 'Hmm, nothing better on a hot African day.'

Kubu was watching Mabaku's patience slowly wearing thin. His fingers were drumming on the table, and his right foot was tapping. Kubu silently urged Ian to get on with the story.

'When Selelo's blood type came back as O, my fears were realised. That's what I was trying to tell you when you left for Dibotelo's. O blood type is the most common and can be from parents who are O, A, or B types. Those three groups account for ninety-five percent of the Batswana peoples. When the kgosi's blood type came back as AB, I was gobsmacked. That's the only blood type that can't produce offspring with O blood.'

No one spoke for a few moments, then Kubu responded despondently. 'That means that the kgosi can't be Selelo's father, right?'

Ian nodded.

'And I believed what Selelo told us.' Kubu gazed at the dirt at his feet.

'Have you told Selelo and the kgosi?' Mabaku asked.

Ian took another large mouthful of beer. 'That's your job, Assistant Superintendent. Not mine.'

CHAPTER 36

After dinner, Kubu looked through the list of names Dibotelo had given him. The only name he recognised was Assistant Superintendent Balopi. That wasn't surprising since he'd claimed to be an old friend of Lesaka, so they would be in the same age group.

His heart sank as he imagined following up with each person on the list. He'd need Abram's help or he'd never find them. And what would he ask them? He could hardly ask if they'd massacred Bushmen and murdered Batswana decades ago.

Then something did occur to him. Suppose he assumed that one of the men who'd taken part in the massacre was responsible for all the murders – Zondo and young Dibotelo twenty-five years ago, as well as the two current murders of Lesaka and Mma Zondo. In that case, he could concentrate just on the current murders and ask each man on the list where he was at the times they were killed. He thought it was a long shot, but at least it was something.

When Kubu explained his idea the next morning at breakfast, Mabaku nodded. 'I think that makes sense. There's really nothing else we can do with the list, and frankly we need some luck to break this case. Everyone from the director to the commissioner is unhappy with us right now.'

'I'll get hold of Abram to help me. Perhaps we can talk to them all today. We can skip the station commander, of course.'

Mabaku smiled. 'Let's ask him too. Stir him up a bit.'

Kubu could imagine what would happen if he tried that, and his reaction must have been clear from his face. Mabaku laughed. 'Don't worry. I'll ask him. You and Abram concentrate on the others.' He checked his watch. 'I need to call the kgosi. Then we can head out.'

~

Mabaku walked to reception, and a few minutes later he had the kgosi on the line.

'Dumela, kgosi. I have some news. The blood tests came back indicating you are type AB, which is quite unusual for a Motswana. Only about five percent of the Batswana population has that blood type.'

'And the Bushman?'

'The Bushman was type O.'

'I told you that I wasn't the father.'

Mabaku decided not to explain the intricacies of blood-type inheritance, both because it would only muddy the waters, and because he wasn't sure he understood it well enough to answer the inevitable questions.

'That is now certain, kgosi. It's not possible for you to be the father, no matter the blood type of the mother. You can put that accusation to rest.'

After a moment, the kgosi asked, 'Do you think that the Bushman is the result of a rape?'

Even though the kgosi was at the end of a phone line, Mabaku shook his head. 'I've no way of knowing. Dr MacGregor tells me that there are now more sophisticated tests that can provide information about the genetic make-up of someone's parents. But that information won't help us find the actual father.'

Mabaku heard a sigh on the end of the line. Of relief, he thought.

'Thank you, Assistant Superintendent. That's the best news

I've had for a while. Now, please can you wrap up your investigations and leave us to finish the water project.'

~

When they reached the police station, Mabaku dispatched Kubu to inform Selelo of the results of the blood tests, then went to the station commander's office. Balopi pointed to a seat and said, 'I want to get that Bushman into a cell as soon as the clinic releases him. I called them this morning, but they said he isn't doing so well. Probably he's putting it on. Enjoying being coddled. He won't get that here, I promise you. Now, what do you want?'

'A few things. First, to update you on the blood tests. Dr MacGregor took the samples, and the clinic did the blood typing yesterday afternoon. The kgosi is AB and the Bushman is O. That means it's impossible that the kgosi is his father.'

Balopi smiled coldly. 'Well, of course it is. It was just another story he made up to pull the wool over your gullible eyes.'

'One story he didn't make up was the issue of the knife. I checked with the protesters yesterday afternoon, and it's theirs. Selelo stole it from them on Monday night. So nothing connects him to the murders of Lesaka and Mma Zondo.'

'Of course they would say that. They'd say anything to cover up for him. To them a lovable Bushman can't be a murderer.'

'The owner of the knife correctly described it before I showed it to her. She said she'd come in and make a formal statement today.'

Balopi frowned. 'Well, so what? So he stole another knife somewhere. It's obvious to everyone except you that he's the culprit. He tried to kill the kgosi and then made up that ridiculous story about the kgosi raping his mother. And remember that he confessed to the Lesaka murder.'

Mabaku sighed and let it go. He was never going to change the station commander's mind until he had proof of the Bushman's innocence.

'I've been pursuing another line of enquiry that goes back to the Bushman massacre. We've been told that four young men from around here carried out the attack, and that it took place about thirty-five years ago.'

'That was the Bushman's story. What on earth makes you believe it?'

'We've heard rumours from a number of sources,' Mabaku responded. 'We think that one of those men may be responsible for all the other murders too – Mma Zondo and her husband, Lesaka, and the young Dibotelo.'

'What have they got to do with the Bushmen? Are you suggesting they were involved in this massacre as you call it? That's ridiculous. Lesaka and Zondo were greatly respected members of the community, Dibotelo was much too young, and Mma Zondo was a woman. It's all complete nonsense. The murderer is down the road in the clinic!'

'He couldn't have murdered Zondo and Dibotelo. He would have been too young,' Mabaku pointed out. He paused, but Balopi had no response for that.

'We've made a list of men still living around here who were young in Ncamasere at the time of the massacre. We're checking where each was on the nights of the murders of Lesaka and Mma Zondo.'

'You're the detective,' Balopi sneered. 'Waste your time however you like.'

'Right. You're on the list so I'd like to know where you were on the nights of the twenty-fourth and twenty-ninth of April.'

For a moment the Balopi looked confused, then he exploded. 'What? You're asking *me* where I was? Treating *me* as a suspect? That's outrageous! I won't let you get away with this.'

When Mabaku responded, his voice was dangerously quiet. 'I'm not treating you as a suspect. I'm following procedure. We're asking everyone on the list for this information. Everyone. I can't make exceptions.'

The station commander took his time before responding. Mabaku had expected more anger, but Balopi seemed to have calmed down.

'Very well. You know where I was the night Lesaka was killed. I was at his house, investigating.'

'What about before that?'

'Before that I was at home. I live alone. I made some dinner, then I watched television. When the station called, I was watching some current affairs programme about the president opening a new shopping centre or something. And, no, no one can verify that. You'll just have to take my word for it.'

Mabaku nodded. 'And last Friday night?'

'I worked here late. Then I went home, had supper and watched some movie on television. Robin Hood. Some stupid American rubbish where the thief is the hero and the police are the villains.'

Mabaku noted it down. He was actually impressed that Balopi remembered what he'd been watching. He could never recall what had been on television.

'Is there anything else?'

Mabaku shook his head and left without another word. He headed out of the station to his vehicle. His next stop was to talk to Tembo, the contractor for the water project.

The duty nurse at the clinic told Kubu that Selelo hadn't eaten or drunk anything since they'd seen him the day before. 'I think he's trying to commit suicide,' she said. 'He keeps complaining that the walls of his room are closing in on him.'

'I think that's a psychological reaction to being cooped up,' Kubu responded. 'I've read that Bushmen can die when deprived of the freedom they're used to.'

'Please try to get him to drink some water, at least. That's the most important thing.'

Kubu was shocked as he walked into Selelo's room. The man was wasting away. He looked on death's doorstep.

'Selelo.' Kubu shook the Bushman's shoulder gently. 'Selelo. Can you hear me? It's Detective Sergeant Bengu. It's me, Kubu.'

At first there was no reaction, but eventually Selelo stirred.

'Here, please drink some water.'

'Selelo want join ancestors.'

'Your ancestors will not like what they see. Please have some water.'

Eventually, Kubu persuaded Selelo to drink half a glass. When Selelo put the glass down, Kubu told him that he had the results of the blood test.

Selelo perked up and pulled himself into a semi-sitting position, lying back on the pillows.

'The kgosi is not your father,' Kubu said gently. 'From what the doctor learnt from the blood test, it's impossible.'

'He my father! I see him on horse.'

'It's not possible.'

'You on kgosi side. Don't like Bushman. All black men same.'

Kubu shook his head. 'No, Selelo, you're wrong. I'm on the side of what is true. I'm not for you or against you. This time, you've made a mistake, or your mother made a mistake, or your uncle made a mistake. But it's impossible for the kgosi to be your father. The blood tells the truth.'

Selelo let out a cry of anguish. 'Mother said was man on horse. Then, who my father?'

Kubu was nearly overwhelmed by sympathy for the Bushman, but realised that it was possible he was being manipulated. 'If we find who could be your father, we'll take his blood too, and test him. But we don't know who to test.'

Selelo slumped back into a fetal position. 'My mother not happy when I go to ancestors. She made me promise.'

When Kubu left the room, he was sure Selelo intended to starve himself to death. He spoke to the nurse, and she said they would put him on a drip. However, Kubu thought Selelo would just tear it out. And if they transferred him to a prison cell, it could only end one way. He'd have to ask Ian if he could intervene somehow.

≈

When he returned to the station, Kubu persuaded Abram to help him with interviewing the men on his list and, with Abram's local knowledge, it went smoothly. All had alibis for at least one of the murders that could be corroborated by a family member.

Eventually, they reached the last name on the list.

'It's a Rra Tshepe,' Kubu said. 'Where does he live?'

'That's an easy one. He lives next to the station commander. They're friends.'

Kubu didn't expect a warm welcome from anyone who counted the station commander as a friend, but Tshepe turned out to be pleasant enough.

'Saturday a week ago? We went out to supper at our daughter's home. We often see them on Saturdays. But I'm not sure about last Thursday.'

He shouted for his wife, 'What did we do last Thursday?' She shouted back that they'd been at home all night. It was clear to Kubu that Tshepe was not a suspect for the murders.

As they left, Abram pointed out the station commander's house. It was a modest home close to the road, similar to Tshepe's.

Kubu had known the whole exercise was a long shot, but he was still disappointed.

'Thanks for all your help, Abram,' he said. 'I'd never have managed it without you. Could you do me one more favour and drop me off at Drotsky's?'

CHAPTER 37

I t was a sombre group that sat down at the table overlooking the Kavango river. They had to admit that they'd spent a lot of time and police money in the Shakawe and Ncamasere areas, and had little to show for it.

What had started as a simple training exercise for Kubu to learn about dealing with old skeletons had blown up into investigations into a massacre, four murder cases and an allegation of corruption. To make things worse, the press was beginning to draw attention to what was going on. Now Mabaku's boss, the CID director, was unhappy, as was his boss, the assistant commissioner.

In addition, on a personal level, Mabaku, Kubu and Ian were all upset by the friction between them and the station commander, who resented both their intrusion into his domain and their rejection of his ideas. Moreover, he was intent on stirring things up in Gaborone, to their detriment.

'The assistant commissioner told the director that he wants us back in Gaborone this weekend if we've made no progress by tomorrow night,' Mabaku said after he'd finished his first beer. 'And I can't say I disagree with him.'

That made Kubu more depressed than he'd already been. 'But that means Balopi will drag Selelo into a cell, where he'll die. Then he'll claim credit for solving the two latest murders, and ignore the massacre and the two murders that happened years ago.'

Mabaku nodded. 'That's the way it works sometimes. No use fretting about something that's out of our control.'

He waved to the waiter to bring another round.

~

After a dinner where they'd imbibed a little more than usual, Mabaku said they'd have one more brainstorming session before heading for bed. 'Let's go back to our table overlooking the river.'

After they'd sat down and ordered a pot of coffee, he kicked things off. 'Let's keep an open mind about each of our investigations. Feel free to throw things into the mix, even if they sound a little crazy.'

They started with the massacre of the Bushmen.

'We know they were murdered,' Ian said. 'No doubt about that.'

'Dibotelo claims four people were responsible,' Kubu added, 'including the kgosi, Endo Lesaka and Mma Zondo's husband. He doesn't know who the fourth was.' He paused. 'The kgosi denies any involvement.'

Mabaku chimed in: 'Selelo claims his mother was at the massacre, that four people attacked them, and that she was raped by the kgosi. Of course, the kgosi denies that too, and we know Selelo can't be his son because of the blood tests. That's about all we know about the massacre, and it's all hearsay.'

'However,' Kubu said, 'it seems likely that the discovery of the Bushman skeletons stirred the pot in some way, because Lesaka, who may have taken part in the massacre, was murdered soon after. No one has come up with a reason why, except for the station commander, who now believes it was Selelo carrying out revenge killings. And, of course, Selelo appeared for the first time soon after the skeletons were found. How he found out about the discovery, we don't know.'

'Then Mma Zondo was murdered,' Mabaku added, 'but that could be related to her accusation that the kgosi is corrupt. It's the only motive that makes sense.'

Ian frowned. 'If we believe Selelo and Dibotelo are telling the truth, and the kgosi, Lesaka, and Zondo were three of the four men who carried out the massacre, then who was the fourth man?'

Kubu explained his idea about checking the men on Dibotelo's list, concluding with the disappointing outcome.

Mabaku nodded. 'It wasn't a bad idea, but the only man who didn't have a verifiable alibi turned out to be Balopi.'

'What about Dibotelo himself? Did you check his alibi?' Ian asked.

Kubu didn't have an answer for a moment, but Mabaku came to his rescue. 'No, that makes no sense. Kill his own son and mourn for twenty-five years? Very unlikely – but just possible, I suppose. But why tell us the story of the four men in the first place? He has no idea we're also getting information from Selelo.'

Ian nodded. 'Okay. So what about Balopi? You said he has no alibi, and that he was friendly with Lesaka and the others.'

Mabaku laughed. 'The alcohol is going to your head, Ian. Balopi is the head of the Shakawe police. And what possible motive could he have?'

After a moment's hesitation, Kubu said, 'If he were involved in the massacre, his reputation and maybe his job would depend on that staying secret.'

Mabaku shook his head. 'Just because we dislike him, we shouldn't—'

'Why is he so keen to pin it on Selelo?' Ian interrupted. 'Surely, any half-way decent policeman would at least look for evidence before giving way to prejudice.'

'He seems to really dislike Bushmen,' Mabaku responded. 'Maybe that blinds him.'

'Dislikes them enough to murder them?'

Mabaku said nothing for a moment, then he shook his head. 'I suppose it's not impossible, but I don't believe it. And Mma Zondo wasn't at the massacre. Why kill her? The only possible motive in her case is the corruption.'

'It may be the only motive,' Kubu said, 'but so far we haven't found any evidence of corruption—'

'Well, I interviewed Tembo, the water-project contractor, this afternoon,' Mabaku interrupted. 'I scared him half to death. I've no doubt that if we can produce some hard evidence, he'll crack. He claims the skeletons have left him behind schedule and seriously over budget, and I believe him. I've been waiting for some results from Gaborone on a forensic audit they've got under way. They promised me something by tonight, but nothing so far.' He shook his head. 'But even so, how did Mma Zondo know about the corruption? What evidence did she have that she could use as a lever with the kgosi?'

Kubu thought for a moment. 'If Mma Zondo knew about the massacre, she could have been using the kgosi's involvement in it as blackmail to stop the water project, which we know she believed Mami Wata disapproved of. The project is the kgosi's baby, his legacy. If she threatened to stop it by revealing he'd killed the Bushmen, that would be motive enough to kill her.'

Kubu changed tack. 'Then there are the other two murders: Mma Zondo's husband, who Dibotelo says was part of the massacre, and Dibotelo's son. His murder doesn't fit in anywhere as far as I can see.'

'It is possible,' Mabaku said, 'that they were both killed by Bushmen in revenge for the massacre—'

'But,' Kubu interrupted, 'Dibotelo's son was far too young to be involved.'

'Yes, but it may be a case of mistaken identity or just indiscriminate revenge. Kill any Motswana in the area.'

Kubu nodded. 'The kgosi, Lesaka, and Mma Zondo all put in strong security after Zondo and Dibotelo disappeared. That's consistent with fearing an attack.' He pondered it for a moment. 'I saw the station commander's house this afternoon. One of the other people on Dibotelo's list happens to live next to him. No security. So he wasn't afraid of vengeful Bushmen.'

Ian shook his head. 'That doesn't convince me. If he murdered Zondo and Dibotelo, why would he need security? I think the whole idea of Bushman revenge is very unlikely. They are peaceful people.'

He took a sip of his drink and swirled it around his mouth.

'Well, I'm not a detective like the two of you, but my money would be on the kgosi. He has the most to lose, the most important of which is his reputation. He's a proud man and wants to leave a legacy. If he was involved in the massacre, as Dibotelo suggests, the unearthing of the skeletons puts his reputation at risk. It's possible that the only people who knew about them were Lesaka and Mma Zondo. With them out of the way, the water project is home and dry, so to speak.

'But he didn't kill Lesaka, so someone has to be working with him. Maybe his son, or maybe Balopi. Then again, perhaps Balopi killed Lesaka to keep the massacre secret, and then the kgosi killed Mma Zondo when she threatened to expose the corruption.'

Both Mabaku and Kubu looked at Ian with surprise. It was the longest speech they'd ever heard him deliver.

The three sat lost in their own thoughts for quite a while. Eventually, Mabaku broke the silence. 'Even if any of this makes sense, we've no hard evidence to make an arrest, let alone get a conviction. The best we can hope for is a breakthrough on the corruption, but whoever committed the murders walks away free.'

Ian pointed at Kubu. 'Laddie, last time you pulled a witch doctor out of your hat to solve the diamond heist. What are you going to do this time?'

'Well, I do have an idea. I don't know if it will work, but maybe it's worth a try.'

First thing the next morning, Mabaku phoned the Shakawe police station and left a message for the station commander, asking him to be available for a meeting at ten o'clock. 'Please tell the station commander,' Mabaku said to the receptionist, 'that I have some new information concerning the murders of Rra Lesaka and Mma Zondo.'

Then he phoned the kgosi. 'Kgosi, I apologise for phoning so early, but please could you meet me at the police station at ten o'clock. I may have some information that you'll be interested in.'

'Is it about the murders?'

'I don't want to discuss it on the phone. Please just meet me at ten.'

The kgosi confirmed he'd be there.

Mabaku hung up and walked over to the table where Kubu and Ian were eating breakfast. 'Stage one successful. They'll both be there.'

He'd just sat down to enjoy a cup of coffee, when a waiter came over and said there was a phone call for the assistant superintendent.

'I wonder if one of them has cancelled already,' Mabaku said as he stood up.

When he picked up the phone, it was the director on the line.

'I have the information you asked for last week,' the director said and proceeded to tell Mabaku what they'd found out.

After asking a few questions, Mabaku thanked his boss and returned to the table.

'That was the director. He had some very interesting information that will make our job a little easier.' He paused. 'I hope.' He took a mouthful of his now-lukewarm coffee and grimaced. Once he'd caught a waiter's attention for a new cup, he turned to his colleagues and filled them in on what he'd just learnt.

'I think I need to pay another visit to the contractor. I'll meet you at the station at ten.'

Mabaku, Kubu and Ian arrived at the Shakawe police station at the same time, a few minutes before ten. After asking the receptionist to tell the station commander that they'd arrived, Mabaku went to talk to Abram, while the others went directly to the conference room.

'Balopi will keep us waiting, of course,' Mabaku said when he walked in. 'And so will the kgosi.'

At ten minutes past the hour, the station commander walked in. 'What's this all about? I hope it won't take long. I'm very busy.'

'I think we have a possible breakthrough in two of the murder cases,' Mabaku replied.

'And what's that?'

'Let's wait until the kgosi arrives, so I don't have to repeat myself.'

Before the station commander could respond, the kgosi and his son walked in. 'Dumela, borra. I apologise for being late.' He turned to Mabaku. 'What have you found?'

'Kgosi, your son is not needed here. Could he wait outside?'

'I want him to stay, thank you.'

Mabaku shrugged. 'There's a lot to cover, gentlemen, so I'm going to record this. Detective Sergeant Bengu, please start the recorder.'

Kubu pressed the record button and gave the date, time, and names of the people present.

When everyone was settled, Mabaku cleared his throat. 'I received a call from my boss this morning. As you may know, the day before I came here, the Department of Water Affairs received an anonymous letter suggesting there was corruption in the water project here—'

The kgosi's son banged his hand on the table. 'That's not true! How dare you say that?'

'Quiet, Raseelo,' the kgosi snapped.

'Please let me finish,' Mabaku said quietly. 'We also know that the letter was sent by Mma Zondo, who was set against the project because of her so-called friendship with Mami Wata.'

'She was totally mad,' Raseelo sneered.

'That may have been true,' Mabaku continued, 'but she was correct. The Department of Water Affairs investigated the project for me and has found major irregularities—'

The kgosi and his son jumped to their feet. 'How dare you!' the kgosi shouted. 'Everything is above board.'

'Please sit down. There's more.'

Raseelo pointed at Mabaku. 'Get out of here. Go back to Gaborone.'

Mabaku waited until the two had sat down before continuing. 'This morning I spoke to Rra Tembo, the contractor in charge of building the pipeline and reservoir. I told him about certain suspicious payments made to his bank account. It didn't take much pressure for him to show me the discrepancies between the plans that had been approved and those he was asked to carry out. He admitted that you'd phoned him with the new plans and paid him to make the changes.'

'Wait till I get hold of the lying bastard.'

Kubu was pleased Raseelo was losing control. Their plan was going better than expected.

'What was of interest to me,' Mabaku continued, looking directly at the kgosi, 'was that the money came from your personal account.'

For a few moments, there was silence in the room, then the kgosi jumped up again. 'Come on, Raseelo. We don't have to listen to these lies.'

'Yes, you do, kgosi.' Again, it was Mabaku's quiet voice. 'If you leave this room, I will arrest you before you've left the building.'

The kgosi turned to the station commander. 'Dammit, Balopi, do something. Why are you just sitting there? You know me and what I've done for the community. Get rid of these people.'

'Let's hear them out. And you need to deal with these accusations about paying off the contractor.'

The kgosi looked thunderstruck.

At that moment, there was a knock on the door and the receptionist's face appeared. 'Phone call for Dr MacGregor.'

Ian frowned, then stood up and left the room.

'Kgosi, please sit down.' Mabaku pointed at the chair the kgosi had been sitting in. 'I'm not finished.'

For a few moments, Kubu thought the kgosi wasn't going to obey, but eventually he sat down.

'Kgosi, we think that Mma Zondo tried to blackmail you into stopping the water project and that you killed her or had her killed to prevent her from doing that.'

'Are you out of your mind, Mabaku? What on earth would she blackmail me about?'

'You were involved in the massacre of the Bushmen, and she threatened to reveal that.' He paused. 'That would have been the end of your reputation.'

'I told you I know nothing about that.'

'You lied to us.'

Raseelo stood up and clenched his fists. 'Are you calling my father a liar?'

Mabaku nodded. 'I am.'

Raseelo took a step forward, but Balopi grabbed his arm. 'Don't be stupid. Sit down and shut up.'

It took a while before everyone was once again seated.

'Despite what the station commander thinks, we're confident that the Bushman, Selelo, didn't murder Rra Lesaka. We think you arranged for Lesaka to be killed because he also threatened to reveal what you'd done. We know you couldn't have done it yourself because you were talking to his son at the time Lesaka was murdered, but perhaps Raseelo here obliged.'

Raseelo's chair tipped over backwards as he leapt at Mabaku.

Again the station commander stopped him. 'Grow up, Raseelo. He wants you to hit him, then you'll be had up for assaulting a police officer. For God's sake, sit down and shut up. They've no proof of anything. Now sit down.'

Kubu glanced at the kgosi, whose face was gaunt and his fists clenched. He's about to blow, Kubu thought.

'Assistant Superintendent Mabaku.' It was Ian returning to the room. 'I have some news about Selelo.'

'I hope he's died,' Raseelo hissed.

Ian shook his head. 'There may have been a mix-up in the blood tests. It's possible that the kgosi is Selelo's father after all.'

'I never touched the woman!' the kgosi shouted. 'I—'

'Enough!' The station commander shouted. 'There may have been a mix-up, kgosi, but can't you see this is just a trick?' He turned to Mabaku. 'This circus is over. There'll be no more questions unless the kgosi has his lawyer present, and you have hard evidence to put forward.'

Mabaku didn't respond.

The kgosi took a few moments to calm himself, then pulled together what dignity he could muster. He turned to Mabaku. 'All right, I did pay the contractor money. There was no more funding available, and we had to have that extra water volume. So I covered the extra costs myself. I admit we cut some corners about obtaining approval from Water Affairs, but I was in the process of sorting that out when all this other stuff blew up. As for your ridiculous accusations about the murders, Raseelo and I have solid alibis. The station commander is absolutely right. You have nothing.'

He turned to his son. 'Come, Raseelo. We're leaving now.'

Kubu's heart sank as he watched them walk out of the door, followed by the station commander. Their plan had failed.

CHAPTER 38

'I thought it was worth a try,' Kubu said quietly. 'I'm sorry for wasting everyone's time.'

'I don't know what you're talking about.' Mabaku sounded far from despondent. 'We learnt a lot from that encounter.'

Kubu frowned.

'The kgosi admitted to the corruption, which is a start, but probably won't go too far. More importantly, your idea of having Ian say there may have been a mix-up in the blood test made him basically admit that he was at the massacre of the Bushmen and that a Bushman woman was raped.'

'I must have missed that—'

'He said something like "I never touched the woman". That implies there *was* a woman and she *was* touched. Probably raped, since we were talking about the kgosi raping Selelo's mother. Saying that also strongly suggests he witnessed it. So, your plan did produce some results.'

'But nothing we can use—'

'Nothing we can use in a court of law, but plenty we can use to move forward.'

'I don't follow,' Ian interjected.

'Well, we also learnt something about Balopi. He was correct, of course, in saying that the kgosi should have legal representation.

But he also warned the kgosi that we were trying to trick him. And when he could see the kgosi was about to break, he cut the interview short. You have to wonder why a policeman would do such a thing.' Mabaku paused for a moment. 'The only reason that makes sense is that he was protecting himself from scrutiny. I think Balopi was also at the massacre of the Bushmen.'

Ian nodded. 'So he was the fourth man. That makes sense.'

'But how does this tie in with the recent murders?' Kubu asked.

'I still can't imagine the station commander would be involved in a premeditated murder,' Mabaku replied. 'The massacre, yes. They were all teenagers thirty or so years ago – young and stupid.'

Kubu mulled that over. 'So then the murderer has to be the kgosi.'

'Yes. With Raseelo's help.'

Kubu said nothing.

'You're not convinced?'

'I don't know. I can't really see any other sensible explanation, but I'm afraid of letting my dislike of the station commander bias me.' He paused. 'So what do we do now?'

'We're going to carry on shaking the kgosi's tree as hard as we can and see what rotten fruit falls out. We'll hit him with the water-project corruption to start with. It all sounds very nice and altruistic for him to pay that additional amount out of his own pocket, but he broke the law. The contractor said it was just the extra cost of the work, but I'm sure there was a payoff involved as well. It was a lot of money, and where did the kgosi get it from?'

'Maybe from his friends, by promising them good land allocations later on,' Kubu put in. 'Maybe that's what Mma Zondo discovered. We should ask her son about it.'

Mabaku nodded. 'Let's head to Drotsky's and plan our strategy there. I don't feel comfortable in the station commander's domain.'

'So we're not going back to Gabs tomorrow?'

'No, we've still got work to do.'

Kubu felt some of the excitement of the morning return, but

at the same time his heart sank as he thought about missing Saturday with Joy again. He was not looking forward to his next phone call to her.

∾

In fact, the kgosi's tree was already well shaken, and Mabaku didn't have long to wait for the result. As he and Kubu planned their next moves, he was called to the phone at Drotsky's reception. He looked pensive when he returned a few minutes later.

'That was the kgosi. He wants to talk to me right now. Just him and me.'

'Will you go?' Kubu had learnt enough to know that a one-on-one was a risk.

'I insisted that he come here. I'm not going to run after him.' Mabaku hesitated. 'I really shouldn't see him alone. He could make up all sorts of stories about what I say. But we don't have a lot to lose at this point.'

'I could be there just to take notes.'

Mabaku shook his head. 'He was adamant that I must be alone. He wanted it to be off the record, but I told him he was talking to a policeman not a journalist. He eventually accepted that. Of course, we'll never be able to use anything he tells me against him. He'll just deny he said it.'

'When is he coming?'

'He'll be here in the next half-hour.'

'So, what should I do in the meantime?'

'You can do some of the legwork we discussed.'

Kubu nodded. Maybe both of them would discover something interesting, but he felt Mabaku had the better chance.

∾

While Mabaku was with the kgosi, Kubu decided to do a little of his own legwork before attending to Mabaku's. Despite the resignation he'd felt as he went to sleep the previous night, Kubu hadn't put Joy completely out of his mind. His big problem was that he believed she would have lost interest in him because he hadn't contacted her for over ten days. He didn't have the courage just to phone her for a chat. Nor did he want to ask her out again as long as the date of his return was uncertain.

As he sipped a cup of coffee, looking over the Kavango river, his mind came up with all sorts of scenarios in which phoning her was perfectly reasonable. What was going on in the trial of the two Bushmen who'd been forced to sign confessions they hadn't understood? Had the Jwaneng diamond-heist suspect been brought to trial yet? Had there been any interesting cases in Gaborone lately?

The problem with all of these ideas was that Joy would see through them in a flash. That made him depressed.

Then suddenly an idea came to him that was plausible. He could phone her on official business at the Records department and ask for any information on people of interest in the cases in Shakawe. He knew that Mabaku hadn't suggested such a thing, but it was showing initiative. At least, that's what he'd say if Mabaku came down on him.

He took a couple of deep breaths, then walked to the main building to find a telephone.

≈

'Joy Serome, please.'

Kubu waited nervously as the call was put through to Joy.

'How can I help you?'

The little speech that Kubu had prepared left his head, and he stammered 'Hello. It's Kubu.'

'Kubu. How nice to hear from you.'

Is she being sarcastic? he wondered.

'The rumours down here are that you've a big mess up there at Shakawe.'

'I hate to admit it, but it is. A massacre decades ago, two cold-case murders, two current murders, an attempted murder and likely corruption. And we're pretty confused about what's going on.'

'Is there something I can do to help?'

Kubu realised this was his chance. 'Yes, there is. Thank you. There are two prominent people up here. I wonder if you could check if either has a record.'

'Of course. What are their names?'

'The one is actually the kgosi of a village just south of Shakawe, called Ncamasere. His name is Rantao. Kgosi Rantao. I don't know his last name. And the other is the station commander at the Shakawe police station, Assistant Superintendent Balopi. I don't know his first name either.'

Kubu heard a whistle from Joy. 'If either is involved, the press will have a field day. When do you need the information by?'

'The usual. Yesterday if possible.'

'Call me back in ten minutes. I'll see what I can dig out.'

∼

Kubu waited fifteen minutes before calling back.

'Neither of the two have any records, not even traffic violations. They are, as we like to say, squeaky clean.'

Kubu wasn't disappointed, because that was what he expected.

'However,' Joy continued, 'there is a Balopi from Shakawe who's had several run-ins. He could be your station commander's father.'

'What did he get up to?'

'Not a very nice man, it seems. A couple of domestic-violence charges, both ultimately dropped; three assault charges, two dropped and one that landed him in jail for a year; cruelty to animals...'

'Is he still alive?'

'No, I checked. He passed away in 1983.' She paused. 'What on earth is going on up there?'

'You won't believe it when I tell you, but unfortunately I'm in someone's office so I can't do that now. I also don't know when I'll be back, but I'll phone you as soon as I know.'

'I can't wait to hear of all the intrigue.'

'Anyway, I've got to go. Thanks for the information. Speak to you soon.'

After he'd replaced the handset, he sat for a moment thinking about the call. It was so much easier to talk about work-related issues with Joy than about his feelings. He sighed. At least they were talking.

~

When Mabaku was told that the kgosi had arrived and was waiting for him at the manager's office, he didn't rush. He was happy to let the kgosi stew for a while. Eventually he headed over to the main building, and the manager took them to a staff office where they could talk privately. After they were seated, Mabaku waited. This was the kgosi's show. Mabaku had no intention of making it easy for him.

After a few moments, the kgosi began. 'Thank you for seeing me, Assistant Superintendent. I'm very worried about the water project. I accept that what I did was wrong, but it was for the good of this community. The project is my legacy. I don't care about myself, but I care about the people here and keeping this town alive. Without proper irrigation, it can't grow. If it doesn't grow, it will die as the young people move away.'

It was a pretty speech, but Mabaku wasn't impressed. 'Perhaps you should have thought about that before you bribed the contractor.'

'The payment wasn't a bribe; it was for the extra work required. The larger dam isn't constructed yet because of the delays with the skeletons. We can simply revert to the original approved plan.'

'I didn't get the feeling the contractor would be in a hurry to pay back any money.'

The kgosi shrugged. 'Maybe I lose the money. That's my problem.'

'What about the other people here who put in money?'

'There were no others,' he said – quickly, Mabaku thought.

'Kgosi, if you want to negotiate a deal, get your lawyer to discuss it with the prosecutor. I have nothing to do with that. My job is to arrest criminals and hand them over to the justice system.'

'I'm *not* a criminal.'

Mabaku said nothing, allowing the silence to draw out. Eventually, the kgosi moistened his lips and said, 'There's another matter.'

Mabaku folded his arms and waited.

'When you spoke with me about Endo Lesaka's death, you warned me that his enemies might become my enemies. I'm afraid that may be true.'

Mabaku nodded. 'Unfortunately, we're not a lot further with finding out who his enemies were.'

'I now remember that I did tell someone about my meeting with his son the night Endo was murdered.'

'You mean apart from Raseelo?'

The kgosi nodded. 'I mentioned it to Balopi.'

'The station commander? Why did you do that?'

'We were concerned about Endo going mad and starting to rave. It'd happened before when he was alone with me, but he was getting worse. I suppose it was somehow connected to his stroke. In fact, I thought that was what his son wanted to talk to me about that night.'

'Exactly when did you tell Balopi?'

'It was after the kgotla. Endo had been saying odd things at the meeting. As his friends, we were both concerned.'

'Thank you for telling me that. I'll make a point of asking the station commander if he mentioned it to anyone else.' Mabaku made no attempt to keep the sarcasm out of his voice. 'Kgosi, you're wasting my time. You tell me about Lesaka having enemies, but you don't say who they might be. Now you say you mentioned your meeting with Lesaka's son to other people. What is the point of all this?'

There was a long pause before the kgosi spoke again. 'All right. Balopi may have been involved in the Bushman killings. I'm afraid of him.'

'You're accusing the station commander not only of taking part in the massacre, but also of being a cold-blooded murderer?'

The kgosi hesitated. 'Yes, I'm afraid that may be the case.'

'And what makes you think that? Were you there?'

'No.'

'If you weren't involved, why are you afraid?'

The kgosi frowned. 'Isn't it obvious? Balopi's worried I'll talk to you. He warned me on the way out of the meeting this morning. He said I should be very careful what I said. That there could be consequences.'

Mabaku shook his head. 'Who was the woman, kgosi?'

'What woman?'

'The woman you said you didn't touch.'

'Whoever the Bushman's mother was – that's all I meant.'

'Kgosi, you're lying to me again,' Mabaku said quietly. 'I don't like it when people do that. Perhaps you didn't rape the woman, but you were at the massacre. And you've made up this whole story about Assistant Superintendent Balopi to try and shift the blame away from yourself and your son. Why would he warn you if you had nothing to do with it?'

'That's not true...'

The kgosi hesitated, then tried to start another sentence, and another, but gave them up. Mabaku could see from the kgosi's body language that he was wrestling with how to proceed, but did nothing to help him out. Eventually, the kgosi spoke. 'All right. I did see what happened with the Bushmen.'

As though he were an innocent bystander, Mabaku thought.

'It was Zondo, Lesaka and Balopi. And myself. Balopi said he wanted a Bushman girl. There were plenty of Batswana girls he could have had in those days, but he wanted to see what a Bushman girl was like. He couldn't keep his pecker in his pants, just like his father.' He took a deep breath. 'I swear I was against the whole thing, but we'd had some beer and...' He trailed off.

'What happened?'

'It all got out of hand. One of the Bushmen tried to stop him, and Balopi knocked him down. Then another man came at him with a spear, and Zondo shot him. I swear I didn't kill anyone, and I tried to stop them, but...'

'And the woman?'

'After it was over, Balopi raped the woman and left her for dead. Then we went home and fetched spades. When we got back, the woman had gone. We buried the bodies and all their possessions. It took us the rest of the day.' He paused. 'Few people noticed the Bushmen had gone; they just assumed they'd moved on. They did that in those days.' He looked up at Mabaku. 'I've been ashamed of it for my entire life.'

'But apparently not enough to confess to it.'

There was a long silence before the kgosi responded. 'We swore a terrible oath – that anyone who spoke about what happened would die.'

'So Zondo was the first.'

'Yes. After he got married, he was happy with his new wife and the farm for a while, but she was a difficult woman, and he wasn't really a farmer. He started hanging around with friends – not with us anymore, but drinking friends. When he got drunk he talked too much, and rumours started to spread.'

'So you had him killed.'

'No. I spoke to him. I warned him. He said he'd be careful, but he carried on drinking. Then one day he disappeared. Balopi said nothing about it, and even helped us search for him for several days. But he seemed strange and avoided me afterwards. It bothered me, and later I found out that he'd also gone out into the desert on that day.'

'What about Dibotelo's son?'

'Dibotelo had nothing to do with the Bushmen, and his son was a child at the time.'

'So he just happened to get killed the same way a few weeks later and buried in the same place?' Mabaku's voice rose. 'Kgosi, if you want me to help you, you have to stop lying to me.'

'I'm telling you what I know. I know nothing about Dibotelo's son.'

Rather to his surprise, Mabaku believed him. Perhaps Tandi Dibotelo had just been in the wrong place at the wrong time.

'So you believe that Balopi killed his old friends, Lesaka and Zondo. What about Mma Zondo?'

'You were right about that. She was threatening me. She said she'd expose me as the man responsible for the Bushman massacre if I didn't cancel the water project. It was an impossible situation. I couldn't cancel the project even if I wanted to, and the scandal of the Bushmen would have put off our funders.'

'So you told Balopi about it?'

'I had to. She'd stop at nothing to destroy the water project. She would have carried out her threat. Before the skeletons were found, everyone would have just laughed her off, but now I would have been forced out, and Balopi would have lost his job.' He shook his head. 'The woman was mad. She drove her husband to drink, and that's where all this started.'

Mabaku shook his head. 'No, kgosi, this all started when you and three other young louts decided to gang rape an innocent women. The question is how is it all going to end.'

'You have to arrest Balopi.'

'On what grounds? You've told me a long story implicating a respected police officer, but given me no evidence whatsoever. For all I know, you made the whole thing up.'

'I've admitted I was at the massacre. Why would I tell you that if I was the murderer?'

'To direct attention away from yourself.'

'Search his house,' the kgosi spluttered. 'Surely you'll find something. That's your job.'

Mabaku shrugged. 'Perhaps if I had a formal statement, a magistrate could be convinced to issue a search warrant. He won't do it on my say-so.'

Mabaku watched the kgosi struggle to take that final irrevocable step, but he knew his fish was hooked, He only had to wait.

The kgosi hesitated before he grudgingly agreed.

Mabaku left the room and asked a waiter to find Kubu and tell him to bring a writing pad.

'The detective sergeant can write it all down for us,' he told the kgosi when he returned. 'He has good handwriting.'

While they waited, Mabaku wondered if the whole story implicating the station commander was a neat diversion that the kgosi had constructed to eliminate himself and his son from suspicion. It was certainly possible, but the kgosi would have to be a good actor to pull it off.

'After this,' he said to the kgosi, 'you go back to your house and stay there until we get this mess sorted out. Tell Raseelo to keep everything locked up. You may as well get some value out of all the security you paid for.'

'What if he asks why?'

'That's your problem. But I suggest you tell him the truth.'

There was a knock at the door, and Kubu came in. 'You sent for me, rra?'

'Yes, have a seat Detective Sergeant. The kgosi wants to make a formal statement.' Mabaku made no effort to hide his satisfaction.

~

The kgosi read the statement Kubu had written and was just about to sign it when the receptionist barged in.

'Kgosi, your daughter is on the line and wants to speak to you. She says it's very urgent.'

The kgosi jumped up and raced out of the room, closely followed by Kubu holding the unsigned statement in his hand. He wasn't going to let the kgosi leave without signing it.

The kgosi picked up the phone. 'Bontle, what's happened?'

He listened for a few moments. 'Balopi did what?'

He listened again. 'The bastard. I'm on my way.' He slammed down the phone and headed for the door.

'What's happened?' Kubu asked.

'The bastard has arrested Reseeleo. I'll show him who's in charge around here.' With that he stormed out of the room.

Kubu raced back to Mabaku and told him what had happened.

'Shit,' Mabaku exclaimed. 'We'd better get over there before someone else gets killed.'

As he rushed out, he spotted Ian at their usual table and shouted for him to come. The three of them ran for the vehicle.

CHAPTER 39

They had started only a few minutes behind the kgosi, and given how Mabaku was driving, Kubu was surprised they hadn't caught up with him. Both Kubu and Ian were holding on for all they were worth as Mabaku raced around corners, not slowing down even when there were cows grazing at the side of the road.

Kubu prayed they didn't hit one. A Land Rover would certainly cause severe injury to a big cow, but in return a cow would likely put a Land Rover out of commission.

After a hair-raising ten minutes or so, they skidded to a halt a short distance from the Shakawe police station. The kgosi's old Mercedes was already there, right in front of the entrance. As they jumped out, they heard a shot, followed by another, accompanied by the tinkling of glass.

'We're not armed,' Kubu gasped as they ran towards the station.

Mabaku didn't reply, but pushed the front door open and headed towards the station commander's office. Abram and a constable were outside gazing at the floor. Mabaku shoved them aside and went in, closely followed by Kubu.

The station commander was standing over the kgosi, whose shirt was stained with red.

'Where's Ian?' Mabaku shouted.

'Right behind you. Let me get at him.'

Ian knelt next to the kgosi and felt his neck. 'Nothing. Someone get me a torch.' He ripped open the front of the shirt and examined the wound, shaking his head slightly. Abram handed him a torch, and he shone it into the kgosi's eyes, one after the other. He rose to his feet. 'The kgosi is dead.'

Kubu tried to take in the whole scene. The kgosi was lying on his back, head against the leg of a chair. His left arm was at his side, and his right arm was extended away from his body. Next to his right hand lay a pistol.

Balopi was standing at the kgosi's feet, his left hand rubbing his neck, and his right arm hanging at his side, a pistol in hand. Behind the desk, a couple of the top window panes were broken, and the frame between them twisted. There were shards of glass on the floor.

'He tried to kill me,' Balopi stammered. 'He stormed in and started shooting. Thank God he missed.' He bent over to pick up the kgosi's pistol.

'No!' Kubu shouted. 'Don't touch it.'

Balopi straightened up, startled.

'You know you shouldn't touch anything, rra. And please put your handgun on the desk.' Kubu prayed he wouldn't start shooting again.

After a few moments, Balopi complied, and everyone relaxed.

Mabaku walked over. 'Assistant Superintendent Balopi, in accordance with police regulations, please hand over your badge. You are now on administrative leave until the assistant commissioner authorises you to go back on duty.'

'You can't do that. I don't report to you.'

'You know the regulations as well as I do. When a police officer is involved in a shooting, they go on administrative leave until the incident is investigated thoroughly. Your badge, please. And go to the conference room. I'll interview you there.'

∾

Much needed to be done before they were ready to start the interviews. Abram photographed the station commander's office, taking a number of pictures of the body. Ian accompanied the body to the undertaker, then went to the clinic to check on Selelo. The office was taped off as a crime scene, and a forensics unit was summoned from Maun. Mabaku spoke to the director, who informed the assistant commissioner, who confirmed that the station commander was to be put on administrative leave and appointed Abram to run the station in the interim. And they decided to leave the kgosi's son in his cell, because they were afraid what he would do when he found out his father had been killed.

Just as they were ready to interview Balopi, Kubu asked Mabaku if they could review their strategy first. Mabaku frowned, but led them outside so they wouldn't be overheard.

'What's on your mind, Kubu?' he asked when they'd found some shade under an acacia tree.

'Rra, I have to admit I'm concerned, even a little afraid.'

'Of what?'

'The problem, as I see it, is that we still don't know who murdered Lesaka and Mma Zondo. The kgosi told us that it was the station commander. The station commander has just been attacked and was lucky not to be shot by the kgosi. That suggests the kgosi and perhaps his son are responsible.'

'Yes, I know. But what's the problem?'

'Rra, I'm worried that the murderer may feel the need to continue murdering – perhaps even us. The kgosi is dead, but what about his son? If he was involved in the earlier murders, he may want to get rid of the station commander or us, because we're closing in on him. And if the station commander is the murderer, he may want to get rid of Raseelo, maybe Selelo, and even us. I don't think we can let either Balopi or Raseelo leave the station today, for everyone's safety.'

'We can't just lock them up without cause.'

'Can't we tell them it is protective custody or some such thing?'

Mabaku turned to Abram. 'What do you think? You know the station commander better than any of us.'

'Well, I've known him for a long time. He's been a good policeman overall, and I still find it difficult to believe he could have been responsible for the murders. I don't think he's a threat to anyone.'

'We know both of them have access to firearms,' Kubu interjected.

'Raseelo?'

'He has access to hunting rifles. He used one to shoot Selelo.' Kubu paused. 'And Balopi is a policeman, after all, with easy access to guns.'

Mabaku thought for a few moments. 'I don't like the idea of impugning a fellow officer without proof. It could end up being, as they say, career-limiting.' He paused, then continued. 'On the other hand, being shot dead is also career-limiting.'

'We have all seen how hot-headed Raseelo can be,' Kubu said. 'I wouldn't trust him after what's happened today, even if he wasn't involved in the murders.'

'All right,' Mabaku said. 'Let's go and interview them, then I'll make up my mind.'

'About time!' Balopi muttered when Mabaku, Kubu and Abram eventually walked into the conference room.

Mabaku started the tape recorder and rapidly dispensed with the preliminaries. Then he turned to Balopi.

'Please tell us what happened this afternoon.'

'I was working in my office when I heard the kgosi come into the station, shouting that he was going to kill me. Fortunately my service pistol was in a drawer in my desk. I was just getting it out when he ran in and shot at me. Luckily he missed, and I was able to shoot him before he could fire again.'

'Why do you think he wanted to kill you?'

'I'd arrested his son an hour or so earlier. His daughter probably contacted him and told him what happened.'

'Why did you arrest Raseelo?'

'For the murders of Endo Lesaka and Mma Zondo.'

'And what evidence do you have that he was responsible?'

Balopi thumped the table. 'For God's sake, Mabaku. Use your head! No one else could have done it. He was protecting his father from the accusations of murder and rape.'

'Rra, we've been through this before, when you accused Selelo of the same murders. You have to have evidence – hard evidence – to arrest someone and accuse them of murder. Now tell me what evidence do you have for arresting the kgosi's son?'

'You're right we've been through this before, dammit. He was the only one who knew Lesaka's son was going to be out of the house the night he was murdered, and he also would have known that Mma Zondo was trying to blackmail his father. What more motive do you need?'

Kubu put up his hand. Mabaku nodded for him to go ahead.

'Rra, did you know that the kgosi was not going to be at home when you arrested his son?'

Balopi hesitated for a moment, then pointed at Abram. 'I asked Detective Sergeant Nteba here to keep an eye on the kgosi. He radioed me when the kgosi left and headed for Drotsky's. So, yes, I knew. It made the arrest much easier. But what difference does it make?'

Kubu turned to Abram. 'Weren't you surprised when he arrested Raseelo?'

'I wasn't there. I'd followed the kgosi, then the station commander told me to return to the station.'

'Assistant Superintendent,' Mabaku continued, 'you were very lucky that the kgosi missed.'

'I was indeed.'

'But I'm puzzled that your pistol was loaded when you took it out of your desk drawer. How did that happen? You know that's against regulations.'

'The regulations allow me to have it loaded if I'm concerned for my life. After this morning's fiasco with the kgosi, I was scared that he would do something crazy. Turns out I was right.'

Mabaku helped himself to a glass of water. 'Actually the kgosi was with me when his daughter called. He was giving me a statement that implicated you in the same murders that you arrested Raseelo for. As well as for taking part in the murder of the Bushmen, and for raping a woman who could be Selelo's mother.'

'Well, of course he'd say that. He's trying to save his son.'

'When he left me, he came straight here. Why do you think he had a loaded pistol in his car?'

Balopi shrugged. 'How would I know?'

After a few more questions, Mabaku cautioned the station commander not to leave the building as they would want to speak to him again.

With a snort, Balopi stood up and stalked out of the conference room, muttering something about Mabaku's future in the police service.

∾

When interviewed, the two constables on duty at the time the kgosi had stormed into the station agreed on most of the details. The one difference was that the man at reception didn't remember whether the kgosi was shouting threats when he ran into the building, while the other thought he heard the kgosi threatening to kill the station commander. Neither saw the kgosi carrying a gun.

Abram interjected that he hadn't heard anything, because he was in a holding cell with Raseelo.

One constable had accompanied the station commander when he arrested Raseelo and recounted that Balopi had to threaten force in order to make Raseelo get into the police Land Rover.

'He handcuffed him and frog-marched him to the car. I thought he was going to break his arm. The kgosi's son was screaming in pain.'

∾

Mabaku, Kubu and Abram debated whether they should interview Raseelo in the conference room or in his cell, given his volatile nature. They eventually decided they couldn't justify keeping him in the cell any longer, so Kubu went to fetch him.

'What was that shooting? Did my father come to get me out of here? He was worried Balopi was going to come after him. Where is he? I want to talk to him.'

'Rra,' Kubu said. 'Please come with me. We'll tell you what's happened, and then we want to hear your whole story.'

'Where's that bastard Balopi? I'll teach him a lesson for nearly breaking my arms.'

'Please calm down, rra. You won't do any such thing.'

'Bloody police!'

Kubu escorted Raseelo to the conference room, where he exploded once again the moment he saw Mabaku.

'You're the most incompetent person I've ever met. Wait until I tell the commissioner – he's a friend of the family. You'll be selling trinkets on Africa Mall when I'm finished with you.'

'Rra, please sit down.'

'Fuck you. Where's my father. I need to talk to him.'

'Sit down, Raseelo.'

Kubu watched Raseelo, unsure as to whether he'd comply or explode, but the tone of Mabaku's voice must have convinced him, because he shut up and lowered himself into a chair.

Mabaku explained that the interview was going to be recorded.

'I haven't done anything.'

'You're not accused of anything. We just need information, need to know what happened.'

Mabaku turned on the recorder and went through the formalities. Then he turned to Raseelo. 'When your father heard that you had been arrested he came to the station. Assistant Superintendent Balopi claims that your father tried to shoot him—'

'He'd never do that. My father's a peaceful man.'

'Balopi says that he had to defend himself and shot your father.'

Raseelo jumped up. 'I'll kill that bastard! Where is the kgosi? I want to see him.'

'Rra, I'm very sorry to tell you that your father is no more.'

Raseelo face froze. 'He's dead? He can't be dead...'

Mabaku said nothing. Kubu moved to block the door in case Raseelo decided to take matters into his own hands, but after what seemed like a long time, Raseelo resumed his seat and covered his face.

'This is all your fault,' he said in a choked voice. 'All your prying and accusations and poking around where you weren't wanted. That's why my father is dead.'

'There will be a full investigation into the shooting and a detailed report. If necessary, the police will take action. Not you. Understand?'

Raseelo said nothing.

'I asked you if you understood that you are to keep out of this whole matter.'

Eventually, Raseelo nodded.

'Please say yes or no.'

'Yes, but—'

'There are no buts, Raseelo. If you interfere, I will have you arrested.' Mabaku paused to let that sink in, then continued. 'Please tell us what happened this afternoon that ended up with you in a cell.'

'What does it matter now?'

'It's part of the investigation into your father's death.'

For the next few minutes, Raseelo told them about the station commander arriving at their house and telling him he was under arrest for the murders of Lesaka and Mma Zondo. 'I told him that was bullshit and that he had no grounds for doing it.'

He then described how Balopi and another policeman had jumped him and handcuffed him, and then thrown him in the back of their Land Rover. 'I thought they were going to break my arms.'

Mabaku changed direction. 'Raseelo, did your father own a handgun?'

Raseelo didn't answer for a few moments, then said: 'No, of course not. He's not allowed to.'

Kubu was pretty certain that he was lying.

Mabaku continued. 'Apparently your father brought a handgun into the station in order to shoot the commander.'

'That's a lie. My father wouldn't shoot anyone.'

'If he didn't own one, how did he have one in his hand?'

Raseelo didn't answer.

Mabaku let the silence linger.

Eventually Raseelo spoke. 'Well, he may have had one, but I've never seen it.'

'Where would he keep it?'

'If he has one, it would likely be in the gun safe with his hunting rifles.'

Mabaku turned to Abram. 'When we've finished here, please accompany Raseelo to his home and check the contents of the gun safe.'

Abram nodded.

'I want to see my father.'

'I'm sorry, but that's not possible right now. We'll let you and your sister know when it is.'

'I want to talk to that bastard, Balopi. Let him look me in the eye and tell me my father was trying to kill him. Bastard!'

Mabaku ignored that. 'Raseelo, this is what we are going to do for the moment. It's my responsibility to keep the peace. I want you to go back to your cell—'

'I haven't done anything. You can't hold me.'

'I'm not arresting you. I think there's a real danger that you will try to injure the station commander, and vice versa. I'm going to put both of you in protective custody until we sort out this mess.' He turned to Abram. 'Detective Sergeant, please escort this man back to his cell. No one – repeat, no one – is to see him or talk to him without my permission. Understood? You can take him home to check the gun safe when we're finished.'

❧

When Abram returned to the conference room, Mabaku turned to Kubu. 'So, what do you think is going on?'

Kubu had been worried that his boss was going to ask him, because he really didn't know. 'Well, yesterday I thought that the kgosi and his son were behind the murders. After the meeting this morning, I thought that the station commander was protecting the kgosi, possibly because of self-interest – that he didn't want it to come out that he was involved in the Bushman massacre.' He paused. 'Then, this afternoon the kgosi was willing to sign a statement accusing Balopi of the recent murders, as well as the rape of the woman and the murder of the Bushmen, many years ago. However, he gave no indication that he wanted Balopi dead. That all seems to have changed when he heard about what had happened to Raseelo. Then suddenly, the kgosi wanted to kill Balopi. I can't work out why. It seems an extreme reaction to his son being arrested, especially since no one has produced any evidence at all that Raseelo was involved. Maybe the kgosi thought Balopi had found some evidence.' He shook his head. 'I'm sorry, rra, I'm not helping very much.'

Mabaku turned to Abram. 'And you?'

Abram shook his head. 'I don't know about the kgosi's statement, so I've no idea what's going on, but I don't see any reason not to believe the station commander's story.'

'I am puzzled by one thing,' Kubu said. 'And that is why the kgosi had a pistol with him when he came to see you, rra. He didn't have time to go home when he heard about Raseelo's arrest. Maybe he was worried about being attacked by Balopi?'

'Abram,' Mabaku said, 'when you followed the kgosi, did you tell the station commander where he was going?'

'As soon as he turned down the road to Drotsky's, that's what I told him.'

'So he knew the kgosi was coming to see us,' Kubu said. 'Maybe he thought the kgosi was going to spill the beans and arrested his son to put pressure on him.'

The three detectives sat lost in their own thoughts, all confused about what was going on. Kubu was replaying what he'd seen in the station commander's office. Something was niggling at the edges of his brain. Something didn't fit. He shook his head as though that would dislodge the thought into consciousness. However, it didn't work. Something didn't fit, but he didn't know what.

'Well,' Mabaku eventually said. 'We may as well get a good night's sleep. Where's Ian?'

'He's back from the clinic and waiting in my office,' Abram replied.

'Please go and tell him we're ready to leave, then take Raseelo home and inspect the kgosi's gun cabinet. You'll have to explain to his sister what happened. That won't be a pleasant task.'

Abram nodded, but clearly he wasn't happy that the job had fallen to him.

'Then bring him back here and let him spend the night in his cell. I'll go and tell Balopi that I'm putting him in protective custody. You'll probably hear his reaction.' He stood up. 'Forensics will be here in the morning. Perhaps they'll find something we missed.'

CHAPTER 40

As usual, it didn't take long for Kubu to fall asleep. However, his brain refused to take a rest and continued to process what had happened during the day.

'My subconscious always helps me work through problems,' he would often tell people. 'I go to bed not knowing what's going on, and I wake up with the solution. It's very efficient.'

On this night, however, he found himself suddenly awake in the early hours of the morning. That was unexpected. He usually slept the whole night through. It must be my brain, he thought. It's discovered something.

However, his brain wasn't ready to tell him about the discovery. Then, just as he was about to fall asleep again, he realised what he'd been worried about. It was the tinkling glass.

He sat up and took a sip of water from the glass next to his bed.

'That's it,' he said out loud. 'That blows Balopi's story.'

He glanced at his watch. Three-twenty! He couldn't realistically go and bang on his boss's bedroom door with his discovery. It would have to wait until breakfast.

~

Selelo was also awake, staring at the ceiling. It seemed just above him, ready to press him into the bed. He didn't turn his head to look at the walls. He knew they were all around him, creeping in.

There was no sound except the drip of liquid falling to the floor. It had done so since he'd pulled out the pipe. The woman who looked after him was kind. She'd tried to explain that the pipe would help him. But he didn't want help. He wanted release. And he felt that now it was near.

But what would happen then? He'd failed in his mission, and that tormented him. Would the ancestors accept him anyway? If they did not, what would become of him? He didn't know and was scared.

From nowhere, the hippopotamus came into his mind, and he managed a hint of a smile. He'd been kind, yet he'd said that the man he'd attacked was not his father. Was that possible?

As he brooded about it, his eyes closed, and he was sitting at a camp fire with his uncle. The desert and the stars were all around them.

'Yes, it is true,' his uncle told him. 'He was not the man, but because of what you did, it will end now.'

His eyes opened, and he was back in the bed, yet he felt that someone was with him in the room. He didn't turn his head, because he knew no one would be there, and he'd just see the walls pressing closer. Nevertheless, he was comforted and no longer afraid.

A while later, he felt himself leaving his body as he did during the dance. As he rose, he looked down at the shrivelled thing on the bed, and wondered how it had held him for so long.

Then he left to join the ancestors.

Kubu was exhausted when he arrived at the breakfast table. He hadn't slept at all since his subconscious had summoned him.

As usual, he was first there and gratefully accepted a cup of coffee from the waiter. A few minutes later, Mabaku and Ian arrived.

'I just called the clinic to check on Selelo,' Ian said by way of greeting. 'He isn't doing well. I told them I'd look in on him when we get to Shakawe. Right now, I need coffee.'

With great restraint, Kubu waited until both had cups of coffee in front of them.

'I think the station commander is lying about what happened in his office,' he said.

Mabaku and Ian looked at him quizzically.

'It was the tinkling glass that made me realise.' He took a gulp of coffee. 'When we were running for the door of the station, we heard two shots. Right?'

Mabaku and Ian nodded.

'What do you remember about the shots?'

'They were a few seconds apart?' Ian ventured.

Kubu nodded. 'What else?'

When that elicited no further response, Kubu continued, 'Do you remember hearing glass falling after one of the shots?'

'Now you mention it, I do,' Mabaku said. 'What of it?'

'Did you hear the glass after the first shot or the second?'

There was silence for a few moments as Mabaku and Ian thought about it.

'Dammit, you're right, Kubu,' Mabaku said. 'Well done. We could have easily missed that.'

Ian shook his head. 'I'm sorry, but you're way ahead of me. I don't know what you're talking about.'

'Balopi told us that the kgosi burst into his office and opened fire. Right?' said Kubu.

Ian nodded.

'Then he said he shot the kgosi in self-defence. Right?'

'Yes.'

Kubu waited for the penny to drop.

'Ah, I see,' Ian said eventually. 'The glass broke after the second shot. We know Balopi's bullet hit the Kgosi, so it must have been the Kgosi's bullet that broke the window.'

'Right,' Kubu said excitedly. 'The kgosi must have been the one to shoot in self-defence. That changes everything.'

A few moments passed, then Ian started speaking. 'However...'

Then a different penny dropped in Kubu's head. 'I see what you mean, Ian. I missed that.'

Mabaku banged on the table. 'What on earth are you two talking about? I don't understand a word of what you're saying.'

Ian glanced at Kubu, who nodded.

'If we're correct about the sequence of shots,' Ian said, 'and the second shot was the kgosi shooting in self-defence, then how the hell did he manage to pull the trigger after he'd just been shot in the heart. He would have collapsed at once and died a few seconds later.'

Soon after breakfast, Mabaku, Kubu and Ian drove to the police station to await the arrival of the forensics team from Maun and to work through a list of items that had to be cleared up.

'First,' Mabaku asked, when they all had coffee in front of them and Abram had joined them, 'how are the two in the cells? I hope you kept them far enough apart that they couldn't kill each other.'

'The constable at reception tells me that they screamed and shouted at each other all night. Each accusing the other of murder.'

Mabaku smiled. 'I hope they're exhausted. That usually makes people more amenable to telling the truth.' He paused. 'By the way, did you hear the station commander's window break during the shooting?'

Abram looked puzzled and shook his head. 'I was with Raseelo at his cell when I heard the shots, but no glass.'

Mabaku indicated that Kubu should take up the story. 'As you know, the station commander said that the kgosi burst into his office and shot at him.'

Abram nodded.

'However, there's a problem with that story. First, as we were running towards the station, all three of us heard two shots, the second of which was accompanied by the sound of glass.' He paused. 'The second, not the first. That means that the kgosi had to have fired second because the window is behind the station commander's desk.'

Abram frowned. 'I see what you are saying.' He shook his head. 'But the shots were close together. You would have only heard the glass when it hit the ground. Maybe it was after the first one. It all happened so quickly...'

Kubu nodded. 'That's the problem. How can we prove that Balopi fired first – he'll dispute the fact we heard the glass after the second shot. And he'll insist that he shot the kgosi only after the kgosi fired at him. So the kgosi was hit after firing.'

'Even if we all agree as to what happened,' Mabaku interjected, 'I don't think what we have will hold up in court.'

'Where does that leave us?' Ian asked.

'I may have something,' Abram replied. 'When I went back to the kgosi's house last night, and Raseelo opened the gun safe, the kgosi's pistol was there.'

'He had a handgun?' Mabaku asked. 'That's against the law.'

Abram nodded. 'I asked Raseelo before he opened the safe what he expected to find. He said the kgosi owned two rifles for hunting and a handgun. He was very reluctant to mention the handgun.'

'And when he found the handgun?' Ian asked.

'He was very relieved. He said his father would never shoot anyone.'

'That's helpful,' Mabaku said, 'but much like the other evidence. Balopi will say that it's obvious the kgosi had two handguns. Only Raseelo could testify about that, and he'd be accused of covering up for his father. Did you bring the handgun in? We can check if it's stolen.'

Abram nodded. 'I'll see if it still has a serial number and send that through to Gabs. But if it's stolen...' He shrugged.

Kubu stood up and went to the whiteboard. 'I've got an idea.'

He sketched the station commander's office, with its desk and chairs. 'The only thing that makes sense to me is that the kgosi walks into the office, angry at Raseelo's arrest. Probably threatening the station commander in some way. Balopi shoots him, then shoots out the window with a second handgun, which he puts next to the kgosi's hand.'

He added a body outline with a gun next to one hand.

'The prints on that gun should tell us a lot. If there are no prints, the only way that could happen is if Balopi wiped them off. He wouldn't do that if he wanted us to think the kgosi fired at him. The only reason for it to be clean would be if he wiped his own prints off.

'If only Balopi's prints are on the gun, then he fired it, and probably didn't have time to clean it and put it in the kgosi's hand. Then my theory is probably true.

'Third, if both the kgosi's and Balopi's prints are on the gun, that doesn't help us because Balopi would say he handled the gun after the shooting, even though from what we saw, that is unlikely. And the last possibility is that only the kgosi's prints are on the gun. That's what you'd expect if what Balopi says is true. If they are, that may blow my theory. However, if my theory is right, Balopi would have had to wipe his prints from the gun, then put it in the kgosi's hand. There wasn't much time for that.'

Kubu took a sip of coffee. 'And finally, we should ask Forensics to work out the trajectory of the bullet that hit the window frame. If I had any money, I would bet that it came from behind the desk, not in front of it.'

Kubu drew two lines on the board, each representing one of the possible trajectories. With a flourish, he put a big cross over the line starting at the kgosi.

Abram looked puzzled. 'Are you suggesting that the station commander had two handguns and the kgosi none?'

'That's exactly what I think, and I hope Forensics can prove it.'

'But then it was premeditated murder.' Abram looked unhappy. After a moment he added, 'If the kgosi fired the gun, there should be gunshot residue on his hand or arm or clothes. If there is, we know your theory is wrong.'

'And if there isn't?' Ian asked.

'Unfortunately,' Mabaku interjected, 'then it would only be marginally useful, because lack of residue doesn't necessarily mean that a gun hasn't been fired. Unfortunately, it'll take weeks to get an answer, so we need to keep looking. Still, good idea, Abram. We'll ask Forensics to check.'

The four men pondered their situation – they were sure the station commander was the culprit, but they didn't have evidence that would stand up in court.

Ian stood up. 'If you don't mind, I'm going to leave you to decide what to do next. In the meantime, I'm going to see Selelo.'

When the forensics team arrived, Mabaku explained the situation to them in detail before they began their work. One carefully photographed the entire crime scene, including the window frame and where the bullet had impacted it. Then she measured the angle at which the bullet had hit the frame.

Another collected fingerprints from the two guns and lifted what he hoped was gunshot residue from the window frame, the station commander's desk, the floor around where the body was found, as well as the general area in front of the desk.

When he was finished, Mabaku took him to fingerprint the station commander, whose mood had not been improved by a night in a cell.

'Mabaku. About bloody time. You can't keep me in here like a criminal. I demand to speak to the assistant commissioner right now. This is an outrage!'

A shout came from a cell on the other side of the passage: 'You've got to hang him. He's a bloody murderer!'

'Shut up, Raseelo. Let us do our job.'

'He murdered my father!'

'If you don't shut up, I'll have you handcuffed and gagged.'

When Raseelo had quietened down, Mabaku glared at the station commander. 'Assistant Superintendent Balopi, we're keeping you here for your own protection, as I explained yesterday. We haven't charged you with anything. Yet. However, if you want a lawyer, we'll arrange that.

'I don't need a lawyer. I need a senior police officer who can stop this madness and throw you out of the police service.'

Notwithstanding his blustering, he allowed his fingerprints to be taken. Mabaku asked again if he wanted a lawyer, and he shook his head, so Mabaku locked the cell door to a torrent of angry shouts.

After that, they returned to the meeting room and were surprised to find Ian already back from the clinic. They could see from his face that something was wrong.

'Selelo died last night. I was suspicious and checked the body myself, but it was definitely natural causes. He starved himself, and dehydration killed him. They put him on a drip, but the nurse said he kept pulling it out.' He sighed. 'We never really understood each other, but I liked the wee chap.'

Kubu was also sad. He felt that somehow they'd failed the Bushman. In the end he'd stung like a bee, and then paid the price.

'Well,' Mabaku said, 'we'd better get on with it.'

He directed the man from Forensics to the undertaker to take the kgosi's fingerprints and collect gunshot residue from the kgosi's hands and a bag of the kgosi's blood-soaked clothes for testing.

Mabaku told Kubu and Abram to stay at the police station and find out what the forensics team had discovered before they left. Then he went to a meeting with the local magistrate.

When Mabaku returned, the detectives gathered in the meeting room. 'What have we got?' he asked when they'd settled round the conference table.

Kubu kicked off. 'Well, Forensics don't believe that the bullet that broke the window frame was fired by the kgosi. The damage was more consistent with a shot fired from behind the desk.'

'Fingerprints?'

Kubu shook his head. 'Balopi's prints are on his service pistol of course, but just some smudges on the other one. Nothing clear. The fingerprint man thought the kgosi's prints would have been on the gun if it was his and he'd fired it in the office. And, as you thought, the gun residue tests will take at least a week. They have to send them to a private lab in Gabs.'

Mabaku looked thoughtful. 'It may not be enough for a judge, but it's enough evidence for me. We're going to let Raseelo go. After that, we're going to Balopi's house, and we're going to take it apart. I persuaded the magistrate to issue a search warrant. We need to find something there to close this out.'

CHAPTER 41

Mabaku decided that the time had come to change the station commander's status. After releasing Raseelo, he informed Balopi that he was now being held as a suspect in a murder investigation and read him his rights. He allowed Balopi to rant for a few seconds before he interrupted, showed him the search warrant, and demanded his house keys.

Balopi grabbed the warrant and read it. 'This talks about the murders of Lesaka and Mma Zondo. You have no evidence for my involvement in those whatsoever!'

Mabaku waited.

'You are not going into my house. My home is private.'

'Nothing's private in the investigation of a serious crime. You know that. Give me the keys right now, or we'll break down the door.'

After a moment's hesitation, the station commander dug a bunch of keys out of his pocket and handed them over. 'Now I do want a lawyer,' he said angrily.

Mabaku nodded, thinking that perhaps Balopi was starting to realise the seriousness of his position.

~

The detectives returned to the police station late that afternoon, bringing with them the items they'd collected from the station commander's home. As they arrived, the constable at reception stopped them.

'Rra,' he said to Mabaku, 'the assistant commissioner is here. He said you must join him in the meeting room as soon as you arrive. He's been waiting a while.'

Mabaku was surprised. He hadn't been told the assistant commissioner was on his way and wondered what that meant. He nodded his thanks, told Kubu and Abram to secure the items and make an arrangement with Forensics to collect them in the morning, and headed straight to the meeting room.

'Good afternoon, Assistant Commissioner. I wasn't aware you were coming, rra.'

The assistant commissioner waved him to a seat. 'It was quite sudden. The commissioner is very concerned about this matter, Assistant Superintendent. It was bad enough with the Bushman skeletons and the media coverage around that, but then add the murders and the rumours of corruption, and finally the shooting right here in the police station. The press is having a field day.' He paused. 'Your reports have been comprehensive, but I want you to go over it all again for me, step by step.'

Mabaku did so over the next half hour. The assistant commissioner was clearly worried by the evidence implicating the station commander.

'Who actually heard the window break?'

'It was myself, Detective Sergeant Bengu and the pathologist, Dr MacGregor.'

'You all immediately realised what had happened?'

Mabaku shook his head. 'The detective sergeant raised it later, and then we all agreed that the glass broke after the second shot.'

'When did he raise the issue?'

'The next morning.'

The assistant commissioner changed tack. 'I gather you searched his house this afternoon.'

'That's correct. I had a search warrant from the local magistrate, of course. The house is very strange. The walls were bare except for a single Bushman bow hanging in the lounge. We thought it might be from the Bushman massacre so we brought it in, but I doubt we'll get anything worthwhile from it. No photographs of family, except one of a man with a heavy scar, who might be his father. Everything was precisely arranged. The clothes ordered by type and colour, all carefully ironed. No books, except a bible, perfectly centred on a bedside table.' He shook his head. 'The man's obsessive-compulsive.'

'All that's very interesting, but did you find anything incriminating?'

'A revolver locked in the drawer of the bedside table. That's almost certainly an illegal weapon. It's not police issue. We also collected a number of kitchen knives to be tested. One is the length that the pathologist specified for the weapon used in the murders of Lesaka and Mma Zondo. It has a wooden handle, so Forensics may be able to find some human blood or DNA.'

'Was that knife hidden?'

Mabaku shook his head. 'It was with the others in one of the kitchen drawers. Hidden in plain sight perhaps.'

'Or perhaps it's just another kitchen knife.'

'That's also possible. The murder weapon may be buried somewhere in the Kalahari.'

The assistant commissioner thought for a few moments. 'So where does that lead us, Assistant Superintendent?'

'I believe Balopi was behind the murders of Rra Lesaka and Mma Zondo, and that the kgosi was telling the truth about it. However, it'll be hard to prove to a judge unless we get incriminating DNA from one of the knives we seized, and that will take weeks, if not months. But we do have a case for murder against Balopi for shooting the kgosi. We can charge him with that.'

The assistant commissioner took his time before responding. 'Assistant Superintendent, do you have any idea what damage the BPS image will suffer from a long, drawn-out trial of a senior police officer? All the lies that these protesters throw at us will stick. One rotten egg will stink out the whole henhouse.'

Mabaku didn't like the direction the conversation was taking. 'I'm convinced the man is guilty, rra, and I'm sure we can convince a judge.'

'I'm not so sure. I want to interview the man myself.'

'Of course. I'll tell the constable to bring him to us.'

'I'll see him alone, Assistant Superintendent.'

Mabaku didn't like that at all, but he could hardly object. 'Of course, rra. He's been cautioned already.' He got to his feet.

'Assistant Superintendent, you've done a good job here in a very difficult situation. We won't forget that. And I trust you'll keep our discussion here confidential.'

Mabaku nodded. 'Of course, rra.'

When he saw the assistant commissioner, the station commander saluted smartly. The assistant commissioner nodded in response and indicated a seat, before instructing the constable to remove the handcuffs. Balopi smiled slightly, guessing that things were looking up for him. The assistant commissioner went out of his way to put him at ease, pouring him water and informing him that their conversation was off the record.

'I hope you've come to sort out this mess that Mabaku has created here, Assistant Commissioner.'

The assistant commissioner took a few moments to respond. 'Mabaku's a good man, but he can be a bit overzealous, shall we say. Why don't you tell me the whole story from your point of view? I've heard his interpretation.'

The station commander launched into his version, first building the case that the kgosi was behind the murders of Lesaka and Mma Zondo, using Raseelo to do the dirty work. By his own admission to Mabaku, the kgosi had participated in the Bushman massacre. After Lesaka had started to speak about it at a kgotla, the kgosi arranged to have him killed by Raseelo. Later, Raseelo had eliminated Mma Zondo, because she was spreading rumours that the kgosi was corrupt – an issue that had been picked up in Gaborone and subsequently confirmed by Mabaku.

Finally, he himself had been the target of the kgosi's anger for doing his job and arresting Raseelo, while Mabaku did nothing. He described how the kgosi had burst into his office and taken a shot at him. Only his excellent BPS training and quick response had allowed him to escape death.

Balopi sat back and waited for the response.

The assistant commissioner nodded. 'I think I have a feel for the whole thing.' He took a sip of his water. 'You appreciate the importance of our public image, Assistant Superintendent. The BPS needs to be kept above any suspicion of impropriety. Your record shows that you've always supported that.' He paused, and then asked, 'Tell me, Assistant Superintendent, was that why it was essential to eliminate Lesaka, Zondo and the kgosi? Was it to prevent them spreading rumours about the Bushman deaths?'

The station commander looked as though he'd been hit in the gut. 'That's not what happened. Surely you don't believe Mabaku?'

'It's not a matter of belief, I'm afraid. It's all quite clear. Witnesses heard the glass of your window breaking after the *second* shot. Since you shot the kgosi dead, he could never have fired it. You set him up.'

'That's all lies! Who are these witnesses?'

The assistant commissioner shook his head. 'It's not only the witnesses. Forensics proved that the bullet that hit the window frame was fired from behind the desk, not in front of it, so you must have fired both guns. It's over, Assistant Superintendent. Mabaku found an illegal firearm in your house, as well as a knife that Forensics will show was used to kill Lesaka and Zondo.' He paused to see if Balopi would call his bluff, but there was no response. 'What lies ahead is a long, drawn-out trial with the newspaper hacks lapping it up, Mabaku gloating on the stand, the name of the BPS sullied, perhaps irreparably. But you don't want that, do you, Assistant Superintendent? That's not who you are or what you stand for, is it?'

The station commander shook his head, weighing every word, wondering if the assistant commissioner was offering him some way out. 'There was the oath,' he muttered. 'We all took the oath, but the others were weak. Someone had to protect our reputations.' Quickly, he added, 'The Botswana Police Service's reputation.

'That was why you had to kill them, wasn't it?'

The station commander didn't respond.

'You don't want that trial, do you? And then the ignominious execution.'

'Certainly not, rra.'

'You will do your duty as you always have, Assistant Superintendent. You won't let us down. Can I take it that you'll find a way to end this, leaving your reputation intact and with no damage to the BPS?'

The station commander realised he was being offered a way out, but hardly what he'd hoped for. 'Yes, rra,' he said in almost a whisper. 'You can rely on me.'

'Excellent. I knew we could. You are a man of honour.' He stood up and offered the station commander his hand. 'We'll release you immediately. After that, the sooner the better to finish this, don't you think?'

The station commander nodded.

～

Mabaku was waiting in a vacant office when a constable arrived with the station commander.

Balopi glared at Mabaku with an expression mixing hatred and bitterness. 'Give me my keys.'

'What are you doing out of your cell? You're not going anywhere!'

'I've been released. Now give them to me at once, or do I have to get the assistant commissioner?'

'Rra,' the constable put in tentatively, 'the station commander is to be released at once. It's the assistant commissioner's orders. He told me himself, rra.'

Mabaku couldn't believe what he was hearing. Was it possible that the station commander had won after all? Yet there was no sign of triumph on the man's face.

Balopi stuck out his hand for the keys.

'It's the assistant commissioner's orders, rra,' the constable repeated.

Mabaku pulled them from his pocket and reluctantly passed them over.

'Rot in hell, Mabaku,' the station commander said and walked out.

Mabaku swore under his breath and stormed back to the meeting room. 'You're releasing him, Assistant Commissioner? The man murdered the kgosi of Ncamasere!'

The assistant commissioner sighed. 'Close the door and sit down, Assistant Superintendent.'

When Mabaku was seated, the assistant commissioner said, 'It would never stick. The story of the timing of the shots would never hold up in court. The defence lawyer will ask you the same questions I did. His summary would be that two policemen who had an axe to grind with his client came up with the story.'

'What about Dr MacGregor?'

'They convinced him too. Look, Assistant Superintendent, the station commander will make the case that the kgosi is the real culprit. It's a reasonable case, by the way. If anything, the kgosi had the stronger motive.'

'And the forensic evidence?'

'That the bullet was fired from behind the desk? They'll find their own expert to contradict that.'

'So Balopi walks away?'

'Not at all. We have an understanding.'

'An understanding?'

The assistant commissioner sighed again. 'I realise this isn't what you had in mind, Assistant Superintendent. It's too easy for him after what he's done. However, we must think of the reputation of the BPS. That must be our top priority.'

'I thought that bringing criminals to justice was our top priority, rra.'

'You caught him, Mabaku. Leave it at that.'

'But if it's all swept under the carpet, what was the point?'

'I've explained that, Assistant Superintendent. You must leave it in my hands now. That's an order.'

Mabaku was fuming. He wanted to tell the assistant commissioner what he could do with his concerns about image and reputation, but he had a family to support and a career he loved. He rose to his feet. 'Very well, rra, I understand.' He headed for the door.

'Assistant Superintendent.'

Mabaku turned back.

'The conversation we had this afternoon was confidential. The conversation we've just had never happened. You understand?'

Mabaku nodded and then left.

CHAPTER 42

'He did what?' Kubu was incredulous. 'He let him go, just like that? How did he justify it?'

'He said there was no way we could win the case against Balopi, and he'd reached an understanding with him. I take that to mean that Balopi is going to leave the force. Probably, he'll end up working for a security company in Gabs.'

'And the murders of Mma Zondo and Lesaka?'

'He didn't mention them. I assume they are ongoing.' He paused. 'My bet is that we'll leave soon, and Abram will take over the investigations.'

Kubu gazed out of the window, watching the scenery go by, as he, Mabaku and Ian drove back to Drotsky's. He was certain that the station commander had killed the kgosi, and was reasonably sure that he'd murdered Mma Zondo and Lesaka. If the assistant commissioner had promised not to bring any charges if the station commander left the force, how was justice served? What were Jacob Zondo and Joshua Lesaka going to think? And, of course, Raseelo? How much confidence would they and their friends ever have in the Botswana Police Service?

I don't understand it, Kubu thought. And I don't like how I feel about it.

Mabaku's prediction came true just after dinner, when a call came through from the assistant commissioner.

'I think things are under control here now,' he told Mabaku. 'The three of you head back to Gabs tomorrow morning. I've a few things to do, then I'll fly back the day after tomorrow. And, for your information, I've told Detective Sergeant Nteba to take over the investigation of the two murders.'

'And the Bushman skeletons, rra? What's to become of them?'

'The skeletons are of anthropological interest only, and Dr MacGregor can send them back to Gabs.'

'But, sir, the kgosi implicated the station commander in the massacre. Should we not—'

'No, you should not. There's no point in pursuing the matter. It'll be time-consuming, and nothing will come of it. There's no possibility of a case, because everything you learn will be hearsay.'

Mabaku decided he'd pushed enough. 'Yes, rra. Thank you, rra.'

When he relayed the latest orders to Kubu and Ian, they were both very pleased that they'd be heading back to Gaborone the next day. It had been a very much longer trip than expected, and they looked forward to being home.

As Kubu was packing to be ready for an early departure the next morning, he thought back to all the twists and turns they'd experienced. From a trip where he'd expected to watch Ian dig up some old bones with little hope of an interesting case, it had morphed into one of multiple murders, an attempted murder, corrupt politicians and corrupt police. Not to mention what he thought was a huge miscarriage of justice.

What an interesting job I have, he thought. And I've so much to learn.

A few minutes later, he climbed into bed, looking forward to eight full hours of sleep.

Bang, bang, bang.

'Wake up, rra. Wake up.'

Bang, bang, bang.

Kubu dragged himself from his bed and opened the door.

'Rra, your boss says you must be ready to go in five minutes.'

'Five minutes?'

'Yes, rra.'

Kubu tried to get his mind into gear.

'What time is it?'

'Quarter past two, rra. You must hurry up. Five minutes, your boss says.'

With that the man walked off into the dark.

This is madness, Kubu thought, as he struggled out of his pyjamas and into his clothes. Why had Mabaku changed his mind? He knows we can't drive all the way to Gabs in one day.

It was more than five but less than ten minutes later that he stumbled across the lawn to Ian's Land Rover, suitcase in hand. Mabaku and Ian were already there.

'You're late,' Mabaku snapped. 'And what's the suitcase for?'

'The man told me we were leaving. I assumed you'd changed our departure time.'

As he said it, he guessed what was happening. 'Another murder?' he asked.

Mabaku pointed at the car. 'Jump in. I'll tell you on the way.'

Mabaku had been roused a quarter of an hour earlier to take a call from the Shakawe police station. Someone had reported a shot being fired in their neighbour's home. Apparently, their dog had barked and woken them, and they'd heard the shot shortly after. A constable had gone out to investigate. When he got there, he found a man dead on the floor from a gunshot wound to the head. It was the station commander. A handgun was lying next to his body. The constable radioed the station, who'd called Abram, who'd instructed them to get hold of Mabaku.

'It looks as though I misinterpreted the assistant commissioner,' Mabaku muttered. 'When he said he had an understanding with Balopi, I assumed he meant that Balopi would resign and disappear from the scene. Maybe he meant that he was going to commit suicide, as unlikely as that may seem.'

'He didna strike me as one to take his own life,' Ian said. 'Too proud, too arrogant.'

'Maybe it was the thought of standing trial that pushed him over the edge,' Mabaku retorted. 'That could be too much for his pride.'

'I don't think he committed suicide,' Kubu said. 'Where would he have found a handgun between being released and shooting himself? We tore his place apart and took the only handgun on the premises.'

'Maybe he got one from a friend.'

Kubu shook his head. 'I doubt it. Everyone knows he was being held on suspicion of attempted murder. Who would lend him a gun? And why would the dog bark *before* the shot?'

They sat in silence until they reached a police car at the side of the road.

'They said they'd send someone to show us the way,' Mabaku said.

They followed the car until they arrived at the station commander's house, where a number of vehicles were parked outside, and a small throng of people was huddled, awaiting developments, despite the ungodly hour.

They walked into the house and were directed to the kitchen, where the station commander lay in a pool of blood near the back door. There were blood splatters on some of the cupboards, the counter and the floor. Abram was standing to one side taking notes.

'I don't think I need to check whether he's alive,' Ian muttered. 'Shot in the head at point-blank range. Look at the residue on his forehead.'

He knelt next to the body. 'And you were right, Kubu. It's not suicide. No one holds the gun in the middle of his forehead if he's going to do himself in. It's either the mouth or the temple. Never the forehead.'

'I'm sorry to get you out of bed at this time of the night, Assistant Superintendent,' Abram said to Mabaku. 'But I thought it was important for you to be here.'

Mabaku nodded.

'I've sent two constables to take the kgosi's son to the station for questioning.' Abram continued.

'Did the neighbours see him?'

'Not to identify, but they saw someone running down the road after the shot. A man, they thought. Anyway, after what went on at the station, I thought Raseelo was the most likely suspect.'

Mabaku thought for a few moments. 'Good job, Abram. Please radio the constables and have them bring him here. I want to see how he reacts. Also, ask them to collect any clothes and shoes they see lying around and put them in evidence bags. If he shot Balopi, there's likely to be blood spatter on his clothes.'

'How did whoever did it get into the house?' Kubu asked.

Abram turned to a constable who was standing at the back of the room. 'Tell them what you found, constable.'

'Well, rra, when I arrived here I knocked on the front door, but nobody responded. I banged on it again, but no one answered. Then I tried the door and it opened. I radioed the station to ask for back-up, then went inside. That's when I found the body.'

Kubu frowned. 'The door was unlocked?'

'Yes, rra.'

'That is very strange. Why would Balopi open the door at that time of night? Especially to someone like Raseelo.'

'We don't think that's how he got it in,' Abram interjected. 'It looks like he jimmied a window on the other side of the house. When he ran out, he probably opened the front door and didn't think of locking it.'

'Well, make sure no one touches the handle,' Mabaku growled. 'We'll have forensics test it for prints, as well as the window.'

～

'I want a lawyer,' Raseelo shouted as he was pushed, handcuffed, into the station commander's living room, where Mabaku was sitting on a couch. 'You are all mad! Balopi killed my father, and you let him go free. How much did he pay you? Or are you just protecting your friends?'

Mabaku stood up. 'Come with me.' He walked into the kitchen and pointed at the station commander on the floor. 'Whoever killed him made so many mistakes.' He turned to Kubu. 'How many times have I told you, Detective Sergeant, that most criminals are incredibly stupid?'

'I'm not stupid!' Raseelo shouted. 'I'm the kgosi's son.'

Mabaku turned to Raseelo. 'You thought we would call it a suicide, didn't you? Because you left the gun next to the body. God Almighty, nobody shoots themselves in the middle of the forehead, Raseelo. Nobody.'

He pointed at the gun on the floor. 'You better hope that you wiped it clean, Raseelo.'

He looked hard at Raseelo and saw a trace of smugness that he was trying to hide.

'You did, didn't you? Well, how about here?' He pulled Raseelo into the next room, where the window that had been forced. 'Did you remember to wear gloves?'

Again Raseelo had the smug look.

'And covers on your shoes?'

Raseelo frowned.

'And a shower cap on your head, so we wouldn't find any of your hairs?'

Mabaku pulled him back to where the gun was lying.

'And the bullets? Did you remember to wipe them too? Most murderers forget to do that.'

Suddenly Raseelo turned and bolted for the door. He elbowed Kubu in the chest and got past him, but the two constables moved quickly, grabbed him and held on. Despite Raseelo flailing at them with his handcuffed fists, they wrestled him to the ground. After a few moments, he stopped struggling.

'Get him on his feet.'

The constables dragged Raseelo upright.

Mabaku pulled himself to his full height. 'Raseelo Moitsheki, I'm arresting you on suspicion of the murder of Tolalo Balopi. Do you wish to say anything? You are not obliged to say anything unless you wish to do so, but whatever you say will be taken down in writing and may be given in evidence.'

'You can't arrest me. I'm the kgosi's son! Balopi deserved to die. He killed the kgosi!'

'Take him away.'

CHAPTER 43

Kubu was excited and nervous as he climbed the stairs to Joy's flat. It had been a month since he'd seen her, with only a couple of short business calls in between. Despite his worry that she may have lost interest in him or now had another man in her life, she'd sounded very happy when he'd phoned her to say he was back in Gaborone and would like to resume their Saturday lunches. She'd accepted immediately, but suggested that they go for dinner instead, which suited him because of the amount of paperwork he had to catch up on at the office.

He knocked on the door, expecting Joy's sister, Pleasant, to greet him. However, he was wrong. It was Joy who stood before him.

'Kubu, it's been so long.' She leant forward and kissed him on the cheek. 'Come in. I'll just be a minute.'

As he watched her disappear into her bedroom, Kubu grappled with his feelings, which were stronger than when he'd gone to Shakawe. How he'd missed her.

∽

'This isn't the way to our usual restaurant.' Joy sounded puzzled.

'It's been so long since I've seen you, I thought I would splurge and take you to a fancy place.'

'I told you before, Kubu, we shouldn't waste money like that. I'm very happy with our old place.'

'Tonight is on me. I've just come into a fortune.'

'You won the lottery?'

'Unfortunately not, but I hardly spent any money in the last three weeks. The Police Service paid for all the board and lodging. So I have some extra cash. Please don't object.'

~

It was difficult to find parking at the Caravela, a popular Portuguese restaurant, and when they did, two men rushed up, offering to look after the Land Rover.

Kubu smiled. 'And who would steal an old Landie like this?' He paused. 'Especially as it's owned by a policeman. Make sure it's here when we get back.'

A few minutes later they were seated at a quiet table on the patio, with menus in their hands.

'Let's order right away,' Kubu said, 'so we can decide what wine we'll have.'

A few minutes later Kubu waved at a waiter, and they placed their orders. Joy was going to have jumbo prawns and Kubu a pepper steak.

'Please order the wine you like,' Joy said. 'I'm happy with red or white.'

Kubu ordered a reasonably priced South African red blend. 'And bring a bottle of sparkling water also.'

'So, tell me what kept you for three weeks in Shakawe, Kubu. I can't wait to hear – the rumours have been flying.'

'In some ways, it was very depressing. Quite by accident, a contractor laying pipes dug up a skeleton of what turned out to be a Bushman. Our pathologist, Ian MacGregor, excavated another eight, including two children. They'd all been murdered sometime in the past, probably thirty or forty years ago.

'That's terrible. Children too?'

Kubu nodded. 'Then, out of nowhere another Bushman

appeared. He called himself Selelo. To cut a long story short, he believed that the current kgosi of the village of Ncamasere was his father, that he'd raped his mother after the massacre. He tried to kill the kgosi, but was shot by the kgosi's son before he could succeed. Fortunately, or perhaps not so fortunately, the shot didn't kill him, and he was taken to the local clinic under guard.'

He paused to taste the wine the waiter had poured into his glass. 'Very nice, thank you.'

When the waiter had filled both glasses, Kubu raised his. 'Cheers.' They touched glasses, took a sip, then he continued. 'We were very worried about Selelo. First, the local station commander blamed him for two murders that happened shortly after he'd appeared, and wanted to arrest and prosecute him even though there was no credible evidence. And second, I'd read that when Bushmen are confined in small rooms, they feel the world is shrinking around them and often just die. They need to have space.'

He took a deep breath. 'And sadly that's what happened. He died a week ago. In the clinic.' He took another sip of wine. 'From what we could piece together, it's likely that he *was* the result of his mother being raped, not by the kgosi, but by the station commander. Can you believe that?'

'How awful. And that's who you phoned me about? The station commander?'

Kubu nodded. 'Yes. Balopi was his name. We believe that the kgosi, the station commander and two others, an Endo Lesaka and an Ezekial Zondo, were responsible for the massacre when they were just teenagers. They swore an oath – a deadly covenant, if you will – to keep quiet forever about what they'd done.'

'That's not surprising.'

'Anyhow, a long time ago, Zondo started opening his mouth when he'd been drinking, so the station commander, who was then only a constable, killed him in the desert and buried his body. Everyone thought he'd just disappeared.'

'You couldn't make this up, it's so bizarre.'

'It gets worse. When I was at the site of the massacre I met an old man, a Rra Dibotelo, who had been looking for his son for twenty-five years. The son had also disappeared, shortly after Zondo. My heart nearly broke.' He paused a moment. 'We're not sure what happened to the son, but we found another skeleton, of a Motswana, who was likely him. We think Balopi killed him too, perhaps because he knew something connecting Balopi to the Zondo murder. But now we'll never know.'

'You said that there were two murders after the skeletons were found. What were they about?'

'Same thing. The first was Endo Lesaka, who'd been part of the massacre. Balopi was worried he was ready to come clean. So he killed him. The second was the wife of Ezekiel Zondo, who'd been at the massacre—'

'I can't believe a woman took part in a massacre, especially if there were children involved.'

'It was only her husband who was involved, but she must have known about it. She was trying to blackmail the kgosi, and Balopi wanted to make sure she didn't say anything.'

'It's unbelievable.'

'Eventually, as we closed in on him, Balopi felt he had to get rid of the only other person at the massacre – the kgosi. He arrested the kgosi's son for the two murders, which led to the kgosi storming into his office. Balopi shot the kgosi and tried to make it look as though he'd fired in self-defence.'

At that moment, the waiter arrived with their meals. 'Let's enjoy the meal without talk of murder. When we've finished, I'll tell you the rest.'

As they enjoyed their meals, Kubu talked about Drotsky's Cabins and how beautiful they were, perched above the Kavango River. 'The birdlife was unbelievable. I've never seen so many different species of bird in one place, and so many of each species.'

Kubu wondered whether he should suggest they go there, but worried she'd think he was being too forward. Plus, he wasn't sure how he'd feel if she turned the suggestion down.

'It sounds wonderful. So different to the desert we have around here.'

The waiter came to refill their glasses. Joy put her hand over her glass, but Kubu indicated he'd like a top-up.

'In a sense, it was the river that was the start of all the problems.'

Joy frowned.

'The kgosi had started a water project up there, and it was when they were digging a trench for it that the first skeleton appeared. If they'd dug a few metres in either direction, nobody would have ever known about them.'

'What happened to the kgosi after Balopi shot him?'

'He died instantly. The water project was his baby, and it turns out he was involved in some corrupt practices with respect to plans and money. He also confessed to my boss that he was involved in the massacre, but obviously that won't go anywhere now.'

'It's all very confusing. I read that Balopi was also killed.'

'Yes, by the kgosi's son, Raseelo, in revenge for murdering his father. He tried to make the killing look like a suicide, and if I told you how badly he botched that, you'd laugh. Raseelo will be tried for murder. There's no way he can wriggle out of that one.'

The waiter reappeared. 'Dessert for you?'

Joy shook her head, but Kubu ordered ice cream with hot chocolate sauce. 'Make sure the chocolate is hot, please.'

'And what happened in Gabs, while I was gone,' Kubu asked.

'Very little actually. Much the same as usual, except for some protests about the Bushman skeletons. Those drew some attention early on, but faded after about a week. But I have to say, the rumours we heard about what was happening up there...It was impossible to make sense of what we were hearing. I was dying to talk to you to get the real story.'

～

When they'd finished their coffees, Kubu put the cork in the bottle of wine. 'I shouldn't drink any more. It would look bad if a policeman was stopped at a road block and found to be under the influence. More than bad, actually. I'd probably lose my job. Please could you hold the bottle while I go and pay.'

When he returned, Joy took hold of his arm. 'That was a wonderful meal. Thank you so much. When we're rich, we'll have to come back here often.'

Did she mean that literally? Kubu wondered. Did she think they were going to be together for a long time?

The thought took his breath away, and he immediately worried that he'd misinterpreted what she'd said.

It was probably just a roundabout way to say thank you.

It was about nine o'clock when they arrived back at Joy's flat. Kubu parked and climbed out of the Land Rover to open Joy's door.

'Will you come up, Kubu? I have a surprise for you.'

His lack of confidence kicked in immediately. He wasn't sure what her invitation was all about.

'Come on, Kubu. I'm sure you'll like it.' She grabbed his hand and led him up the two flights of stairs to her flat.

'What about Pleasant?' he stammered.

'What about her? She's with a friend tonight. She won't be back until tomorrow evening.'

Joy unlocked the door and walked in. Kubu took a deep breath and followed.

'Sit down anywhere. I'll be right back.'

The elderly armchair had a couple of dresses over the back, and Kubu thought the other single chair looked unstable, so he sat down on the sofa. A few minutes later, Joy returned with a bottle that Kubu didn't recognise. It certainly wasn't a wine bottle, as far as he could make out.

'A friend of mine was in South Africa last week. I asked him to bring this back. He'd told me that you probably would enjoy it.'

She handed it to him, and he looked at the label: *KWV Five Year Brandy*

'He actually recommended the ten-year, but it was too expensive.'

'I don't know what to say. But thank you. I've never had a brandy like this before. I'm sure I'll like it.' Kubu inspected the bottle carefully. 'I think we should try it.' He looked up at her.

'Definitely.' She took the bottle and went to the kitchen. When she returned, she held two tumblers, each with a very small amount of brandy. 'I haven't had it before either.' She said as she handed one to him.

She sat down next to him and tucked her legs under her. 'Cheers, Kubu. I've had a lovely evening.'

With a little flourish, they clinked their glasses and took a sip.

Joy gasped. 'Whew, it's strong! It burnt all the way down.'

Kubu didn't reply, but continued to swirl the liquid around his mouth. Eventually he swallowed.

'I think you are meant to leave it in your mouth for some time, not just swallow it.' He sniffed at the glass. 'It has a lovely nose. Try it. First just sniff, then breathe it in. Just like wine.'

She followed his directions, then nodded. 'That's good.'

'Now take another sip, but this time swirl it around your mouth. Try to reach every part on the tongue, under the tongue, around the cheeks. Let your whole mouth taste it.'

She did that. Eventually she swallowed. 'That's different. Much softer than the first time.'

As Kubu sniffed and sipped and swirled, Joy looked at him with interest. When he's talking about something he knows, she thought, he loses all his shyness. She put her hand on his knee, and he immediately stiffened.

Joy laughed. 'Relax, Kubu. Touching someone you like is natural.'

Kubu was at a loss for words. She'd just told him that she liked him. He hadn't expected that. And she'd bought him a bottle of expensive brandy. He wasn't sure what to do.

Fortunately, Joy solved the problem for him. 'You can hold my hand, Kubu. I won't be offended.' She paused. 'In fact, I'll be offended if you don't.'

He reached out tentatively and took it.

What to do next?

He'd held his mother's hand, of course. But this was different. His stomach began to hurt as he felt more and more out of his depth.

Joy snuggled closer and entwined her fingers with his. 'Touching should be enjoyable, not terrifying.' She started gently massaging his hand.

It took a while and several more sips of brandy before he started to feel the tenseness leave his shoulders. He wondered if he should try to kiss her. He frowned. Did one ask first? Or did one just do it? And what if she pushed him away? He'd be mortified.

'I think I'd like another brandy,' he said. 'I really like it. Thank you so much.'

She took his glass and returned a few moments later. She sat down and took his hand once again, and Kubu once again had to decide what to do next. To defer the decision, he took another sip of the brandy and took some time swirling around his mouth. The pain in his stomach increased.

As he was contemplating his situation, Joy let go of his hand and snuggled closer. She took his head in both hands. 'Kubu, you have no idea how attractive your shyness is. Most men by now...' She shook her head, took the glass from his hand, and put it on the side table.

She leant forward and put her lips on his. She kissed him. Then kissed him around the mouth, then back on it.

Kubu started having feelings he'd never had before. His breath became short, and he started to reciprocate, kissing her hard.

Eventually she broke off, breathing heavily. 'I like that.'

Kubu nodded, unable to speak.

'I think we should try it again.'

This time she kissed him gently, their lips barely touching. He could hardly stand it.

She's teasing me, he thought, cradling her face in his hands.

She pulled back. 'Easy. There's no rush.'

She brushed his lips with hers.

This is driving me crazy, Kubu thought.

Still, he resisted the temptation to crush her head against his.

She kissed him harder. He reciprocated. Suddenly he felt her tongue exploring his lips, pushing forward, her mouth opening.

He gasped. What to do? His mother had never kissed him like this.

He opened his lips a little, letting his tongue touch hers. He felt all the air had left his lungs. He pushed her back and took a deep breath.

My God, he thought. What's happening to me?

He looked at the beautiful face in front of his, with its gorgeous smile.

I'm in love, he thought.

He kissed her gently on the forehead.

She leant over him and picked up the glass. She put it to his lips. He took a sip. She took one too.

She turned her head left then right, then back and forward. 'I'll need to go for a massage tomorrow if we sit all twisted like this. Let's go to the bedroom – there's not enough room on the sofa for both of us to lie down.'

'But...' he stammered. 'I've never—'

'Relax, Kubu. We're not going to have sex, just get more comfortable.'

She took him by the hand and led him to her bedroom. He was very conscious of his erection and wondered if she could see it. It was so embarrassing.

He sat on the bed and took off his shoes, then lay down next to her, rolling on his side to hide the bulge at his groin.

She snuggled up to him and kissed him. 'Hold me,' she instructed.

He wrapped his arms around her and pulled her close. She kissed him gently and stroked his face. 'I've dreamt about this ever since our first date.'

Kubu couldn't believe what he was hearing. 'I've been so scared of talking to you, except about work. I didn't think you would see anything in me that you liked.'

She kissed him again. 'And I thought you'd think me too stupid to be with. Just a clerk in Records. Not knowing much about anything.'

Kubu digested that. If only I'd known, he thought, I could have avoided all those days of uncertainty and despair. 'You're not just a clerk in Records, Joy.'

Neither of them felt the need to say anything more, so they lay there, content in each other's arms.

And it wasn't long before Kubu was fast asleep.

GLOSSARY

Bakkie: pick-up truck (Southern Africa)

Batswana: the Tswana people. Plural of Motswana

Bomma: women (Setswana). Plural of mma

Borra: men (Setswana): Plural of rra

Botho: the idea of gaining respect by giving it (Setswana)

BPS: Botswana Police Service

Calcrete: carbonate deposits formed by groundwater near the water table in arid areas

Ditsala: friends (Setswana). Plural of tsala

Ditshwanelo: the Botswana Centre for Human Rights (rights, Setswana)

Dumela: hello (Setswana)

Gabs: short for Gaborone

Jackalberry: (Diospyros mespiliformis) a large evergreen tree found mostly in the savannas of Africa. Jackals are fond of the fruit, hence the common name.

Ke: I (Setswana)

Ke a go rata: I love you (Setswana)

Kgosi: chief (Setswana)

Kgotla: a meeting of the community. Also the location where meetings regularly take place (Setswana)

Knobkierie: a short club made from hardwood with a knob on one end, used as a weapon (Afrikaans)

Kubu: hippopotamus (Setswana)

Landie: affectionate name for a Land Rover vehicle

Lechwe: (Kobus leche leche) water-loving antelope found in the Okavango region

Lithops: a genus of succulent plants, often known as pebble plants or living stones because they blend in with surrounding rocks

Lobola: bride price paid by the groom to the bride's family (Southern Africa)

Mami Wata: water spirit, sometimes depicted with a mermaid tail. Known in many parts of Africa by different names

Mantis: the praying mantis is one of the Bushman gods and is known as a trickster

Mma: respectful term when addressing a woman. Mrs, madam (Setswana). Singular of bomma

Motswana: a Tswana person. Singular of Batswana

Pula: Botswana currency = 100 thebe

Rra: respectful term when addressing a man. Mr, sir (Setswana). Singular of borra

Setswana language of the Tswana people

Shake Shake: brand of sorghum beer in Botswana

Slàinte mhath: good health (Gaelic)

Stoep: veranda (Afrikaans)

Thebe: Botswana currency (see pula)

Tokoloshe: an evil spirit

Tsala: friend (Setswana) Singular of ditsala

Tsodilo Hills: a group of hills in north-west Botswana sacred to the Bushmen. A World Heritage Site, it contains a wealth of wonderful rock art

Uisage beatha: water of life (Gaelic)

ACKNOWLEDGEMENTS

Many people have given us their help and encouragement with this book.

We thank our agent, Jacques de Spoelberch of J de S Associates, for his continued support.

We are delighted to be published outside North America by Orenda Books, winner of the 2020 Publisher's Dagger from the Crime Writers Association, and thank Karen Sullivan, West Camel and the rest of the team for their valuable input and enthusiasm for our stories.

We benefitted greatly from the valuable input of the Minneapolis writing group – Gary Bush, Barbara Deese and Heidi Skarie. Also, Steve Alessi, Linda Bowles and Steve Robinson read the completed novel and gave us very helpful feedback. Steve Alessi also came up with the title for the book. Tracy Khatenje helped enormously with the social media campaign.

With all their comments, it's hard to believe that the book still has mistakes, but it probably does, and we take responsibility for any that remain.

CPSIA information can be obtained
at www.ICGtesting.com
Printed in the USA
LVHW031436130323
741500LV00002B/72

9 780997 968989